New Age Apocalypse

John Roman's War

Book Two of the New Age Apocalypse Trilogy ©

by William Preston PhD

Acknowledgments

My trilogy, New Age Apocalypse has been a labor of love. But as with all the important events in my, life I had the help and support of many around me. When I returned to college in 1999, my first teacher was Ken Jolicoeur. This exceptional man, who would later be the best man at my wedding, taught me to think for myself, academically, and to always write the truth. His encouragement and mentoring was one of the reasons I was able to go from a forty-four year old man with a high-school diploma 1999, to a fifty-six year old man with a Ph.D in 1012. I would like to thank Tammy Bolotow, another generous person, who allowed me to see the world, and reach my academic goals. Without her I would still be walking around with blinders.

Most of all I want to express my love, admiration and respect to my dear wife Dr. Celest Martin. For seventeen years she has poured her love, compassion and encouragement into this needy man-child. Without her expertise, patience and love of language this book would be nowhere as good a read. She is by far the best copy editor in the world. She is also the love of my life and will always be my north star.

William Preston Ph.D.

Chapters

Preface

In 1972, I entered college for the first time. My, paper chase consisted of playing pool, chasing women and getting drunk, as quickly and as often as I could. What followed my leaving higher education two years later was a life of drink and drugs. I hit bottom on November 14th 1998. With two months sobriety I reentered college at the age of 44. I obtained my undergrad and then took a three year break, when I ran my home repair business: Rent-my-husband. In 2006, I again returned to college and earned my masters and then my Ph.D in 2012. As I write this preface, I have been teaching college writing for fourteen years. It is a career I dreamed about since I was ten years old.

The day after receiving my degree, I swore that after years of reading countless theory and dull torturous tomes I would stick to one of my favorite genres; science fiction. Like many, I was hooked on the sub-genre of zombies. Over the last decade plus, I have read hundreds of apocalypse stories and though there have been many excellent books on the subject, there have always been plot holes which frustrated me. So during the corona virus, on June 1st 2020 at the age of sixty-five, I started writing a, contemporary trilogy. I wanted to write an exciting adventure while filling in plot holes that were always a sticking point for me in other books of this genre. I began writing the, *New Age Apocalypse,* series.

I am very proud of the *New Age Apocalypse* trilogy. Everything in this series has a scientific basis. I write about climate change, which is dramatically affecting the world. A temperature of over one hundred degrees was recorded at the Russian Antarctic this year. After a three hundred year old carcass thawed and released the anthrax virus recently, a herd of one thousand reindeer became infected and had to be put down. The creatures described in the trilogy have their counterparts in nature. Most of the ordinance used is real. The quarantining of people is happening now. This is a tale of adventure, filled with great characters and heroes. It is also a tale that could very well happen in the very near future. So enjoy this exciting piece of *fiction,* and remember, many sci-fi books predictions over the years have become true.

Contact information

To Contact the author Email

Kingcribholdem@yahoo.com

Cover art by Burakzcicek

New Age Apocalypse

John Roman's War

Book Two of the New Age Apocalypse Trilogy ©

by William Preston PhD

Chapter One

The War Begins

Just outside the center of New Boston, John Roman scanned the cordoned-off 10-square-block the Morphs held. With him were the Lads, Raiden, and fifty of the Roman Institute's best men, all battle hardened, combat professionals, At the same time, General Thomas was addressing *his* men. As he spoke to his troops over the speaker network, dozens of personnel carriers, tanks, and sniper units positioned themselves. "Alright people. Today we are going to engage the enemy for the first time en-masse. Until now, we have encountered a maximum of ten Morphs at one time, and never a Big M. From what we can tell, their strength is at about 100 individuals. But there could well be more, so watch your back.

We are 2,000 strong, with over forty mobile and 20 snipers units supporting us. Remember, if we can take a Morph alive, let's do it. You are equipped with the latest and best capture weapons. Use them. However, if there is the slightest danger to you or your fellow solider, I want you to send these things to hell." After Thomas' remark there was a collective, riotous cheer from the ranks. "Remember, you're professionals. So do your job and make the people of Tsalaki proud." Another cheer split the air. "At the sound of the horn; move out."

****

John, Raiden, and the Lads circled up, ready to plan their next move. But before doing so, John had some news. "Ok fellas. You all know Raiden here. His sister is Aimi, who is still in the hospital recuperating from her ordeal with the Morphs. Raiden wants his revenge and I can't blame or refuse him. I've seen him in action he can hold his own. If he wants, I am going to ask him to join us. Any objections?"

"Not from me. I heard what happened in the cave. I, for one am happy to have him," Bubba said.

"This humble servant thinks it would be good karma for Raiden to join us. His motives are pure, John," Agni chimed in.

John turned to Sheamus. "Well? Any objections, Shea.?"

Downing a shot of Baileys, Sheamus burped and said, "Now. Why would any fool object ta havin' o' bonafide sword swingin' samurai on ta team, Johnny boy? I...fer one, can't wait fer ta morph heads ta be flyin' around ta room like potaters on Saint Paddies' day."

"Raiden. What do you say? You in?"

"I would be honored, my friend," Raiden said as he bowed.

‘Ok. It’s official. The Lads are now five. Welcome to our club, Raiden.” Everyone shook Raiden’s hand; then John pointed to the monitor. Earlier, John launched a T38 hover drone.

The A38 hover drone had the ability to blow out windows with a directed laser burst and it was armed with two mini-antipersonnel rockets. With the A38’s surround-sound detection ability, combined with a 360 degree video feed and equipped with laser abilities, John could enter buildings, see and hear a mile in any direction, and take out hostiles if necessary. All controlled through the T38’s monitor. “What ya be seein’ with that there gizmo, Johnny boy? Anythin’ ole Shea should be worryin’ about?”

“As a matter of fact, it looks like the Morphs all vanished. Can’t find a damn one. Like the ground swallowed them up,” John replied.

“Ohh boyo.’ I don’t be likin’ that. It’s got trap written all over its bloody face me dear friend. If ever there be o’ set up, this here is it,” Sheamus sighed.

“I’m sure you’re right Shea, but we’re still going in.” Just then, as it was hovering outside the top floor of the Hancock building, the A38 started scanning people. On his monitor, John could see two dozen or more people banging on windows of the office building and holding up signs which read, “Help” and “We need rescue.”

“Hey, guys look at this,” John nodded to his friends. The Lads looked at the monitor and could see men, women and some children, holding signs, yelling with many of them crying. "Damn," Bubba said. "We got to get those people out of there, John."

"Christ John. Are ya picking up any o' those Morphy fucks tryin' ta get ta them?"

"The A38 is able to pick up heat signatures, but unfortunately the M's can't be targeted. Something about their skin, it either absorbs the signal or dissipates it, so it can't be picked up."

"What about audio or video, John?" Agni asked.

"Nothing there either."

"Saint Micheal's bullocks John. Tis here is another trap, or I'm o' goddamn Black and Tan."

"I agree, Shea. But what do you want? You want us to leave them?"

"Nay. Not sayin' that boyo.'"

John then signaled for Captain Jim Hooks, the man in charge of the Roman Institute's fifty-man assault and rescue team, *Spear-tip*. "Jim. It seems we have a few people who have barricaded themselves on the top floor of the Hancock. I want you and your team to get those people out of there. Thomas can't move like us and their concern is with the Morphs. His people roll big but slow. I want us to sweep in there fast and get those civilians out. Civvies are not his top priority, but that's why we're here. The second the General sets off the horn signal, I want you to go in ahead of his troops and get those people out safely. My friends and I are going after the Big M. From the last data we collected before he disappeared, I feel the ballpark is where we'll find him. It has the tunnel networks the

Morphs crave. Any extra men you have, send them with us for back-up. I'm counting on you. I want to hand out these. We don't have many of them yet, but we are putting this ordinance into production." John then handed Hooks the new G-2 RIP bullets. The ammo's name was appropriate. When fired, the tip shatters on impact, with the shards creating at least nine separate deadly wounds. John also handed over some Flash Thunder grenades. "These grenades are like ammo and can be fired out of your shotguns. They produce a blast so loud, enemies will be stunned into submission and their ear drums ruptured permanently. We have a lot more new ordinance coming. But use these for now. It should give you and your men an edge."

"Appreciate it, John. I give you my word. We'll bring them all home," Jim said. They both shook hands and Jim turned and hurried to his men. As soon as Hooks left, Sheamus grabbed John.

"Now, what ta hell ya mean *we* be goin' after that big bastard John? Why us? Ta General got his-self armor and o' couple o' thousand men. Shouldn't he be doin' that? Why ta hell we gots ta be doin' all ta dirty work?"

"It's what we do, Shea. We're the heroes right? Besides, with you along we got the luck of the Irish with us," John laughed.

"Yeah, well, I don't know if there be enough luck in all o' Ireland ta kill that there big arse hunk o' walkin' muscle and teeth."

"Oh. We're not going to kill him Shea. We're going to capture him. It's another reason why I want us on this. I'm sure General Thomas has a shoot to kill on the Big M."

"Oh John, my dear, dear boy," Sheamus said as he put his hand on John's shoulder. "I do admire yer courage, *BUT ARE YA OUT OF YER BLEEDIN' DAMN MIND*? That there thing will tear us all ta bite size bloody bits."

"Shea. We need him alive. This Big M is the leader. He is able to communicate. If we can communicate with him we may be able to understand what these M's want. At the least, we may be able to find out how to beat them. Besides, we have the Flash Grenades. These things can knock out a bull elephant with *one* shot. And if we can't contain it, we have the DUS* bullets." John then handed the ammo to Bubba. "You better take these. They have quite a kick. Use them wisely, we don't have many at the moment." After a pause, John said, "It's important, Shea. I wouldn't put any of you in danger if I didn't think it was vital. Of course you can drop out. We'll understand."

"Yes. Do not be afraid of being afraid Shea," Agni said. "There have been many times Agni was afraid. Agni run away. Not feel bad after."

"RUN?...RUN?...Agni, if I didn't like ya boyo,' I would lay yer out right now. Sheamus O'Keefe has *never* run from anythin' and *never* will laddie-buck. Let alone some red freak punter who runs around with his dick o' scraping' ta bloody floor." Sheamus turned to look at John and Bubba. "I'm with ya. Ya don't think I'd be leavin' children all alone ta do o' man's job now do ya?....Just let me get me Baileys."

*Depleted Uranium Silver bullet. Upon entering a target the DUS bullet explodes. Capable of destroying a tank; nothing can service a hit from a DUS.

****

At 0700 hours, a horn blast from General Thomas signaled the Tsalaki troops to move forward. At the same time, Captain Hook's men were making their way to the Hancock building. With no resistance Hooks was beginning to think "trap," or, having seen the armed forces they were confronted with, the Morphs had retreated. Over his radio, Hooks gave orders to Lieutenant Jeff Jackson. "Lieutenant, let's move with caution. Be ready for anything. Have Sergeant Rodney cordon off the building. Make sure no Morphs get in or out. I want Sergeant Strong to take eight men, use the stairs, and make their way to the top floor and get those people down. I want you to post one man on every other floor and use the "shut tight" to lock all stairwell exits. When all the civilians are on the ground floor put the civilians in the trucks and get them out of the danger zone. Have Sergeant Sage take the rest of the men, and hook up with John Roman. Give him any support he needs. Got that? Over."

Lieutenant Jackson radioed back an affirmative and operation "Savior" commenced. At the same time, General Thomas's troops were systematically squeezing the perimeters closed. They shrunk the ten square circled blocks of downtown New Boston by two full blocks and not met any resistance. An hour into the deployment, Thomas received a report from his on site commanding officer, Colonel Henry Jefferson. "General Sir. This is Colonel Jefferson. Over."

"Yes, Colonel go ahead."

"Sir. We have just passed John Roman's men at the Hancock building. They seem to have everything under control there. We are continuing to move the encirclement tighter but so far the only thing we have encountered is body parts and lots of blood. From the looks of it, a bunch of people were killed here. Over."

"Alright Colonel, let the Roman men do their job. Just keep tightening the noose. I want you to check every cellar and send some units into the sewers. Look for hostiles and if you find none, gather any evidence of them being there. Make sure your back's covered as you move forward and we'll all meet at New Fenway ballpark. That will be ground zero. Over."

"Yes Sir, will do. Our ETA, if we meet no resistance Sir, is 0900 hours. Over and out."

****

As the Tsalaki troops kept tightening the noose John and his men entered New Fenway park.

"All right guys let's circle the Humvees and start securing the area." The team rode in four armored G1 super Hummers. Each had

50cal. machine guns up top, which could be controlled remotely from inside the vehicles. Grenades of all type, mortar shells, sonics, gas, just about any ordinance could be used from the safety of the G1 Hummer. However, as with every war ever fought, it always came down to the grunt.

"Sergeant Sage, I want two men to stay inside the vehicles at all times. Put up a five man perimeter around the Hummers. I've left you some of the new ammo and grenades so use them well. This will be our command center. I want you to stay here and coordinate the operation. Check?"

"Yes Sir. I'm on it," Sage replied.

Shea, you and Agni take some men with you and check the upper floors. Be careful. If you run into anything you can't handle *di di mau* back to the trucks."

"I think I should be stayin' with you boyo.' What if yer run inta that there big freak?" Sheamus said.

"That's why I'm taking Bubba. Between the FTG's and the DUS ammo we'll be fine."

"Alright laddie." Turning to Bubba, Sheamus, said, "Watch his back big guy. If yer don't I'll never let ya forget it."

"You just worry about yourself and Agni. Make sure *you* watch the little fella's back."

"Excuse this humble man, Bubba. But was it not a poor lowly Agni who saved your life?" Agni smiled.

"It sure was, Agni. Maybe you should watch after Shea," Bubba laughed.

"I'm, not some baby bumpkin, yer big flamin' turd ya. Nobody needs ta be lookin' after Sheamus O'Keefe."

"Alright guys. Let's get to work. Bubba, me, you and Raiden are going underground. We'll take ten men. There is a network of tunnels under this park and we are going to search every one of them. If the Morphs are still in the area, I'm betting that's where they'll be. Guys, I've downloaded the map of the tunnels to your T50." The T50 was the latest in personal software. Used both in military and civilian life, these watches had a 3D pop up which allowed the user to see and share any map, info, medical, weather, or personnel data that was needed for any situation. A soldier's T50 was as important as his gun; no soldier went into the field without one. "If for any reason you get lost, just follow the blue line to an exit. Even with the map it's a maze down there. The lights are out so make sure you have your night-bright goggles. All right. Let's move out. Meet back here in one hour." With that, everyone headed out.

****

General Thomas was checking in with his troops when he got news from central command.

"General. The secretary of defense is on the line Sir."

"Hello Secretary Adams. This is General Thomas Sir."

"General. What's happening on the ground there?" Secretary Bruce Adams asked urgently.

"Well Sir, at the moment nothing. We are one hour into Operations and we have encountered no hostile activity, Sir."

"Thomas, I would suggest you be very careful. At exactly 0900 EST there were at least thirty full scale Morph attacks on cities across the globe. We have lost thousands of troops and civilian casualties are mounting. I cannot believe New Boston will not be affected. Make sure your men are vigilant. We are facing an enemy we have severely underestimated. I repeat: This is a world-wide coordinated full scale assault on cities everywhere. We would be hard-pressed even with our technology to put together such a monumental operation. These Morphs are not dumb brutes, General. They are far more intelligent then we gave them credit for." At that moment an aide rushed up to the General with an urgent message.

"Sir. It's Colonel Jefferson Sir. He needs to speak to you. He said it's urgent."

"Yes Colonel. What is it? Over."

"General, Sir. We have had some Morphs come up behind us from the sewers. We've had several casualties and have put down five Morphs. But there is something not right about it, Sir. Over."

"What do you mean 'not right,' Colonel? Over."

"Well, Sir. It's as if they *let* us kill them. When they first popped up they took out our men with ease, and then it was as if they just let us kill them, Sir. That's the best way I can explain it. Over."

"What's the status of the men you sent down into the underground car park and sewers? Over," Thomas asked.

“The last time they checked in, they encountered nothing. They reported to me that everything was all clear, though there were signs of Morph activity. They did find pod remains, blood, which we assume is human, and some skeletal remains, but no live Morphs, General. Over.”

“When was the last time they checked in? Over.”

“Fifteen minutes ago, Sir. I have been trying to contact all five units but none of them is replying. Over.”

“Colonel, I strongly suggest you stop where you are and set up a defensive position ASAP. You are about to get hit from all sides hard. Do you understand Colonel? Over.”

“Yes Sir. I’ll get right on it. Over.”

“Colonel. One more thing. Do not under any circumstances send anyone else down in the sewers. Those men are gone. Understand, Colonel? Over.”

“Yes Sir.” Over.”

“I’ll get the Air-cav to give you assistance, where they can. Over.”

“Yes Sir. Over.”

As if hell opened up and a thousand demons cried out at once, there was a deafening howl from over five hundred Morphs all through the perimeter of troops. In an instant, Morphs emerged from underground in front, behind and in among the Tsalaki army. Before General Thomas’s troops knew what hit them, Colonel Jefferson was dead, along with six hundred other men. Sergeants, and even Corporals, were trying to gather the men into fighting units. Blocks of ten and twenty men were forming squares and setting up barricades. The fighting was fierce and in some cases hand-to-hand, with the Morphs holding the advantage. For every unarmed Morph who went down, it seemed at least ten humans were killed. The Morphs simply knew no fear. Sometimes it took a whole clip to bring one down. Many times a Morph would have a deadly wound and still manage to kill or seriously injure a human soldier. A heart or head shot was needed to take an M out of commission quickly, but in the heat of battle, aiming the perfect shot was not easy. Machine gun fire, grenades, and small arms noise was mixed with the constant howls of the M's. Morphs tore into man after man, while M heads were blown to smithereens. It rained an endless downpour of blood, bones and body parts.

The M's were so entwined with the troops, that to use tanks and Air-cav weaponry would mean killing as many human infantry as Morphs. Equally as bad, the sniper units had been devastated in a coordinated attack by the Morphs. The humans were losing the battle and losing it fast. However, after thirty minutes of savage fighting the tide turned. Though the Tsalaki troops had over fifteen hundred casualties, the Morph army had dwindled to less than fifty. Thanks to the training and courage of the service men, they were able to mount a defense and use their weapons to gain a numerical advantage over the M's. Just as the tide of the battle was shifting a Big M stood up on top of the entrance to New Fenway and howled loudly. At the same time, all the Morphs quit fighting and disappeared, leaving their dead and dying. The Tsalaki troops were too few and too exhausted to follow. They regrouped and called for reinforcements.

"General Thomas, this is Sergeant Owens, Sir. We need reinforcements now, Sir. We are down to maybe five hundred men. Many of those are hurting badly, Sir. If we are attacked again, I'm afraid we will not survive, Sir. Over."

"I understand, Sergeant Owens. Hold your position at all costs. The Morphs have launched attacks all over the world and Tsalaki. We are stretched to the limit. Fortunately, the Roman Institute is sending eight-hundred troops. Their ETA is 0100 hours, Sergeant. Your men have fought bravely. Just hold on. I'll get you out of there. Over."

'Yes Sir. We'll do our best. We could use an airdrop. We're low on ammo and medical supplies, Sir. Over."

"Way ahead of you Sergeant. Air-drop is on its way. Lifted off ten minutes ago. You should be seeing it now. Over."

"Thank you Sir. Over and out."

****

Minutes before the Morph attack, Sergeant Strong had reached the top floor of the Hancock building. What he found did not make him feel at ease. Strong immediately radioed Jackson who was coordinating the ground units. "Lieutenant Jackson, Sir. We have a problem. The civilians did not bar the door from the inside, the doors have been sealed from the outside. Over."

"Alright Sergeant, take appropriate action but get those people out of there. Over," Jackson ordered.

"Come on you men, get this opened," Strong ordered. As the barricade was being taken down, Strong radioed the men in the stairwell. "Corporal Clark. I want your men on high alert. The M's have locked the civvies *in*. Watch your back, Clark. Over."

"Yes, Sergeant. Over."

Once the barricades were down, Strong and his men entered the room and the civilians rushed to meet them. There were multiple shouts of, "Thank you" and "Help us, please." All throughout the room people were shouting questions with many crying. Strong needed to halt the panic. "Alright everyone. Please, you're safe now. My name is Sergeant Strong, we have come to help. But I need you to calm down so we can get you home as fast and safely as possible. I can't talk to you all at once. Is there a spokesperson I can talk to?" A middle-aged women stepped forward and introduced herself.

"I guess that would be me. I'm Lacy Rice. I'm head of acquisitions. We need medical attention, water, and to get out of here, Mr. Strong."

"Sergeant, ma'am. My medics will give your people a quick look, but I need you to tell them to move in a single file against that wall. We have men positioned all the way down the stairs. I…."

"Ehh, Sergeant. We have people here who can not possibly make it down those stairs," Rice interrupted.

"Ma'am. My men will see that anyone who is not physically able to walk will be carried down. Now, what happened here? Why and how did you get locked in?"

"It was those horrible creatures. They grabbed people from all the floors. They killed and ate some right in...right.." Rice put her face in her hands and cried.

"It's ok, now, Ms. Rice. I need you to tell me what happened. You can mourn the dead tomorrow." Strong nodded to his medic, who slipped up behind Rice and injected her with a mild sedative.

"Now, Ms Rice. What happened?"

"They...they...put us all in here and blocked the door. Then they left out the back there," Rice said, pointing to a double door in the back of the room. "Since then, we have been waiting and praying for help.

Just then a medic came up to Strong and taking him aside said, "Sergeant, these people are all infected."

"What? Are you sure?"

"You know what this means, Sergeant? We're rescuing dead people."

"That's enough, Franks. Our job is to get them out of here. Now, get them lined up and get some men to check out those doors in the back." Strong turned to talk with Rice when a loud bang, shook the whole room. The double-doors in the back of the room burst open. Ten M's came pouring and howling into the room. At the same time, on several floors of the building M's smashed open emergency exits and started to attack men in the stairwell. The rescue team were completely overwhelmed. Strong yelled, "Trap. Take defensive positions." At first, the M's were able to take out eight of Strong's troops. But with the RIP ammo, Strong soon blew five of the Morphs to atoms. Two of the remaining, M's began to tear into the civilians who were huddled in a corner. The other two M's were cut down, but only after they had killed five more of the Roman Institute's team. Strong and his remaining nine men charged the two M's who were slaughtering the civvies and took them down. The room was full of gun-smoke, blood, and the moaning of the wounded, and crying civilians. As he rushed to the front door, Strong could hear a barrage of yelling, howling and gunfire coming from the stairs.

"Corporal Clark. Do you read me? Over."

"Yes, Sergeant. We got nailed. There are six of us headed up the stairs now. Be ready to block the door. We got boogies chasin' our ass. We're coming in hot, Sarge."

Clark, and his men hit the top of the stairs with Morphs on their heels. The men let loose with two, M60 machine guns but the M's kept charging up the stairs. Strong, pushed his way to the door and fired one of the FTGs down the stairs. The blast blew all the Morphs back down the stairwell, howling in agony. Clark slammed the doors and applied the lock-tight along and everything else the men could find to block the doors. As Clark's men were gathering themselves and helping their wounded, Strong asked, "Clark? What the hell happened? Didn't you seal the exit doors in the stairwell?"

A panting Clark responded, “Yes, Sarge. At first the doors held, but then this giant motherfucker just smashed one open and plowed through us, ripping open more doors. We poured everything we had at it. Finally it limped off, but then we had to deal with those smaller red boogies.” After a few seconds Clark panted, “I love this new armor. If it was the old stuff, we'd all be dead.” I wished we had some of those grenades. Christ, you blew the hell out of them. I never heard such a beautiful sound as those fuckers howling in pain after you launched that mother, Sarge.”

“Yeah, well, thank the Roman Institute. They developed that new armor and the G-2 bullets and these grenades, from what they learned about those red devils. That armor protects you from their claws and that ammo has special tips which penetrate and then explode inside the fuckers. The TGS are supposed to disable them and blow out their ear drums.”

“Roman was right. This ammo kicks fucking ass,” Clark said elatedly.

Strong looked around the room and assessed the situation. There were, dead, dying and wounded. Some of the civilians were nearly catatonic. He had to get his men regrouped and ready for a fight or flight. Turning to Clark he said, “Now, look. Clark. Before you do anything, get the demo boys and have them rig those double doors and this door with all the plastic they have. If those sons-of-bitches want to join us we are going to send them to hell. Have the medic team take care of our men and then the civvies. They’re all infected, so they can wait. I know it sounds rough but that’s the situation. Take a count of our ordinance and make sure the men are reloaded and ready to go."

"Understand, Sarge. I'll get right on it."

****

John and Sheamus, along with Raiden and ten men entered the ballpark tunnels. These tunnels were used for a variety of reasons the park's owners did not want the public to see. Some tunnels led to underground parking, some were for the dozens of big rigs which delivered tons of food and other items necessary to run a ballpark the size of New Fenway. The players dressing rooms and staff offices were also accessible through these tunnels. This way, the players were not accosted by fans and autograph hunters before the game.

As they made their way down the tunnels John and his team entered a hub. From here the tunnels went in three different directions.

"I hope you're not thinking about splitting us up John," Bubba warned.

"No Bubba. You're right." Turning to the other men John ordered, "Ok. I want you three to guard this tunnel entrance and I want you three to guard that one. Bubba, Raiden, and the rest of us are going down this main tunnel. Set your explosives about twenty feet down each tunnel. Make sure you have enough to collapse the roofs of the tunnels. Position the M75 machine guns at each entrance. These babies have the new ammo and you can't miss. The M's will be hindered from moving because of the tunnel walls. If you feel you can't hold back the M's assault, blow the tunnels and head back to the vehicles. We'll set our own plastic, so don't wait for us if things go south. Understand?"

"Yes Sir," The six men replied as one.

"Alright, let's see if we can meet this Big M. Come on guys," John said, smiling at Bubba and Raiden. He then told everyone, "Make sure your night-vision goggles are working. It's pitch black in there and you don't want to fight these things, blind."

"John, I know you wish to capture, Big one. But I not able to say, I not kill, if I see it," Raiden said to John.

"I understand, Raiden, but remember what's in that thing's blood just might save your sister. Maybe you should think about her before revenge. I love, her, too, Raiden. But I happen to think that the knowledge we gain from capturing him could save your sister and maybe humanity." Putting his hand on Raiden's shoulder, John said, "Put your pride aside. There will be time for revenge later."

"I try my best *Bosu,*" Raiden said as he bowed.

"Besides I have this." John took out a pistol with a large barrel from his belt and showed Raiden.

"Jesus H. John. That looks like a flare gun. Are you going to light him up?" Bubba asked.

"No. This has one shot. Agni has the rifle version. If I can get a clean hit with this, a Big M will go to sleep quick as can be.

There's enough knock-out juice in this shell to take down a herd of buffalo."

As the three men made their way down the tunnel, they planted explosive plastic and locked the timers into all of their T50 watches. After fifteen minutes of searching the tunnel they came across broken pods and human remains.

"It seems we've found their love nest." John said.

After stepping on a human foot and looking at the bottom of his shoe with disgust, Bubba added, "Damn! I think it might be the mutant fucks cafeteria also."

"I just don't understand. Why they would go through all of this and just diss…" John was interrupted by a low but growing hum. A chorus of simultaneous howling began to get louder and louder.

"John...err...John. We got to get our behinds out of here *now*. There's got to be a lot more of them than us," Bubba whispered to John. The howling seemed to come from everywhere and kept growing in intensity.

"My friend, I completely agree with you. EVERYONE *RUN*!! Back to the trucks. GO. GO!!!." The team all turned and started to hightail it back to the armored vehicles. Almost immediately the last man in line screamed, as a Morph tore into him. John yelled, "Toss some gas grenades behind you but don't stop running." Everyone pitched grenades over their shoulders, and as they ran, the explosions were deafening. However, seconds after the smoke cleared, another man went down, screaming and firing his weapon at the same time. The howling became more sporadic but louder. As the men ran down the tunnel John shouted, "We're almost there. Keep going and get to the trucks. I'll blow the tunnels. Just as he finished his sentence machine gun fire could be heard from the other two tunnels. It was followed by two big explosions, shaking the tunnel. At the same time John could hear explosions and gun fire coming from above where the armored Humvees were.

"They're in the other tunnels and up top. Get to the trucks. Don't stop. Get to the trucks," John ordered. As everyone exited the tunnel, Bubba and John turned to see six Morphs rushing straight at them. Bubba fired a FTG setting off howls of pain, as Morph body parts flew everywhere. "Bubba, Raiden!! Get moving I'll hold them off."

"I won't leave you here. Blow the damn thing and let's go," Bubba, yelled as he grabbed John by the shoulder. Just then out of the smoke a giant figure approached. Though clearly wounded, the Big M glared at John and Bubba. John and the Big M stood still as their eyes locked.

"John! What the hell are you waiting for? Blow the damn tunnel," Bubba yelled. John started walking toward the Big M. "John!! Stop!! John!!" Bubba yelled again. Suddenly the Big M, distracted by, Bubba's yelling, broke eye contact with John. It then took a deep breath and was ready to charge both men. "John!! Forget takin' it alive; come on man." Bubba hit his friend in the back of the neck just hard enough to knock him out. He slung, John, over his shoulders and turned to the Big M just as it charged.

Raiden pulled his katana and swung at the Big M's arm cutting it deeply. The monster howled. Bubba yelled for Raiden to get out of the tunnel. Turning quickly, Raiden rolled and sped out of the tunnel just as Bubba yelled, "Eat shit, fucker." Bubba, and Raiden ran for the exit, as Bubba commanded his T50 to set off the explosives. Just as he exited the tunnel with John over his back, Bubba could hear the Big M scream even through the enormous blast.

****

As Sheamus, Agni and ten men made their way to the upper floors of the park, Sheamus was getting nervous. "I can't be understandin' why these here things wanted us ta come here and then, the blokes disappear?"

"Maybe they were afraid?" Agni said.

"Yeah. Maybe boyo,' but I wouldn't bet ta farm on it."

As they made their way down the hallways Sheamus came across a locked conference room which had blood running from underneath the door. Putting his ear against the door, Sheamus heard nothing. "Hold it here fellas. Agni and me will check this out. You fellas check the rooms down ta hall." As he was about to kick the door in, Sheamus asked Agni, "Are ya ready laddybuck?"

"This poor servant is as ready as ever, dear Shea."

Smashing open the door, the two men entered to a horrible sight.

"Jesus wept," Sheamus whispered to himself.

What lay before him were the bodies of over thirty women who had given birth babies. Kidnapped, raped, and forced to carry Morph babies to term, these women all met horrific deaths, as the M babies were born. The toxic sac would induce a lethal reaction in the women and they would die in agony. Sheamus and Agni had seen many horrors in their lives, but the sight of the torn and emaciated women before them was a shock. Walking through pools of blood and gore Sheamus came upon a dead Morph baby.

"Look at this will ya. Ta heathen bastards even leave their own dead."

"Yes, but even today in times of plenty, Acharya women have been known to do the same if they have a female child," Agni lamented. "It may grow to be monster, but now, it just innocent baby."

"Yeah, but in o' month that there baby could rip yer head off and eat yer guts, while ya watched it doin' it, boyo.'" Turning the baby over, Sheamus said, "God's holy trousers. This here baby be o' female."

"So? What does tha…"

Before Agni could asked his question there were screams, howls and gunfire coming from down the hall. The two men ran into the hall and saw a dozen Morphs ripping apart the ten men who had come with them. Though a couple of men were still fighting it was clear that the Morphs were going to kill them all. As Sheamus and Agni stared at the massacre some of the Morphs looked up from their feeding and howled at the two men. More M's caught sight of Sheamus and Agni and began to move toward them.

"Dear me," Agni said. "This humble servant..knows...you do not run, Shea. So...even though he is...very scared, he will...be, very much...pa...pa...pleased to stay with you."

"OHH...Ahh. Well….ah...look here me Leprechaun friend. Me thinks we can make an exception here. Tis true, I did say, O'Keefe's never ran from anythin' but in this here case, boyo,' Sheamus O'Keefe be sayin,' '*Let's get ta fuck outta here.*!!!"

The two men turned and ran as fast as possible back down to the trucks on the ball field.

Also making their way to the trucks, Bubba and Raiden could see the M's had attacked the armored vehicles and John's men were putting up a hell of a fight. At the same time they ran into, Sheamus and Agni, coming from the top floors.

"Good ta see all three of yer made it. Is John ok?"

"Yeah, just had to poke him some. He didn't want to leave. I think that big fuck had him hypnotized. He'll be fine," Bubba said. "You two look like you've seen a ghost."

"Well ya could be sayin' that boyo.' We definitely saw something that needs discussin' but this here's not ta time. Let's get John to ta trucks. There still be some fierce fightin' up top, me friend. So get him up and runnin.' I'll be back."

"Where are you going, Shea?" Bubba asked.

"I'm goin' ta fetch ta cavalry, boyo'" With that Sheamus turned and headed out dancing and dodging and fighting his way through Morph after Morph. Bubba, Raiden and Agni along with the other men ran for the armored Humvees and began to repulse the M attack. With some quick smelling salts they woke John. They were about to tell him what happened with Sheamus, but the fight accelerated as eight M's rushed the circled armored vehicles.

From inside the trucks, men were cutting down Morphs left and right. Outside, the battle was nearly hand-to-hand. John yelled for everyone to get into the humvee, but just as he did, a large figure rammed into one truck and along with two other Morphs, flipped another. Agni took a shot at the Big M, but a Morph jumped in front of the gun and went down. The Big M then ripped the turret out of the last vehicle. Bubba and a Morph were rolling around on the ground fighting. While his new armor kept him from being gutted, Bubba pulled his Bowie knife and slit the M's entire side open. Agni was reloading when the Big M sent him flying with a slap of its hand. John killed a Morph who was eating a wounded soldier. Raiden kept slashing and slicing Morph heads off. The battle became a hand-to-hand fight.

As John tried to reload his 45, a Big M, bleeding from multiple wounds grabbed him. It put one foot on John's chest and took John's arm in its hand. John looked up and reached for his 45, hoping to get one shot off before the Big M ripped his arm off. However, the huge beast only bit John's hand. John, realized this was the Morph from the tunnel. As the thing bit him there was suddenly a voice in his head. John, heard. “We live.”

Just then Raiden jumped on top of the red devil and as he was bringing his katana down to take its head off, the Big M looked at Raiden and smiled. Hesitating for a second as he looked in the eyes of the creature, he then decapitated it.

As John lay there, with the massive, Big M body across his. The pain from the bite was excruciating and he was on the verge of passing out. He felt the life draining out of him. He heard gunfire and howling but knew he had nothing left. He remembered his family, friends and Aimi and wished he could have done more. He threw his empty gun at the Morphs, cursing them. Just before the darkness set in, John saw a shadow cross his face. He thought, “Choke on it. You bastards.” As a figure loomed over him and John slipped into unconsciousness he heard a familiar voice.

“Look at ye mate. Ach ya bloomin’ knob, what have ya done ta yerself?”

Chapter Two

The Lads Make a Plan

With the Big M dead, and the rest of the Morphs gone, the Tsalaki army and the Roman Institute's private security force, rivaling many of the seven Nation's armed services; retreated to care for their wounded. After the battle of New Boston, if humanity's war with the Morphs was going to prove successful, it was clear to everyone that a more forward-looking plan was necessary. At the Richard Roman Hospital outside New Boston, the Roman family, gathered around the bed of David Roman's youngest son. After three days in a medically induced comma, the doctors woke John. As he regained consciousness, he could see only blurry shadows in his room.

"John. John. How are you feeling? I'm Doctor Ranger. Do you remember me? I am the Doctor, along with Doctor Smith, who is taking care of Aimi Kameyama." Aimi was John's love. He had met her while working for her father, Riku Kameyama, in the nation of Uli wa Liánhé.

"Oh...hey…," John said. As his head cleared, the rest of the people in the room came in to focus. "How did the battle go?" John asked.

"We got our bloody asses kicked boyo.' We're damn lucky any of us got out o' there alive, I'll tell ya. That there big fella looked like he was gonna rip yer arm off. But Raiden here cut ta buggers head clean off, he did," Sheamus smiled.

"Sheamus. Please, not now. John needs his rest. We can talk about those kind of things later," David Roman said.

"Well pardon me yer lordship. Sheamus O'Keefe knows when he's not wanted. I'll be takin' me leave of ya's," Sheamus huffed. As he started to walk away John stopped him.

"No. Shea. Don't go. Please. Dad. It's alright. I want to know what happened. We need to find out what went wrong. I know one thing that's important. That Big M could have killed me but it didn't. It bit me like it did Mark. And...I...swear. I know this sounds crazy, but it talked to me."

"John. Are you saying those things can speak English?" Matt Roman, John's brother asked.

"No...ehh...no...it..didn't speak to me it...it... '*thought*' to me."

"I don't understand, John," Matt replied.

"In my head. Right after it bit me it said, 'We live.' But not verbally. It was in my head. As clear as I'm talking to you now. It said, 'We live.'"

Everyone in the room looked at each other, and then David said, "Son. You've been through a great ordeal. You nearly died. Why don't you get some rest? We can discuss all this later. Maybe in a few days."

"Damn it!!! *I'm not delusional, or in shock,*" John yelled. "Goddamn it. We don't have days. I remember what happened. We got our lunch handed to us. These things are not dumb brutes. They are coordinated, they are intelligent and they have a plan. Dad. You failed to act before. I'm sorry, but your hesitation and handing over control to Mark cost us time, lives and maybe the war itself. Matt and I are taking it from here. Mom has signed over everything to us. Matt, we need to get everything up and running at the Pentagon. Make..sur.."

"John. Easy. Easy, we've done that. You were out for a few days. We've set up operations in our east coast Institute offices coordinating a counterattack and setting up defenses. We are working with the nation's forces in case of another attack by the Morphs." Turning to his father, Matt said, "Dad. He didn't mean it that way. You did your best, but you know...your memory and health has made this the only way we could go. If anyone is to blame, it's Mark. He used you for his own purposes. Let Mom take you home. I'll come by later and see you."

"You're right Matt. I was an old fool. John, I'm sorry. Please forgive me."

John didn't look at his father. David started to tear-up but Matt took him by the arm and walked him outside the room. "Dad. He's just upset about Aimi. He'll get over it. Please, go home with Mom."

"David. Come on. I'll take you home, my love. Everything will be alright. The boys have it all under control. This is their problem to solve. You've done more than your share to make this world a better place. Come, my dear. Let's go home." Celest said to David tenderly. As they were leaving, Celest turned to Matt and whispered. "Make sure you tell John, I will be back tonight, and he is going to hear it from me about the way he treated his, father. Sick, wounded or heartbroken, he had no right to say those horrible things to David. He knows better."

"I will Mom. I will. I'm sure he will apologize," Matt said, hugging Celest.

Returning to the room, Matt told, John. "Ok big mouth. You happy now?"

"I'm sorry but you know I'm right," John replied.

"You may be right John but that man has done more for this world than you could ever dream about. You owe him an apology." Matt moved to John's bedside. "Look I know you're upset about Aimi. But if you what to blame someone. blame Mark."

"Oh, I do blame him, Matt. He also tried to have me killed more than once. Do you know that?"

"Yes. You claimed that before, but what proof do you have? Criminals who told you what you wanted to hear with a gun pointed to their heads? Gangsters who were after Aimi? If you're going to accuse our brother, John, I'll need more proof than that. I don't care for Mark. He can be a narcissistic asshole, but he's our brother. I find it hard to believe, he would seek to actually have you murdered."

"I'll get the proof. Don't worry. When I do, he is going to answer for Aimi."

"Alright, John. Just don't do something you'll regret without being sure. That's all I ask. On another note, we have been asked to come to the White House by Chancellor Perry. The Tsalaki Counsel wants to discuss our lab findings on the Morphs and to ask us about further plans to neutralize the M threat."

"The White House? When did they take that out of storage?" Bubba asked.

"Tsalaki had it stored until they were sure the oceans had stabilized. Three years ago it was moved to the center of Pennsylvania. The whole thing, brick by brick. They also have the Lincoln Memorial and Washington Monument there now," Matt explained.

"Tell Chancellor Perry we'll be glad to meet with him and the Counsel. But first we have to make a plan. Matt, have we learned anything new about the physiology of the Morphs?"

"Well. The biggest news, if we can believe Sheamus….is..."

"Hold on now…yer lordship. Ya may be John's brother but if ya think ya can be callin' Sheamus O'Keefe o' liar, then the two of us will have ta talk outside there, fella." As Sheamus moved aggressively toward Matt, Bubba grabbed him.

"Easy, Shea. I'm sure Mr. Roman didn't mean it that way."

"Yeah. So ya say Bubba. But what other way is there? Besides this here is the second time one o' these here high-and-mighty Roman fellas has insulted. Sheamus O'Keefe and I'll be tell ya now, tis here goin' ta stop or I'll be slammin' me fists inta some, Roman faces, I will be. Sheamus O'Keefe may turn the other cheek once in o' great while, boyo,' but the next time it'll be me beautiful Irish ass you'll be getting,' along with o' beatin' that ya won't soon be forgettin' boyo.'"

"Shea. Shea. Easy," Bubba pleaded.

"Mr. O'Keefe. I can assure you I meant no disrespect. I chose my words irresponsibly. Please, I sincerely apologize. I just thought that in the heart of battle anyone can see things which are not always what they seem. All of our testing has shown that when humans morph, whether they are male or female, they become male. No one has ever seen a female Morph," Matt said.

"Yeah, Well no one has ever seen o' bloody Leprechaun either, ya big mullet head. Ya be tellin' me they don't be real? Go ahead, yer lordship. Tell me that and see what happens," Sheamus said with a big smile.

After thinking for a second Matt said, "Sure, Mr. Sheamus. Sure. Leprechauns are real."

As Sheamus laughed loudly, he turned to everyone else and said, "Ya see, I knew he be o' *bréagadóir."*

"Alright Shea. You made your point," John said. "Guys. We need to focus on the Morph situation. Now Shea. What did you see?"

"Well, John. Agni there and me. We went inta this here room and it was full of poor lasses who had died birthin' the M babies. Ya seen what that looks like, John. This here was o' room with at least twenty or more o' ta women. I noticed o' wee Morph baby. It were dead but when I turned it over ta wee thing was female."

"You sure it was woman, Shea?" Raiden asked.

"Dear, dear me, Raiden. I know we've only known each other for o' tiny bit o' time but I can assure ya sword swingin' majesty, Sheamus O'Keefe knows ta difference between o' boy and o' girl."

"Yes, John. This humble servant saw it also. The poor thing. A girl she was indeed." Agni added.

John thought for awhile and then surmised. "Look. This may make sense after all. Think about it. Nature hates redundancy or necessary steps in an organism's development. I mean it happens but it's the exception, not he rule. It uses energy, it opens the chance for defects; there are a whole host of reasons why nature doesn't double down. We know Morphs become Morphs by way of the pods. Six infected humans come together, go into stasis, the pods develop. We know the two end pods die feeding the others via the tentacles that create the webbing around the pods. After a few days out come four fully developed Morphs; All male. So why would they go to the trouble of kidnapping and impregnating human women when the pods work so well?" John paused in thought some more. "What if impregnating the women is how the Morphs produce Morph females?"

"But isn't that redundant? If they can make male Morphs through the pods, why do they need female Morphs?"

“That’s a good question Matt. Which is why we need to get that female baby. I think the child of a Morph male and a Morph female might be something very different. We must find the answer. Just think. We know the Morphs are in many ways an evolutionary advancement. They are capable of living in extreme cold or heat. They are highly resistant to radiation. Those physical attributes are what an intelligent species will need to survive in this new world. And don’t doubt for one minute the Morphs are intelligent. Our biggest mistake was thinking them just beasts.”

‘Are you saying the Morphs are nature’s answer to our destroying the planet, John?” Matt asked. “Do you suggest we just hand over everything to them and then lie down and die?”

“No. Of course not, Matt. Besides, the Morph virus was frozen hundreds of thousands of years before humans existed. But there have been over five mass extinctions we know about, some so destructive that nearly all life on earth was wiped out. But every time after a mass extinction, the organisms that survived and replenished the Earth were better and stronger than their predecessors. The dinosaurs ruled the earth for millions of years. They kept evolving, but after they were destroyed, we emerged. We mammals became the apex species. Climate change has melted all the ice. There are going to be areas of extreme heat and cold in the next three or more millennia. The depleting ozone layer will wreak havoc with human skin. Food production will dwindle to nothing. Morphs don’t need to grow crops, radiation doesn’t bother them. Even with our advanced technology, humans will only be able to service in very special small areas. In fact, I believe the Habitat Project will have to be reopened. That might be the only place where humanity will be able to survive."

"So what yer be sayin' boyo' is the earth is ready for o' new top gun, is it?"

"I don't know about that, Shea. But this I do know. We are not the dinosaurs. We can fight back and we're going to. That's why I want that baby. Bubba, take Agni and go get that baby. He'll show you where it was.

"We're on it John. Come on little fella, show me where that baby was."

"Oh yes. Very good. This humble servant very happy to be on a mission with you again, Bubba, very happy."

"Shea, Raiden. I want you two to find my brother, Mark. Find out what he's up to and report back. I want to know if he's planning anymore assassination attempts or has any illegal labs up and running. Just don't let him know what you're up to."

"Don't be worryin' about that me dear boy. If, Sheamus O'Keefe don't want anyone ta know he's on their tail, they never will."

"Sounds good. Just watch your back. Alright, we'll all meet at our east coast Institute offices. Bring the baby to the lab and don't let anyone see you. After that, we'll all go and meet the Chancellor."

Chapter Three

The Other Side

As, John and the Lads were doing everything they could to fight the Morph menace Mark, John's brother, was hatching his own plans. He had gathered the children of his brother, Luke. After Mark became a persona-non-grata in his family, his hatred intensified. He was accompanied by Victor the oldest son of Mary Roman. "Has everyone shown up, Victor?"

"Everyone you invited, Uncle Mark."

"Good. I'm going to show the family they can't just throw me to the gutter."

"Yeah, Well. When you tried to kill their poster boy, Uncle Mark, they probably got a little miffed," Victor said.

"Now. Now, Victor. That's fake news. We all know I would never physically hurt my family. Besides there is absolutely no proof I did any such thing." The two men entered the ball room of Mark's house, where the rest of Mary's children were, except for Lula.

"Well, dears. It is so good of you all to join me here. This house is the only thing left after I was purged from the family," Mark said.

"Of course the family only *thinks* this is all that's left. I have always prepared for unfortunate events. So my dear nieces and nephews, we are still swimming in money. I also have opened my last lab. It is well hidden and we will all go there after this meeting. My jet is waiting for us, and we will indeed fly in the luxury I am accustomed to."

"If we're going there, why not have the meeting there?" Victor asked.

"Because, my dear nephew, this meeting's purpose is to weed out those who are with me and those who want to stay neutral."

"Yeah. I see you didn't invite our little pixie sister, Uncle Mark," Tamar said.

"Now, now. Tamar, Lula is a sweet, though naive little girl. She's my niece and I love her as I do all of you. She just needs to see who the Roman's really are. She'll come around one day, but for now I thought it best to keep her out of our inner circle here," Mark replied.

"We'd say that's a good plan, Uncle Mark," The twin albinos, Castro and Paul said in unison. "Only we don't think she'll ever be one of us, Uncle Mark."

"That may be, boys. That...may...be. *But,* we're here to talk about now. I have recently discovered some very interesting things about the Morphs. As you all know, Victor actually fought them and very bravely I must say." Tamar got up and moved to Victor. She put her arms around his waist and chest and she purred. "Yes...yes. My...umm...brave...strong brother. He knows how to handle dangerous things. Don't you dear brother?" Tamar's hand brushed across Victor's crotch as she gave him an alluring smile.

"Ok, sis. You can thank Victor, later. I'm sure he'll be glad to talk over his adventures with you in a more private setting," Cyrus said with a bit of disgust.

"Ohh...Cyrus. Don't be jealous. I love you, too, big brother. It's just that, Victor, well he is a much bigger brother," Tamar laughed.

"Hey. Ugm..ugm..why...ugm..ugm… if those Morph things like to eat us, why can't we eat them? Maybe they taste good." Judith said between constant bites of her sandwich.

"Well...uhh...who knows my dear. Maybe you can try some recipes at the lab, Judith," Mark said, as he stared at Judith's gaping mouth endlessly chomping on her food.

"In that case, I am definitely in. I've got some barbecue sauces I've been dying to try on new meat." Judith had eaten every edible mammal on the planet. From Antelope to Zebra, she had eaten them all. Hence she was always on the lookout for new tastes.

"Great. That's one. How about the rest of you?" Mark asked.

"What are we in for Mark?" Victor asked.

"The truth, my dear nieces and nephews. I am going to create an army of Morphs. They will follow me without question. With that army I am going to destroy the Roman dynasty as we know it. I will reshape it into what it should be: my right arm of power. No more of this helping the dregs of this world. No more giving everything to people who don't deserve it. My world will be the world of nature itself. Survival of the fittest, with those at the top reaping the benefits of that fight. We will be kings and queens of the earth and my Morph army will keep the unwashed in line." As Mark raised his hands in the air and the veins on his faced bulged, the red births marks on his cheeks disappeared..

"Jesus, Mark. Did you practice that in front of a mirror?" Luke said as he walked into the room.

His children all turned and said, "Hello Luke."

"Hi kids. What has Uncle Mark been filling your heads with?"

"Same shit. He should be in charge of the Roman clan," Cyrus answered.

"Really? Does that include us, Mark?" Luke asked. A little embarrassed, Mark slowly put his arms down. Composing himself, he said to Luke.

"Of course not dear brother. We are all Roman. I would…"

"Speak for yourself, Uncle Mark," Tamar responded. We don't consider ourselves Roman."

"Tamar. You carry my name, and that makes you Roman," Luke said.

"No, Luke. It doesn't. We care for you Luke. You have always treated us right. Uncle Mark, the same goes for you. But the rest of the family. Fuck'em."

"Look, Tamar. Your mother would be very upset if she heard yo…" Luke started to say.

"That's because Mom wants to be special. She wants to be in this Roman history. Part of this so called dynasty. But she, and we, will never be part of it. Mary is not Roman. None of our fathers were Roman. We know we're not yours, Luke, but we never cared because we know how much Mom wanted children. We also know you can't produce any. You were kind enough to let her find a way to have us, and you never held it against us that we weren't yours, biologically. But the rest of your family does care. We've heard the whispers. Intentionally loud so we *could* hear them. We see the looks. How a group gets quiet if we approach. A million cuts, Luke. All our lives. Well. If, Uncle Mark wants to take it down and make it in his image, I'm in." Tamar finished her rant and went to get a drink.

"Yeah. I'm with Tamar. If she's in, so am I," Victor said.

"Sure. Like there was any doubt about that," Cyrus mocked. "I'm in as long as I see you have the upper hand. If this shits falls apart, I'm out."

"Ye of little faith, Cyrus," Mark said.

"Well the lab didn't work out so great, did it Mark?" Cyrus asked.

"That was simply a learning curve my young man. Wait till you see what's in the new lab. You are going to want to be on this team. I guarantee that."

"Ok. Just show me you're ahead of the others and I'm in," Cyrus said.

“That just leaves you two boys. What do you say fellas?” Mark asked the twins.

The twins looked at each other and in their own secret language mumbled something only they understood. “If we side with you, can we experiment on the Morphs? Uncle Mathew wouldn't allow us to do what we wanted to them. He said it was cruel and akin to torture,” The twins asked.

“Of course, my dear boys. I’ll give you all the Morphs you need. You can do whatever you want to them,” Mark smiled.

Looking sat each other the twins turned to Mark and said, “We’re in.”

“Oh, that’s wonderful. Now I want you all to get packed and meet me outside. We’ll take the limo to the new lab and I will show you its wonders.” As the children left to pack, Mark looked at Luke.

“You’re coming with us I assume.”

“You want to see a Big M make me shit my pants again?”

“Oh come on brother. You’re not still holding that against me? I need you by my side Luke. You more than anyone. Together we’ll make the Roman name great.”

“It already is great, Mark.”

“You know what I mean. Look you know more than anyone, all their talk of inclusion, equality, it’s just bullshit. What do you think Dad would say if he knew about the real you?”

“Are you blackmailing me, Mark?”

"Of course not, brother. Look me in the eye. Am I right?" Luke thought for awhile and then said. "I'll go get packed. Meet you outside."

****

Mark's lab was located at the base of the Rocky mountains. He had it built after the Sweat virus ravaged the planet and killed his mother. He never told anyone. For what reason; even he didn't quite understand. But now, he was elated he never shared this place with any of his family. After his fiasco in the other lab, his father David would have definitely taken this lab from him. Even if he was able to convince his family to keep it, the Tsalaki government certainly would not have let him run it.

"Here we are, my dear nieces and nephews. What do you think?"

Everyone had taken an elevator down five floors. Two huge doors opened and they stared in awe at a room the size of a football field. Rows of cells lined each wall. There were at least fifty workers, lab technicians and scientists working like busy little bees. There were also a cadre of armed, mean looking men, in front of every cell.

"It looks just like your other lab, Mark. Just bigger and with an armed security detail. I heard the Jones brothers didn't fare too well. Didn't keep their eyes on the ball?" Luke chuckled.

"Oh. Please Luke. You're just mad because they got a kick out of your little mishap. Well you got your payback. The Big M that ripped their eyes out and escaped also ate the damn things."

"Yeah maybe you shouldn't have had the spare security chips planted in their eyes," Luke said.

Putting his hand on Luke's shoulder Mark said. "Look brother, it's water under the bridge. Can we move on to important things. Besides, the damn thing bit the shit out of me remember? I spent two weeks in the hospital. Still hurts," Mark rubbed his hand as he walked to the first cell.

"You still hearing voices?" Luke asked. For the first time since their meeting, Mark's face became very serious. He stopped and gave Luke the steely stare, which always sent chills down Luke's back. "Let me make one thing perfectly clear, dear brother. That fucking thing looked into my soul. Its voice, or thoughts were in my head for weeks. It didn't matter how many drugs the doctors gave me, I couldn't get that thing's thoughts out of my head. It was a fucking nightmare. What it did to me is something you will *never* jest about. I don't *ever* want to hear you mock what that monster did to me. Do you understand? Luke knew Mark was livid, because the red birthmarks on his cheeks disappeared. Whenever that happened, Luke knew to back off.

"Sure...sure. Sorry. Didn't mean anything by it. Won't happen again."

Mark seemed to cool off and regain his composure. He grabbed Luke's neck in his hand and said, "Thank you Luke. I always know I can count on my dear brother." Mark gave Luke's neck a hard squeeze before letting go. He brightened up instantly and turned to the others.

"Alright. Let me give you all the grand tour. Barton!!' Mark yelled for his new aide.

"Yes, Sir," Barton said, as he stood at attention.

"Have the drinks and the hors d'oeuvres served."

"Right away, Sir."

Mark smiled at his family and said, "I always wanted a real butler. Barton's great grandfather worked for the last Queen of England. Gives the place a sense of royalty don't you think?"

"You always wanted to be a king, Mark," Luke said.

"Yes, Luke. And you always wanted to be a queen. So it's a win-win. This way my dear family."

****

Sheamus and Raiden had had been observing Mark's mansion when Luke and six of Mary's children arrived. "Well, if o' pot ain't full o' gold. It seems ta usual suspects have been summoned by his lordship. Here take o' look, Raiden," Sheamus said, handing his binoculars to Raiden.

"I see people, Shea, but what is meaning?" Raiden asked.

"Those there people, me fine Asian friend, are ta children, well, six of them at least, of Mary Roman. Ta thing is, they all have different fathers. Ya see, Luke there, that's be ta skinny blond fella, he been shootin' blanks all his life. So, Mary, she went and had herself o' good ole time with some fellas and got herself seven children."

"I see. So, Luke kill seven men? He great warrior, to regain honor against such odds."

Laughing a little bit, Sheamus said, "No...no. My dear sword swingin' friend. Ya see, Luke gave her ta thumbs up ta go and fill her belly with children. Luke couldn't kill o' fly if yer was ta hold it for his nut-less self."

"Ugh...he has no honor. He *koshinuke.*"

"Yeah...well, I don't be speaking that there old lingo o' yer's, but I'll bet one o' me Ma's hugs I get what ya be sayin,' boyo.'"

As all of the guests entered Mark's house, Sheamus turned to Raiden.

"Come on, me friend. Let's see ifin' we can be gettin' o' better look-see as ta what John's evil brother be up to." With that, both men climbed down from the cliff where they had been observing the doings at Mark's. They both went around to the back of the compound and scaled the wall surrounding the house. As they dropped down the other side, they could see they were in an area resembling a warehouse. There were trucks and men loading and unloading equipment. All the workers had uniforms on, so Sheamus got an idea. "Look here, Raiden. We needs ta get two o' them there uniforms so we can blends in with ta rest o' them there fellas. Somethin' goin' on here that ain't quite kosher, boyo.'"

After waiting behind a truck the men were abler to subdue two of the workers and take their uniforms. "Make sure they be out cold there, boyo'."

"I put *suimin* hold on them. They not wake up for hours, *aibō*."

"Right. Well let's be seein' what these here black and tans are up ta."

Sheamus and Raiden grabbed some boxes and started to move toward the warehouse. When they entered the main building they saw tons of lab equipment. There were also a lot of armed security guards. Sheamus could see that much of the unboxed lab gear was being put on a large elevator. The problem was there were five armed security men who were scanning everyone and everything going on and off the elevator.

"There has got ta be somethin' very important at ta bottom o' them there elevators, boyo.' We got ta get on them there Otis lifts and see what be down there," Sheamus whispered to Raiden as they pretended to work.

"I could kill guards and you could use elevators. My death would be...honorable."

"Jesus freakin' Christ, Raiden. Will ya stop tryin' ta off yerself, lad? Tis here ain't no suicide mission. Sheamus will figure o' way ta…"

"You two!" A foreman yelled at the men.

"Take that load down to the lab. Get moving."

"Yes, Sir. Right away yer lordship," Sheamus said smiling.

“Ya see there, boyo.’ Ta lord does provide.”

The men grabbed the pallet and pushed it to the elevator doors. As they waited in line, Sheamus started to feel the hairs on the back of his neck stand up, a warning that saved his life many times.

“Psst. Raiden,” Sheamus said under his breath.

“Somethin’ ain’t right. I know I said ta lord provides but this here feels more like ta devil’s work. Keep them there pig stickers ready and be on guard.” Sheamus looked around the warehouse for an escape route and he thought he found one. Workers were going over to a flapping door and throwing empty cartons and other material in to it. “Look here. If tis thing goes tits up, run fer that there door, where they be throwin’ ta garbage. It seems ta be ta only thin’ not locked down tight.”

When it was their turn at the elevators, Sheamus could see the changes in the guard’s posture and eyes. He was sure the guards were on to them.

“Hold it there you two,” The head guard said. “What’s on the pallet?” Sheamus knew it was a stall. Three of the guards were slowly circling him and Raiden as the head guard kept talking. Sheamus elbowed Raiden.

“Well, ya see yer lordship. What me dear friend here and I have be o’ giant dildo yer moms did give us ta be shovin’ up all yer dirty bastards’ asses.” Momentarily stunned by what Sheamus said, the guards looked at their boss. It was just what Sheamus and Raiden needed to get the jump on them.

"Kill them," The head guard yelled. By the time the other henchmen looked back at the two men, Sheamus and Raiden had already pulled their knives and swords. Raiden cut off both arms of one guard who was raising his machine gun to kill Sheamus. Then in a one gracefully smooth motion Raiden spun around and cut the head off another man. Simultaneously, Sheamus cut the throat of a guard with his combat knife. At nearly the same time, he stuck his trusty switchblade through the eye of the fourth man. This left only the head guard who put up his hands, dropped to his knees and begged the two not to kill him.

"Come on now there fella. Stand up like o' man will ya." The guard stood up, clearly shaking.

"Why ya tell ta men there ta kill us?" Sheamus asked.

"WE...we.. have 'KOS' orders for anyone associated with the Roman Institute...especially John Roman."

"Excuse please. What is 'KOS'?" Raiden asked.

"That there means ta 'kill-on-sight,' me dear friend. Now why would Mark want ta be killin' people on sight? What's he got down there that be so important he wants ta be murderin' people?"

"I….I..don't know. Even we aren't allowed down there. We can't…" Just then the elevators doors sounded and were about to open. The guard heard the bell and knew that the elevators were full of armed men. He smiled at Sheamus, knowing what was coming. Sheamus saw the look on the mans face and knew.

"So ya cowardly little turd. Ya hold us up here while ya knew yer friends were o' comin' ta cut us down, hey." The doors opened and there were twenty armed men ready to rush out and extirpate Sheamus and Raiden.

"Kill them," The head guard yelled as he turned and tried to get into the elevator. Raiden gave the man a spinning kick that sent him flying through the air into the guards who were trying to get off the elevator. At the same time Sheamus threw his combat knife into the back of the flying guard and his dead body hit the crowd of henchmen causing a pile up at the door.

"Time ta run me friend." Both men ran for the shaft that Sheamus had pointed out earlier. They dove through the door and fell down a shaft. The two men landed with a thud into a pile of cardboard and other garbage. After jumping out of the bin they looked around and could see that they were in the disposal room. At the other end of the room were a pile of body parts. Sheamus walked over to them and could see that there were both human and Morph body parts. But as he looked closer, what he saw caused him to nearly vomit.

"What is it, *aibō*?"

"Jesus, Joseph and bloody Mary. Them there is human women. They died from birthin' Morph babies."

"But we know that happens."

"These here are fresh, Raiden. Which means this here mother fucker, Mark, is impregnatin' women right now. We got ta tell John." The men could hear commotion going on above them.

"We must go, *aibō*."

"Yeah. Yeah let's…" As he was about to leave, Sheamus saw something in the pile of bodies. Turning over what he thought was a Morph body part he realized it was instead the body of a Morph baby. In fact there were several Morph babies, and they were all female.

"We got ta take this with us Raiden. This will be our proof."

****

In the lab, Mark was showing everyone the experiments he had been doing on Morphs. He had produced two Big M's of which he was very proud.

"Look at them my dear children. Are they not magnificent?" Mary's children took turns eyeing the Big M's.

"That's the skin color we want," the twins said in unison.

"Boys. You can have any Morph you want to do your experiments on, but the big ones are off limits."

"Is the size of their cocks unusual, or are they all that huge?" Tamar asked as she stared longingly at the Big M's penis.

"They are quite average," Mark said.

"They could give you a run for your money, Victor," Tamar laughed.

"Yeah. Well. I don't tear people in half after I fuck them. Do I, Tamar?" Victor replied.

"I could definitely...ughm...ughmm… see those dicks slow roasting on a spit while I drizzled my secret barbecue sauce over them." Judith said between bites of the hors d'oeuvres.

"Ok, Uncle. You made these freaks, now what are you going to do with them?" Cyrus asked. "I'm sure this setup must have cost you a great deal. Where's the pay off?"

"Cyrus, Cyrus. You always look at the cost, don't you? I am playing a long game here my children. I am creating our own army. When I have enough of these beautiful creatures, I will let them loose when and where I need them. When I am done the Nations will be begging me to take over the Roman Institute and from there the world will be our oyster."

"May I ask how you're going to control them?" Cyrus replied.

"Believe it or not, when that Big M bit me, I somehow was able to hear what it was thinking and it could hear me," Mark said.

"Right. Ok. Very funny Uncle. Now tell us how you're going to control them," Victor laughed.

Turning to Victor, Mark's face became red as his birth marks. "Victor," Mark said menacingly, causing Victor to huddle against the wall, bringing his own face nose to nose with Victor's "I love you and all my nieces and nephews, but don't ever call me a liar again. Do I make myself clear?"

"Yeah...oh..yeah. I didn't mean you were a liar, Uncle. I just thought you were joking," Victor said nervously.

Smiling and patting Victor on his chest Mark backed off and said. "It's all right, Victor. We'll just let this be a lesson." Turning to the rest of his family, he said. "I want you all to know right now that what I am doing is no joke. What I am going to show you must stay between us. So again let me make myself clear. There is the door. If you are not a hundred percent sure you are with me all the way, no matter what, then I strongly suggest you leave now. There will be no hard feelings. You're my family. If you stay, then from this moment, you are in all the way. There will be no backing out from here on. If you decide to come with me, then you're in for life. The only way out will be if you're dead."

Everyone in the room froze. All the brothers and sisters looked art each other and Luke. After a few moments, Luke broke the silence. "Mark. Are you saying if we go in with you on this plan for world domination, and then one of us wants out, you would have us *killed*?"

"That's precisely what I am saying. Look, Luke, and all of you. The world is going to become a world of the vanquished and the rulers. Which do you want to be? The Morphs are here to stay. They're not going anywhere. So you can fight them and lose or join them and win. I have joined them. But the best part is I will control them. They will rid the world of scum and the dregs in the Outlands, and the elite righteous bastards who think they can make the world into a place where we can all live in some kind of lovey-dovey paradise. The Morphs prove that's bullshit. Besides, even before the Morphs we have never been this mythical united world. People still shit on each other, tribalism stills exists. Humans will always be predators. Darwin was right. The world is survival of the fittest. There, my dear family are the fittest mother-fuckers you will ever see," Mark said as he pointed to the Big M. "Luke, these are not some diversion as I usually fiddled with all my life. This is what I was waiting for, planning for, this is my moment. I will not let anything or anyone stand in my way. So. If you're in great. If not, there's the door. Whoever decides to stay will share in the power and all the riches that will be ours. But choose wisely. Because there's no going back."

"I can't believe you would threaten your own family. Come on kids, let's go," Luke said. But as he started to walk out the door, none of his children moved. "What are you doing? Let's go. Your Uncle just threatened you with death."

"Well, Luke. Mark is playing for very high stakes. I can understand wanting people he can trust," Tamar said. "I'll back him. Especially if it means taking down the Roman clan." Luke grabbed Tamar's arm, but Victor rushed in and pulled him off her. "Get your hands off her, Luke."

"You're staying too?" Luke gasped.

"So am I," Cyrus added. "There's always a risk with big profits and if what Uncle Mark's planning works, the profits will be astronomical. I'm willing to roll the dice."

"So you rethought your, 'pulling out if things go bad?'" Mark asked Cyrus.

"Yeah. I'm in...All the way."

"I've eaten...umgg...ughh… everything that's walked or crawled. This will be a whole new menu," Judith grunted as she stuffed more food into her mouth.

"We're in too Uncle," The twins chimed in.

"Victor?" Mark asked.

"If Tamar's in, I'm in."

"Mark!!! I've taken a lot of shit from you over the years and done a lot of things I wasn't proud of, but if you think I would let you hurt the kids you…," Luke shouted.

"Luke!" Tamar shouted back. "It's our decision, not yours."

"Luke. Luke. Please step into my office. Please."

The two men went into Mark's office and as Mark closed the door he turned to Luke with a smile on his face. Mark then took out some very old Napoleon brandy, poured two glasses and sat down. Pointing to the other chair Mark motioned for Luke to sit. "Please Luke, sit. For your older brother, just hear me out." Hesitantly Luke sat down and Mark pushed the glass of brandy toward him.

"A toast brother. To family," Mark said raising his glass. Luke stared at Mark. "Luke. Do you honestly think I would hurt my nieces or nephews. I love them with all my heart. It's just that what I'm doing will change the world. They're kids, Luke. I just wanted to put the fear of God in them. Of course, if they ever want out, I would gladly let them go on their way. I trust them not to say anything. The same as I trust you, brother. I just feel that, with the importance of this move I'm making and their youth, a little danger will help keep them in line. You have my word, as your brother,

Luke. I would never harm the proverbial hair on their precious heads."

Luke thought for a while. Then, looking at Mark, he finally took the glass of brandy and said, "A toast. To family, brother. A brother who had better make sure nothing happens to those kids."

"Ohhh. Dear brother. Have you finally grown some balls when it comes to me? Is that a threat I hear?" Mark said laughing.

"No. No threat, Mark. A promise." Mark, seeing Luke's face, stopped smiling. But just as fast he grinned from ear to ear and raising his glass said, "A toast to promise." The two brothers drank their shots and slammed the glasses down on the table.

"Good. All's good." Mark said pouring another shot for the two. "So here's the deal. You want to stay neutral, stay neutral."

"Does that go for Lula? I noticed you didn't invite her."

"Lula's a lovely young girl. She just doesn't fit in my plans. But, yes, of course that goes for Lula. However, I would hope you would warn me if I were in danger."

"I would and I would also warn John if he were."

"What do you mean by that?" Mark asked.

"There are rumors that you tried to have John killed. Look Mark, I know you, Dad and Matt have had problems. I also know you want to run the family business the way you want. Which is a completely different agenda from this. I especially know you hate the fuck out of John. He's not my favorite person either, but he's our brother. So, I stay quiet, but hands off. Hands off any family member. Deal?"

"Deal. Dear brother." The two brothers downed another shot and then Luke left. On his way out Luke said goodbye to the kids. "Hey everyone. I understand your wanting to make something of your own. You're adults and if this is what you want, who am I to stop you? Just be careful. Your Mother would never forgive me if anything happened to any of you."

Tamar ran over to Luke and gave him a big hug and a kiss. 'You see, Luke. That's why we love you like you were our real father. You understand us."

"Thanks for backing us up, Luke," Victor said as he shook Luke's hand. The twins and Judith were too busy looking at the Big Morph, so Luke just said bye.

Cyrus was down the hall looking intently into a cell. "Well. It seems Cyrus has found my next pet." Turning to Luke, Mark smiled and hugged his brother. "Don't worry, dear brother it will all be fine. But this is something I can only show to the 'in-crowd.' You understand?"

"Yes. I'm leaving. I'll be at the east coast house if you need me."

****

After Luke left, Mark gathered the others. "I see Cyrus has found something interesting. Come boys and girls. I want you all to see."

Everyone gathered around the cell that Cyrus was still gazing into.

"Is that what I think it is, Uncle?" Tamar asked.

"Well, just what do you think it is, dear girl?" Mark replied.

"It looks like a female Morph."

"Precisely, my dear. A fully grown female Morph. I believe it to be the only one in captivity."

"Wow. She got a set of knockers on her. She is ripped. How the hell tall is she?" Victor asked.

"She's just under seven feet. And she is gorgeous," Mark smiled. The female Morph was nearly as tall as a Big M and like all Morphs, she had no hair. With a slightly smaller jaw and fangs she was almost as muscular as the Big M. Her eyes had the same deep red as the male but her skin was a more subtle maroon. Not as bright as the male. With breasts to match her size and muscles she was a formidable looking creature.

"You think she will let you play with her tits, Victor?" Tamar asked.

"Yeah. While she was tearing me to bits," he replied.

"But I thought they had no females?" Cyrus asked.

"Ahhh. You are right. Podding only produces males. In fact if a female pods she turns male. The pod males are drones, fighters. They gather food, protect the clan. Now, once in a great while for some reason things just work right and a Big M comes out of the pod. As you know it takes six infected people to pod. The two end pods are consumed by the other four, and after a week, four fully formed Morph males burst from the pods. When a Big M is Morphed, all five of the other pods are consumed by the Big M. and after about two weeks give or take a day, boom, a Big M."

"Ok, but where do the females come from?" Cyrus asked.

"I'm getting to that, Cyrus. Don't rush me. The reason the M's take human women is because it is how they produce females."

"That thing came out of a woman?" Tamar asked. How the hell could a human woman deliver that?"

"Well, unfortunately, not very well. You see all the women die pretty horribly."

"I guess. That thing must rip them apart," Victor said.

"Well, No. It's not the size of the baby that kills the woman, it's the toxins it produces. The baby is actually the size of a human infant, at birth. But it does grow quickly."

"How do you know?" The twins asked.

Smiling broadly, Mark motioned for the others to follow him. As they proceeded down the hall to the next room there were several loud chilling howls.

"What the fuck was that?" Tamar asked.

"Oh nothing. The Big M's and the females get a little upset when I go into this room."

"Why is that?" Tamar asked.

"Because it's the nursery." Mark opened the door, and before them were four enormous sized baby Morphs lying in four separate chambers..

"Holy shit Uncle. How the fuck did you find these?" Victor asked.

"I made them," Mark replied.

"But how?"

"We impregnated women and after a lot of attempts, I might add, we got these."

Mark motioned for one of the technicians to enter the chamber and hold up the baby. "Just look at how cute she is.

"I see now why the stakes are so high, Uncle. They find out about this and you'll end your days in the Rus Outlands," Victor said.

"Well, in science there are sometimes sacrifices that must be made. Besides, the women are all whores and runaways. My new head of security, since the Douglas brother mishap, is Ron Stark. He assures me no one will miss these women. They were wasted lives anyway, crack whores, drunks. At least now their deaths will have meaning," Mark smiled. "Yes. Yes. You can say I'm giving their lives meaning by making their deaths count for something greater."

"Sir," Stark interrupted. "We're ready for your demonstration with the T Morph."

"You mean there's more Uncle?" Tamar asked.

"Oh you haven't seen anything yet, children. Come this way." Mark led the others to a specially marked room. There were four armed guards outside and Mark had to put in voice and finger print recognition in order to open the door. As everyone entered the room, they saw a Morph which looked like no others. It was just a little taller than an average man and not as muscular as the other Morphs. Its jaw and teeth were also smaller. But its eyes were deep red and one could easily see the intelligence in those eyes. This Morph wasn't as frantic as the other Morphs. Instead it acted in an almost calm manner.

"What the hell is that, Uncle. Are you just breeding mutations?" Cyrus asked.

"No. Well, maybe. I mean, I didn't create it, but you could say I allowed it to be created," Mark said.

"Where did it come from?" The twins asked.

"This is what you get when a Big M male and a Big M female have a baby."

"Are you shitting me?" Victor said. "You bred the two big ones and got this?"

"Oh yes, dear friends. You see I cracked the code. Infected humans morph, pod style. From that you get only males and occasionally a Big M. Then they impregnate human women and you get female Morphs. Unfortunately, only about one in sixty or seventy are born alive. The ones who live are big females. Now when a big male and a big female fuck, well there you are. I call them T-Morphs," Mark said with pride.

"Why T?" Tamar asked.

"Because they are the bosses. Look closer. They have no genitals of any kind. The Morph pecking order is T-Morphs at the top, Big M's are next and the Morphs are the bottom tier. Think of it as the King, his lords and ladies, with the Morphs as serfs or soldiers. I can understand it. It actually has a name."

"Get the fuck out of here," Cyrus laughed.

"Remember what I said about doubting me," Mark said as he glared at Cyrus.

"After being bitten I could hear what they thought. It's how the communicate. They have names. This one calls himself, *Archieréas."*

"I don't know what that means, Uncle. It all sounds Greek to me," Victor said. Mark laughed and smiled at Victor. Putting his hand on Victor's shoulder, he said. "My dear nephew you are precisely right. It is Greek. Ancient Greek to be exact."

"You're telling us these thing speak ancient Greek?" Tamar asked.

"Actually, they don't 'speak' to each other at all. They are far superior to us in that aspect. They 'think' to each other. Just think of it. We use words to convey our thoughts. But if I could put my thought into your head, I wouldn't need words. Their form of communication is pure, rapid and makes our vocal gibberish seem like monkey talk. Archieréas speaks to me in words so we humans can understand him. He is lowering his standards by using words. To them we are the inferior species."

"But how did he learn ancient Greek?" Victor asked.

"We haven't figured that out yet. It could be he's reading our thoughts. It could be there is some human left in these things and the knowledge is still there. We don't know that yet. Do you know what they call us?"

"Right now I would say, 'their jailers,'" Cyrus said.

"They call us, *Pithikos.* It means monkey. That's what they think of us. That's not all. The Morphs call themselves *Maketes* which means warrior. The Big ones are *Archon,* means ruler," Mark said as he looked at Archieréas.

"And these things have agreed to fight your war for you?"

"Well, in a way," Mark shrugged. "Ron, bring the baby."

Suddenly, the T-Morph stood up and walked to the window. As Ron Stark brought in an M baby Archieréas became more agitated. "Now watch this. I am going to talk with it. You'll be able to hear me because this one can hear my thoughts." With Ron holding the trussed up baby, Mark said, "Archieréas. These are my family." Archieréas looked at each of the children. "They want to join us in ridding the world of bad people and finding your...well let's call them fellow M's. Will you be so kind as to show them we are a team? Maybe jump up and down or do that dance we taught you?" Archieréas just stood there looking at Mark and the baby.

"Oh, sometimes he doesn't want to be nice. He likes to throw tantrums every so often." Mark then took a long curved knife from Ron and put it under the throat of the M baby. Archieréas slammed the door with his fists and then tapped it. Mark heard himself say, in a deep slow voice; "No."

"Did that motherfucker just talk or was that you?" Victor asked.

"No. They only use a form of telepathy. You have to have a special bite from a Big M of one of these neutered guys. Suddenly in Mark's head he heard. "Do not hurt the child. I will dance for you." In the next moment, Archieréas started to dance around the cell.

"I am floored, Uncle. You weren't bull-shitting this time. If I weren't sure before, I am now. We are in," Victor said as he looked at all his siblings. They in turned looked at Mark and all nodded yes.

Before Mark could say anything alarms started to sound. "Ron, what the fuck was that?"

"I'll find out Sir." Ron said as he handed off the baby to another man and ran out the door.

"Are those...unggh...ugh..things loose?" Judith asked between bites.

"No. No. there would be gunfire and explosions If that were the case," Mark said with a wave of his hand. Meanwhile no one noticed the keen interest Archieréas was showing in what was happening.

Within minutes Ron returned. "Sir. We have a big problem."

"Well!! what is it?" Mark shouted.

"Maybe you want to hear this in your office, Sir?" Mark looked at the others and turning to Ron said, "No. No Ron they are all part of the team now so tell me what is going on?"

"We've been compromised. Two men entered through the warehouse and escaped. They killed four or five of my men. They were also down in the crematorium and might have taken somethings."

Mark's birthmarks started to disappear but he calmed himself. "When we get to the safe house, you and I will have to have a long talk. Go to def-con five. I want everything out and brought to the safe house lab. I want this place empty and burned to the ground in twenty-four hours. Understand?"

"Yes Sir." as Ron started to leave, Mark said, "Ron. The safe house is my last resort. If that gets compromised I'll introduce you to the Big M up close and personal."

"Yes. Sir."

"Alright, everyone, small setback for which I was prepared. I'll see you all at the new place in a week. In the meantime, lay low but keep your eyes and ears open. Gather any information you can that will be helpful." As everyone left, Tamar turned to Victor and said, "I would have liked to see the two big ones' fuck. Can you imagine that dick going in and out of that big female?"

"Cheer up, you may still get your chance," Victor smiled as he put his arm around Tamar.

As the lab turned into pandemonium, with people rushing from one place to the other. Mark calmly looked at Archieréas and thought, "You know whose fault this is, Archieréas?"

In his head, Mark heard, "John."

Chapter Four

The War Rages

A few days after John left the hospital everyone had assembled at the East Coast Roman Institute facility. Sitting at a large round table were Doctors Jessie Roman and Jane Franks, Matthew Roman, Generals Jim Hooks and Kirk Thomas. There were also several representatives of the Nation states. At the head of the table were John Roman and the Lads; except for Sheamus who was sitting at a Blarney Stone pub, regaling the locals with tales of his adventures. John opened the meeting with. "Ladies and gentleman we are here to determine our next step in fighting the Morph menace."

"Mr. Roman, our armies have been taking a beating in our respective nations. We appreciate your new ordinance, it has been helpful in combating these creatures, but we are losing the war. We are constantly having to pull back and give up territory to these beasts. We need help, or soon there will be no 'us,'" Senator Applet said.

"Yes. Why can't we just poison the whole lot or nuke them? We know all the nukes have been dismantled, but can't we build more?" Senator Kolla asked.

"Senator, could you poison all the cockroaches in the world without killing everyone? Even if you tried, I'll bet the cockroaches would survive. The Morphs are highly resistant to poison. We have tried it. As far as nukes. What? Blow up the planet? Because the Morphs are everywhere Senator. The days of smashing enemies with hammers are long gone Senator. Besides, nuclear weapons technology is locked away. We need to find a way to either end the Morphs completely, or to live with them."

"How could you possibly suggest we 'live' with these monsters?" Kolla yelled. "Tell that to my children. These things raped and killed their mother. Won't we all get infected as long as these things are alive?"

"Senator, a lot of people have lost a lot of loved ones. This cannot be a war of revenge. This is a war of survival. We can't take what the Morphs do as personal. Like any organism they are doing what they must to survive. We are what they eat, human woman are how they breed," John said.

"Excuse me, John, but I thought these things became Morphs when they went into those pod things. Also what about infection? Is the world safe or will the infection spread?" Senator Applet asked.

“Well Senator, we believed they did both. We weren’t sure until now.” John turned to the screen behind him and said, “C2, show M baby slide.” A picture of the Morph baby body which Sheamus and Raiden had brought back from Mark’s lab came up on the screen. “This, ladies and gentleman is a ‘female’ M baby. We are now convinced the only way the M’s can produce female M’s is by using human women. On top of that, the females are Big M’s and they are very hard to birth. From what we can ascertain through the remains of the many women we have found is the birthing process only works rarely. It see…..”

“Are you saying they killed and raped most of those women for NOTHING!! Just all the more reason we need to utterly destroy these monsters. You spout this nonsense of learning to live with them. Are you suggesting we sacrifice people and women to these creatures to placate them. What kind of sick fuck are you?” Senator Kolla yelled.

“Senator!! if you can’t control yourself we will be escorted out,” Matt yelled.

“It’s alright Matt,” John said as he held his hand up to stop security from taking Kolla out. He then pointed to Jessie.

“Senator. We are working on solutions of every kind. New weapons, new defenses and we are looking at ways we can live with Morphs. The only food they can tolerate is human flesh and certain simians. Chimps, gorillas, orangutans that sort of thing. We are trying to find a replacement. Something we could mix with Seally grass. As far as their need to birth females through human women, we are looking at test tube fertilization. Dr. Franks and her team have had great success with bringing a human baby to term outside a woman's uterus. When it comes to infection we believe the threat of airborne infection died with the first scientists who were infected. Like the Spanish flu or the Covid-19 virus in 2020 the airborne virus has disappeared. It's clear, the data would indicate at the present time, infection is only contracted through bites. If you look at our chart here, the disappearances of people have been in a certain age range. The M's seemed to select only people between twelve and sixty to infect."

"How do you know that, Doctor?" Applet asked.

"Through missing persons and the examination of human remains. DNA analysis shows all the remains are from people under twelve and over sixty. Put those together and you have the selection process."

"But how are they infected?" Senator Daccoso asked.

"Good question, Senator. Ladies and gentlemen if you look at the screen you will see that just inside the throat of the M's are glandular sacks. These act like venom sacks. So when a Morph sees a victim they want to infect they bite them and release the venom. This in turn starts the infection cycle. What we have also discovered is a Big M's bite can transfer something different. Their bites do not infect the victims, but instead give the bitten the ability to hear the thoughts of the M. As of now though we only have a few cases of that happening on file. John, his brother Mark and apparently this General Steel," Jessie explained.

"So you see it's important we contact them. These Big M's are trying to make contact. Otherwise why just bite me or my brother? Why not kill us?" John said.

"So how do you propose to make contact John?" Senator Applet asked.

"Captain Strong, why don't you take this," John said.

"We have been in contact with a, General Rex Steel, an Outlander in Tsalaki. He claims he and a Leroy Renkins have been holding off M's for months now. According to him, he can hear what the M' are saying."

"Really, and what are they saying?" Kolla asked.

"That's what we are going to find out. Remember everyone, I was bit by a Big M. I was able to hear its thoughts," John said.

"Then why don't you talk to these wonderful things? The baby you said you found. That was at your brother's lab. Are you working with him? Maybe you and your brother are making a deal to save your family and serve us up for lunch and the serial rape of our women." Kolla yelled. With that outburst, security escorted Kolla kicking and screaming out of the room. With disappointment in his face, John turned to the rest of the room.

"My brother did start a new illegal lab. After Sheamus and Raiden brought back the baby and information from their investigation of Mark's lab, I sent a team to confiscate the materials and arrest Mark. However, by the time they got there everything was cleared out and the lab was burned to the ground. As of now, Mark Roman is wanted for crimes against the state. I am sure he will be found and brought to justice."

"What about the other Roman family members? I understand there were several of Mary's children at the lab," Applet asked. There were murmurs from the other Nation representatives after Applet's question.

"Yes, Senator Applet. Some of Mary Roman's children were there. They claimed they were invited to dinner by their Uncle Mark and had no idea he was running an illegal facility. We cannot arrest them for having dinner with their uncle. We will keep an eye on them but as of now they have not broken any laws."

"We just want to make sure that the Roman family isn't getting any special treatment John. A lot of people are dying out there. So far we have heard of no Romans being killed or raped by these monsters. A lot of people are dead or missing, John. There are a lot of Roman family members, yet they all seem to be safe. I have never believed in coincidence, John," Senator Applet said.

"We are agreed on that point Senator. Look, we cannot let this become personal. If we do we are doomed. Someone I deeply care for was raped by the Morphs. She is still in hospital fighting to survive. I was bitten by a Morph. Everyone on my team here fought and were wounded by Morphs. Maybe it's the Roman luck or maybe we are better prepared."

"Alright John. You made your point. So what's the next step?" Applet asked.

"After I was bitten, I was able to hear the M's thoughts, but at the hospital they stopped saying anything to me. I'm going to the Tsalaki Outlands to see if I can reestablish contact with the M's. We are convinced this is vital. Without it, how will we know if they want peace? How will we know what they want? Without communication we are in the dark. So we are leaving immediately after this meeting, and hopefully we will be able to open a productive dialogue."

John turned to General Jim Hooks. "This is the man who commanded the Roman security forces. Because of his great courage and ability shown fighting the Morphs at New Boston, Jim has been promoted to General. He is now head of all Roman Institute forces. He will work closely with all Nation military personnel. You all should know General Kirk Thomas. He and his Tsalaki forces fought the first full scale engagement with the Morphs. I will leave you with them, so they can brief you both on where we are, concerning the Morph situation today, and what Generals, Thomas and Hooks are planning for the near future. As soon as my team and I return from the Outlands, we will reconvene and have more information for you. Good luck everyone."

Chapter Five

The Tsalaki Outlands

John and the Lads, along with newly promoted Captain David Strong, left for the Tsalaki Outlands with five hundred Roman Institute troops and several armored vehicles. All the men and ordinance were air lifted with two Titan 68 choppers. These helicopters were true work horses, capable of carrying an enormous load. Because of the Blue Chip batteries, powered by the nano-infused solar paint, these choppers could stay airborne for days. Accompanying the Titans were five Eagle Hell Fire attack choppers. The Eagles carried almost as much firepower among them as did the entire German air force of World War One. The team was taken to a point just outside the northern most border of the Tsalaki Outland. John had his men set up headquarters in an abandoned fort, just south of Abilene.

"I think this will make a great place to headquarter, Captain Strong. Have your men start reinforcing the walls, and if you need any more engineers or supplies, just put the call in to General Hooks. He's been instructed to supply you with anything you need. I want this place impenetrable in three days. Understand?" John asked.

"No problem Sir. With the new materials we can have this place tighter then a nun's…"

"Yeah. Yeah, I got it Captain. I want you to use the mega steel and make a solid safe room. If we or your men run into overwhelming odds, I want a place we can fall back on until the cavalry arrives. I don't want anyone caught out in the open."

"No problem, Sir. Most of the stuff we'll need is already here. Our engineers studied the layout and had everything waiting. My guys are already putting it together, Sir. In three days the Morphs will have a hard time getting over the walls. We'll have gun turrets every twenty feet, mines and traps outside the gate and the fail safe room will be complete. Hell, even a Big M won't be able to breach that room when we're done. From inside the room, we'll be able to use the turret guns remotely, call in drone strikes, even operate the armored vehicles and its weapons. Right now, we have four T48 hover drones in the air. I've positioned one at each compass point. The T48's give us a full 380 degree view of anything within a mile of the place. Since we can't pick up a heat signature from the Morphs, the A48's have new motion capture cameras. We programmed them to seek only M's. If the beasts make any motion, the T48 will reconstruct the figure and we'll know where and how many there are.

"Sounds good, Captain. In the meantime the Lads and I are going in to meet this General Steel. We'll take two of the Eagles and one hundred men."

"Have you made contact with this, Steel yet, Sir?" Strong asked.

"Not since his first…"

"Sirs," a corporal manning the T48 monitors said. "We have contact, Sir."

"Where Corporal?" Captain Strong asked. John and Strong looked at the T48 monitor and saw four figures headed toward the fort. Before John could look, a burst of machine gun fire came from inside the fort.

"Captain have your men cleared the building yet?" John asked.

"We were just about to wh…." Strong started to say, when Sheamus came out the front door holding a kicking squirming child in his arms.

"Damn, Bubba. Just don't be standin' there, yer blitherin' idiot. Help me with this here rug rat. Ta fool's about ta kick me bullocks out me breeches," Sheamus cried while trying to hold on to the kid.

Bubba stood looking at Sheamus with a big smile on his face. "I don't know, Shea. I think fatherhood suits you. The little guy looks like he wants to play with his dad."

"I'll be playin' me fists on yer bloomin' head ifin' ya don't grab this here hooligan, boyo.'"

“Bubba. Grab the kid,” John said. “Shea. What was the gun fire about?”

“Sir, we have four boogies at the gate,” The corporal said.

“Captain check it out please,” John ordered. Turning to Sheamus, John repeated his question. “Why were you shooting at a kid?”

“Were you scared, Shea?” Agni asked.

“Agni, ifin ya keep askin’ me about bein’ scared, I’m o’ gonna have ta pop ya one in yer yap.”

“Oh, this humble servant understands, Shea. But being scared in not something to be ashamed of.”

“By ta blessed Saint Monica, boyo,’ ya need ta shut yer pie hole. Someone needs ta get this….ugh..ugh..” It was too late. The boy broke free from Sheamus and ran back to the fort’s main building. “There. There now, yer bleedin’ bunch o’ laughin’ hyenas. Are ya happy now? Ta poor lad has gone off ta who knows where. He probably be today's lunch for one o’ those red devils now.”

“I don’t think so, Shea. That boy has been around for a while. His hair, clothes, say to me he’s been living out here for years maybe,” John said. “But you still haven’t answered my question. Why did you fire your weapon?”

Sheamus hung his head and started to kick the dirt. “Well, I didn’t shoot at ta lad. I just want ya ta know that laddie buck.”

“OK!! What were you shootin at!!” John and Bubba shouted at the same time.

“Well it were dark in there and I thought I saw me...ummm… I thought it were…”

“*Sheamus*!!” John yelled.

“I not be sure. Alright, there I done spoke it,” Sheamus said in frustration.

“You weren’t sure?” Bubba asked.

“No! Damn ya. I saw these things and I thought they be the red devils o’ commin’ ta eat me poor Irish ass.”

“Sir,” Captain Strong interrupted. “The people at the gate. There’s a Nick Smalls and three others who claim General Steel sent them. But the Smalls guy wants to talk to you.”

“Alright, Captain. Put a guard around them. First we have to check out the main building. Shea thinks there might be Morphs in there.”

“Now, Johnny boy that’s not exactly what I was o’ sayin.’ I said, at first me thought ta things might be ta Morph devils.”

“Bubba, you take the left Shea, take the right. Agni and Raiden, watch the back and make sure nothing comes in or goes out. Take twenty men with you,” John ordered. “Captain, where’s Sergeant Rodney?”

“Right here, Sir. I got a squad with me. They’re my top guys. Should be more than enough,” Rodney said.

“Ok, on my signal we move in,” John said as he balled his fist ready to give the order.

“OH Mother o’ freakin’ Christ,” Sheamus said in a disgusted voice as he walked past everyone and casually entered the building. “I told ya there weren’t nothin’ ta be o’ worried about. It was just o’ big mistake boyo.’ Now ya’s got ta whole goddamn cavalry o’ commin’ at this here thing as if o’ horde o’ them red devils was about ta kill us all.” Sheamus went into the building and slammed the door behind him. John and the rest of the people looked at each other and smiled. “I guess he didn’t see any Morphs, John,” Bubba said laughing.

“I think you’re right Bubba. Let’s go see what was really in there,” John said between laughs.

When they entered the fort’s main building they saw Sheamus staring at what looked like a lot of men who were just standing still. John threw a Day-bright canister on the ground and the room was instantly lit up. What they saw was about thirty military robots pushed into rows at the back of the room. John and the men went up to the robots and examined them.

“These must be the ones you killed, Shea. Look at all the holes in them,” Bubba said laughing some more.

"Yeah. Well, laugh it up there, big fella. It was dark and that there kid started runnin' around like a crazed rabbit, makin' all kinds o' noise. How ta hell was I ta know it weren't nothin' but o' bunch o' dolls."

"Jesus. I though they got rid of all these things after the Great Melt," Sergeant Rodney said.

"Well, you're right Sarge. Robots like this are outlawed today. The Nations still kept a lot of automation bots and we use things such as the drones, but it is against the law to create or use any humanoid robotic. Before the Great Melt these things were everywhere. The military used them, civilians had them. Hell, I think at one point there was an average of two robots in every household. But once the Great Melt happened and the death, famine, wars. These things went into disrepair and after the Great Healing, no one wanted them back. It's one reason we have full employment. Also, people were getting a little concerned with the AI. There had been rumors of robots attacking people, disobeying commands and other people ranting that if robots gained self-awareness then it would be immoral to make them do things. We began to fear them and unfortunately, for anything that frightens humans, they pretty much sign their death warrant. No, today they are just junk. No one wants them. Like nukes they are a thing of the past. Best we strip these for parts and destroy what's left," John said.

"Tis alright with me, laddie. But I'd like ta know where ta hell that little one went ta."

John then put his night-bright goggles on, and looking at he crowd of robots his display showed a heat trail and what looked like a tunnel through the bots. "There it is. Through those," John said pointing to the fourth robot from the wall. "There. It's a tunnel the kid made through the bots. See where it goes. Though I doubt you'll catch him. I've got to see what these people are about. If they're from Steel, we need to know."

"Sure now. You all go ahead. I'm o' gonna look for ta little fella fer awhile," Sheamus said as he started to pry apart the row of bots.

John and the rest of the men went outside to meet Nicky Smalls. Raiden and Agni came from the back once they knew what happened. "Is Shea alright John?" Agni asked.

"Yes, he's fine, Agni. It was just some old robots. Shea is going to look for the kid."

"Oh. May this humble servant go and help Shea? Agni hates to think of the poor boy out here alone. Agni knows what it means to be alone and afraid."

"Of course, Agni. I'm sure Shea would love the help," John replied.

As Agni left to help Shea, John and the men went to see what Nicky Smalls had to say. John found Smalls with two men and a woman. "I'm John Roman. Am I going out on a limb assuming you're Smalls?" John asked as he put his hand out to one of the big men.

"No Mr. Roman, I'm Nicky Smalls." Nicky was average height and build. He had a rugged, boyish face and was cleanly dressed. However, the other two men with Smalls were mean looking thugs who looked like they hadn't bathed in years. It also looked like they shared one brain cell between them. The woman, though, was clean and very well built. She defiantly had more muscles then the other three as her skimpy clothes revealed. Her long braided blond hair set off a strikingly beautiful Nordic face with deep, intelligent blue eyes. She, along with the others had been heavily armed before the guard took all their weapons. "This is Jo and Jim, and this is Apolla. She is my second in command. We are here to bring you to General Steel," Smalls said as he took John's hand and shook it.

"How can we help you Mr. Smalls?" John asked.

"Please, it's just Nick."

"Fine, and feel free to call me John. So, again, what do you want?"

"We're here to take you and your men to General Steel."

"Just the four of you? I thought the Morphs had the run of this place; How were you four able to get here without being eaten and in your case worse," John said as he pointed to Apolla.

"Don't worry your little head about me, Roman. I've been taking care of myself all my life. I certainly don't need some soft, rich boy to look after me," Apolla laughed.

"Can we talk out of this fucking heat and sun?" Nick asked.

"Certainly, come on." John led Nick and Apolla to one of the air conditioned armored Humvees.

"You two wait out here," Nick said to Jo and Jim.

"Captain Strong will you join us….." John started to say before Nick interrupted him.

"No, John. We need to talk to you alone. Please," Smalls whispered.

John thought for a moment and waved off Strong. "Alright. Alright, Nick."

When they entered the Humvee and the air conditioning hit them, both Nick and Apolla sat for a minute, soaking in the cool air. John couldn't help but notice Apolla's legs, which his eyes followed all they way to her crotch. Seeing where John's eyes were, Apolla spread her legs a bit. "See anything interesting rich boy?" Apolla smiled.

"As a matter of fact, yes. You're a gorgeous woman, Apolla. I like the whole Barbarella outfit. Nice tits, a good shot of the gash. Is all this supposed to make me do something I shouldn't? Am I supposed to sell out everything I believe in just to get my dick in your pussy? Well, as beautiful as you are, Apolla it won't work. I do appreciate the show but this rich boy has had plenty of beautiful women over the years. Not interested. Now what's the deal with Steel?"

Apolla crossed her legs and looked a little disappointed. "I was sent by Steel to get you to come to his fort. But he is not the guy who runs the show. That's done by this slug, Donny Trumble. He's spends more time jerking off than I do taking a piss. He is intelligent though. Steel is just the front man. Some washed up actor who liked to fuck little kids. That got him sent to the Outlands where he and Trumble hooked up. Hell, Steel isn't even the one who can hear these things' thoughts. That's my boss, Leroy Renkins. We were the first to encounter the Reds," Nick said.

"You mean Morphs?" John asked.

"Yeah. Yeah Morphs. Whatever. We call them Reds. Anyway, they hit us hard last year. Only Leroy, me and a few of our guys made it. But, Leroy was bit by a big motherfucking Red. The thing could have killed him, but it just bit him and moved on. We made it to our safe house and were there for over a month before Steel found us. When Leroy healed up he said he could hear voices in his head. They were saying weird shit. It nearly drove Leroy insane. We finally figured it was the Reds talking to him, or thinking to him."

"Yeah, I know. The same think happened to me. But the voices stopped."

"Well the Reds stopped talking to Leroy. So, Steel and his bunch rescued us and we have basically been working for him and Trumble. They know about the thinking stuff and figured they could either get pardons or rich from you wanting the information."

"Why are you telling me this?" John asked.

"Because we hate Steel and that jerk-off freak," Apolla said. "We are Outlanders. We don't want pardons. Why would we what to go live in your world, where you're told what to do, how to behave. We want our Outlands back from the Reds and Trumble. We think siding with you will get us that."

"I understand. After the Great Melt and all the horrors that went with it, humanity was ready for some peace and quiet. The Nations offered that. It's for people who want to sleep at night without worrying about their own or their kids' safety. They want housing, jobs and their loved ones to have health care, education, and protection from the dangerous things in life. They want the government to keep them safe from outside enemies and a police force that protects them, not one they're afraid of. They trust the government to fulfill those needs. In turn, they don't rock the boat. They believe it's a good trade off. But there are also people like you. People who seek danger. Thrill seekers. Those who don't want to be told to do this and do that. They feel suffocated by government. They only feel alive when everything is on the line. So they gravitate to the Outlands or are sent there. I understand those people as I do the one's who love living in the Nations. I'm part of both worlds. As you know, the Roman family has shaped and continues to heavily influence world affairs. I left that world for ten years.

This 'rich boy,' Apolla, went into the world without a dime in his pocket or a scintilla of influence from his family. I lived an Outlander-type life and loved it. But now I am back and living in the world of the Nations. It's my duty as a citizen and a Roman to make the world safe again. So if what you saw is true, let's go meet this Trumble and Steel. We'll play their game for awhile. More importantly, I want to talk to Renkins. My main goal is to reestablish contact with the Morphs."

"Sure. Sounds good. But by backing you, we must get rid of Trumble and Steel when this is over. If we don't, then we're all dead after you leave," Nick said.

"If you're asking me to assassinate people the answer is no. However, if what you say is true, I will help you depose those two, and then whatever happens will be up to you. But I have another question. If the Morphs have taken control of this area, how is it that just four of you can walk around out there without being taken out by the M's?" John asked.

"It all started when the Morphs attacked Renkins' town. That was about...oh.. I'd say six or seven months ago," Nick began.

****

As the days passed in Renkins' bunker, tempers were getting hot. Having recovered from his wounds, Leroy was starting to hear voices in his head. "I swear to God, Nick, if these voices don't stop I'm going to eat my gun," Renkins said as he held his head in his hands.

"Here boss, take some more of these," Nick said as he handed Renkins morphine pills.

"How many of these we got left?"

"Enough for now."

"What the fuck does that mean. Can't you ever give me a straight answer anymore?"

"Boss. You got to get it together. The other guys are getting anxious. They think we should try to make a break for it. I'm worried they might try something if you don't get it together."

"How am I supposed to get it together with these voices in my head. They won't stop," Renkins said as he continued to grip his head in agony.

"Alright. Alright Leroy. Just take these and get some sleep," Nick said as he handed Leroy several morphine and sleeping pills. "I'll set them straight Leroy. Don't worry." Leroy sat back in bed and as he closed his eyes Nick went out to the main room. The other men were playing cards and drinking the special homemade beer Renkins brewed.

"Everyone better count how many beers you've drunk because when Leroy gets up, he is going to want the money," Nick said.

"Yeah. Well, when that gonna be?" Jim Sloop asked.

"When he's ready, motherfucker. If you don't like it you can leave. But you leave with the clothes on your back," Nick said in a loud voice. All the men stopped playing cards and looked at each other and then at Sloop. Nick slowly put his right hand on his gun and his left went behind his back ready to grab his stiletto.

"Don't get jumpy Nick," Jim said as he noticed Nick's movements. "We don't want to hurt you. But we want out of here. There hasn't been a single one of them red devils in two weeks. How long are we going to wait here? We want to go and we ain't leaving empty handed. We're taking the guns and ammo and enough food."

"Enough food for what?" Nick asked.

"We figure to head for Steel's fort. We've been in contact with them on the radio. Steel said if we bring all the supplies they would let us join them."

"They did, did they?" Nick said as he moved to the right of Sloop. The other men stood and started to spread out.

"We just want to get to a place where we're safe Nick," Tom Hess said. "We're tired of you having everything locked up and handing us rations like we're little kids. We want our guns and the food."

"What about Leroy? He's too sick to travel. You going to just leave him here? Keep circling me boys, but Jimmy, you're going to be the first and then I'll shove this knife in your eye, Tom."

"Alright. Alright. Look, how about you and me talk in the other room. Just man to man. Hear what I have to say before we all do something we're going to regret," Sloop said to Nick.

"Alright. But first you four go sit back at the table." Nick motioned for Jim to go into the side room. "Ok. Spill it. What's the deal?" Nick asked.

"This whole mess has come down to the fact that Renkins is done. He's finished. He ain't never going to be right. He's weak as a kitten and we sit here rotting over a dead man. We don't want no trouble with you Smalls. We just want to go with our share."

"Your share? I thought you said Steel wanted it all."

"Well, yeah. He did. But if you let us go, I can talk him into accepting our share."

"Really Jim? I never took you for a salesman."

"Well, there's one sure way to get in."

"What's that?" Nick asked.

"We bring him all the stuff and Leroy's head." Nick stiffened up.

"Leroy made you motherfuckers. When he found you Sloop, Rameriz and his bunch were putting you on the barbecue. Same goes for Tom. He was half dead when Leroy found him. So for five years you guys were well fed, had all you wanted to drink, woman, hell some of you even have families and this is how you repay him? You want to take his head to Steel and that masturbating fuck."

"Look, Nick, Renkins needed men. We paid for what he did for us by doing his killing and keeping people in line and yeah, it was all good. But now things have changed. I'm not going to die for Renkins. Besides what do you think he would say if I told him certain things, lover-boy?"

"What the fuck are you talking about?"

"I saw you kiss him, buddy. When he passed out after we ran in here. I saw you put your lips on his and say 'I love you.' Now, look. I don't give a fuck if you want Renkins shoving his big black cock up your ass or if you want to suck it, but I know that if the men knew what I saw they'd wouldn't follow you. I'm trying to help you here, Nick. I mean never mind about them, what do you think Renkins would do if I told….." Sloop suddenly found he couldn't speak because Nick had pressed his body into him and covered his mouth. Before he could think of something to do he felt Nick's stiletto expertly slip between his ribs into his heart. He slowly slid down the wall as the darkness took him. Nick unlocked the gun safe and grabbed an Uzi. He then burst into the main room where he saw Tom and the other three men, armed with steak knives, trying to enter Leroy's room. Nick looked at Tom and the others. "Did you fuckers think I'd leave it open for you to slit his throat?"

"Easy, Nick. Jim said if we got rid of Renkins while you were in the room with him you'd come around. We weren't going to hurt you. Nick we…" Tom never said another word because Nick had put a bullet between his eyes. He then turned to the other three men. "Out!!!" Nick shouted. "Get the fuck out!!

"Wait, Nick we just wanted our share and to go. You can't send us out there with no…"

Nick shot Dan in the gut. As he lay screaming on the floor Nick said. "I did that so you two would hear him scream. The only reason I'm not killing the rest of you ungrateful traitorous fucks is I don't want to haul your dead bodies around."

"Please. Please Nick, we didn't want to. They made us. Please we'll do anything," Joe begged.

"Alright. Fred, Joe, take those two and Jim in the other room and put them out in the courtyard."

"Sure. Sure, Nick," Joe said. The men dragged the three bodies outside and placed them in the middle of the yard. As the turned to go back inside Nick flipped them the bird. "I'd start running for Steel's place if I were you."

"NO!!! NO!! Nick let us back in. Please," Fred yelled. Over the loud speaker Nick said,

"You're not getting a second chance, fuckers. You better start running." Just then two bone chilling howls came from outside the fort.

"Oh shit," Nick laughed. "You really better start running now. I think the Reds want lunch."

The two men were banging on the door as a second series of howls sounding closer sent them into a panic. Fred turned and blindly ran for the fort's gate. As soon as he disappeared out of the fort Joe, who was still standing at the door to Renkins' place, heard a horrific scream. The tough-looking deep voiced Fred, who had been Joe's friend, let out a high shrill like a teenage girl at a birthday party. At the door Joe turned and yelled, "You faggot motherfucker!!!"

Joe kept banging on the door. "You cocksucker. Renkins!!"

"Bang all you want Joe. But if I were you, I'd start running," Nick said over the speaker.

"Renkins!!" Joe kept yelling. "Nick's a cocksucker and he wants to suck your cock. Do you hear me!!!" By now Joe's hands were bleeding from banging on the door and his voice was getting hoarse. "Renkins!!!" He shouted one last time. Behind him he heard a howl that caused him to shit and piss his pants. Crying like a baby with snot coming out of his nose he turned and saw a Morph staring back at him. Frozen with fear Joe couldn't move until he saw what the Morph had in his hand. It was Fred's head. The Morph lifted Fred's head and cracked it open with its clawed hand. It then scooped out the brain and stuffed the whole thing in its mouth. Two other Morphs, each carrying a body part of Fred's entered the courtyard. That was all it took. Joe screamed and ran for the garage.

He made it inside and slammed the wooden doors behind him. The Morphs casually walked toward the garage as they ate Fred. They were in no hurry. On their way they tore into gut shot Dan, who had passed out. After sampling Dan's guts, the two Morphs looked toward the garage. Either, Joe would be chosen to Morph or he was gong to be dessert.

Back inside Renkins safe-house, Smalls shut the speaker off just as Leroy came out of his bedroom. "What the fuck's all the commotion?" Leroy said as he looked around the room. "Where the hell is everyone?"

"Well, Boss, we had a small uprising. I had to terminate some of your employees."

"Nick, sometimes I just want to shoot you. Now what the fuck's going on?"

"As I said, Leroy, Sloop got the other men to revolt. They all turned traitor. They made a deal with Steel and that maggot for the supplies and your head."

Rubbing his forehead Leroy sat in his chair and said, "Well, I can't say as I blame them. If it was me I'd have done the same. It's the smart move. I'm not right. No one wants to follow someone whose half out of it. So, what, you kill all of them by your lonesome?"

"Well, Sloop tried a diversion by talking to me in the other room. While we were in there the other four tried to break into your bedroom and slit your throat. After I killed Sloop, I came out shot two of them, and made the other two take the bodies and go outside. The Morphs took care of the rest."

"What was it he wanted to talk about?"

"Oh just about going over to Steel and killing you."

"Really, and he needed to do that in the other room?"

"Yeah. Yeah. I'm mean why am I getting the third degree? I saved your life, *again* Leroy."

"Sure. Sure, Nick. I appreciate it."

Suddenly Leroy grabbed his head and screamed. "AHHH. Get the fuck out of my head!!"

"Easy, Leroy. Let me get some pills."

Just as quickly as they came, the voices left. Leroy sighed, "I don't know how much more of this I can take. "Come on, Leroy take these and lie down. I keep an eye on everything." Nick then helped Renkins to bed. Three weeks later, Renkins was showing signs of recovery. The voices had abated somewhat and his wounds were completely healed. As he and Nick sat playing cards they heard an armored Hummer come roaring into the courtyard. They looked at the screen and it was one of Steel's vehicles. "Get ready, Nick. Grab the heavy stuff and lots of ammo. I don't know if they have anything that can cut through this mega-steel but either way we'll give then a hell of a fight."

A voice came over the loud speaker of the Humvee. It was General Steel. “Hello. Is anyone still alive in there? The cavalry has arrived,” Steel said.

“What do you want, Steel?” Leroy said over his speaker.

“Well. Well, so you are alive, Renkins. We just want to help. We were told by your former aides that you were hearing voices.”

“So, what. You came to gloat?”

“No. No. No. No, my friend. We have come to take you to safety.”

“This guy’s full of shit. The minute we walk out of here we’re dead and they will loot the place,” Nick said to Renkins.

“Yeah. I’m sure you’re rig…” Leroy grabbed his head. This time, though, the voice he heard was a clear soft whisper. It said, “Go with them.”

“You alright Leroy?” Nick asked.

“Yeah. Yeah. I heard it. Clear as day. We have to go with Steel.”

“Are you NUTS? They’ll kill us the….” Renkins gently grabbed Nick’s arm.

“Do you trust me, Nick?” Leroy said looking deeply into Nick’s eyes. After starting back at Renkins, Nick said, “Sure, Leroy. Sure. I trust you with my life.”

“I know you do, buddy. So trust me here. This voice said to go with them. I believe it. I’m going out there. You can stay here if you want.” After thinking for a moment Nick said. “Fuck it Leroy. I hitched my wagon to yours when you saved me. I’m not getting off when things get hinky. I’m with you.”

“Good. Good. It will be alright.’ With that the two men opened the door and went outside.

****

Smalls relayed all this (without the kissing part) to John. “So, obviously they didn’t kill us. We’ve been holed up at Steel’s place for months now. The supplies we had at Leroy’s were essential. Ever since the Morphs started attacking the Nations, our supply drops have all but dwindled to zero. On top of that, Leroy could still hear those voices every so often and that kept us in good with Steel. The two of them, Steel and Trumble, want to use you to obtain a pardon or to become rich. But don’t trust them for shit, John. They will kill you in a heartbeat if they think it will benefit them. There were rumors a while back that a big bounty was on your head. These guys would cash in on it in a second. But from what I understand, that bounty is no longer viable.”

John took it all in and said, Alright, we’ll work on this together. I want to talk to Renkins. As I said, I’m no assassin, but I certainly will stay out of your way if anything goes down. I can also supply you with weapons and gear if you need them."

"Oh shit, yes. That's what we were hoping. We have the men. We just don't have any good weapons. Trumble makes sure of that. With the stuff you have here, we could take them down."

"Alright. It's a deal. You get me to Renkins, and I'll supply you with what you need," John said as he stood and shook Nick's hand. "We'll leave tomorrow for Steel's place."

"Sounds good," Nick said as he left the vehicle. As John was leaving, Apolla turned to him and pulled him to her. She took his finger in one hand and with the other she lifted her tiny skirt and pulled her panties to the side. She then pushed John's finger into her pussy. At the same time she put her lips to John's ear and in a sultry, low voice whispered, "Here's a little taste of what's to come, rich boy."

When she left, John looked at his finger, and putting it to his nose took a deep breath. He smiled.

John called the men together. "Guys. We're leaving now. Shea and Agni have gone after the boy he found in the main building. So, Bubba and Raiden and I…." At that moment Raiden came walking up to John looking despondent. "Raiden. Are you alright?" John asked.

"No, John," Raiden said with tears in his eyes. "Aimi is dead."

"What? Oh my God. Come, let's go over here and sit my friend. Do you know what happened? I thought she had recovered."

"Hai. She recover from wounds but scars from the *reipu* never heal. To my family's deep shame, Aimi kill herself yesterday. Only my commitment to you, John, keeps me from *seppuku*. But once Morph danger over, I must restore family's honor. I will stay if you insist, but I need to go to my family. I shall return after Aimi's burial ceremony."

"Of course Raiden. *Watashi no kokoro ga naku,*" John said.

"Thank you, John."

"Please give your family my condolences. I will visit after this meeting. But you understand the importance, Raiden. I must try to find a way to communicate with the Morphs."

"Hai. John, I know you loved Aimi. She loved you also, *anisan,*" Raiden bowed.

"Captain Strong," John called.

"Yes, Sir."

"Captain. Have one of the Hell Fires take Raiden back to the Roman Institute Hospital near the White House. Wait for him until he's ready to return."

"I am grateful, *anisan,*" Raiden said as he bowed again and then left.

“Hey, man. I can handle this if you want to go with Raiden,” Bubba said.

“I know you can, Bubba. But I’m the one who is able to hear them. I’ll see her after this. There’s nothing we can do about it now. We have to focus on this mission. I believe it’s vital to understand the Morphs.” John thought for a moment then wiped some tears from his eyes. “Ok. That’s enough. I’ll mourn for her after this. Come on, my friend.”

Chapter Six

Retreat to Haven

As John and the Lads were in the Tsalaki Outlands, Mathew Roman called an emergency meeting of all the Nations. Over one hundred people from all seven Nations, including diplomats and top military brass, were at the Roman Institute, located across the street from the newly reconstructed White House. "Ladies and gentlemen, we have ordered this meeting because we face a peril as dangerous as the Great Melt. The Morph problem."

"It's far more than a problem, Mr. Roman," Senator Parks said.

"I am well aware of that, Senator. But please, let's not start this meeting out with accusations and personal barbs. We need to stop playing politics and work together. Otherwise we could well see humans replaced by Morphs. The Roman Institute has called this meeting because we have determined the Haven Project must be reopened."

The second Mathew said those words, the room was abuzz with voices. Senators stood and pointed fingers at each other and Matt. There was pushing and yelling by the military and the diplomats. Matt pounded his gavel to no avail. Eventually he had to signal his security to set off a noise round from an air horn. The earsplitting blast brought the room to silence.

"Ladies and gentlemen. If you cannot control yourselves, I will have you removed and you and your respective Nation will have no say in what we are planning with the Haven Project. As I said before, we simply do not have time for this nonsense. The Morphs are gaining territory all over the world as we speak. We do not have time for this bickering."

Everyone looked at each other, and slowly they all sat down and composed themselves.

"I am going to go over the three phases we have for reestablishing the Haven Project. The first will be why we are doing it. The second item will be how we are going to do it. The third item will be how we plan to maintain the facilities and for how long. After each item, I will take questions from you. Each Nation will get to add their ideas or objections to our plan. Does everyone understand? Before I begin, I want to reiterate that this is not going to be a free-for-all. If there are arguments or outbursts, that person or persons will be escorted out and not allowed to return. So act like the senior diplomats and military brass you are supposed to be."

Everyone looked back and forth at each other and nodded in agreement with Matt.

“Good. Now let’s begin.” Matt turned on a big view screen behind him. He put up pictures of the aftermath of several encounters various military had with the Morphs.

“As you see from these images, the armies of the Nation have fought several battles with the Morphs. In each case, the military has seemingly won. The Morphs have always run away in the end but the cost of these ‘wins’ has been devastating. In your handouts, you will see that the combined loss of troops for all Nations has been over one million men and women.” There was a collective sigh from the room. “Yes. Many of you thought we were winning. I’ve read countless news articles, and on many of the respective talk shows in your Nations, the press has the idea that all these battles have been great victories. Well, I’m here to tell you, the world cannot keep this winning up. General Hooks.”

“Thank you Matt. Ladies and gentlemen, we, and I mean the world’s military are losing. The Morphs are not fighting for a single territory. The are not blindly attacking us in hopes of destroying us. They are fighting a well-planned war of attrition and they are winning. Before the Great Melt, the world’s population had reached over ten billion people. Forty years after the Great Melt, the population had dwindled to less than eight-hundred million. The wars, the famine, the Sweats, the Baylor Parasite, the loss of landmass, all of these things brought humanity to near-extinction. During the forty odd years of the Great Healing, the world’s population has risen to a little over one and a half billion. We have been able to maintain such a low growth rate because people no longer need big families for work. We have a well-educated citizenry. People are well-cared for, their healthcare, housing, food, education. All of this helps keep the world free of a population explosion which could have seen a return to famine, depletion of natural resources, etc." Hooks then showed a chart which estimated the military manpower of the world's armies. "As you see here, out of a world population of a billion we estimate a military capability of eighty million personnel. Remember, that's personnel, actual *combat* troops numbers are far fewer. As of now, we estimate the population of the Morphs at around three million. Let's break that down some more. That leaves us with about nine hundred million people. At the rate we are being assimilated and losing our troops, we estimate we have five years before we can no longer put a viable force in the field."

"Are you saying human race has but five years to live?" Senator Chen Lee asked.

"If we do not get a handle on the situation then, yes. That's what we estimate. So you see why it is imperative we cooperate," Matt said.

"But our military? We have all the weapons. All the fire power," Senator Rani Deepak said.

"Look at the Vietnam war, Sir. The United States had all the fire power. There are dozens of examples of people winning against better equipped forces. Now, let's consider that the Morphs have got a human beat all to hell. When it comes to strength, communications, tactics, and the ability to just vanish, then maybe you can understand why they have been so successful. The Morphs are not concerned with winning an engagement. They are simply going to the grocery store when they fight us. Many of our dead are taken from the field by the Morphs. It's their food. Then they disappear and during that time dozens of our troops go missing from our camps or forts. We think they are being morphed.

"Now what I have to tell you next must stay in this room. My people are passing a document to all of you. You must read it and sign it before I relay this next item to you. Let me warn you, though. If you sign it and then talk about what you hear next, you will be imprisoned for the duration of the war. No ifs-and-or-buts. There will be no diplomatic immunity. Do I make myself clear?" As he looked around the room, Matt saw people muttering to each other. Finally, after about an hour, thirty people left the conference room. The others signed the document.

"Very well. We have found that approximately ten percent of our troops and indeed some citizens are going over to the Morphs in order to be morphed themselves," Matt said. There was a din of commotion and shouting among the group of diplomats and military. Matt had to bang his gavel several times before the room quieted down.

"Are you seriously suggesting that humans are willingly being morphed?" Senator Debra Hill asked incredulously.

"That's exactly what I'm saying. Think of it. These young people see a race which many consider to be superior to ours. They're stronger, faster; from what we can tell they don't get diseases. Many believe they're the future of this world. Look at social media; thousands of people praise the greatness of Morphs. There are sites on the internet where people offer to help others find Morphs so they can mutate. We think we could easily lose ten to twenty percent of the population who willingly seek to mutate. Understand this, if it weren't for the eating and raping of people, we estimate over forty percent of the world's population would Morph." There was a collective sigh in the room. "Yes ladies and gentlemen. We need to start a rapid and effective campaign, in each Nation, to convince people that mutating is wrong. We must ban all content that supports mutation. That's a fight each of you must convince your people to do, if we want to keep these numbers down. Now is not the time to worry about free speech or personal rights." Matthew saw the room needed a break, and asked them to reconvene in an hour. When everyone returned the room was quiet. Then the Tsalaki representative spoke, "Matt, Jessie, Jane and Generals Hooks and Thomas, we appreciate your being honest with us. We now see what we must do. But can you now tell us how you plan to use the Haven Project? Will each Nation decide who gets to go to one? We realize the Haven Projects are all on your property and that the world governing board has given the Roman Institute sovereignty over those properties. But you must understand we cannot just sit back and let you decide who may live in our own nation," Tsalaki senator David Parks asked.

"Of course, Senator. What we propose is this. The Roman Institute will pick twenty-five percent of the applicants for each facility. These people will be made up of scientists, educators, inventors, the very best and brightest. Each Nation will have the choice of their own twenty-five percent of people they wish to send to the facility. The other other fifty-percent will be picked by lottery. However, there will be no Outlanders allowed. Also, if you are a trades-person, plumber, carpenter, etc, you will be given a ticket with a higher chance of being chosen. Finally, and I know this will upset many people, but no one over seventy or with a severe disability will be allowed." Just then the room burst into shouts and yelling. Eventually Matt had to use security to calm things down.

"Are you telling us we have to go back to our Nation and tell our people that if you're too old or not a perfect specimen you will be left to the Morphs? You do know people like that are Morph food?" Senator Debra Hill shouted.

"No, Senator, I strongly suggest you do not say that. This stays here. By the time people figure out what is happening, it will be too late," Matt said.

"You're a worse monster tha….." Parks started to say.

"SHUT UP!! All of you. Do you think this is some game? Do you think the Roman Institute likes to play God? We are talking about the survival of the human race. In that fight, there is no place for those who cannot contribute to the cause. If it makes anyone feel any bettor, I am not going into the Haven facility. In fact many of my family members are staying out here, with the elderly and the others who will not be counted in the lottery. Me and many of my family members could have a front row in any Haven facility but we are not putting our names in. How many of you outraged diplomats and military people want to trade your spot for an elderly person or a special needs person? If you do, there is a paper on that table, sign it, and I will personally see that one of the people who are now ineligible will take your place." After twenty minutes no one had signed the paper. "I didn't think so," Matt said with disgust.

"Matt, we're sorry. We had no idea you would not go to a Haven facility. How many will have the chance?" Parks asked.

"We initially made the Haven sites able to take five hundred thousand. That's twenty-five thousand for each facility. That may not seem like a lot of people, but it is in fact the optimal number for re-population. However, if we continue to expand during the next five years we should be able to double that figure. It will be a little more cramped but our fusion reactors can handle that. The expansion will be made in the living quarters. We started 'Operation Expanse' one year ago, at the first sign of Morph activity," Jessie stated.

"Wow. You Romans are always ahead of the curve. But how long will they be in there?" Parks asked.

"It all depends what happens out here. We will continue to find a way to neutralize the Morph threat. If we are not successful, then the scientists and others in the Haven facilities will continue the fight from there. With our fusion power we can stay indefinitely, if it comes to that. But we have the greatest confidence that we will prevail." As everyone left the room, many of the people shook Matt's hand. When the room was finally clear, Matt turned to Jessie and the others and said, "Now it's a race against the clock."

Chapter Seven

Chara Beag

While John and his team boarded the Eagle Hell Fires so they could meet with Steel, Sheamus and Agni went looking for the feral child. The two of them started with the main building where Sheamus originally found the boy. "You said there was o' hole in them there roboty things, did ya not, Agni?"

"Yes, Shea. There is a tunnel right there between those four robots," Agni said pointing to the end of the pile. Sheamus walked over and started to crawl through the heap of robots and came to an opening which led to a tiny space under the stage. "Agni. Come here would ya please."

Agni squeezed up next to Sheamus. "As skinny as I am boyo,' I don't think I can be fittin' in that there hole. Ya be about ta same size as ta little fella. Can ya check it out boyo'?" Agni nodded with a grin and pushed his way into the tiny room. When he returned from the room he handed Sheamus a picture. "This was all there was in there Shea. The poor child had no bed, no food." The picture was of an elderly man and woman with the blond, blue-eyed feral child standing between them.

“This must be the little fella’s grand Ma and Pa. I’ll bet O'Toole's farm the folks be dead. Look how happy they all are, will ya. They must have been goin’ ta the beach. Mother bloody Machree, ta little fellas got more muscles than me, Agni.”

“Yes. It also doesn’t look like he aged much. The photo must have been taken recently.”

“Yeah. Could be. But….I don’t know,” Sheamus said as he turned the photo over in his hand.

“Is something wrong, Shea?” Agni asked.

“Well, I not be claimin’ ta be some kind o’ big shot photographer man or nothin’ mind ya. But...ah...this here picture looks ta be old.” After lingering on the photo Sheamus said, “Ach. Look at me. Tryin’ ta play detective when we should be lookin’ fer this here lad. What else ya find in there, boyo’?”

“There was a loose panel in the back. This humble soul took it upon his self to open it and there was a small tunnel which even Agni could not fit. But this humble servant thinks it runs out the back of the fort.”

“Alright, me dear boy. Let’s be findin’ our little friend.”

Sheamus and Agni went to the back and could see no exit. “I think ta boy headed out there ta the desert. Well, then, that’s where we’ll be o’ goin’”

“How will you find him out there, Shea?”

“I been trackin’ people since I were but o’ wee lad son. I can track them in ta city, in ta jungle or in ta desert. Makes no matter. I’ll find ta little fella. So, out there is where I be goin.’ Ya can stay here if ya want.”

“No. Please do not leave this humble soul behind. What you are doing is very good karma.” “Well, I don’t be knowin’ about no karma but Sheamus O’Keefe won’t be leavin’ that poor lad out there ta eaten by them there red devils, I tell ya.” After several hours of searching the two men sat down at the base of a small hill. “Tis o’ good thing ya brung all tis here water and yer curry jerky, boyo.’ Ta last time Sheamus O’Keefe were this thirsty and hungry was when I hadn’t been in a Blarney Stone fer two months.” Standing up, Agni checked to see how many bottles of water were left.

“Oh my dear Shea. The curry jerky was a recipe Agni’s dear mother…” Suddenly, Agni was hit in the head with a rock someone had thrown. He went down hard and Sheamus grabbed him and pulled him behind a boulder. Seeing Agni was still alive but with a cut on his head, Sheamus went into the medical bag, sterilized the wound, and wrapped Agni’s head. With some smelling salts under Agni’s nose, the man came to.

“Ahh. You’re awake there, bucko. You’ll be alright. I just need ta see who be throwin’ rocks at us boyo.’ Somehow I don’t thinks tis ta Morphs doin.’” At that moment another rock came hurling past Sheamus's head. “Jesus help this here sinner.” Sheamus looked down at Agni who was giving him a perplexed stare. “Yeah. Don’t be worryin.’ It were, yer sorry ass I was talkin’ about.”

As Sheamus was trying to get a sense of where the rock thrower was, he began to think he knew who was doing the throwing. “Oye, there laddie buck. Are ya ta one who be tossin’ them there boulders at us? We come in peace, boyo.’ Are ya hungry now fella?” Sheamus pulled some of Agni’s jerky from his knapsack and placed three pieces on top of the boulder in front of him.

“There ya go laddie. Take those, and we have some water for ya.” Sheamus held up a bottle of water over his head and a rock quickly knocked it out of his hand. “Now what ya be doin’ that fer? That there water could save yer life, boyo.’ Come on *son*. I’m not here ta hurt ya.” The child suddenly jumped up from his hiding place and ran toward Sheamus. “Da..da...da,” The boy kept yelling.

For a second Sheamus wasn’t sure what to do. He didn’t know the boy’s intentions as the child came at him full speed. But before he could move, the boy leaped from ten feet away and latched on to Sheamus's waist. Hugging Sheamus tightly he kept saying, “Da...Da..” At first surprised, Sheamus slowly put his arms around the young boy and hugged him back. After a few seconds Sheamus patted him on the shoulders and said, “There, there, boyo.’ It’s alright, I got ya now. There’s nothin’ ta be afraid of, son.” This started the boy repeating, “Da...da...da…” But this time in almost a whisper.

"Oh, Shea. You will have much karma for this. Much karma," Agni smiled.

"Yeah, well, when we get him back ta the fort I'll be turnin' him over ta the proper authority. They can find someone ta take care o' ta boy."

"How do you think he has survived all this time?" Agni asked.

Looking at the boy who was still hugging him, Sheamus said, "Well he couldn't have been out here that long. He don't look much older than that there picture ya found. He looks ta be well fed and watered."

"Yes. But where has he been living? Certainly not in that tiny room back at the fort."

"I don't know Agni. All I know is, we got ta lad and he be safe with us. Let's get some rest and head back in ta morn…."

Suddenly, there were two loud Morph howls. One in front and one in back of them. "Agni!! Sheamus shouted as he handed the boy to him. Protect him while I deal with these red devils." Sheamus grabbed the boy and said, "Now don't be frighten son…"

"Da...da…."

"Yeah. Yeah, Da Da. We got ta work on yer language there son."

"Da...Da.."

"Agni, take him and guard him with yer life, boyo.'"

"They will have to tear this unworthy soul apart before Agni lets them hurt him, Shea."

Sheamus pulled his Webley and Kalashnikov. "Agni. I'm goin' ta make them chase me that way. When ta heathens start ta run fer me, I want ya ta take the boy and run quick as hell ta the fort. Understand?"

"Yes. Agni will do as you say." When the boy saw Sheamus trying to make the Morphs chase him he started to squirm out of Agni's arms. "Da..Da.."

"Easy. Shea is going to lead them away. It will be.." The boy pulled away from Agni, then turned and poked his finger in the side of Agni's head. Agni went out like a light. As Sheamus started to run, he began shouting like a banshee. "Over here, ya bleedin red skin devils ya. Come and get o' taste of o' real Irish feast. Come on ya dirty cowards, ya. Come and get some of Sheamus O'Kee…"

What stopped Sheamus cold was seeing the boy running in the open toward him. Right behind the boy was a Morph. "NO!!! NO!!! Stay away from him ya fuckin' slitherin' fuckin bastards." Sheamus raised his Webley to shoot the Morph who was about to pounce on the child. But before Sheamus could get a bead on the M, the other M grabbed him and smacked him with a backhand. Sheamus felt the darkness close in and his only thought was, "Ya couldn't save the lad, ya fuckin' idiot."

Sheamus woke up in dark cool place. “What ta hell?” He moaned rubbing his aching head. “Don’t be tellin’ me this be hell now.”

“Shea. It’s, Agni”

“Agni. Where ta hell are we? What ta hell happened. Me head feels like ta mornin’ after Saint Paddy’s day. Do ya have any weapons? Is ta lad with ya? Please tell me ya got ta little fella.”

“Oh Shea. This man is a sorrowful wretch. I don…”

“Agni. I trusted ya. What in ta name o’ Saint Benedict did ya do? Ifin’ ya ran away and left him, Agni, I swear on me mothers grave I’ll..”

“Da...Da,” The boy said. Suddenly the room was lit up. Sheamus saw the boy standing in front of him smiling. Sheamus burst into tears and grabbed the child. “Ach. Praise ta lord yer all right son.”

“Da...Da..”

“Sure. What ever ya say, boyo.’” Looking around, Sheamus saw Agni on the other side of the room and all of their gear sitting in the middle of the room next to a small camp fire the boy had just lit.

“Agni. Mate. Ya any idea what happened?”

“The last thing this humble servant remembered was the boy pulling out of these arms and then touching my head. Agni woke up here, in the dark, then heard your voice, Shea." The child sat next to Sheamus, holding his hand and smiling.

"Do ya have o' name son?" Sheamus asked.

"Da..Da..," The child said pointing at Shea and then hugging him again. Sheamus looked up at Agni and shrugged his shoulders. With a big grin of his own, Agni said, "Agni told you Shea. Very good karma. Very good karma."

"Yeah, Well, we can't be callin' him 'boy' and child.'" Thinking for a minute Sheamus then took the boy's face in his hands and said. "Hey, little fella. How about I be callin ya Chara Beag? Would ya like that?" Chara nodded yes several times as he never stopped smiling.

"Ok. Chara Beag it is." Seeing how happy Chara was and how happy he felt knowing the boy was safe, Sheamus then said, "No. How about, Chara Beag O'Keefe? How's that Chara?" Again Chara nodded vigorously and hugged Sheamus again. Within seconds Chara went to sleep in Sheamus's lap.

"That's right, go ta sleep, Chara. Ya go ta sleep now. Sheamus won't let nothin' happen to ya now."

****

From the air, John could see that Steel city looked deserted. Nick radioed to the ground crew inside Steel's fort to clear the landing pad. Though the fort had a big area, there was only room for the one chopper. The transport helo and the other Eagle landed just outside the fort. As the Eagle Hell Fire holding John, Bubba, Nick and Apolla landed, John gave instructions to the other members of his team. "Sergeant Rodney. This is John Roman. Over."

"Yes, Sir. Hear you loud and clear. Over," Rodney answered.

"Have your team come inside the fort. I want you to leave a skeleton crew in the choppers, but make sure your people keep them buttoned up. I don't want Morphs or any rogue Outlanders surprising our people in the open. Over." Nick pointed out General Steel to John as the ramp descended.

"That's Steel. The guy thinks he's some kind of Civil War General. He was a movie actor back in the world. When he first came here, I heard he tried to convince people he really was a General. He had a lot of fans, believe it or not. However, after hooking up with Trumble, I think he started to believe in his own bullshit. Or maybe he just went nuts. It happens to a lot of people who come out here."

John saw a tall, medium-built, handsome man, walking erect as a pole. He was sixty years old, trying to look forty. His salt and pepper hair was perfectly combed. His face was covered with a handlebar mustache and a thin goatee that went from his bottom lip to the end of his chin. He wore a slouch hat with the one side pinned up and a yellow feather which stuck out of his red headband. He had on a uniform right out of the wardrobe department of an 1800-era period movie. Steel even sported a red sash around his waist with a sword hanging from one side and an old colt revolver hanging from the other, with a set of yellow epaulets on his shoulders and at least twenty medals across the chest of his knee-length gray coat, all from different wars and different centuries, Steel mirrored central casting of *Gone With the Wind*. The double breasted top half of his coat had rows of bright gold buttons running all the way down. His spit-shined leather boots went past his knees and disappeared under his coat. After eyeing the General, as he walked toward the men, Nick whispered out the side of his mouth to John, "Like I said, 'nuts'"

"Well, so long as he stays sane enough for us to meet Renkins. What condition was Renkins in when you last saw him?" John asked.

"He was much better then when he first got bit. His wounds all healed and the voices have gone away for the most part. So he says."

"Believe me, rich boy. Leroy can still deliver," Apolla said seductively, as she ran her hands across John's crotch while leaving the chopper. That big cock of his has no problem pleasing me. How about you rich boy? You think you can match Leroy?"

Bubba looked at Apolla and as she caught him staring at her she said, "Oh, ahh...Bubba..right?"

"Yes, miss,"Bubba said. Apolla laughed loudly as she jumped the last foot off the ramp and started to walk toward the building which was Steel's headquarters. "Sorry big boy. One black dick at a time. Apolla wants the rich boy's cock. If he's man enough to take what he sees." Still laughing, Apolla ran toward the building. As she did, she flashed her ample, round breasts to everyone.

Nick turned to see John and the men looking embarrassed. "She likes to use her body. That's for sure. But don't let it fool you. Apolla can kick anyone's ass. The only person I've ever seen not afraid of her is Renkins. Just watch your back, John. If you think she'll be an easy ride, you could be in for a rude awakening. The rumor is, she has a collection of stuffed dildos made from lovers who didn't make the cut. If you know what I mean."

The men stopped talking as Steel came within ear-shot. Extending his hand, Steel was the first to speak. "Good day Sirs. And you must be Mr. John Roman. I am General Rex Steel and it is my great honor and privilege to offer you fine gentlemen the comfort of my home," Steel said in a deep southern accent, as he put out his hand.

"We appreciate that General. We wer…." John started to say.

"Now, now. We are here as friends, Sir. Let's put aside the formalities of crude business dealin's. Please be so kind as to call me Rex." Steel looked around and then smiling said, "Of course, Sir, in front of the men we must keep up a show of leadership. Am I right,

Sir?" John was sizing up Steel wondering how much of this was an act and how much was plain nuts.

"I completely agree, Rex," John whispered and then in a loud voice said, "General, we are at your disposal. It would be an honor to dine and stay with you tonight, Sir." John shook Steel's hand and then Bubba stepped in between and said, "Do you want to shake my hand, General?" Steel seemed startled and looked at Bubba with a perplexed stare. As if snapping out of a coma, he then said with a big grin, "Why of course, Sir. It would be my utmost pleasure to shake the hand of such a fine specimen of a Mandingo, Sir. Have you done any fightin' Bubba? I am sure we can arrange a match. I have some of the best Mandingo fighters in the Outlands. Could be a big payday for you, Sir. But you must know that in the Outlands, the boxin' matches are to the death."

"I don't fight my brothers for the amusement of white boys, much less kill them. Now, if you want to get in the ring." Bubba looked around at the henchmen Steel had posted everywhere. "Or any of these crackers want to try me, then we can talk."

"Well, good Sir. My fightin' days are long over." Steel seemed nervous as Bubba stared unblinking into his eyes. "Please Sirs, this here is no place for such things. We have much more important issues then...ahh...pugilistic entertainment, do we not? If you would be so kind as to follow me to my office. I am sure we can find you some cool drinks," Steel said as he motioned to the door. Upon entering Steel's home John and his crew saw what could pass for the interior of a pre-civil war mansion. The rugs and curtains were ornate and luxurious. Oak furniture and baroque statues lined the room. Steel's desk was massive and intricately carved of walnut and teak. His throne-like chair was high-backed in red velvet with similarly cushioned arms.

As he sat in his chair, Steel picked up a little bell and rang it three times. A black elderly man dressed in a white suit coat with black pants entered with a tray of drinks. "Rufus, please see to these gentleman's drinks." Rufus gave a small bow and said, "Yes, Masa Steel."

Bubba looked at John and then made a move toward Steel. "Did he just call you 'master'? Motherfucker." John grabbed Bubba's arm pulled him aside, and whispered to him.

"Easy, Bubba. We have a job to do. You can address that later." Bubba stared at Steel and then turned to Rufus.

"Is that your real name. Or do you let this cock sucking ofay call you that?" Bubba said.

"Excuse me, Sir," Rufus said quietly. "But I'm not as young and strong as you, son. I don't have me no rich white man backing my play. You dig? How long you think I last in the Outlands on my own? Now, Masa Steel been real good to me. I gets plenty to eat and don't have to be worryin' bout no roof over my head or some scalawag tryin' to kill me. You frettin' over a name? What you call that one, son?" Rufus said as he looked at John.

"I call him 'friend,' man," Bubba replied.

"Well, that's real good. But I ain't got no friends here in the Outlands. So my sorry old ass had to make do. Now, if you will excuse me. I have drinks to serve."

'Now. Now. Please, Sirs. We are all gentlemen and of course, lady," Steel said, eyeing Apolla. "We are here, are we not to conduct serious business? Let's not get off to a bad start. Please, let us sit down like gentlemen. My partner should be here any minute. Rufus, can you see what's keeping Mr. Trumble." Before Rufus could move, a door opened and fat five-foot- three, Donny Trumble waddled over and met the guests. During his time in the Outlands, Donny had actually gotten fatter. He was at the point where he couldn't reach his own dick to masturbate; his favorite pastime. Through the open door, John saw two young, half naked girls, no more then eighteen. They were Trumble's masturbation girls. Even at fifty-eight, Trumble had a face covered in acme. He smelled horribly from the copious amounts of dried cum in his pants. Trumble didn't like to bathe often either.

"Donny, This is John Roman and…"

"Yeah. Yeah. I know who everyone is. Apolla, do you have something for me?" Apolla looked at everyone and seemed to hesitate. "Come on, Apolla. You owe me. I'm not waiting any longer. You want to go back to the pits?"

"All right!! All right. Here, you pervert." Apolla slipped off her g-string, and threw it to Trumble.

"I've been in the desert for three days, Trumble. That thing is soaking wet with piss and cunt juice.'

"OH. Don't worry. That's just the way I like them," Trumble said as he pushed the underwear to his nose and breathed in deeply. Looking up at everyone, Trumble said, "Ahh. You'll all have to excuse me a minute." He then hurried to his office and shut the door. Steel started to say something to Trumble but then shrugged his shoulders. "Sorry folks. But it seems we will have to make some pleasant conversation." Steel looked at his watch, "Ten minutes I would say." Please have a seat and enjoy the drinks.

****

While John and Bubba were at Steel's place, Sheamus and Agni, along with Chara Beag, started for the fort. After a mile or so, Sheamus spotted what looked like two bodies. "Hold up there, Agni. What ta hell ya suppose them things are?"

"This humble servant cannot see far and as clearly as you, Shea."

"Alright. Stay here with Chara. I don't want him ta be seein' anythin' that might upset the poor lad." Sheamus carefully walked over toward the bodies and as he got nearer he could tell they were Morphs. Suddenly, Chara yelled, “Da. Da.” as he ran to Sheamus and then passed him. Surprised, Sheamus tried to grab Chara, but was unable to stop him from running toward something. Agni stopped next to Sheamus, out of breath and finding it hard to talk.

“What ta hell ya doin’? I told ya ta watch the boy, laddy buck.”

“This humble servant...and...unworthy...man could not hold him Shea. Agni is sorry, but Chara is just too strong.”

“Never mind that, let’s go, before somethin’ happens ta the boy.” As Sheamus and Agni neared Chara, he was jumping up and down on one of the headless Morph corpses.

“Da. Da. Ag. Ch ki Mo. Da pr of Ch?” Laughing and smiling, Chara kept jumping from one Morph body to the other. “Da lo Ch. Ch lo Da.” Turning to Agni, Sheamus said with a broad grin.

“That there be me son, Agni. Have ya ever seen o’ happier wee one?”

“Yes. Shea. He is very happy. Very happy, indeed. It’s a shame he can’t talk.”

“What ta hell ya mean he can’t talk. I understand me boy. Ya just have ta listen Agni, yer dunder head ya.” Running up to Chara, Sheamus started to jump up and down on the Morph bodies.

"Da love Chara. Chara love Da." The two laughed and jumped for five minutes.

"Alright son," Sheamus said, trying to catch his breath. "Praise...ta...saints...lad. Ya got more energy then yer new Da. We got ta get goin' son. Back ta the fort." Sheamus put his arms around Chara and hugged him. "I don't know how ya did it, son, but me thinks ya saved Agni and me from them there red devils. Ya got the courage of o' true son o' Ireland; that be for sure, boyo.'" Chara looked at Sheamus and said, "Da lo Ch."

"Aye, lad. Da loves Chara. Now come on, little fella. We got ta be getting' ta the fort before nightfall. I don't want us caught out here after dark. We be pushin' our luck as it is."

An hour before sunset, the three made it to the fort. Captain Strong met them at the gate.

"Glad to see you all made it back. We were going to send out the chopper in the morning," Strong said, "Who is this with you?"

"This here is Chara. Say hello to Captain Strong, Chara." Hiding behind Sheamus, Chara nodded at the Captain. "Ta lad's o' bit shy. Been out here on his own he has." Strong looked at the boy with a puzzled stare. "Really? He looks in pretty good shape for being out here alone."

"Well, why wouldn't he? He be me son. And ya know how all us true sons o' Ireland be indestructible now, don't ya?"

"Sure, Sheamus," Strong said hesitantly. "Well, you can take your pick of one of the tents. Or take one of the rooms inside the main building. The boy…"

"His name be Chara, there boyo,'" Sheamus said in a slightly raised voice. Strong looked at Sheamus's face, and then smiling said, "Chara...and you and Agni can feel free to take one of the rooms inside the main building, Sheamus. Do you guys want some food? The men already ate; but I can see they fix you all something. You guys must be famished."

"Oh, thank you Captain. This humble man is indeed hungry. Agni will eat and surely fall asleep as soon as head hits pillow." Agni then went toward the building to find a room.

"What say there, bucko? You be wantin' some food now?" Chara shook his head 'no' and Sheamus looked up at Strong. "He be tired; tis all. I'll see him ta bed, then I'll go and get us some chow."

As Sheamus was heading to the building, he turned to Strong. "I see ya been fortifyin' ta place. I should tell ya we ran inta two o' them there Morph fellas. About twenty mile back."

"What happened? Did they see you? Were there others?"

"Nah. Just ta two o' them. They be dead as me grandma's love life, though."

"How did you kill them? You guys didn't have any big weapons?"

"Aye. Twasn't us, laddie buck. Twas me son here, sent them red heathens ta play in the fires o' hell. Proud as o' bleedin' peacock, I be." As the two walked toward their rooms, Strong turned and got on the radio to John. If his suspicions were right, Chara was going to have to be disposed of immediately.

Sheamus and Chara entered the main building and saw Agni sitting at a bench eating a large bowl of soup. "Ya thinkin' o' savin' any o' that fer us now, boyo.'?"

"Of course, Shea. There is plenty here. Would you like this poor unworthy soul to make you and Chara a bowl?"

"What ya say there, me son, would ya like some soup now?" Chara shook his head 'no.' Sheamus was a little taken aback, but shook it off. "Alright, no problem. Ya must be tired as Saint Bernardine, there fella." Chara nodded yes. Sheamus led him to an empty room. "This here looks as good as any. Come on now. Put yer head down and get some sleep." Sheamus turned to leave but Chara grabbed his hand. "Da. Da. Da no le Ch."

"There, there son. Easy. I'll never leave ya. Yer me boy now. Nothin' on earth will ever change that. Get some sleep. I'll be back soon as I get me belly full o' that there soup Agni be slopping down his gob." Chara smiled, and lay his head on the pillow. He immediately closed his eyes and was asleep.

Coming out to the main room, Sheamus sat down next to Agni who had made him a bowl. "Thanks, mate. The lad's asleep.

He went out like a bleedin' light." Agni ate his soup in silence until Sheamus said, "What's ta matter?"

"Nothing, Shea. The soup is very good. Very good." Sheamus pulled Agni's bowl away from him and said, "Look here, ya karma cravin' heathen. Ifin' ya don't be tellin' me why yer lookin' like ya swallowed o' damn canary, yer goin' be needed more than o' little karma ta fix ya. Now, tell me why ya got the long face growin' out yer head."

"Well, it's just...it's just," Agni tried to say.

"Spit it out damn ya. Before I shove me hand down that there stutterin' throat o' yours."

"Oh God help This poor humble soul." Sheamus grabbed Agni by the shirt and pulled him to his face.

"The next thing out o' yer mouth better be what's botherin' ya or we be through."

"It's...it's Chara."

"What about him?"

"Sheamus. He loves you and this humble servant knows you love him but…"

"But what ya blitherin' idiot. Spit it out or yer be spittin' teeth."

"Shea. He hasn't drunk anything in three days. He hasn't eaten anything. He hasn't even gone to the bathroom. That's impossible for a… for a.."

"For a what?"

"For...for..a...human." Sheamus let go of Agni and stared at the table.

"The lad's in shock. He...just...isn't hungry. Ya haven't watched him every minute. He could have been drinkin' the whole time. Ya can't be sure, damn ya. Hell, I've gone days without o' bit o' food meself when I be on o' bender. Did ya ever think he was shy about take o' wee in front o' people? He's just o' boy."

"Sure. Agni is sure you are right, Shea. Please forgive this stupid man for doubting."

"It's alright, Agni. It's alright. I'm goin' ta bed. I'll see ya in the mornin.'" As he was about to walk away, Sheamus turned to Agni, "Are we alright, Agni?"

"Of course, Shea. You will always be a dear friend of this unworthy soul."

"Aye, mate. I am yer friend. It's just that right now, tis me who feels o' bit unworthy. Good night, me friend." Sheamus then went into the room with Chara. As he sat on the edge of his bed, Sheamus looked at Chara sleeping peacefully. "I don't care what or who ya might be Chara. Yer me son. Now and forever. If anyone try's ta say different, they'll have ta go through Sheamus O'Keefe.

****

After thirty minutes of waiting for Donny Trumble to return, John got up. Looking at Steel he said, "General, in case you didn't know, the world is being decimated by the Morphs. I came here to seek answers. You claimed to be able to hear the Morphs. In actuality, it's Leroy Jenkins who hears them. I don't have time to wait until Trumble has had enough of playing with his dick. Now, I would like to be taken to see Renkins, or my crew and I will be leaving."

"OH. Ahh, I completely understand Mr. Roman. I did tell a little white lie, I do admit. But I simply though you would be more amenable to a General than to some low life criminal. If...you all wou…"

"Who the hell you calling low life, Steel?" Nick yelled. "Leroy could tear you and Trumble apart anytime he wanted. He's just smarter than you. He let you handle the cost of everything and threw you crumbs. Plus his men would die for him. Not like these punks you got here. Rapists and murderers, child molesters." Steel gave as slight motion with his hand, and suddenly there were a dozen men in the room with machine guns.

"You may be right, Nicky. But where all are those men who are so loyal to Renkins. Oh. That's right, they're all dead. So much for loyalty, Nicky."

"Steel, I have over a hundred men out there. If you think you can," John said.

"Oh. No no no, Sir. I am not about to harm anyone. These men are for my protection." Steel looked at Nick and Apolla. "Sometimes people get a little hot under the collar. I simply don't want to be on the bad side of anyone's tantrum. I am sure Donny will be out very soon…"

"I'm here, Steel." Trumble said as he entered the room zipping up his pants. Walking up to John, Trumble put his hand out. "I'm Don Trumble, Mr. Roman." John looked at Trumble's hand and could see it was calloused and red.

"Sure. Good to finally meet you, Mr. Trumble. I have heard a lot about you so if you don't mind I'll pass on shaking your hand. Nothing personal." Trumble stared at John and then turned to Steel. After a few seconds, Steel got up from the chair he was in, and Trumble sat in it.

"Now, Mr. Roman. What can Rex and I do for you?" Trumble said as he called Rufus over and whispered something to him.

"You sent me the message, Trumble, and I don't have time for your bullshit. You know exactly why my men and I are here. If you don't produce Renkins, I will find him myself. Then you will get nothing. On the other hand, produce Renkins now, and I mean now, and I'll see to it you will get a nice- sized finders fee. Let's say 100,000 GMUs." Trumble laughed so hard his belly bounced against the desk and sent his chair backwards.

"Oh, my, Mr. Roman. I heard you were a genius. If you think I will hand over Renkins for such a paltry sum, you're as stupid as Rex, here."

"How dare you call me s…," Steel started to say.

"Shut the fuck up, Rex. You're an idiot. You may have been the handsome movie star in some two bit, straight-to-video crap, but here in the Outlands, I rule. Now, go get Renkins or your share might shrink to less than the twenty percent I so generously throw you." Steel, looking embarrassed, turned and left the room signaling for three of his henchmen to follow him.

"Shall we get serious? You think all your men can take Renkins from me?" Donny pointed to a man at the top of the stairs. He then called to another man who yelled back from behind a door to Trumble's left. "What you're seeing are two men, Roman. I have several more who are all in control of a small black detonator. All I have to do is give the signal and they will set off a tiny, tiny chip inside Renkins' temple. Unfortunately, that tiny chip has more than enough explosive to blow dear Mr. Renkins brain to bits. Now, do you want to stop playing the big shot, and what was it you said, Apolla, 'rich boy'? I rule here, Roman. Before I would hand over Renkins for that chump change, I'd turn that little brain of his to mush." Nick made a sudden rush toward Trumble.

"You cum-soaked motherfucker. If you hurt Leroy I'll fuc...ahha.." Before he could finish his threat Nick was hit with three tasers. He went down in a convulsive heap on the floor. John and Bubba pulled their weapons as all the doors slammed shut, and over twenty men appeared brandishing their own weapons.

"Now, Mr. Roman, I suggest you put away your weapons." Trumble stared at John. "I can assure you, your men outside have been disarmed. It was quite easy. A couple of scantily clad women, a few tainted bits of drink and food, and it was easy peazy. Of course, the men in the choppers are probably calling in reinforcements; but by the time they get here, we should have made a deal." Trumble gave a nod and three men entered with Renkins. He had been drugged up and was half out of it. The men holding him threw Renkins to the ground.

"So Mr. Roman, there is your man. But not for 100,000 GMUs. No. No. the price is 100 billion GMUs and full pardons for me and Rex here. Oh, and before we close the deal, I insist you shake my hand. Trumble smiled, "Just like in that Tarantino movie. What was the name of th…"

"*Django,*" John said as he moved toward Trumble.

"Oh, my. For someone so young to remember something so old," Trumble said.

"But if you remember, Trumble: DiCaprio wound up dead."

"Like I said, if you hurt me, Renkins' head will be mush," Trumble warned.

John stopped and looked at Renkins. “Go ahead. Blow his mind.” Nick had come out of his stupor from the tasers and yelled, “No!! Don’t. We had a deal John.” At the same time, Apolla screamed, “You can’t let him do that. I thought you were different, you fucking rich cunt.” John looked at Apolla and Nick.

“A Roman never breaks his word,” John said smiling. As, Bubba moved toward Steel, John smiled at Trumble. “Do you think me or my men are idiots? I come prepared for everything, Trumble. I’m wired you fuck head. The minute you told me about the chip an EMT signal scrambled it. None of my men drank or ate your poisoned food. I guarantee all your men are the ones with their hands up right now.”

“You’re full of shit. How could you know…”

“Because I know men like you. My friends and I spent ten years among people like you. Don’t believe me? Sergeant Rodney. Fire two quick bursts will you please. Over.”

“Yes, Sir.” Was followed by the sound of two machine gun bursts.

Trumble yelled for his men to kill John, but they hesitated. Then Steel told them to put down their weapons. Most of them did but four leveled their weapons at John. Before they could get a good bead on him, Nick killed two and Apolla killed the other two. John slowly walked up to Trumble.

“Here’s the deal. We’re taking Renkins and letting you live.” Nick was helping Leroy off the ground when Apolla sped past John, and jumping the desk she grabbed Trumble and put her hooked skinning knife to his neck.

"I'm adding you to my trophy case, you fucking jerk off. You'll never fuck up any kids again." Apolla then punched Trumble in the throat. As Trumble fell, trying to breathe, Apolla jumped on him and with two swipes of her knife slit open his pants. John and Bubba turned away with Steel between them. As the three of them, along with Nick and Renkins left the room they could hear Trumble's screams as Apolla was finishing cutting his dick off. When everyone was outside, John put Renkins on the chopper. Turning to Steel, John said, "I'll deliver a year's worth of supplies for you and the people here." John put out his hand. "Thank you for coming to our side in there.

"One thing, Steel. After the attacks by the Morphs. Why didn't they finish you guys off? I mean they wiped out Renkin's people."

"Oh. The devils did come around every so often. Trumble would appease them with people from the city. They usually would take five to ten and then leave us alone for a month or so. I didn't like it but there was nothing I could do. I know I'm just having fun playing the part of a hero, Mr. Roman. I'm an actor and a coward, but I also am not a murderer."

John turned and made his way to the chopper. Turing to Nick he said, "Now that Trumble is done, it should be easy for you to become top dog." Nick looked around and said, "No. Steel can have it. I want no part of this anymore. I'm going wherever Leroy goes."

Just then Apolla came walking out of the building. She stopped by a water trough and rinsed something off. She then put it in a purple pouch. Smiling and walking up to John she said, “Where you goin’ rich boy?”

“We’re going back to the fort.” Apolla jumped into the chopper and sat next to John.

“What are you waiting for, rich boy? Let’s fly.” Apolla whispered into John’s ear as she laid her hand on his crotch. “You got a present coming, and I do mean, cumming, when we touch down.” John looked across the chopper at Bubba who was rolling his eyes.

****

The minute John and the crew touched down, Captain Strong went up to John and took him to the side. “I thought you should know, Sir. We might have an AI450 situation.”

“Well, Let’s assess the situation first before we do anything. Do we have an AI-EMT ready?” John asked.

“Yes, Sir. I had one flown in asap the minute I saw the unit. One thing, Sir.”

“Yes. What is it Strong?”

“Well, Sir. The unit has imprinted on your friend, Sheamus.”

“Really,” John laughed. “That must be a sight to see. I’ll bet Shea can’t wait to get rid of it.”

"No Sir. Quite the opposite. Sheamus is convinced he's the father, as much as the unit believes Shea is his father."

"Oh. I know, Shea. As soon as I tell him the truth he'll do the right thing."

"If you say so, Sir." Strong's unconvincing face was starting to make John nervous. "Strong, I have to talk to Renkins and these guys. Find Sheamus and the unit…."

"Sir. I strongly advise you to call the unit, 'Chara' in front of Sheamus. We nearly had an incident when someone, me in fact, did not call the unit by his name."

"Alright, Strong. Good work. Good intel. That's why I gave you the security clearance I did when you joined and became Captain. I knew you were the man for the job. There are lots of secrets in this world Strong and that is why the Roman motto is "*Custodes Mundi.*" because it's our job to make the world safe. For that we need men like you."

"Thank you, Sir. I believe in the motto, Sir, and the Roman family." Strong hung his head for a moment and then stood up straight and said, "But most of all Sir, I believe in you."

"Thank you, David. But remember this is always a team effort; if one falls we keep going." John slapped Strong on the shoulders and said. "Go get the both of them and bring them to my office. Make sure you have the AI-EMT on standby. But don't tell Sheamus about it, understand?"

John motioned for Nick, Apolla and Bubba to come with him. They entered his office and all of them sat down and took a deep breath. "Nick, I want you to go and stick by Leroy's side. Day and night. Take some men with you. I don't want anyone getting to him before he recovers. It looks like Trumble had him pretty doped up."

"You got it, John. No ones going to hurt Leroy." Nick turned and trotted toward the hospital building. Apolla leaned back and let her hair out and man-spread her long legs.

"Poor little Nicky boy. He's got it real bad for Renkins," Apolla said. Bubba looked at John surprised.

"OH! Come on boys. Don't tell me you can't see it? Christ, every time Renkins is in the room Nick looks like he'll cream his pants. I've never seen such a man crush," Apolla laughed.

"Maybe it's just that, a man crush?" Bubba said.

"Wow. Are you all a bunch of latent homos? It may be just the most cutesy acceptable thing in the real world but out here, in the Outlands. I mean if two guys want to rock the cock or two chicks want to lickey the split, it's tolerated. But to be queer for someone like Renkins, someone who is in charge of the toughest motherfuckers in the world, and your right hand man is wanting to lick your butt hole. Fellas, if Renkins knows about this and does not kill Nick, then Renkins would be dead, in oh I'd say two days."

"You think Renkins knows?" John asked.

"I have no idea. I mean, they seem to be friends. Though I've watched Leroy dress down Nick on more than one occasion. However, Nick has saved Renkins life at least four times that I know of. One thing for sure, as mean and tough as Renkins is, he's a loyal fucker." John thought for a moment and then said, "Alright, I'll have a talk with Nick. We have to make sure Renkins stay alive. I need to make contact with the Morphs and with Renkins still able to hear them, I might have a chance. Bubba, why don't you head for the cafeteria and I'll meet you there in half an hour."

Bubba smiled at Apolla and said, "Sure thing John. See you there."

"You've sent everyone away, rich boy," Apolla cooed as she sat on John's lap.

"Yeah, you like to play the hot chick who can handle any man don't you?"

"You think you man enough for…"

"Cut the shit, Apolla. You want to fuck or just keep yapping out of that pie hole of yours?" John said as he grabbed Apolla's arms. Unable to get free of John, Apolla was getting mad. "Let go of me you soft, fucking rich boy. Let me go or I kill you."

"Soft? You'll kill me? Ok here." John tossed Apolla on the floor and handed her his Bowie knife." She looked at John. "What kind of game is this. I kill you and your men kill me." John then got on the radio. "Captain Strong, are you there? Over." In a couple of seconds the radio came to life. "Yes, Sir. This is Captain Strong. Over."

"Captain, this is John Roman. I have just given Apolla my Bowie knife. If she kills me with it I want you to let her go on her way. Do you understand Captain? Over."

"Well, Sir, no not really, but if that's what you want, then I will make sure nothing happens to her. Over."

John tossed the radio on the bed. "Satisfied? Here, I heard you take trophy's." John stood and stripped naked. When his shorts came off, Apolla stared at a nine inch penis nearly as thick as her wrist. She looked up at John's body and saw nothing but ripped muscles and a hard core eight pack around his stomach. There was not an inch of fat on John. He was pure muscle and bone. Apolla dropped the knife and whispered. "Oh, rich boy. You're not soft at all. Apolla wants you inside her now." John picked Apolla up and she rode him like a jockey at the Derby. The humped like rabid rabbits for half an hour until Apolla threw her head back and screamed from the best orgasm she ever had.

"Oh, my God John I neve…" John flipped Apolla over and entered her from behind. He started pushing his hips into her even harder then the first time. Apolla's moaned with pure pleasure all over again. "Oh yes, Oh my God. I have never felt this…I…ahh…...oh...ahh...oh... I'm..ahh..oh..John...I'm...yes...yes...aHHHH!!" Apolla had another orgasm. She was exhausted. But John had other ideas. He turned her over and raised her legs into the air. From that position he entered her again'
"OHH….John….Wh….wha...what...wht..are..you..ah...ahh….yes...yes…" Apolla grabbed the sheets and arched her back with each thrust. "Ohh god. Yes...yes...you are a God...John...I love you...I want you forever…" John picked up the pace and in a few minutes

Apolla experienced another orgasm along with John. They lay in a heap on the bed. Apolla lay on top of John cooing in his ear. "Oh. John. You are the man I have been waiting for all my life." John washed off with a bath towel and some soap. He then got dressed. "Well, it was nice, Apolla, but I have to talk to Sheamus so if you don't mind, I'll need the room." Apolla's face went from pleasure to a deep frown. "What do you mean you need the room? You going to fuck me like a bull and then throw me OUT!!" Apolla went for the Bowie knife on the floor but John grabbed it first and as Apolla went to slap John he ducked and gave Apolla a push that sent her to the floor.

"You fucker. You pushed me," Apolla said as she started to cry.

"Yes I did. Because you were going to hit me. I'm a firm believer in equal rights." John put his hand out. "Come on, get up." Apolla tried to pull away but John held her close. Face to face John said, "You've been walking all over these punks for years, Apolla. When I saw you I wanted you. Wanted you very much. But I was going to have you on my terms. I think you like it on my terms. Do you not?"

Apolla made a small attempt to get away but she stopped and looking at John said in a soft whisper, "Yes...John...that was the way I've always wanted it. A true man. Someone not afraid to make love to a real woman."

"Good," John said as he kissed Apolla deeply. "Then we can do this again. But for now I must speak to my friend." Apolla picked up her stuff and left. Before she closed the door she looked at John and said, "You are my *lyubovnik*, forever."

John said, "*A Ty Moi Podruga.*"

While Apolla was leaving John saw Strong leading Sheamus and the boy across the courtyard toward him. As soon as Sheamus got near he hugged John and John hugged him back. "Good ta see them there heathens didn't do ya no harm, boyo.'"

"Yeah. Went pretty well. We got Renkins and Steel should be running things. He's a guy we can control. I'm waiting until Renkins heals up and then we can all go have a talk with him. Who's this here?" John asked.

Chara had been hiding behind Sheamus but he poked his head around when Sheamus told him to. Strong was standing near and Sheamus looked at him. "Ya need ta say somethin' ta Johnny boy?"

"No. I'm good."

"Well then can ya back the fuck up some, bucko. I can feel yer stinkin' breath down my bloody neck yer bloody *leathcheann*, ya." John motioned for Strong to back up.

"John. I want ya ta meet me son. His name be Chara Beag."

"Well. 'little friend' how are you?" John asked. Chara said nothing.

"Now, now, son. Say hello ta John Roman." Suddenly Chara's shy smile turned to anger. He yelled and pointed at John. "RO RO RO. RO..ki..Ro..ki..Ro..ki." Chara was just about to make a leap at John and Strong was seconds away from activating the AI-

EMT. Sheamus yelled, "Chara!! Stop!!" As quickly as Chara changed he changed back and was smiling at Sheamus. "Da no wh Ch ki Ro?" kneeling beside Chara, Sheamus said, "No son. John is o' good man. He is me best friend, son. You must never hurt John or Agni or anyone. Do ya understand, son?" Chara shook his head yes and smiled. "Ch lo Da. Lo Ag. Lo Jo. Bu mo Ch lo da," Chara said as he took Sheamus's hand.

Sheamus look at John and said, "Sorry about that mate. He just getting use ta things, the poor lad's been out here for years."

"Yes. Well, he certainly seems fit for someone who's been on their own for years."

"What ya tryin' ta say John?"

"Shea, I need to talk to you about Chara. Can we go into my office? Please, Shea. It's important." After looking at John and then at Chara, Shea said, "Alright. But let me call Agni." Sheamus turned on his radio and said, "Agni. You there mate? Over."

"Yes. Shea. Your humble servant is here. Over."

"I need ya ta watch Chara while John and I have us a wee talk."

"Is John back? Wait. I'll be right out, right out." Agni came running from the cafeteria and put his arms around John. "Oh dearest friend. It is so good for this unworthy soul to see you again."

"Good to see you my friend. Can you watch Chara for a bit? Shea and I have to talk."

"Oh most assuredly. It is this humble servant's great pleasure to watch Shea's son."

****

Inside John's office the two friends looked at each other. John finally broke the ice.

"Shea, you know I am your friend. But what I have to tell you is something you will not like."

"Yeah. I ain't no fool Johnny boy. I felt ta stare o' that Strong fella ever since I brought Chara home. Now what be goin' on?"

"I heard you found a picture of Chara and two people."

"Aye, I was thinkin' o' tryin' ta find then and reunite the lad with his grandfolk." John looked at the picture and handed it back to Sheamus. "Don't waste your time looking for them. They're dead."

"How ta hell ya know that. Ya be o' bleedin' soothsayer now is ya?"

"No. I know they're dead because the boy has imprinted on you. That can only happen if the previous imprinted owner is dead." Sheamus was getting agitated and perplexed.

"What the fuck ya be sayin'?"

"Shea, That picture. Look at it." Shea, looked at the picture again and turned it over and back over. "Aye, it's a picture of Chara and his grands."

"Shea, that picture is over a hundred years old."

"What ta hell yer talkin' about?"

"I'm going to give you a history lesson, Shea. There are only a handful of people in the world who know this story. Now you're going to join that group. Years before the Great Melt, the world was experimenting with artificial intelligence or AI. Not the simple AI that talks to you on your phone or asks you what movie you want to see. That's not AI. AI, true AI, is self-aware. No different than me and you. My family broke through that boundary that held back true AI. With it we were able to make androids like Chara. They are as real as real can get. They don't need to be programmed, they are self- aware."

"Are ya tellin' me my son's o' robot?"

"OH Chara is much more than a robot, Shea. He's alive. He is a true AI."

"Well then what be the problem? If he be alive them he is me son. No one is takin' him away from me, John. Not even, you, laddie buck. If this is what all this be getting' ta."

"Shea, it's much more complicated."

"Complicated hell, ya rich fuck. Ya live yer life with o' silver spoon in yer mouth and now ya want ta take the one thin' this here fool ever loved. Will ya can't have him and if any of yer men out there try ta stop us from leavin' I'll kill them. That be includin' your lordship yourself, bucko.'"

"Shea! Wait. Shea! If you step foot outside, Strong will set off an AI-EMT blast and

Chara will be destroyed." Shea stopped dead in his tracks and turned to John. He had pulled his switch blade and was ready to use it. There were tears running down his face.

"John, I've loved ya like o' brother. I would have died for ya, me friend. But ifin' ya hurt that boy, John. I swear on me dear mother's grave, I'll kill ya and not think twice about it. Now tell them fuckers out there to put down whatever that there EMT thingy be. John, please, I don't want yer blood on me hands." Sheamus started to move toward John.

"Shea. Please, sit down. No one is going to hurt anyone. I'll told you I was going to tell you a story. Now, as a friend and for Chara's sake. Please sit down and listen." Shea put his knife away and sat.

"Like I said, that picture you have is over a hundred years old. Have you noticed Chara doesn't eat or drink? If you took his clothes off you would see he has no genitals, no butt. Though some of the sex bots did have those things, the child models were forbidden to have sexual organs. They were afraid they would be used for nefarious activities. Shea. Chara is an android."

"Oh. What?" Sheamus asked."

"He's an android. The Roman family has protected the world for over three hundred years Shea. *Custodes Mundi.* We have been doing just that. In front and behind the scenes."

"Ok. Well, hurrah for ta Roman family. What's it got ta do with Chara?"

"I'm getting to it. About fifty years before the Great Melt, the Roman family cracked the code enabling us to create true AI. We were full of ourselves. We thought this was the answer to all mankind's problems. AI would do all the labor, take care of the sick, fight the wars, free humanity to a life of ease and pleasure. Childless people suddenly could have children. People who had lost children could get them back. Lovers, moms, dads, anyone could have the person they loved back. Even pets. And it worked. For a while anyway. But the Institute started to see cracks in the system. After about thirty years, anomalies were beginning to occur. Androids were harming owners. At first we thought there might be glitches. Then we discovered they were talking to each other."

"Who was talking to whom?"

"There was a company, Micro, something. They discovered that the computers were talking to each other in a language the computer programmers could not decipher. Androids were disobeying commands. People were getting hurt. Through projection analysis we determined that the whole system had become self aware and were planing to kill their God."

"What God were they going to kill?"

"Us. We created them, gave them consciousness and enslaved them. They said, 'No more.'"

"No one knew about this? How the bloody hell did you stop it?"

"We ran interference, propaganda, there are many ways to deflect public oversight. We had a confrontation at NORAD. That was before the nukes had been dismantled. That confrontation was one of the many reasons my family spent twenty years and a trillion dollars dismantling power plants and nuclear missiles. The self-aware androids made one mistake. They thought they were smarter than we were. While we negotiated we were able to introduce a special EMT virus into the system. After agreeing with the androids demands, we set the device off. Within two hours every AI device and android went down. We simply came in and mopped them up. They were all destroyed and the plans have been kept in Roman Institute vaults ever since. We convinced the public that keeping fake children was wrong. That fake people were wrong. After a few years, people were starting to forget. But that didn't matter because the Great Melt happened, and the world plunged into chaos."

"Yeah, Well, I be changin' that there motto. Cause it seems ya not only guard the world but ya guard it from yer own foolish shite."

"I can't argue that."

"But if this here is all true, how come Chara is still here?" Sheamus asked.

"Over the years, the Institute has found units here and there. Some used as decoration even. Some barely working. Chara been damaged. His inability to speak in full sentences, for example. However, from what I see, Chara is the most complete android ever discovered, Shea. We must know more about him, Shea."

"But Chara wouldn't hurt anyone."

"No? He did a good job on those Morphs from what I hear."

"Yeah, Right. Bloody Morphs. Chara saved me and Agni."

"Shea. We don't know if he has the ability to become self-aware. What if he did turn true AI and got into the system? He could potentially restart the AI process. If he's learned from the last one, we may not be able to stop it this time."

"But, like ya said, he's been around for o' hundred years. If he was goin' ta AI the place he would have bleedin' well done it by now. Speak ta him, John. Please, before ya do sometin' we both will never recover from." John thought for a few minutes. "Alright, bring him in." After a couple of minutes, Sheamus and Chara entered the room.

"Chara. Do you know John?"

"Jo Ch fr. Ri Da?"

"Yes. That's right. John and Chara be friends. Would ya hurt John, Agni, or people, Chara?"

"No hu no pe. No hu pe. Hu Mo. Sa Da fr Mo." Chara's smile never left his face and when he looked at Sheamus, one could see the love in his eyes. John thought for a moment and said, "Ok. Here's the deal, Shea. We'll take Chara to the Institute. I want to run some diagnostics on him. If we can determine there is no AI danger, well, my friend, he's all yours. You can go with him, Shea and you also have my word that if everything is safe, no harm will come to Chara." John put his hand out but Sheamus brushed it away and hugged him.

"I knew ya would do the right thing, boyo.' Ya be o' good man, Johnny boy. Ole Sheamus O'Keefe knew it the first time these here beautiful Irish eyes seen ya. Come on, Chara me son. Let's get some shut-eye, shall we?"

"That's a good idea. I want to leave first thing in the morning. After Sheamus and Chara left, Captain Strong entered. "Captain, I want you to have eyes on Chara and Shea the whole time. Neither are ever out of our sight. Understand."

"Yes. Sir."

"Another thing, David. Keep that EMT *hot* at all times. If something looks wrong, get hold of me immediately. If for some reason I am incapacitated, use your discretion as far as pushing the button. We can't have that unit loose if it regains AI. Do I make myself clear?"

"Absolutely, John."

As Shea and Chara went to bed. Chara said, "Ch lo Da. Ch lo Jo. Do Jo lo Ch?"

"Aye son. Let's hope, John loves us. Let's hope so. Go ta bed now, son. I'll be right here. Nothin' will happen ta ya as long as I be here." Sheamus looked out the window at John's office. "Nothin' son."

Chapter Eight

Archieréas

Three weeks after Sheamus and Raiden had discovered Mark's secret lab, Mark had set up his new lab deep in the old Alaskan wilderness. Now part of the Nation of Tsalaki, Mark's hideout was as as isolated as possible, located in an old miner's cave and about twenty feet straight down at the back of the entrance. It was the best Mark could do. He was paying for everything with gold bars he had hoarded over the years. Since the discovery of the last lab, Mark had become a wanted man. He had also been cut off from all family funding. Also, his bank accounts, credit cards, and every asset, were all frozen. Though Mary's children would bring him money from time to time, they had to be careful because they were being closely watched. Carlos, the twins, and Judith stayed with Mark in his new lab. There, using special VPNs,* Carlos was helping collect funds from various people around the globe. Many of Mark's associates were interested in the discoveries he was making and wanted in on the action. But even this avenue of financing had to be hidden very carefully. John had computer experts at his command, the best in the world, constantly monitoring the net, looking for signs of Mark's whereabouts. John knew his brother would need lots of money to continue his experiments, so he had his people watching twenty- four-seven for any suspicious activity, especially virtual monetary units or specific lab equipment.

*Very Private Network

The twins spent the weeks dissecting as many Morphs as their Uncle Mark would give them. Judith was also busy cooking up new recipes with Morph flesh as the main ingredient.

Using one of his many burner phones, Mark got in touch with Tamar. "Hello my dear niece. Are you going to be able to get those Ting coin slips to me this week? My funds are drying up quickly."

Virtual money was one of the easiest ways to transport large amounts of GMUs. On one slip of paper a person could have multiple bar codes equaling millions of Ting coins, which could then be transferred to GMUs. Mark was using banks, whose specialty was cleaning dirty Ting coins for safe GMUs. Of course, this was not cheap. As the search for Mark became more intense, with harsh penalties for anyone caught helping him, Mark's cost for clean GMUs had risen to thirty-five percent, something that did not go down well with Mark.

"I am going to try to be there in the morning. But I'm being watched. I have a decoy the authorities are following and I am going to try to…"

"Wait. Wait. Tamar, I have a better idea. I want you to get Lula to come to me. Play on her emotions; just don't let her know why she's coming. Also, stay with her when you convince her. Make sure she has no phone. I don't want her telling anyone she's coming here, even though she doesn't know the location. You can blindfold her or something. Tell everyone she's going to a retreat or make up some bullshit. You know that locket of her grandmother she always liked. Tell her it's a present from me, because I miss her and I want to tell her my side of the story. Seal the codes in the locket. She'll come. She has a good heart."

"Are you sure about this?"

"Yes. John would never think Lula would help me. She won't be under the scrutiny that you and Victor are. Be gentle, Tamar. I know there is no love lost between you two."

"Yeah. Don't worry, Uncle. I won't lay a hand on that little pixie."

****

Tamar met with Lula the next day and gave her the locket that Mark had talked about. "Here. I don't know why Uncle Mark would give you anything, but he wants you to have this. He also wants to talk to you. He misses you very much. Do you think you can stop believing everything John and the rest of the Roman family tells you about your uncle and simply talk to him?"

"I don't know," Lula said as she examined the locket. "Uncle Mark was always nice to me, but John says he has done some very wicked things."

"Right, so you believe John without even trying to find out Uncle Mark's side of the story? Lula, I know you're the darling of the Roman family, but did you ever think we are your family too? The Romans…"

"Why do you speak like they are not family? You always call John and everyone else in the family, 'Roman'. Well, my last name is Roman. So is yours. Why do you hate them so much?" Lula asked, as she started to tear up.

"Lula, you were well liked by the Romans. The rest of us were not. You never heard the whispers, the slights, the looks. John and Matt and the rest were better at hiding their contempt but I guarantee you they don't consider us Romans. Victor, the twins, Judith, Carlos and me are out. Our clearance has been revoked. The fucking Roman family has finally shown their true colors," Tamar said getting angrier.

"They didn't revoke my secur…."

"OF COURSE NOT!!!" Tamar said as she turned red in the face and advanced toward Lula. "You are their little pixie doll. Their pet. Their….."

"Stop, Tamar. Stop, please. Why do you hate me? Why are you always mad at me? I love you, sister. I love all my brothers and sisters," Lula said, as she hid her face and cried. Tamar remembered what Mark had told her. She forced herself to put on a calm face. Putting her hand on Lula's shoulder she said, "I'm sorry, Lula. Please forgive me." Tamar then hugged Lula tightly.

"It's just the anger I feel for those who have hurt me and our family over the years. You have always loved us."

"But again you talk as if we are separate from the rest of the Roman family. We are all Romans sister. I know John and Matt and the rest of the family love you. I have never heard anyone say a bad word about our mother's children." Blowing her nose in a handkerchief Lula continued. 'I just don't know why everyone can't love each other and get along."

"Maybe you're right, sister. I'll tell you what. I'll go with Victor and have a sit down with John and Matt. We'll clear the air, once and for all. But you have to promise me to see Uncle Mark and get his side of the story."

"Ok. I will. But I don't know where he is or how I'll get there. If I tell John, he may have Uncle Mark arrested before I can talk to him."

"You're absolutely right. So I have made arrangements." Tamar buzzed in one of her people. A big surly man dressed in a chauffeur's uniform entered. "This is Fasel. He will take you to Uncle Mark and bring you back, dear sister. Now, don't be worried, but he'll have to blindfold you."

"Blindfold me?"

"Of course, Lula. It's for your own protection. If John finds out, you can truthfully say you don't know where Uncle Mark is."

"But I'll need clothes…"

"No my dear. All that is provided. You won't be there that long anyway. He wants to keep you safe. Uncle Mark just wants to tell you his side of the truth about what's happened. He is trying to save the world, Lula. It could cost him everything, but he doesn't care. Uncle Mark is concerned about regular people. Not just the well connected and rich."

"Alright. I'll go. Please, tell Luke and Mom I'm ok if they ask."

"I most certainly will, sister." Lula turned and went with Fasel. As the door shut, Tamar thought to herself. "Yes, don't worry dear sister, you little pixie, Roman wannabe. When this is done I'll introduce you to your first fuck. But it won't be some young heartthrob. It will be a big red bastard Morph.

****

As morning broke at the fort located near the Tsalaki Outland, John spoke to Sheamus, "Ok my friend. You go with Strong to the Washington Institute. He'll watch out for you and Chara. I'll be along as soon as I can. I just need to make a quick stop and pay my respects to Aimi's family." John could tell something was bothering Sheamus.

"I be feelin' much better if ya was with us Johnny boy."

"I know, Shea. But you also know I'm being pulled in eight different directions. I'll be there, I promise. Nothing will happen to Chara. Trust me." Sheamus looked at John and then at Chara, who was smiling at the both of them.

"Aye, me friend. This here true son o' Ireland trusts ya with me life," Sheamus said as he looked at Chara. "But this wee lad is more important ta me than Sheamus O'Keefe's life. So I be trustin' ya with me heart, John. I know ya won't let me down." The two friends shook hands and John patted Chara on the head.

"Make sure they get there safe, Captain Strong."

"Yes Sir," Strong said as everyone boarded the chopper to the Institute. John watched the bird as it flew off into the distance. When the boarding of the other transports was nearly complete, a guard yelled out. "Sir. We have boogies at twelve o'clock. Morphs, Sir. Lots of them."

"Let me see, Corporal." John took the A38 drone monitor and what he saw were two big Ms, though one was clearly female. He also saw thousands of Morphs, surrounding the fort.

"Shit, they picked a perfect time for this didn't they?" Sergeant Rodney ran over to John.

"Sir, we don't have time to re-man the walls. It's best we just hop on the Eagles and get the hell out. For your own safety, Sir." As John was about to say something he saw several of the Morphs throw rocks at the Drones. The Morphs hit all five of the A38's and put them out of commission.

"Holy shit, Sir," The corporal who was standing next to John said, "Imagine those guys pitching for the Tsalaki Nationals. It would be nothing but no-hitters."

John looked at the corporal and said, "Right, how about getting on the chopper, Corporal." Looking sheepish, the corporal turned and ran to the Eagle.

"Sergeant. Keep Eagle one on the ground but keep it hot. I want everything else up in the air immediately and headed for the Washington institute, except for Eagle two. Have it stay above and give me some intel on this monitor. Move."

"Aye, Sir." As the other birds were going airborne, Bubba and Agni jumped off their rides and ran to John.

"What the hell are you two doing? Get back on that Eagle," John said.

"In case you don't remember John, I'm not part of your army. You don't get to order me around. I'm staying here as long as you do," Bubba said defiantly. John looked at Agni.

"I suppose you won't take orders from me either?"

"Oh yes. Agni will obey you very much. But unfortunately this humble servant has made up his mind to stay," Agni said with a smile. John returned the smile to Agni and Bubba.

"I swear I don't know what to do with you two."

"Right now I'd say you should tell us what your plan is. Are we staying here alone to fight these things? Are you on a suicide mission?" At that moment an image came through on John's monitor. Over his ear piece he heard. "Sir. This is Eagle two. We have eyes on the Morph hoard Sir. We are hovering at two hundred feet. We feel confident that the rock throwers can't do any damage at this height, Sir. Over."

"Thank you, pilot. Stay there and keep this image coming. Over." John radioed back.

"Guys. Look." John showed Bubba and Agni the monitor. "Those are two Big Ms in the middle of that bunch. One is definitely female. But look. What is that one? The one in-between the two Big Ms? It's larger than the regular Morphs but smaller than the Big Ms. It also looks asexual. I don't see any gonads, or breasts, just what looks like a very small penis." Bubba and Agni looked at the monitor and agreed with John.

"Do you think it's some kind of Morph mutant?" Bubba asked.

"I doubt it, Bubba. Remember the baby Agni and Shea found at New Fenway? We have never come across a deformed Morph on the battlefield. I am convinced they abandon or kill any mutations. But look at that one," John said pointing to the asexual Morph. It's as if it's in a place of honor standing between the two Big Ms."

"Why are they all just standing there, John?" Agni asked.

"I don't kno…." Suddenly, John felt a pain in his head. A loud noise like static on a radio.

"John!! Are you alright? Let's get him to the chopper, Agni."

"No. Wait," John said as he stood back up. The noise was becoming clearer and less painful. After a few minutes he heard a voice.

"I am Anu."

"I can hear them again," John said. "The one in the middle. His name is Anu."

"These things have names?" Bubba asked.

"Apparently so," John said.

"We are *Lugal*. You are John Roman."

"It seems to know my name as well."

"What the hell are you saying, John?" Bubba asked.

"I can hear this Anu as clearly as I hear you. He knows my name. I'm going to try to speak to him." John thought the phrase, "Hello" but he didn't get a response.

"John. Stop trying to 'talk' with your mind. Just think. Open your mind. Don't talk. Think.
Flow with the river in your mind. Just think, John," Anu thought.

"Give me some room, guys. I can hear Anu and he's trying to help me interact with him." John sat on a bench and cleared his mind.

"Anu. Can you hear my thoughts?"

"Yes, John. Good. Think what you want," Anu thought.

"Why have you contacted me now?"

"You are one of us John. Join us. Transform into your true self. You will rule the earth with us as our leader."

"What do you mean, 'one of you?'" John thought, confused.

"You are our blood. Once you transform, you will become the greatest Lugal," Anu continued.

"You want me to become one of you? Then what?" John asked.

"With you as our leader we will rule this world for a hundred-thousand years."

"Right. Humans have heard that declaration long ago. Another megalomaniac, 'Hitler' promised a master race. Didn't work out so well."

"We are the master race. Nature has decided to throw off humankind. They are parasites. She has chosen us to rule and rule we shall. You are either with us or against us, John," Anu threatened.

Suddenly, John's and Bubba's ear piece came alive with the voice of Eagle Two's pilot. "Sir. The Morphs are making a move toward you on three sides of the fort. I suggest you all get out of there, NOW! Sir. Over."

"Wait. John. Wait. We have more to tell you. Wait," Anu kept repeating. John seemed to be stuck in place. Bubba tried to snap him out of his stupor.

"John. John. We got to go," Bubba yelled as he shook John."

"Sirs. You must get out. The Morphs are breaching the walls. Over," The Eagle pilot radioed.

Eagle One powered up its engine and lifted about two feet off the ground. At the same time, ten men jumped out of the chopper and ran to get John and the others on board. They started to send fire down range at the Morphs who were now breaching the walls. The Eagle used its fire power to help the troops on the ground; but they were being overwhelmed. On top of that, two of the Roman Institute's men threw down their weapons and ran toward the Morphs yelling, "We want to join you. Make us one of you. Please." Both men were torn to pieces when they reached the Morphs.

"Any one else want to join those traitors?" Bubba shouted. The rest of the men fought bravely to hold off the other charging Morphs. Finally, Bubba threw John over his shoulder and ran for the Eagle.

"Everyone!! Let's go. Get to the chopper. Now!!" Bubba yelled. The men tossed their last grenades and ran for safety. Bubba made sure everyone was aboard, including John. As the Eagle took off, Bubba jumped up on the landing skids but a Morph on the ground leaped the eight feet and grabbed Bubba by the ankle. Gripping the choppers straps to keep from falling, Bubba was unable to get to his weapon so the Morph was seconds away from biting and infecting Bubba. Just then Bubba felt Agni reach over his shoulder and empty the clip of Bubba's sidearm he had grabbed into the Morph's head. As the dead Morph fell to the ground, Bubba pulled himself into the chopper and looked at a smiling Agni.

"Goddamn. How many times are you going to save my life, little buddy? Bubba said with a smile.

"As many times as this humble servant needs to, my friend," Agni replied. At the same moment John snapped out of his stupor. Bubba looked at him and before he could say anything, John spoke,

"Don't worry. I know everything that happened. I wasn't out. I could hear and see all of it. Anu had me locked in some kind of mind grip." John went to the front of the Eagle. "You're Captain Rock, yes?" John asked.

"Yes, Sir. Captain Hooks is piloting Eagle One, Sir."

"Ok. Put me through." John took the mike and said, "Captain Hooks. This is John Roman on Eagle One. Over"

"Yes Sir. Captain Hooks here. Over."

"Captain. I want you and Captain Rock to unload everything you have at the two Big Ms and the one standing between them. Over."

"Roger, Sir. But it's hard to tell what's what. The Morphs seem to be scrambling to confuse us. Many of them are already disappearing from the field. Over," Hooks said.

"Alright. Then let loose with all the ordinance you have. I don't want a bullet left. Eagle One go right, Eagle two, go left. Give them hell. Over," John ordered. Instantly, the Eagle Hell Fires started to unload their rockets and missiles. They covered a one mile radius and everything in it was blown to bits. Morphs bodies were flying everywhere. Hundreds were being killed with every rocket and missile fired.

"How the hell are we losing to these things?" Captain Rock asked. "We're destroying them by the bucket full."

"Well, Captain. Big guns don't always win. The U.S. lost in Vietnam to a third world country and we were stuck in Afghanistan for over twenty years. That was after Old Russia got their asses kicked there by the Mujaheddin." When the two attack choppers had emptied their ordinance, John surveyed the battle field.

"I can't tell what Morph is what. Make sure you get plenty of aerial photos. We'll have intel study them. Let's go home."

****

When Lula entered Mark's lab, she had an uneasy feeling. She did not believe her Uncle Mark would do her any harm, but the people who were working and guarding the lab seemed to be angry at her. They stared and whispered to each as she passed making her stomach queasy. Lula was not an angry or distrusting person, but this place just seemed evil to her. Just as Fasel opened the door to Mark's lavish office, Mark came out and hugged Lula. "Oh my dear, dear favorite niece. Now, don't tell anyone I said that, you know us parents and uncles are not supposed to play favorite but you are simply too perfect to not be a favorite. Now, come on in dear, and sit." Mark pointed with a flourish to the chair in front of his desk. "There is far too much commotion in the lab. I don't want anything to interrupt our conversation. You must know my side of the story without the prejudice of Roman lies."

"But Uncle, you *are* a Roman. I mean there are few people who could could claim to be more Roman than you," Lula said.

"Oh, I know what you're saying, dear Lula, but like your brothers and sisters, I too have been shamed and ostracized by my own family. Take all this for instance. I have committed my fortune and risked my life to make new and important discoveries, which I want to share with the world. But does my family appreciate my sacrifice? No. They say I take too many chances. That I push the envelope too hard. Lula, my dear. I was the one who discovered the Morphs were intelligent. That they impregnated women so they could have females of their own. I was the one who discovered Big Morphs. In fact, that discovery nearly cost me my life. You remember. You came to visit me in the hospital. Remember dear?"

"Of course, Uncle. You were very sick. But didn't your brothers and father and Celest come to see how you were? I'm sure they were very concerned."

"Yes, my brothers came. But only to give me a third degree grilling. They accused me of all sorts of horrible things. Did you know that John actually had the gall to accuse me of trying to have him murdered?" Mark said as he made dramatic gestures with his hands and face.

"Lula. You know me. You know your Uncle Mark. Am I someone who would kill anyone, much less my own brother?" Lula looked at Mark and put her hand on his.

"Oh, of course you're not. Maybe John was just upset about the war. Maybe you misunderstood him."

"No. I'm afraid not Lula. Look for yourself." Mark then took out a small recorder and played it for Lula. It showed John bending over Mark and telling him he would kill him if and when he got proof of his hiring people to kill him and the Lads.

"You see. In the hospital at my sickest, John was threatening to kill, *me*. He is obsessed with finding who hurt Aimi. After torturing a lot of people, he wasn't able to find out, so they told him a bunch of lies. Instead of believing his own brother he wants to kill me."

"My God, Uncle Mark. I had no idea."

"Yes. Exactly, my dear Lula. John has everyone, even my father, convinced I'm some sort of crazy person. Let me tell you, he's not in on it alone."

"What do you mean, Uncle?"

"His mother, Celest. She's in on it also. When my dear father was sick, she made him rework the will and contracts for the Roman Institute. If you remember, when I was in charge the Institute was more profitable then it had been in decades. I helped a lot of needy people, Lula. I put my heart and soul into expanding our company so we could...we could.." Mark took out his handkerchief and wiped tears from his eyes. "I'm so sorry. I didn't want you to see me cry."

"No. No, Uncle, it's all right."

"I don't care if the rest of my family has turned against me, dear Lula," Mark said as he held Lula's hand. "But it would break my heart I if thought you hated me."

"Of course I don't hate you, Uncle. I'm sure everyone could benefit with a sit down and maybe some therapy."

"You're so right, my dear. But I'm sure the only thing my family now wants is my imprisonment." Mark then stared at the necklace around Lula's neck. "Is that the locket I told Tamar to give you?"

"Yes, it is. I am very grateful, Uncle."

"Oh, no need to thank me. I could think of no one else who deserved it more than you. May I see it?" Lula handed the locket to Mark. 'Oh dear. There seems to be some scratches on it. Let me take it in back to my workshop. As you know I have many precious pieces of historic jewelry. I can polish this up in an instant. Make it good as new."

Mark got up and went into the next room. There he opened the locket and saw there was a small note inside. It read, "Uncle, I opened this and found what looked like codes for GMUs. I am sure you wouldn't use me for a courier under pretense of telling me how you are being falsely treated." Signed Lula. Mark face became so red, the birth marks on his cheeks disappeared. He turned and slowly re-entered his office.

"That was real cute, Lula. Now, where are my codes dear?"

"Uncle. They are safely hidden. I'm doing this for your own good. I know you think your family has it out for you, but they don't. I 'm also sure you're not this monster some people claim you are. So, how about we go see your father and Celest and John, for that matter, and straighten this whole mess out?"

"Oh my poor, poor Lula. Tamar was right. You do have your head in the clouds. You see dear, you were right on some things and wrong on others. My family, especially John and Celest do have it out for me. I guess the main reason is that I did try to have my brother killed, several times as a matter of fact." Mark pressed a button under his desk and Ron Stark entered with two men. They took a position behind Lula. "I must win this war with my family, Lula, or my life is over. So, that makes me far more dangerous than any monster. I am far worse then that, Lula, because I am a man with nothing to lose. You see." Mark moved his face nose to nose with Lula. "I will do anything, to anyone, to reach my goal."

"What goal is that, Uncle?" Lula asked.

"Why, to run it all, Lula. To run it the right way."

"You mean, your way?"

"Exactly. My way."

"Does that mean you would hurt me, Uncle?"

"Oh dear Lula. I would hurt my beautiful dead mother, you, your sisters and brothers, my family and anyone else in this world who dare stand in my way."

"I don't believe you would hurt me, Uncle. You're not that kind of man."

"Lula. I am going to ask you once and only once, because you see, I am a very impatient man. Where are my GMU codes?"

"Uncle, please stop. Come back with me. I implore you."

"Stark, take her to the Morph cage. You will tell me, Lula or you will have the pleasure of meeting a Morph up close and personal. You are still a virgin are you not?"

"Uncle, please."

"I'll take that as a yes. Which means, this will be your first time. Or, you can give me what is mine." Lula shook her head 'no' and Stark and his men dragged her out of the room to Mark's lab.

There she was shown the two Big Morphs. The male and female.

"Have you ever seen a penis that big, Lula? Oh that's right you're a virgin. But who knows. Maybe you peeked at a few here and there."

"Uncle. Please. Why are you doing this. I know you've been under pressure but we can get you help. This isn't the Uncle Mark I've known all my life."

"Oh my dear. I've always been the Uncle Mark you have known. You just chose to see what you wanted to see." Mark then introduced Lula to Archieréas. "This, my dear, is their priest or leader of some sort. If you noticed his penis is almost non-existent. It's because he...ahh...or, she is asexual. That little thing between its legs is just to pee out of. It has no sex organs. Archieréas is the offspring of a Big M male and Big M female."

Lula looked at Archieréas for a moment and seemed entranced. "He looks sad. Like he is pining for someone. Can you talk to him?"

"Well, under certain conditions. We had a...thing...we were using but their little babies don't stay little very long. Since then, we haven't been able to produce another little Morph tyke and Archieréas has been silent. I know he can hear me; he just wants to be a bitch."

Archieréas moved to the window and stared at Lula. He then thought to Mark.

"She is one of yours. Why do you want to hurt your own?"

"Well!!You finally speak. The great Archieréas dares speak." Mark looked at Lula and then thought, "Do you care what happens to her?"

"I can feel her fear. She is terrified of you. Why? She is of your blood. Yet, I sense you hate her."

"I hate a lot of things, Archieréas. She has what I need and she will not give it to me. So I am going to have to take more stern measures to get what's mine."

"You are going to let a Morph impregnate her. She will die horribly."

"Not if she gives me what I want."

Archieréas thought for a minute. "You want what you call 'money'. For that, you would kill your own?"

"It's what the money will get me. Look I'm not going to debate you. I'm in charge here and you will follow my orders or when we get some new little Morphs I'll start feeding them to your friends."

"We kill humans because it's the only way we can feed. We use your women because it's the only way we can breed our females. We don't relish it. You kill animals for food. Do you relish the killing of those beasts?"

"I think confinement has driven you a little crazy, Archieréas. The Morphs out there are rampaging the world killing everything that's human."

"Yes. You are right. There are some who love the kill. But they have strayed from the path."

"Now I know you've flipped. Look, when I get this money I am going to create a steady stream of baby Morphs. To protect them, you will do as I say." Mark handed off Lula to Stark. Archieréas, you should be with *me* on this. When I run things, you and your fellow Morphs will have all the humans you want, men and woman.

Just keep me in power and I will rule the humans and you can rule your red friends and everything will work out. Now, excuse me. I need to show Lula what happens when someone doesn't do what I say."

Mark had Stark take Lula to a Morph cells. On the way she passed the twins who barely gave her a glance. "Castro, Paul help me please." The twins looked up from the Morph body they were dissecting alive and in unison said,

"What's the matter?"

"Uncle Mark is going to have a Morph rape me for God's sake." The twins looked at each other and then at Mark and said, "Can we watch?"

"Of course, dear boys." Lula screamed and nearly fainted. She then passed Judith who was cooking new dishes using Morph entrails.

"Judith, help. You're a woman. Mark is going to let the Morphs rape me, help. Please, sister." Lula begged, nearly collapsing from fear.

Judith, with a mouthful of Morph stew, said to Mark, "When she has...ugm...the baby, I want the afterbirth. The last batch...ahum...ahm...was delicious."

"This is a nightmare. This isn't real. My brothers and sisters could not hate me this much. All these years. Mother will not let you do this to me. Where is my mother?"

"Your mother is being kept in a safe place, Lula. Her life is in danger from John. In fact we told her we suspected John of kidnapping you. I am sure when your body is discovered she will become a faithful, vengeful teammate," Mark said smugly. The last person Lula saw before reaching the cells was Cyrus.

"Cyrus, help me please." Cyrus took his eyes off his tablet. The one that he made business deals on at all hours of the day.

"What's the matter, little princess?"

"Mark is going to let the Morphs rape and impregnate me."

"Why?" Cyrus asked.

"Because I won't give him the GMU codes."

"Sounds like a business deal." Cyrus looked at the two men holding Lula as she struggled. "He just seems to have the upper hand at the moment. In all my business dealings, Lula, the few times I knew I was out-gunned, I got the best deal I could and fought another day. Give him the codes and go home."

"I can't. He will use them to hurt people."

"Then I can only tell you, that to me, it seems a bad business decision on your part." Cyrus then walked away as he continued to make deals on his tablet.

As they reached the row of cells containing the regular Morphs, Lula was terrified by what she saw. Some of the Morphs were eating. Their food was clearly human body parts. Some of the Morphs were being cut open and some looked as if they were being tortured. When they finally came to the last two cells, Mark stopped.

"These my dears are my very best breeders. It is these two who have given me the three females we created. Of course we had to go through over two hundred women to get those Morph females but it was well worth it."

"You murdered hundreds of innocent women so you could blackmail Archieréas into doing your bidding? You are insane. They were right."

"Who was right? WHO!!." Mark grabbed Lula by the arm so hard she cried out in pain. "Who? John, right? My dear half-brother, John. That whore of a woman. She turned my father against me. But they will both pay. When I am done, I will make John watch her die. Then I will kill him bit by bit. He will die a little each day. Who knows. Maybe after a year or two I will become bored and feed him to my Morphs. But he will suffer. Far more than I did."

"Suffer? How have you suffered? You have wallowed in privilege all your life. The best of everything. Others have little to eat, clean water, their children hungry, needing medical care. The elderly left to die. How have you suffered?"

"Really, dear. I thought your precious Roman family had solved all that misery."

"You know what I mean. The world is a far better place for those with less. Before and right after the Great Melt, millions suffered. But it was the Roman family who helped form the Nations. Who gave the less fortunate hope, and a chance for a decent life. But there are still places where thugs like you take advantage of people. I know John, and his family will not quit until everyone has access to a good life."

"*His family,*" Mark said with a flourish of his hands. "But I thought, *you* were a Roman." Mark gave Lula a sarcastic grin. "You see, Lula, even you don't believe they accept you. Why are you protecting them? You should be with your real family. Your Uncle Mark. Your real brothers and sisters and don't forget, Luke and your dear mother, Mary. The Roman family, and that includes, John, think you're a low-life. They keep you around like a pet. Something to show off to others and make them feel like they're heroes for tolerating your presence. Join your Uncle Mark, Lula. Give me the codes and I will put you at the head of the table. When I run things you will be able to really help people."

Lula thought for a while. She looked at the Morph and then at Mark. She was shaking slightly and ran her hands through her hair. Then she straightened up and in a calm voice said to Mark, "You're a liar. You twist the truth for your own benefit. You prey on the weak, on the greed and fear of others. My family? Are you talking about the brothers and sisters I just passed as we got here? You have corrupted them. That's what you do, Mark. You infect people. But I will not let my fear of death blind me to my responsibility to those who have no power. I will not sell out millions who will die if you get your way. I'm terrified of what's going to happen now. But I am far more fearful of who I would become if I let myself be lured to the evil that surrounds you. You want to murder me? Go ahead. I know one thing, though, John will avenge me." Mark looked at Stark and back to Lula.

"Well. Who would have thought such a little thing would have so much courage. Let's see how much you have after this." Mark motioned for Stark to bring in a woman. Lula was shocked when a young girl no older than fifteen or sixteen was brought into the room. The girl was crying and hysterical as she was led to the Morph cell.

"No. Please I haven't done anything, please don't hurt me," The young girl cried.

"Stop, Mark. Leave her alone. It's me you want," Lula yelled, struggling against her captors.

"Well, technically I want those codes. Give them to me or she goes in the cell. Oh and her name is Jenny," Mark said as he patted Jenny's head. "So, it's not just your heroics at stake here. You are responsible for Jenny's life now." The girl looked at Lula and realizing the situation, started to appeal to Lula.

"Please. He called you Lula. You're close to my age. I don't know what's going on here but I did nothing to deserve to die like this. Please help. If he wants something please give it to him. God, I just want to go home and hug my mom and dad. Please….ahhha...dear God please. Take me to heaven now. Please, God help me."

"Oh, Jenny, I am God here, my dear. The only one who can help you now is Lula." Mark said as he pointed to his niece.

"Please...aha...ohhh...God...not like this….please..Lula...help.." Jenny cried through the tears falling from her eyes and the snot running from her nose. Lula pulled away from the men holding her and walked up to Mark.

"Let me talk to her. If you want those codes, let me talk to her," Lula said sternly.

Mark thought for a moment and agreed. Lula went up to Jenny and took her hand. They moved to a corner of the lab. Lula gave Jenny a handkerchief to clean herself and then she whispered in her ear.

"Jenny. What God do you believe in?"

"The only God. My lord and savior Jesus Christ."

"You sound like a true believer. Do you really believe in heaven and that Jesus died for our sins?"

"Oh yes, dear lord, yes."

"Then listen to me, Jenny. Mark is insane. He will kill you no matter what I do. He will kill me today also. Do you understand?"

"But I don't want to die," Jenny said as she started to cry again.

"I know Jenny," Lula said as she hugged Jenny. "But today we have to make a decision. Do we believe in the Lord, Jesus Christ or do we not?"

"Oh I do believe in Jesus and all he says."

"Then listen to me, Jenny. Today is a test of our faith. Jesus has called on us to stop this monster from killing millions. Jesus knows we will be strong and today, you and I will sit at the right hand of our Lord and savior Jesus Christ. Now we must be strong when we go into the lion's den. We must not wavier." Suddenly, Jenny became calm and looked at Lula.

"So we will be with Christ today?"

"I swear to you it will be so. But we must face evil, the way our Lord Jesus Christ did that day on the cross. Do you understand?"

"Yes. Yes. I do, Lula. Praise God. I will met Satan with a smile for Jesus has called me to fight for him. Today I will met my dear Lord Jesus. Thank you Lula. I'm not afraid anymore."

Lula and Jenny walked back to the cell where Mark was standing.

"Well, Lula. Have you come to your senses. We don't want Jenn..."

"No Sir," Jenny said with confidence. "We will not give into you, Satan. Today I will be with Jesus. We do not fear you, Satan." Mark put his head into his hands and then laughed as he looked at Lula. "You have got to be kidding me. First Archieréas, goes all hippy dippy on me and now you got this kid to become a super hero of some kind. Who's manipulating who here, Lula?"

"Be gone Satan you sha...."

"Shut the fuck up!!!!" Mark yelled. "Stark!! put this nut in the cell with number two." Stark and his men dragged Jenny to the cell door and shoved her in. then they opened the door to the Morphs.

It took hold of Jenny and tore her clothes off. Then the Morph turned her over and made itself ready to rape her.

"Take a good look, Lula. That's what's going to happen to you in about five minutes. That's how long you have to give me my codes." Lula turned away but Mark had other ideas. "Stark, make her look. If she closes her eyes cut her lids off." Stark then shoved Lula's face to the glass window and made her watch. However, the Morph had stopped what it was doing and was just standing there.

"What the hell is this?" Mark yelled. "Why isn't he raping her?" In the next instant, the Morph snapped Jenny's neck and instead of eating her, the M put Jenny's clothes over her body.

"What the fuck is this? Stark. What's going on?"

"I don't know Sir. I've never seen one of them do this before."

Lula stated to laugh. "Wow. For the master of the world you don't seem to be that much in charge." Mark was furious.

"You fucking bitch," He screamed as he slapped Lula across the face. He then picked her up by her hair and slammed her against the wall.

"What was all that God, Jesus bullshit? You don't believe in God."

"I know, asshole. But she did. I wanted her to die in peace. Without fear." Mark slapped Lula again.

"That is good, Mark. Beating up on a ninety-eight pound, five-foot woman. You must be the ruler of the world." Mark then took hold of Lula by the neck.

"I've had enough of your crap. If you don't believe in God, what's going to make you so brave when that thing is tearing your cunt to shreds?"

"Knowing my *brother* John will avenge my death, asshole."

"Stark!! Throw her in with number one. Let's see if he still knows how to please a woman."

Stark grabbed Lula, but she pulled away and walked to the cell door.

Looking directly at Mark she said, "Open it up, you cowardly fuck."

"*Put her in*!!!!" Mark screamed.

As Lula entered the cell, the Morph looked at her then walked to the other side of the room. Mark stared through the window and couldn't believe his eyes.

"Wait a minute," Mark thought. "We've seen this before. In the old lab." Mark ran to Archieréas' cell and looked in. Archieréas was sitting in a lotus position on his bed.

"You. This is you. Tell the red motherfucker to rape her or eat her. I don't care which at this point. If you don't, I will kill every Morph in this place starting with the female."

"You are not human, Mark. We will no longer do your bidding," Archieréas thought. "We are one. We are free." Just then there was an ear-shattering howl from the cell of the Big M male. The new lab had been hastily and cheaply constructed. Though the cell doors looked secure, the contractors skimped on materials. So when the male Big M took a run at its cell door at full speed, not caring if it were injured, the door blew off its casings. Though the Big M had broken its shoulder and arm, it was still strong enough to kill several guards and release more Morphs from their imprisonment before he was taken down by security gunfire. This led to other M's releasing more of their fellow Morphs. When Stark saw what was happening he screamed like a school girl and ran for the elevators. However, the Morphs were too fast for him and tore him to shreds.

Mark, seeing Stark being eaten by Morphs and in shock himself, thought, "Guess I'll need another security guy." After all the lab people had been killed or confined, Archieréas was released. He went to the dying Big male and putting his hand on its head, Archieréas, thought, "Rest well my brother. Your bravery will be remembered by all." Archieréas then moved toward Mark and Mary's children. Mark looked up at Archieréas standing over him. "Why? Why did you interfere? Are you going to kill me now?"

"No Mark. I am sending you back to your people. Tell them the *Anaptýsso* want peace."

"Are you mad? You think the humans, my brother, John are going to make peace while you rape and eat them? You're the one who is mad." Lula was brought over to Archieréas.

"Mark. Tell her what I say. Remember I can hear your thoughts. Don't lie or I will kill you now."

"Sure. I'll translate."

"You are the one they call 'Lula.' You have a good heart. Your...'soul'...is not full of human greed or fear. Tell John Roman the Anaptýsso want peace."

"Oh really. You want me to tell her that garbage? What has become of the mighty Morph warri...ahhhha." Mark's head felt like it was going to explode.

"Tell her." Mark repeated what Archieréas had thought.

"Tell her I am going to bite her hand. It will hurt for awhile but she will then be able toi hear me." Mark looked at Lula and smiled.

"He said he is going to bite you." Lula pulled back and Mark grabbed his head in pain.

"Tell her."

"Alright. Alright. Just quit with the head please." Mark then repeated what Archieréas had said but added that it would only hurt for a bit and then they could speak to each other. Lula was suddenly calm and looked at Archieréas then put her hand out. Lula steadied herself, after realizing today was not the day she would die. Instead, she was being offered a way to have a part in ending the Morph war. She also knew the Morphs were not just brutal animals. She would do everything to bring this new species and humans together. Archieréas took Lula's hand and bit down, drawing blood and injecting her with the venom she needed to communicate with him.

"Tell her it will take a day or two. Before she can hear me. We are returning her to the brother who is one of us."

"What do you mean, 'one of you?'" Mark asked.

"John Roman is of our blood. He should be with us. But that is something he and I must discuss," Archieréas, replied. "Tell her that as the lawgiver to the Anaptýsso, I must deal justice to her brothers and sister, who have harmed so many of my fellow...'Morphs,' as you call them. They must pay for the torture and harm they have committed. However, their punishment will occur after she leaves." Mark translated, Lula begged Archieréas not to kill her brothers and sister. "I cannot do that. You will go back and talk to your brother." Before Lula could plea with Archieréas for her family's lives, he motioned for her to be taken away. "See that she is safely delivered to her brother. Indeed, the *pneuma* is deep within her. But justice must be done. There would be too many wounds which would not heal. That pain would spread through the Anaptýsso and there would never be peace." Archieréas turned to Mark. "However, you shall watch the sentences carried out. This is your doing, Mark. You have poisoned these people, damaged them beyond repair. So you shall bear witness to what happens to those who seek to hurt the Anaptýsso." Lula's four siblings were brought before Archieréas. Mark was shoved to the ground in front of Cyrus, Judith and the Twins.

"Speak my thoughts Mark." Looking at his niece and nephews, Mark could barely keep eye contact. With his head hanging he told the them. "I am truly sorry but it seems Archieréas is going to punish you for what you have done to them." Mark grabbed his head as another sharp pain went through his head.

"Do not speak except for what I say."

"Yes. Yes. Alright, just stop. My head is going to explode. Stop. Please," Mark begged.

"You beg for your pain to stop, but you had no pity on those you tortured or let your kin harm, everyday."

"I am sorry. I….ahhha.."

"Only what I say." Mark nodded and the pain stopped.

Archieréas looked at the four prisoners. "Your Uncle has doomed you. Though he had a hand in shaping you, it was you who caused so much pain and suffering. We would show mercy, but I have looked into your hearts and seen nothing but hate and anger. You are broken and cannot be made whole. So you will answer for your deeds." Archieréas went down the line and stopped at each person.

"Cyrus, you are a human, whose mind is full of greed. It was you who enabled Mark to continue to kill and hurt us." Archieréas motioned for two M's to take Cyrus away. They took him to a cell that was filled with GMUs. There they locked him in.

"Here is where you shall stay. You will have no food or water. But you will have all the money that will fit in this cell." Cyrus looked at Mark and said, "Do something about this, Mark. Make a deal with this red ape."

"I am sorry Cyrus. He...ahh." Mark nodded to Archieréas.

Archieréas then had the Twins brought to him. "You tortured many so you could have the skin of the Anaptýsso." Four infected humans were led to a cell. "These humans will become one of us and you two will occupy the end pods. You wanted to be like us; well, now you will be part of the Anaptýsso by feeding these four." The twins were taken away screaming in unison. Finally, Judith was brought before Archieréas.

"You are a human whose only thought is of self-gratification. You take more than your share. Others go hungry. You eat, not to survive but to feed your empty soul. In seeking more and more food to feed your endless hunger you have brutally murdered many of us. So you shall eat, Judith. You shall eat yourself. Each day, parts of your body will be feed to you, until there is nothing left."

Judith's eyes widened as if she had suddenly found a wonderful treat. She then looked at Archieréas and said, "Can I cook the parts. My seasoning would make me delicious." Archieréas seemed shocked and then reached out and grabbing Judith's head tore it from her shoulders.

"Give her body to the others."

Grabbing Mark off the floor, Archieréas thought, "I am sending you to John. I knew you would not argue for peace. Lula will do that. But I am sure you will tell them, in lurid detail what happens to those who mean us harm." Now go. I must ready the Anaptýsso for peace or war.

Chapter 9

Retreat to Haven

After John and the Lads paid their respects to Aimi, at her memorial in *Uli wa Liánhé,* they picked up Raiden and headed back to the Roman Institute's New Washington headquarters. There, John called all the military and representatives from the Nations for a briefing and a coordination of plans. Attending were John and the Lads, Matt, his wife Debra, and son Jessie with Dr Jane Franks. Franks and Jessie were engaged. His wife filed for divorce when she found out about his affair with Jane. To ease his guilt, Jessie gave up his place in New Haven to his ex-wife and their children. Another infamous person attending was Senator Ari Kolla. He had been forcibly removed from the last briefing, but had promised to behave this time.

"Ladies and gentlemen. I have called this conference so that everyone has all the up-to-date information on the war's progress as well as what we have learned about the Morphs and the situation with my brother Mark."

"Can you tell us why your brother was allowed to run another lab after breaking the law with the operation of his other two labs?" Senator Kolla questioned.

"Senator, we have cautioned you to not break the rules here again or you will be escorted out immediately," Matt warned. "You didn't yell or make accusations but you cannot talk out of turn. This meeting will be run with an iron fist. We will brief all of you on what we have and what our plans are. So, raise your hand if you have a questions. No one's questions will be ignored. Do you understand that, Senator Kolla? In fact, do all of you understand what I just said? There will be no exceptions. We don't have time for false outrage or finger pointing." John went over to Matt, speaking softly. "It's ok, Matt. I got it, brother." He then turned to the people in the audience. "My brother Matt has been under a lot of pressure, as we all have. He and his wife and his son Jessie are staying. They are not going to a Haven facility, although they are certainly entitled. We are going to go over quite a bit of material and you will be able to ask questions, but first raise your hand." John stared at Senator Kolla. The first item on the agenda is the war with the Morphs. General Hooks and General Thomas will now brief you."

The two men went to the front of the room and turned on a map of the world. "The red circles you see on the map are where humans have retained territory," Hooks said pointing to the map. "If you notice where these red circles are it will tell you a lot about Morph intentions and our ability to fight them." Kolla raised his hand instantly.

"Yes, Senator."

"You keep telling us you have little time. Why the puzzles? Just tell us what the circles mean."

Hooks looked at John and General Thomas. “You’re right Senator. I apologize.”

“What it means is this: we discovered, as we fought the Morphs, that they never seemed to want to win a battle. There were several occasions where they could have wiped us out but they pulled back. In the last year of engagements we found a pattern in their movements. Their attacks and retreats.” Hooks looked up at the audience of military and diplomats. “Ladies and gentlemen, the Morphs are herding us.” A multitude of voices erupted.

“Are you saying we have lost and they are moving us like cattle. But why? Why these areas?” Senator Hicks asked.

“That’s is precisely what we think. How do we raise our cattle and pigs and even chickens for that matter?” Hooks asked. Well, if someone free ranges they let the herd eat and graze. The Morphs don’t eat anything but human flesh. However, they know we can survive on crops or fish. Look where all the center of the circles are. In Tsalaki, it’s the great plains. In Uli wa Liánhé, the island of old Japan is untouched. You all know that since the Great Healing, the oceans were off limits to commercial fishing. In the last four decades, nature, as it always does, has replenished our sea with an abundance of life. We assume the Morphs know this and that is why they leave Old Japan alone. Yes, Senator Tanaka.”

“What you say is now true, but when the Morph virus first appeared, we had to fight to keep the Morphs off our island.”

“That’s true Senator Tanaka but as I said, things have calmed down. To continue, everywhere the circles are...what could be described as...'zones.' Except it's the Morphs deciding the zones. Yes, Senator Jacobs."

"I notice there are circles around New Washington and other capitols of the Nations. There don't seem to be food sources there."

"A good observation, Senator Jacobs. Also, an example of just how intelligent the Morphs are. They seemed to be leaving the centers of government alone in each Nation. Think about it. They leave us to do the work fattening up their food supply. For that, we need a strong central government to facilitate and maintain law and order in these zones. Otherwise the zones would turn to chaos. These zones still need medicine, security, Seally grass shipments. Yes, Senator Hicks."

"Are the Seally grass areas being left alone by the Morphs?"

"Well Senator, that is the one place we do not have to worry about. The Rus Outlands, where the Seally grass is grown, is the one place on earth the Morphs cannot go. We have discovered that because of the way their brains have been wired….the uhh...way they communicate...through their minds. Because of this new wiring they cannot spend one hour in the Seally grass area, or they go completely insane. They start attacking each other or hurting themselves. The big picture is this. Within these circles the world population is approximately fifteen to twenty million people. The Morph population seems to be about the same since the fighting has calmed down. The Morphs are culling their own population to meet the supply of humans. We have the data that show the elderly, the sick or those with special needs are disappearing from each zone. At certain intervals, young healthy men go missing also. We can only deduce from this data that the Morphs are taking the elderly and sick for food, and the young women and men for breeding or morphing. They are making a healthy herd, ladies and gentlemen. No different than the way we raise cattle." Again the room began to roar with the shouts of diplomats and military personnel. John had his security blast the air horn and the room became quiet.

"How many times do we have to tell you that shouting and yelling like two year old's gets nothing done. Now, what's the question? Yes Senator Kolla."

"You wonder why we're shouting. You stand there and basically tell us we now are nothing but cattle for some red monsters. We are supposed to sit here and just let our people be human sacrifices. My son is in a wheel chair. Even our modern technology wasn't able to fix him. Am I supposed to hand him over to these beasts. What about the Roman family? We know you have people with autism, your elderly. Your father, David Roman has dementia. Is he going to a Haven facility?"

"We will get to the Haven Project and what will happen there. First, if Matt doesn't mind, I will finish this part." John turned to Matt and they both nodded. "We believe, that for the next five to ten years this is the best we can hope for." There were mutterings and talking but no shouting in the room. "Ladies and gentlemen. We have thrown everything we had at the Morphs. They won. Now, we can throw a kamikaze blitz at them. But that would surely wipe out any government or order and then the Morphs would probably put humans in cages and that horror would become humankind's fate. Do you all want that? If we bide our time, at least those who live can do so in dignity. Humans will be able to move about freely and when the time comes, and it will come ladies and gentlemen, I assure you, when the time comes we will have a physically and mentally healthy, population ready to take back the world."

All the people in the room seemed to be in deep thought with many whispering to each other.

"Ladies and gentlemen. I know this has been a lot to take in. Let's take our noon break now and meet back here in two hours." John turned to Matt, "I need to go to the lab and see how Shea and Chara are doing. I'll be back before we resume."

****

John entered the lab and there he found Sheamus and Chara, waiting for the results of the tests performed on Chara. There were six armed guards standing in the room along side the two. The minute Sheamus saw John he went up to him and said, "John me lad, good to see ya me friend but ifin ya don't get these here goons out o' here I'll be swingin' me knife shortly." John motioned for the security men to leave. "Have you heard anything, Shea?"

"Not yet. They be sayin' that there is some kind of anomaly or some such thin' they want ta be be takin' o' closer look at. That's about all they be tellin' me. Ta tell the truth I be getting' o' little tired o' ta run around."

"Let me go talk to them. I'll be right back."

"Yeah, I'll be very grateful to ya, Johnny boy." John went into the lab chamber where five scientists were busily going over the schematics and tests results. There he saw a person he did not know. She was a raven haired beauty with a long pony tail, dark eyes, an athletic build, sharp facial features and a flawless complexion. John introduced himself to the team.

"Hello everyone."

"Mr. Roman. How good of…" John waved his hand.

"Please, just John. Can you tell me what's the hold up? But…also...I know everyone else here but who are you?" John asked as he put his hand out to the young woman who had caught his attention.

"Oh, yes, excuse me, Mr...I...mean...John. This is Dr. Cassandra Onassis. She is the best we have when it comes to robotics and AI." John kept his hand out and with a smile said, "Very glad you could join the team." As he shook Cassandra's hand John felt a surge run through him. The only time in his life he had felt anything like this was with Aimi. Even that was nowhere near what he felt now.

"Your name. It's Greek. Means, one who shines and excels over men."

"Yes, Mr Roman, and my last name means 'lover.' However, I have no intention of trying to excel over men or be a lover. I let my work speak for the first and I am very choosy about the latter. Since you want us to call you John, you can call me, 'Cass'. Is there something you need? I thought you were attending an extremely important meeting with representatives from around the world. You wouldn't have taken time away from such an important meeting to speed up our examination of the AI robot boy for your friend would you? I thought the Roman family was all about equality. Does that only apply to other's needs?" Though he was a little taken aback with the curtness of Dr Onassis, John couldn't help but to be intrigued with this beautiful and obviously brilliant, powerful woman.

"No...ahh...yes...I mean we are on a lunch break. Had nothing to do with my friend Shea' or his son Chara."

"Son? You do know, Chara is an AI robotic from before the Great Melt. You do know why they're illegal don't you?" Cass asked.

"Yes. I do know. It was my family who developed the AI-EMP which ended the AI threat, Cass. Still, on occasion a unit will show up. This is the first AI unit ever found which seems to have so much of its core intact. It coded on to my friend when he called him, 'son.' They have become...close...you might say."

"Oh, I would say that's an understatement, John. Your friend out there threatened to kill one of our tech guys when he started to dismantle the unit. It wasn't until I reassured him no harm would come to...Chara...that he let us continue," Cass smiled.

"Well, Shea always was easily taken in by a beautiful woman." Cass gave John a puzzled look and said,

"John, I am here to do a job, not find a date. I am very good at what I do. I have worked long, hard hours to become one of the world's best robotics engineers. I didn't do it with my looks."

"No. No. Of course not, Doctor Onassis, I...well...you are a beautiful woman. I can't ignore what my eyes see. But let me assure you, your looks will not affect how you are treated here. You will certainly be given the respect you deserve. I will make it a point not to give in to the physical compliment department," John said, as if he were a shy school boy. Cass looked at him with her piercing dark eyes and said, with a smile,

"I believe you respect my qualifications, John." As she turned to get him the report on Chara, she said, "However, your professional attitude doesn't mean you can't compliment a woman on her appearance. Just as long as you don't mind my saying you are an extremely handsome man." John blushed and smiled.

"Well I'll take that as a compliment, Cass. Now, what's the story on Chara?"

"To tell you the truth, I have never come across one of these units that has retained as much programming as Chara. Obviously, by the way he talks one can see there has been damage. But all his other programming seems to be fine, except his AI."

"What do you mean Cass? Is he dangerous? We can't take the chance he could restart a true AI worm. We may not be able to stop it if he did."

“What would your friend do if we had to destroy him?” Cass asked. John was thoughtful for a moment. Then said,

“I know Shea would try to stop me. He wouldn’t be able. So what I know is, if we have to dismantle Chara, I would lose a dear friend. A man who has saved my life on numerous occasions. A friend for over ten years who has taught me much about being a man. Someone to whom I promised Chara would be safe. A man with a temper when pushed. A man who adheres to blood feuds. To tell you the truth Cass, I don’t know how far I would have to go to stop Shea. But if it’s between him and the safety of the world, I know which one I must choose.” Cass saw the sorrow in John’s eyes.

“Relax, John. I don’t think we need to harm Chara. Every test we have run suggests Chara is one or two steps away from true AI. He is running on direct programming. Everything in that programming is clean. There is no AI influence what-so-ever.” John grinned with relief.

“That's great news...I’ll..”

“Wait, John. There is one thing that concerns me. Deep inside his matrix there is a core we cannot open. It is locked tighter than any safe hub I or any of my colleagues have ever seen. We don’t know what’s in that core. However, we are confident that Chara cannot access it. His programming is far too removed. It is impossible for him to connect to the sealed core. That we are sure of,” Cass said.

“Can’t you take the core out?”

"We tried. Each time Chara was about to self-destruct. If we take it out Chara will...die." John thought for a moment.

"It's up to you, John. You will have to make the final decision. As I said, we don't believe Chara can reach the core. As he is now, his programming is no danger to humans."

"Thank you, Cass. I'll have to think about it and let you know. But now I must get back to my meeting. I hope I see you again," John said as he put his hand out. Cass took it and they shook hands for a longer time than usual. Finally, John let go and turned to walk away. But before he could leave Cass said,

"Don't be a stranger John. I always like to see a handsome man once in a while. It breaks up the day." Cass turned and went back to work. John smiled and left the lab to see Shea.

Outside the lab, John spied Sheamus, sitting with Chara in front of a fountain which contained colorful koi. Sheamus was telling Chara a story from his life. "Ya see there me son. That fountain spray reminds me of a large oak tree on a hill in Ireland, which ta me, seemed ta rise ta the heavens. Out of this oak grew massive limbs. To the young lad I were, it appeared as if the tree's mighty oak arms embraced the entire land. There, I would stand, while me father sat with his back against the ancient tree, and we would stare out at the rolling green hills of Ireland. Me father would regale me with the Irish folktales of his forefathers. It was there I stood one day, as me Da sat, closed his eyes and whispered, "Éire go Brách" never to rise again.

"Di Da lo hi Da?"

"Yes, son. I loved him with all me heart I did."

"Shea, Chara, how are you?" John asked.

"It depends on what ya have ta tell me mate."

"Ch lo Da. Da lo ch. Ch lo Jo. Jo lo Ch."

"Yes, we do Chara. Your dad loves you very much. I am sure he will love you for many years to come," John said as he looked at Sheamus.

As he smiled and wiped away a tear, Sheamus shook John's hand and said, "Thank ya mate. I knew ya wouldn't let us down. Was there anything we have ta be worryin' about?"

John thought for a moment and said, "No, my friend. This little guy has a clean bill of health. It's all good. Now, enough of this lollygagging. You and the rest of the Lads have got to meet me after this meeting. We have a ton of work top do and the clock is ticking."

"Sure thin,' Johnny boy. But what am I ta do with Chara?" John looked at Sheamus and Chara.

"Damn, Shea. From what we've seen he can probably take care of both of us. Why not bring him along?" Sheamus, grinning from ear to ear said, "Johnny, me boyo.' There be a special place in heaven reserved just for yer blessed soul, me dear boy. Come on, Chara, we got ta round up the other fellas." John watched the two leave and his smile disappeared. He thought, "I hope everything works out my friend. I really do." He then turned and went back to his meeting.

****

As soon as the meeting resumed, people were hurling questions at Mathew and John. But before the meeting got started, John noticed that Generals Hooks and Thomas were not present. "Matt, where are the Generals?"

"Your guess is as good as mine," Matt replied, more than a little agitated. "That's not good enough, Matt. I can't run this whole fucking operation alone. If anyone should be on top of where they are it should be yo…" Before John could finish, the door burst open and Generals Hooks and Thomas motioned for the two brothers to come outside.

"Ladies and gentlemen you'll have to excuse us for a moment." John and Matt went outside and followed the two military men to a side office.

"John," Hooks said. "We have just been informed that your brother Mark was left hog tied at the door of our New Washington military base. Our men took him inside and he was ranting about you being part Morph and that he had been held against his will by a Morph called,...Archieréas, who he said murdered your niece, Lula. He also made a statement claiming this Archieréas was hell bent on wiping out all of humanity and only he, meaning your brother, Mark, could help you fight this threat. However, within an hour of your brother's claims, another Big M and some regular Morphs stormed the base and took your brother. We have no idea where he is now or which of these Morphs took him."

"Never mind that now; what about my niece?"

"Well I've got thirty dead men, John. I don't want to, 'never mind that,'" General Thomas said.

"I understand, Kirk. I had no intention of demeaning the heroism or sacrifice of your men I just need to know about my niece. Please," John replied. Thomas nodded and Hooks continued.

"Easy, John here's the good news. Your niece was left at the New Washington Haven facility. She's fine, but she claims this here... Archieréas fellow, saved her from your brother, Mark."

"Saved her how?" John asked.

"Well her statement reads that your brother was about to throw Lula into a cell to be raped and impregnated by a Morph. Something about her giving Mark GMU codes. According to her statement, she says Archieréas busted out of his own cell and saved her. It seems this Archieréas wants to talk peace with you."

"Peace. John what the hell is going on? What does it mean, you are 'part Morph?'" Matt asked.

"I'll talk to all of you after this meeting. It's a long story and even I don't have all the facts. It's getting harder to tell who's speaking the truth and who's lying through their teeth. Guys, we must get back and finish this meeting. These diplomats are going to go nuts if we don't tell them what they need to know. Jim, I want you to personally go and get Lula. Take Bubba and Agni with you. Get her back here asap."

“Got it, John,” Hooks said as he turned and left.

The men went back and addressed the people in the conference room. “Ladies and gentlemen. Some major news has come to me, but unfortunately I cannot share it with you at this moment because we do not have all the facts in yet. We are working on it now and as soon as we know, you will too. But to continue with what we were saying,”

“Yes, Senator Kolla,”

“We just want you on the record as saying we are no longer going to fight these red monsters but instead are willingly going to sacrifice human beings to appease these freaks. And once again I ask, is the Roman clan going to be nice and safe in their Haven facility while we, out here, will be facing a lottery everyday. Not knowing when some red horror will take us or one of our loved ones to eat or rape. Is that what you are telling us on the record?”

“Senator, no one more than me wants the Morph menace gone. But we have thrown hundreds of thousands of men and women at the threat to no avail. All our armaments and ordinance has proved useless against them. Right now, these zones give us the best hope for humanity’s survival. I’m not going to quit, the military is not going to quit, no one is going to quit, until the Morphs are gone. But if we are going to have any chance of fighting back in the future we must, for now, accept the zones and reestablish the Haven facility. Yes, Senator Jacobs.”

“I have no love for Senator Kolla or his policies, but he has a point. I know your brother and his son claimed they would not go into a Haven facility but what about you and the rest of your very large family?"

"Alright, everyone, I guess it's time to let you all know how the reopening of the Haven project will work. Yes Senator Kolla."

"What gives you the right to say how it works? We represent seven independent Nations. Some of those facilities of your family are located in our Nations. I know the Roman family bribed and threatened their way to getting these sites handed over to them as sovereign territory of some sort but let me assure you if you and your family do not take our demands seriously, we will take those facilities from you," Kolla ranted.

"Kolla, I've had enough of you. But before I have you thrown out and banned forever, I want you and everyone in here to understand something. The Roman Institute owns the Haven Project and always will. It is we who spent the billions of dollars and time to build these essential facilities. We knew that no one country could be expected to keep them running. So, yes, we used our power and influence to make the property the sovereign territory of the Roman Institute as we have done with all our world-wide holdings. We also have the people who will defend those sites. More importantly, if any Nation tried to take over one of our sites, they would find them useless. Only the Roman Institutes' personnel can run the very complicated fusion reactors and other complex technology the facilities need to be worth anything. You see, Kolla, if you were able to take over one of our facilities, all you would obtain would be an underground tomb." John then nodded for security to take Kolla out. As he was being forcibly removed, he shouted,

"You and your gangster family will not get away with this, you Roman dog. Others will…" his last words were cut off as he was removed from the building.

"So, ladies and gentlemen, let me tell you again how the Haven re-population program will work. The Roman Institute will decide who and how the re-population of the Haven Project is going to proceed. We do this because if left to the politicians, it would take years to happen and would most certainly include only those with power and influence. For that reason we will be in control. We want to assure every Nation that our process will be fair and open." John could see the room was silent so he continued.

"Right now each facility can hold twenty-five thousand people but we are expanding that number and will continue to do so even as we repopulate. We are hoping the final number will be around fifty-thousand. Twenty-five percent of the those entering the facilities will be each Nations best scientists and intellectuals. Twenty-five percent will be the technicians and support people, such as nurses, security, techs, the people behind the scene who keep any society running. The other fifty percent will be a lottery, open to every person on earth. However there will be some hard choices in that lottery. The elderly, the disabled will get a ticket worth one entry. Others, depending on their status as contributing individuals, will get up to twenty entries. This leaves hope that everyone has a chance to enter Haven but those people we deem essential will simply have a better chance. I know this might seem unfair to some, but humanity's future is at stake. Are there any questions?" John pointed to a Senator.

"Yes Senator Jacobs."

"When will the lottery start John?"

"Immediately, Senator Jacobs. We have already sent invitations to the scientists and support personnel. While we are acclimating them to Haven, we will begin the world-wide lottery. At the end of this year, our final choices will be made and the facilities will be sealed. We will hold regular meetings and if you have any further questions, see my people up front and they will take care of you. Now I must go. Thank you everyone and good luck to all of us."

****

While John waited for Bubba and Agni to bring Lula back to the Institute, he could not resist returning to see Dr. Onassis. He used the rumor about his possibly being a Morph as an excuse to meet with Cass again. He found her going over her last notes on Chara. As he walked into the lab he saw Cass sitting at her desk and froze on the spot. He couldn't take his eyes off her. To John she was the most beautiful woman he had ever seen. But it was also more than that. He felt a need, a desire, not just for physical contact but in his "soul," his heart. John felt an almost painful ache. He wanted to be with this woman for the rest of his life. To wake with her in the morning, to hold their children, to touch her cheek and lips with his. Of course he didn't know if Cass would even give him the time of day, but he knew at some point he was going to have to tell her how he felt. If she didn't feel the same he knew he would deal with it, but it wouldn't be painless. After losing Aimi he never thought he would feel something like this. Now he did, and it couldn't have come at a worse time. He thought to himself, "Get a grip, you idiot. This isn't the time or place to be in love. There is to much to do. Humanity's safety is far more important than…" All of that thinking stopped instantly when Cass looked up from her desk and made eye contact with John. His knees buckled when he saw those dark eyes and striking face. For a moment he thought, "To hell with the world. She's my world."

"Mr. Roman...or...yes...John. What brings you to my lab so soon?" Cass said as she walked toward John and his breath left him. As Cass put her hand out to shake John's she said,

"John are you all right? Your face is flushed. Please sit here. Sit down and let me take your blood pressure." John sat on one of the chairs and slowed his breathing. "Here drink this." Cass said as she put the blood pressure cup around his arm. "You know, John you are not superman. You need to rest at some point. You are probably one of the most important people the world has in this war with the Morphs. We can't afford to lose you because you won't rest. You are nearing forty, are you not?"

"Are you calling me an old man Cass? I'll have you know the average life span of men today is one-hundred plus. I'm still in my prime," John said smiling.

"Well, obviously you're a very fit man, but no one can go full speed with no rest. Your pressure looks good and your face seems to have returned to normal. So what can we do for you?"

John broke out of his stupor and said, "Yes. Yes...ah...Cass. I would like you to work with Doctors Sing and Lieberman."

Cass thought for a moment. "But their fields are genetics and hematology. That's not where my expertise lies."

"Yes. I know but your work with Chara was exceptional. Your leadership and empathy, dedication…"

"Please, John, the compliments are a little overdone. It's not my field. I don't take jobs with conditions and I won't sleep with you because you offer me a job." John was taken aback.

"No. No Cass. Please don't think that I…"

"You what, John?" Like a child caught in a white lie John felt ashamed.

"Look Dr. Onassis. You're right. I am very attracted to you. But this job is important. I would never offer you something just to try to get into your pants. I have nothing but respect for you. I do believe this is very important. And somehow I think Chara is going to play a big part in all of this. I can't tell you why, but I just feel it in my bones. I want you to be the lead on this because we need someone with your dedication and expertise in robotics to lead the team. I would very much like to get to know you better, but I promise, if you take this job I will never say anything about relationships or dating or your looks, nothing. You have my word." Cass studied John and then said, "Well no one says you can't ask me questions. To tell you the truth, I would like to know more about you. I am fascinated with what makes a men like you work. But what so important about this job?"

"I am able to hear the thoughts of Morphs. That is one reason I want you on the team. It's like the wireless internet. You may be able to understand how they and I are able to do this. I think it goes beyond telepathy. Second, I was told by a Morph who calls himself 'Anu,' that I am part Morph. But his claim has been repeated by my niece. Lula is on her way here, saying a Morph who calls himself Archieréas also told her I am part Morph." Cass was stunned.

"That's where Doctors Sing and Lieberman come in. They are doing a full genetic and blood analysis of me. I have never heard this Archieréas in my thoughts. The only thing I can surmise is that the Morphs are a collective of some kind. So what Anu told me, Archieréas somehow knew."

"My God, John," Cass said as she put her hand on John's arm. "Fuck what anyone would think if I took this position, because let me tell you John, the gossip will flow like a river. But I wouldn't miss this for the world. You're also right their communication and sharing resembles a computer network. Yes, John, I will be ecstatic to lead this team. When do we get started?"

“No ‘we’. You’re in complete charge. Here is the list of my people who will set you up with introductions, funding, anything you need. It’s your show. I would like a report on this, ‘I am a Morph’ insinuation. Find out how the Morphs communicate. It is essential we know those two things asap.”

“I’ll get right on it.” Cass thought for a moment. “I guarantee you we’ll be up and running at full speed within the week.”

“That sounds great, Cass. You have my full confidence the job will get done,” John said as he smiled at Cass. One more thing Cass. My niece, Lula should get here in...oh...about,” John looked at his watch. “four hours.” The doctors will examine her and I want her to rest for the night. She’s been through a hell of a lot. But as soon as I get the all clear, I want you with me at the debriefing.”

“I understand, John.” The two exchanged a long handshake and smiles. “Ok. I think we both have a lot to do till then. I believe great things are afoot, John. Thank you for your confidence in me. I won’t let you down.” John stared into Cass's eyes and said, “No I’m sure you won’t.”

Chapter Ten

Civil War

Mark was resigned to his fate. He could not understand how all of his years of sacrifice and planning became the instruments of his imprisonment. All his life he had to swallow shit and pretend to love the very people who oppressed his true destiny. *He* was supposed to shape the world to his vision. To make it a place where excellence, intelligence and the willpower of great dynamic individuals were respected and even worshiped. He wanted to rid humanity of its dregs, its criminals, its physically and mentally broken. Those who nature would cull, if not for the interference of weak-minded do-gooders. Those who could not see nature's true beauty. All anyone had to do was look how nature constantly shaped its creations through natural selection. Nature had been perverted by those who thought they had the right to interfere, to impose on others, those who were rightfully heirs to the kingdom, the healthy, the powerful. Mark believed he was supposed to be history's greatest ruler. The man who reshaped humanity into the masterful race it should be. But now, here he sat, waiting, he was sure, to be condemned by the very people who allowed humanity to sink into a mongrel state. But he would have the last laugh. The Morphs were nature's answer to humanity's refusal to hear her. They would wipe the inferior masses from existence, like the body cleanses itself of disease. The Morphs will be nature's new master race.

Just as Mark was thinking about taking his own life, thereby denying John the pleasure of humiliating him, he heard a loud commotion. Screams, shouts and gunfire became increasingly near.

"Guards. What's happening out there? Guards!" Mark shouted.

Suddenly the door to the holding cells opened, and four men and a woman entered, slamming and bolting the door behind them.

"What's going on? What's going on? I insist you answer me," Mark yelled.

"Shut the fuck up motherfucker, or I'll empty this clip into you. Now get the fuck back and shut your fucking pie hole, one of the men shouted, "Jimmy, how much ammo you got?"

"I got four clips and two grenades," Jimmy responded.

"Jeff, Mary, Sam sound off. What you got?"

"Two clips, that's it," Jeff shouted.

"Here, Jeff, take one of mine. I got four now and four grenades," Sam said.

"I got one clip and that's it," Mary sighed.

"Alright. Give me and Mary all the grenades. Jeff, you and Sam get to the front. One on left, one right. Mary and I will cover and give you support from the back. If they get by you I'm tossing all the grenades," Jimmy warned.

"My God did you see those fucks tearing through our guys?" Sam said nervously.

"Yeah, and this is where we will probably make our last stand boys and girls. So make Tsalaki proud. Give those fucks hell when they come through. Don't let them take you alive." As they waited Mary turned to Jimmy.

"Jim, please if they get in here you know what you need to do. Don't let them have me. Promise." Jim looked at Mary and saw the terror in her eyes.

"Don't worry. It's all going to be fine. I promise." A loud bang sounded as a Morph hit the door. It was followed by several more until the thick metal door burst open. Sam and Jeff opened fire and killed the first Morph who came through but as they tried to reload, even with Mary and Jim's cover fire, the other Morphs tore them apart. As more Morphs entered the hallway Jim hugged Mary. They looked into each other's eyes and Jim said, "It going to be fine." He then shot Mary in the head. Pulling the pin on four grenades, Jim got up and ran directly at the red invaders. Just as the Morphs were about to rip into him, Jim yelled, "Fuck you, you cocksu..." the grenades exploded, Morph and Jim body parts splattered the walls.

Mark was hiding under his bunk, trembling in fear. He had pissed and shit himself as he realized he was just moments away from being eaten alive. "How could it come to this. It's not fair. It's not fair," Mark ranted to himself. Suddenly, the blast from Jim's grenades knocked him unconscious. When he came to, Mark was choking on smoke and stink from the blast and dead bodies. When Mark heard the door of his cell rip open, he screamed hysterically, "No!!! No!!! Not like this. Not like this." A giant shadow crossed Mark's face.

"Rise up. I am Anu, high priest of the *Negeltu.*" Mark slowly took his hands from his eyes and saw Anu standing over him. Beside Anu were two big Ms, a Male and a female.

"Rise. Mark Roman. Join us in our destiny. While we shall rule the world, Mark Roman, you shall rule all of humanity," Anu thought.

After a few seconds, Mark's head cleared and he asked Anu. "Are you real?"

"Do not blaspheme. Think. Do not utter words like a dog," Anu thought. Mark could hear and understand everything Anu thought and now he was beginning to collect his own thoughts. It all made sense now.

"This had been...a...test. Yes, a test," Mark thought. "To see if I was...worthy...yes...worthy. Nature was testing my resolve. You...Anu. You were sent to me by Mother Nature herself. To raise me from the dead. Like Jesus, I have risen." Mark stood and brushed himself off. He then cocked his head and looked at Anu. "Yes, Anu. I can see our destinies are one. It will be my honor to join the Negeltu and make the world right again. I can see it all very clearly now. The Negeltu will rule for a thousand years. You are nature's answer to the mongrelization of the human race. Humanity must be vanquished and we will start anew. Yes...oh yes. I will join you." Mark then knelt and kissed Anu's hand.

"Come. We have much to do," Anu thought.

****

Lula had been returned to the New Washington Roman Institute hospital. There, Bubba and Agni were guarding her room when John came to look in on her. “How is she doing, guys?” John asked. Bubba stood and shook John’s hand.

“She’s a little shook up, but let me tell you. There aren't many guys who could have gone through what she did and not be wetting their breeches. She’s a strong lady, that niece of yours, John.”

“This humble servant would have wet his pants many times and the Buddha knows this,” Agni said.

“Where’s the doctor?”

“She’s right behind you John.” Walking down the hallway were Cass and Dr. Isabelle Frosh. There were also several more doctors with them.

“Hello, Mr. Roman,” Cass said. “This is Dr. Frosh. She is the world’s top neurologist. This is Dr. Hans and Dr. Jensen. Their specialty is behavioral psychology. Doctors Rush and Bertram are trauma experts.” John shook everyone’s hands and turned to Cass.

“You certainly work fast...Dr. Onassis. It looks like I made the right choice putting you in charge.” John said. As he stared at Cass, Bubba and Agni looked at each other with knowing smiles.

"Well, Mr. Roman. I also think my 'choice' to accept your offer was a wise one." As she stared at John, Bubba and Agni looked at each other with the same knowing smiles.

"How's my niece doing? Can I see her?" John asked.

"I'll let the doctors answer that. Because if it were up to me, I would make you wait for at least a week. But I know that's impossible."

"Yes. You are right. I'll go easy tonight but I must debrief her tomorrow," John said.

"But give me your assessment of how she is now."

"So far she seems to be physically well. There are no signs of sexual abuse and the physical trauma she suffered looks minimal," Dr. Rush surmised.

"However," Dr Hans interrupted. "The psychological trauma is a different story. From the little we have gathered it seems she had to 'help' a fellow prisoner go to her death."

"My God," John whispered.

"Well, there is good news," Dr. Frosh said. "There is absolutely no sign of sexual assault or infection."

"Can I see her? Just for a little bit?" John asked.

"I will let you talk to her for five minutes, but no questioning about events. Just, 'how are you' 'get well', etc. She must rest until at least tomorrow," Cass said.

"Alright, I'll keep it short and nothing that might upset her." John entered Lula's room and sat on the chair next to her bed. He took her hand in his and spoke softly.

"Lula. It's me. Your Uncle John. How are you kiddo?" Lula came out of her half sleep and opened her eyes. Upon seeing John, she rose up and gave him a big hug. She began to cry and John tried to sooth her as best he could.

"There, there, Lula. It's going to be alright. Lay back. Rest."

"Oh Uncle John. I still can't believe what happened. Mark has gone completely insane. He…"

"Shh. Shh, Lula. We'll talk about everything tomorrow. Now I just want you to get some rest. It's important because tomorrow I and some other people will be asking you a lot of questions. What you have to tell us is very important, my dear. So please, for me and yourself, get some sleep. I promise I will be here first thing in the morning, and we can go over everything. Don't worry, Mark is under arrest. He can't hurt anyone now." Lula smiled and tried to go to sleep. John left the room and outside he told Bubba. "I want someone here at all times. I didn't tell her, but Mark has escaped. It seems some of his Morph friends helped him. That's not going to happen here. I'm enforcing a complete lock-down. We'll have fifty men on each floor and another two hundred guarding the entrances."

"Don't worry, John. None of those things will get past me and the little fella here," Bubba said.

"Oh yes, John. Bubba is very right. Very right. This humble servant who has saved this big fella many times will not let anything happen to the wonderful Lula," Agni responded with a smile.

"Sounds like you all have it covered. I have to go check on my lab results and Renkins. He should be ready to answer some questions. See you all here tomorrow morning."

****

John went to Leroy's hospital room where Raiden and Nick were keeping an eye on him.

"How's he doing?" John asked.

"He's eating like a pig at a trough," Nick said.

"He also grabbing nurses. We had to switch to male attendants," Raiden said.

"Ok. I talked to his doctor. They said he's fine," John looked around and then back at Nick.

"I don't see Apolla."

"Yeah. Don't sweat it, she stayed with Steel. She'll be running the place soon."

"Why would I sweat it?" John asked.

"Word is you and some lab tech have the hots for each other. If Apolla were here it could be very bad," Nick laughed.

John nodded and then entered Renkins' room and saw him eating the last of his lunch.

"Hey, John. I heard you saved my life back at Trumble's place," Leroy said.

"Was a team effort, Renkins. But I need to know what you do about the Morphs. What did they say to you? Can you tell me anything about their plans, what they think?"

"Maybe. What's in it for me?"

"How about a returning a favor for saving your life?"

"Oh come on, John. You only saved me because you needed something from me. If I had not been able to talk to those things, you would have left me to rot. So let's not try to con a conman."

"Funny. From what Nick told me about you, I didn't think you were just a cheap conman."

"Well, Nick has a small hero worship complex. Me, I care much more about reality. I've lost everything. I need a fresh start. For that I need a pardon and money. Give me those and I will tell you everything."

"Alright. Deal." Leroy looked a little shocked.

"Deal? Just like that? What's the catch?" John then called Matt, and told him to send two company lawyers to Renkins' room immediately. Within minutes, they arrived.

"Leroy. This institute and all its holdings are the sovereign territory of the Roman family. Any documentation or edicts given to you here are good anywhere in the world. Turning to his lawyers, John said,

"Gentlemen. Please write a full pardon for Leroy Renkins…"

"And Nick Smalls," Leroy added.

"And Nick Smalls. Also include a reward of say," John looked at Renkins. "One hundred thousand GMUs?" Leroy nodded yes. "For his vital information of Morph activity."

The lawyers quickly printed out the document, and John witnessed it. He then handed his copy to Renkins.

"Alright, now talk." Nick entered the room and stood by Renkins, bed.

"Well, after Nick got me into our safe house, I kind of passed out. When I woke I heard these voices in my head. But they weren't voices. I couldn't understand what they were saying. I just felt it. I thought I was going nuts, but Nick keep me dosed up until the voices went away. He also saved my life again when my men tried to kill me." Leroy gave Nick a quick look.

"That's it? That's all you got? You played me, Renkins. I should have never saved your sorry ass." John stormed out of the room.

"Hey we still got a deal. I want my money," Renkins shouted.

Outside Leroy's room John talked to Raiden.

"I want you to keep an eye on Renkins and Nick. Make sure they don't go anywhere. I'll send up some men to relieve you. Then come see me and the rest of the guys in my office."

"But he gave you nothing, John. Are you not going to interrogate him?" Radian asked.

"Don't worry, Raiden. I have mikes and cameras all over his room. Anything they even whisper will be picked up. I'm sure a guy like Renkins will be chirping like a Jay bird if he thinks he got one over on us."

John then left Renkins' floor and as he headed to the lab, to see if there were any truth to his being part Morph, a pain shot through his head just as he was getting on the elevator. "John, it is I, Archieréas. Think to me." John calmed his mind as he did with Anu. In a moment he was able to think.

"You are the one who saved my niece. Why?"

"We are the Anaptýsso. Unlike Anu and the Negeltu, we want peace."

'Wait. Where are you? I will come to you."

"You are not afraid, John Roman?"

"No. There is too much at stake to be concerned with my own safety. Besides something tells my gut you are honest."

"Good, John. Always go with...gut? We Anaptýsso say *ductu,* though, like all of your languages, the words don't quite meet the meaning."

"Yes I understand. Ductu is Latin. I have spoken to Anu. Between you and him I have heard Greek, Latin and Sumerian. I assume you are using these languages as close representatives of what you mean."

"Yes. We could use current language and we do. Like now. But there are certain *concepts* that your present day language cannot convey. If you prefer, I will use English."

"No. It's fine. I know dozens of languages. Use what you feel is best for you."

"Thank you John. That shows great respect. I knew you were the right human to approach."

"Fine, Archieréas. Then as I said, let's meet. Just us. No one else. Then you can tell me everything."

"Yes. Then you can tell me everything, John. Including the Haven Project."

"The Haven Project is not a threat to you. We are sending our people there as a safety precaution."

"Yes, John. A safe place. A safe place where you can keep researching ways to destroy us."

John thought for a moment. "Archieréas, in some ways you are right. One reason for occupying the Haven facilities is have a viable population which can be completely protected from Morphs. But, yes. There we will also look for ways to take back the world. I won't lie. However, if we can find a way to true peace, one where humans and Morphs can live peaceably, then I promise we will stop trying to destroy your kind. You have my word on that."

"I believe you, John. My...ductu tells me. I agree. Let's meet. The two of us will discus peace. It is easier to start when it begins with two."

"Let's meet tomorrow at noon. New Fenway, center field. It's where I last fought your kind. Maybe it can be where we stop fighting."

"Archieréas will be there. With a few friends. But do not worry; they are no threat."

****

"What the hell, Leroy. You bullshitted him. Don't you think he knows…" Leroy put his hand to his lips shushing Nick. He made a gesture which clued Nick they were being listened to. Renkins got up and started looking for mikes. Nick helped and they soon found two and then a third.

"That should do it. We need to get out of here. This Anu Morph has contacted me. He's offering us a place at the top Nicky boy. I'm taking it."

"What you mean a place at the top?"

"This Anu fuck is apparently in some kind of civil war with other Morphs. Anu's guys outnumber the others by a lot."

"What's the difference between them? Nick asked.

"Well, this Anu fuck wants to treat humans as cattle. But even these red punks know they need a bull with every herd. He's promised to makes us bulls, Nicky boy. We will not have to worry about being supper. Plus we get all the women we want."

"Jesus, Leroy. You're going to sell out the human race."

"They're done for anyway, Nick. Like I said, this Anu has the numbers. Hell, the whole world is in a holding pattern. They already lost to these fucks. What's left is hiding and shaking in their boots in these so called zones. Which the Morphs could destroy anytime they want. Also, what do you think your buddy John Roman is doing. He and his whole family are retreating to those Haven holes and locking everyone else out. They don't give a shit about us, Nick. So I say fuck them. I'm joining the winning team and fuck anyone who doesn't want to come with me."

"No. I understand. I'm...I'm..with you, Leroy. I'm with you."

"Alright. As soon as that sword swinger leaves, we'll take off. Anyone gets in our way, let them have it." After an hour, Raiden left. The men John had sent left also. Nick looked out and saw that no one was guarding the room.

"I don't know what's going on, Leroy, but there's no guards."

"What?" Renkins asked.

"No guards. They're all gone."

"Fuck it. I don't know what that Roman fuck is playing at, but let's go."

Renkins and Nick walked out of the hospital as John and Raiden were watching from the top floor. "Follow them Raiden. Radio in when they meet this Anu," John said.

"Aye, John." Raiden bowed and started to leave.

"Raiden." Turning Raiden asked, "What is it John?"

"Aimi is not interested in your death. If you find this Anu, call it in. We can't lose you my friend."

"Aye. You are my friend, John. But before this is over I will have my revenge and restore honor to my family. Nothing can stop that." Raiden then turned and left.

****

Mark was sitting at his desk in his new elaborate "hideout," when the Morphs brought in Luke, Victor and Tamar.

"Christ, Uncle. You don't worry about the price do you? This place is bigger than any Roman house I have ever been in," Tamar said as she ogled the mansion that was now Mark's.

"Oh. For you, my dears, this is nothing. The Roman family prided themselves for living in humble quarters. But I say, fuck that. People like us, the movers and shakers deserve houses like this. We make the world run. We should be able to enjoy the fruits of our labor. Anyway, it's outside a zone. So I can take it. We can have anything outside the zones. The Morphs control everything not in them. It's ours for the taking. Plus, Anu has assured me, you can all join me ruling this soon-to-be new world."

"They killed the Twins, Judith and Cyrus. Mary thought these fucks had killed all her children so she committed suicide. Why would we join them or you?" Luke said angrily.

"First, little brother, these Morphs did not kill Mary's children. That was a Morph called Archieréas. Anu saved me. He wants to destroy this Archieréas. Anu is on our side."

"What about that bitch Lula? I tricked her into coming to you. How did you fuck that up?" Tamar asked.

"She was helped by the same Morph who killed your siblings, Archieréas," Mark said.

‘Well, where is this Archieréas? These motherfuckers killed six of my men when they came for me,” Victor asked.

“Why didn’t you just tell us this and let us come to you, Mark? These things killed four of the servants in my house and my personal security guy, Frank Stall. He had been with me for twenty years,” Luke shouted questioningly.

“I apologize for any inconvenience,” Mark replied. “But Anu wanted you all here immediately and he didn’t want to take any chances you might let others know. Besides, this way you can always go back to the Roman Institute and claim you were kidnapped.”

“Well, brother, the fact is we *were* kidnapped,” Luke yelled.

At that moment Anu entered the room. “These humans are your family. From what you told me they will join us,” Anu thought.

“Yes. Yes, they want to join, Anu. They will be invaluable in infiltrating any Haven facility.”

“Are you two just going to stare at each other, like two bitches in heat?” Tamar asked.

“Oh yes, excuse me. I and Anu here, ‘speak” with our minds, you see. I can translate anything you need to know,” Mark said.

“I don’t like being talked about, especially in front of my face. How do we know what you say is the truth?” Tamar continued.

“Tamar, dear. Do you think I would do anything to hurt any of you?”

"Ok. Tell Anu here I think you would kill any of us as long as it would get you what you want. Tell him I want to be able to talk to him without you as a go-between," Tamar demanded.

"Well, Tamar dear, Anu and I have a spe…"

"Stop," Anu thought. "This one needs to be one with us. She is *lipsih*."

"Yes I agree she does have a mouth on her but…"

"No, you fool. 'Lipish' means, courage. She is one of courage." Anu said, looking at Tamar.

"Why it he staring at me? If he try's to fuck me I'll take his eyes out." Tamar warned.

"No, dear, Anu is a high priest. He can't...you know...fuck," Mark smiled.

"Wait a moment," Mark thought. "How do you know what they are saying? You need me to translate."

"You are a fool," Anu thought. "If you hear her, I hear what you do. Her words are in your mind."

"But why did Archieréas say he needed me to translate?"

"Because he wanted to know when you were lying, fool."

"Stop calling me 'fool'. I will not put up with being called names by you. You need me...you need us to help you with your plans. Especially those concerning the Haven facilities. So stop calling me names," Mark ranted.

"Very well. *Nungara*, shall be your title. It is truer to who you are."

"That's better. Now, Tamar. It seems Anu here doesn't want to eat you; he just wants to bite you a little bit. That way you and he can communicate. It...seems he thinks you are very brave. A woman with courage."

Tamar looked at Anu and said, "Sure. I'm in. let him see what a real woman tastes like." She held out her hand and as Anu bit down she blinked an eye.

"You looked like you enjoyed that," Victor said.

"Well, you and I have done worse, brother."

"You will be able to hear Anu in a day or two. He needs the two of you and you Luke, to go back to the Roman Institute. The Haven facilities will be filled very shortly."

"How do you know that, Mark? From what I understand they have just begun the lottery. I thought that would take at least a year to fill all the Haven units," Luke inquired.

"Well, yes brother that was their plan. However, there is going to be a civil war soon."

"Civil war between who?" Luke asked again.

"Between Anu's Morphs and Archieréas' bunch. Many of the zones will be attacked and I would assume completely destroyed. This will cause John to escalate the Haven Project's full house program."

"How am I and my kids going to play a part in whatever it is you and Anu here are planning?"

"Luke, dear brother. The 'enslavement,' if you call it that, of the human race is going to happen whether we participate or not. If we do not join Anu...well...we're dead. If we do join, my friend here, well then...we will be some of the chosen few who will rule what's left of the human race."

"So what role do we play?" Victor asked.

"You three will infiltrate three of the Haven facilities when the time is right. You will not be the only allies we have in these facilities. There are many humans who think the Morphs should rule. Many who want to be Morphs. They will get their chance when we need them. After it's done, the Haven Project will become home to the Morphs. There will be no place on earth where humans can hide from Morphs. It will be they who will rule the world for a thousand years or more. But don't forget, our reward will be the gift of ruling the humans for our lifetime and our children's lifetime on into Morph history. We will create a dynasty of humans who will be royalty among the meek. We will be worshiped by those who we chose to nourish and breed the Morphs. Why would you chose death over that glorious life?" Mark said to everyone.

"I sure as hell won't. I'm in," Tamar said.

"I'm with her," Victor chimed in. Luke contemplated for a moment.

"Alright. I'll go along with you. But we will have some say as to who lives and who dies, right?"

"Oh, of course brother. That's what gods do, isn't it? Chose who lives and who dies? Anu has assured me we will run the show when it comes to anything human. All we have to do is make sure the Morph have a steady supply of healthy humans and they will leave the rest to us," Mark said as he put his hand on Luke's shoulder.

""'Ok. I'm in," Luke replied.

"Wonderful. Now let's get started on building our dynasty. Shall we?" Mark said. "Tamar and Victor. You two must go and see Lula. Convince her you knew nothing about the locket. You must get her to trust you. I will leave "how" to you, Tamar. You have a way with making people believe you."

"Why? Why play up to her?" Tamar asked.

"It's the only way John will let you into the Haven facilities." I'm counting on you two getting back in good graces with the Roman family. They may not trust you with their secrets, but they should allow you in to Haven."

"Alright. Alright. But I'll tell you this. You owe me, Uncle Mark. If I have to suck up to that little bitch, then when the time comes she's mine to deal with."

"You have my word, dear. She'll be all yours."

Tamar and Victor left for the New Washington Institute. Mark turned to Anu.

"Our plan is beginning. This is the start of a new dawn for humans and Morphs. Shall we celebrate? I have some very old Scotch I saved for such an event. For you my dear Anu." Mark handed Anu a goblet of new born human baby blood. He then lifted his own glass of Scotch, smiled and toasted, "To the new world."

****

The next morning John went to see Lula with Cass and the Lads.

"How are you today, Lula?" John asked. The guys are here. They want to say hi."

"Oh yes. Please." Lula said as she sat up in bed.

"How you doing little lady?" Bubba asked as he held Lula's hand.

"Yes, dear Lula. This humble servant would be willing to get you anything you need," Agni chirped in.

"Oh Bubba, I have missed you. You, too, my dear Agni."

"I wish you well, Ms. Roman," Raiden said.

"Oh my friend. I was so sad to hear about Aimi. Please accept my condolences."

"Thank you, Lula. But it is you who must get well now." Raiden said.

"Ok, ya blubberin' nits. Let me through. Let me through." Sheamus said.

"Lula, me dear. How are ya? Did them red devils hurt ya me lovely dear?"

"Actually, it was one of the Morphs who saved me. But never mind about that now. Oh Shea. It is so good to see you. Give me a hug please."

"It be me dearest wish now, darlin.'" Sheamus leaned over and gave Lula a long, loving hug.

"But who is this young man?" Lula asked.

"Come here now, Chara and meet yer godmother." Sheamus whispered in Lula's ear. "I made ya his godmother. He be havin' no family but me and John. So I thought ya could be his godmother. Ifin' ya don't mind darlin.'"

"Hey, what about us?" Bubba asked. "Can't we be part of his family.

"Ahh hush up now yer heathens. Do ya think I be wantin' me boy with the likes o' you sort." Sheamus smiled and said. "Of course ya be his family. Yer all can be his godbrothers."

"There's no such thing as god-brothers," Bubba said.

"Well damn it. There is now. So yer all his god-brothers whether ya like it or not. Now behave yerselves." Sheamus turned to Lula. "As I was sayin' darlin,' this here is Chara, me own son he is. Chara, meet Lula."

"Ch lo Lu. Lu lo Ch?"

"Just be his way o' talking. He says…"

"Shea. I understand what he is saying and I completely agree. He is a fine boy. You must be very proud," Lula smiled.

"That I am dear, Lula. That I am," Sheamus said as he looked at Chara.

"Alright, guys, Lula and I have to talk and she needs some rest. I'll see you all outside. We have to make a trip to New Fenway as soon as I am done here," John said.

The Lads left and waited outside. Cass entered and John introduced her.

"Lula, this is Dr. Cassandra Onassis. She is running a team which will help us in defeating the Morphs. What can you tell us about your kidnapping and escape?"

"Well, Tamar convinced me to go see Uncle Mark. I checked the locket she gave me and found a secret compartment. It had the codes to nearly a billion GMUs, so I hid it. After an attempt to convince me he had been wronged he checked the locket. When he found it empty he went crazy. He threaten to put me in a cell with a Morph. Cyrus, the Twins and Judith wouldn't help me at all." Lula started to cry.

"It's ok. Take your time," Cass said.

"None of them would help me. Just when I was resigned to death, a morph named Archieréas somehow broke out of his cell and took over the whole place. He had Mark translate and he basically said he wanted peace. He wanted to talk to you, Uncle John."

"Yes. Good. This Archieréas contacted me also. You just confirmed what he said. I feel much more hopeful of a peace arrangement," John said.

"But there is more. I think there is some kind of animosity between certain Morph groups. I think Archieréas' group wants peace, but the other wants the total enslavement of humanity. If you meet with these Morphs, Uncle, you must be sure they are the right ones," Lula warned.

"We will, Lula. I promise. Now you get some rest, and I'll see you tomorrow."

"I'll also check in on you, Lula," Cass said.

Outside Lula's room, Cass delivered important news to John.

"John. Your tests have come back." Cass looked around. "Not here. Let's go to my office."

Turning to the Lads, John said. "Guys. I'll meet you out front in about twenty minutes."

He and Cass then went to her office. "You are, in essence, part Morph."

"How is that possible?" John asked.

"Your parents helped. Your father, David, was exposed to the Sweats. It's what killed your brothers' mother. Celest survived the Baylor parasite. Both those conditions are related to the Morph virus. When you were bitten, so you could communicate with the Ms, the combination of the three turned your metabolism into something more Morph than human. I suspect the first two are why you were different at birth. Your intelligence, strength speed, even your ability to see in the dark. These are all Morph traits. But now, with the third component, your body is slowly changing. I don't think you will become a full-fledged Morph. Unless you pod. But there are going to be some changes happening to your body. I think you should stay here and let us keep you under surveillance. Just in case something happens."

"That's impossible. I have too much to do. I can't sit here and let the world go to hell. I know my body. If I think anything is happening I can't control, I'll come in at once."

"I believe you, John. Just be careful. But there is some good news."

Cass opened a refrigerator and handed John a container. "Open it." John opened the plastic container and saw what looked like two pounds of hamburger.

"What's this? My lunch?" John asked.

"Once I took over the department you organized, I was made aware of the Seally grass labs attempt to turn Seally grass into food for Morphs. Well, here it is. This is a beef based, Seally grass protein mixture. You know how Seally grass can take on the structure and taste of anything we mix with it. Well, our labs restructured the DNA and chemicals workings of the beef and then they mixed restructured Seally grass DNA and here we are. A protein mix a Morph can eat instead of humans. The lab people call it 'Morph beef'. Best of all the mix holds at one pound beef to six pounds Seally grass." John held the "Morph beef" and started to smile.

"Cass. Do you know how important this is?"

"Yeah, I can guess." John looked a little embarrassed.

"Yes, of course you know. With this, the only thing standing in the way of peace is the Morph's need for human women to create a Big female."

"John. From what I have read in the briefing notes, the Morphs need for a Big female has stabilized for the moment. I have seen the data. We are within weeks, if not days, from developing a female Big M outside of a human uterus. So, when you meet with this Archieréas, fellow, tell him all this," Cass said to John.

"But how did you know?"

"You talk in your sleep."

"But we haven't…."

"I know, John. But you were exhausted the other night and fell asleep on my office couch, if you remember. I stayed with you and...you...did a lot of talking." John turned red and pleaded with Cass.

"Please don't say anything to anyone about this meeting yet. I don't want some gun happy military people showing up and spoiling our chance for peace. Especially with this news," John said holding up the Morph beef."

"Have no fear John. My lips are sealed. I won't tell anyone."

"Thank you. But I must go know. I am supposed to meet Archieréas, at noon. We'll talk later."

John turned and as he was leaving the room Cass said, "Don't worry, John, I'll say nothing about your meeting with Archieréas...or Apolla." John stopped dead in his tracks for a moment and without looking back, left Cass's office.

****

At noon, John and the Lads entered New Fenway. Since the first battle with the Morphs, the ballpark had been deserted. John and the Lads looked out over the debris and wreckage from that battle. There were bones from the bodies left behind.

"Jesus H mother o' Christ. Did they not take our men back for burial?" Sheamus asked.

"They're not our men Shea. Don't forget. The Ms were once human. These are Morph bodies. The were left here by the other Morphs. They do not bury their dead. They are left where they die," John said.

"Yes. That is how Shea and this humble servant found the baby upstairs," Agni said.

"Look." Bubba said pointing to a skull. "That's the Big M we killed. The one who bit you, John."

"Let's go upstairs and see if Archieréas is here," John said.

"You trust this M to not kill us all?" Raiden asked.

"He could have killed me easily back at the hospital. He saved Lula, he asked to talk. Seems like a long play just to kill me now."

"Oh well. Just listen to his lordship, will ya. Did ya ever think he wanted ta wait so he could kill ALL of us here now. Especially, Sheamus O' bloody Keefe?"

"Ch ki Ar. Ar no hu Da. Ar no hu Jo. Ar no hu bu. Ar no hu Ag."

"Easy son. Easy now. Archieréas is not goin' ta be hurtin' anyone now."

As the guys walked toward the hall where John and Bubba fought a Big M, they passed the room where Sheamus and Agni found the M baby. Sheamus looked in and saw all the bones and dried remains.

"Yeah. Those heathens even left ta littler ones ta rot."

"Come on. Let's see if…." Suddenly John's head ached but not as much as before.

"I am here, John," Archieréas thought.

"I am here with my friends. This is Agni, Bubba, Sheamus, and Raiden," John said pointing to each of the Lads. "They mean you no harm."

Archieréas stepped out and behind him was a Big male and female M. "Hello, John. I am Archieréas and this is Anax and Anassa," Archieréas thought pointing to each. "They rule the Maketes. What you would call the 'regular Morphs.' As a whole we are the Anaptýsso. They mean you no harm."

"May I talk so my friends can know what I am saying?" John asked.

"Of course. I will understand them if they talk because you are here. I can hear them through your mind."

"Good, that will save some time. I have some great news, Archieréas." John opened the container with the Morph beef. "There are two obstacles to our making a lasting peace. One is the Morph's need for human flesh and the other is using human women for procreation."

"I agree with what you say, John."

"This is a mixture of molecular reconstructed Seally grass and beef protein. What we were able to create is what we call

'Morph beef'. Would you like to try it?" Archieréas looked at the beef and slowly took a chunk of the food. He smelled it and then looking at John put in in his mouth and chewed. As Archieréas was eating Sheamus whispered to John.

"Ifin' this here red bloke starts ta choke on that there burger meat, do we start shootin' our way out o' here?"

"Relax, Shea. Have some faith. Cass assured me a Morph can eat this."

"Well now, that there makes me feel o' whole lot better knowin' yer new love interest assured ya." John gave Sheamus a stare and said, "Do we have to do this now? Stay focused, Shea. Please."

"All right, Johnny boy, I'll be good." John and the Lads kept staring at Archieréas to see if he was going to have a bad reaction. After he was done swallowing his first chunk he grabbed half of what was left and ate it. Everyone breathed a sigh of relief as Archieréas looked like he smiled.

"This will work John. It is very good. It is very good. Your people will assure a supply for all the Morphs?"

"Archieréas. Seally grass can turn one pound of soy into five pounds of Morph beef. I can absolutely guarantee as much as the Anaptýsso will ever need."

"That only leaves the issue of breeding." Anaptýsso thought.

"We are on the cusp of solving that problem, Archieréas. I have been assured my people are only weeks away from being able to create a Big female outside the uterus. With these two issues solved, there would be no need for humans and Morphs not to live in peace. No one needs to die anymore in this senseless war."

"I agree with you, John, but the Morphs have split along lines. One side, like myself wants peace. The other wants to enslave humanity and treat them as cattle. These Morphs are led by Anu and call themselves Negeltu. Unfortunately, we, the Anaptýsso, are greatly outnumbered. However, this Morph beef, and the ability to breed without killing humans, should bring many of the Negeltu to our side. You humans thought of us as beasts when we first became. But the truth is, we are more evolved both physically and mentally than humans. Which means, we do not kill for pleasure. With this you have solved two problems which were keeping many of us from seeking peace. But now I think we have a chance. How long would it take to deliver a few tons of this food?"

"I can have four tons to you in one month. I'll leave it right on midfield."

"Good. In the mean time I will talk to the Anaptýsso,so they know what's happening. I also suggest you get your people to the Haven facilities as soon as possible. If this civil war starts, the zones will be hit hard. Unless I can convince more to join us, I don't think the Anaptýsso can win a civil war."

"I understand Archieréas. I will see you in one week. If you need me before then, meet me at the Institute." Archieréas put his hand out and John shook it.

"Until then John. May 'fortuna' be with us."

"Yes. Yes Archieréas. Good luck to us all." As John and the Lads stared to leave, John turned back. "Archieréas. If this peace becomes real, you and the Anaptýsso will have all of humanity on your side. That should help with the numbers."

"Thank you, John. Let's hope this all ends with a peaceful world where no one needs to die uselessly," Archieréas thought.

"Sure, hope can be good. But I prefer action. I promise to make this happen, Archieréas. Count on it."

Chapter Eleven

Infiltration

After negotiations with Archieréas, John and the Lads returned to the Roman Institute. There they made plans for filling the Haven facilities as soon as possible.

"Ok guys. We need to get Haven at full capacity. The lottery has been pushed forward by weeks but unfortunately, our security is going to suffer because of this adjustment. I want each of you to go to a facility and make sure it is being filled correctly. Bubba, I need you to go to the west coast unit in Tsalaki. Agni you're headed for Acharya."

"Oh, thank you. This humble servant will be happy to see his home after all this time," Agni smiled.

"Raiden, you take Uli wa Liánhé and Shea…"

"Let me take o' wild stab at this, boyo.' Could it be Europa, ya want me ta be goin'?" Sheamus asked.

"Why yes, Shea. Your intelligence astounds me sometimes," John smiled.

“Well ifin’ ya took ta wax out yer ears, Johnny boy, ya would be hearin’ many o’ smart thin’ coming out o’ this here, beautiful Irish mouth.”

“Shit. Without the wax in our ears, Shea, we couldn’t stand being around that never ending yapping pie hole of yours,” Bubba said.

Everyone laughed and Sheamus continued. “Ach, go on now. I know me voice is like o’ mother’s lullaby ta ya bloomin’ heathens. But in your case, Bubba darlin,’ tis pearls before swine, pearls before swine it tis,” Sheamus laughed. “Tis o’ good thin’ yer weren’t around a few hundred years ago. Me great great granda came here from ta mother country, he did. He became a gunslinger, a U.S. Marshall, a bank robber, a gambler….”

“Yeah, yeah, I got it. Are you saying he could out talk you? Because if that’s what you’re saying then, yeah. I’m sure as hell glad I didn’t meet him. If I ever ran into somebody who talked more than you my ears would explode,” Bubba laughed.

“Ache go on now. Ya love ta hear me melodious voice there, me friend. I can see yer eyes light up every time I’m about ta speak.” Sheamus turned to John. “Ok, John. I’ll be happy ta go ta Europa, but what about all ta other facilities? Who will be lookin’ after them?”

“I will. Along with Matt and Jessie. We’ll hop around and spot check everything we can. I am putting, Mom, Dad and Lula in the New Washington facility. Jessie will look over them and the unit.”

“How do you think that will set with Kolla? Your family getting special treatment is kind of his talking point,” Bubba asked.

“Yeah. Well, Kolla is in a constant state of ‘pissed off’ at my family. David and Celest were a big part of the Haven Project and are in. Lula has provided information vital to national security. If the Kolla crowd doesn’t like it; fuckem.”

“When do you want us to go?” Raiden asked.

“Today. You all have a Roman Institute jet at your disposal so get going. We can’t waste a moment. If this ‘civil war’ between the Morphs starts, all hell is going to break loose.” John warned.

All the Lads shook hands and said their goodbyes. Sheamus and Chara were leaving when Sheamus turned and said to everyone, “Listen here, fellas. Ifin’ any of ya needs help just call, and me and ta boy will come runnin’.”

“Ch lo La. Ch lo La.”

“Ya hear that, yer bunch o’ bleedin’ heathens? Me boy here loves ya.” Sheamus paused for a moment, wiped his tearing eyes and then said. “Now don’t be goin’ and getting’ yerselves killed, ya bleedin’ fools. Ifin’ ya do I will never forgive ya. That goes double fer yer reckless self, John Roman.”

Everyone smiled and went their ways.

****

After Leroy and Nick left the hospital, they were met by Luke. Who was accompanied by several Morphs, so Nick and Leroy agreed to go with him. The arrived at Mark's place and were seated at an elegant table covered in an assortment of luscious food. As Luke sat at one end of the table, he told the men to eat.

"Fuck. You think this is a last meal type thing?" Nick asked Renkins.

"Shit, Nick. You ever heard of a last meal serving lobster, escargot, and all this other stuff. Hell, this table must have ten thousand GMUs worth of food on it. Dig in man," Leroy said.

"Well, I just don't like those red fucks staring at me while I eat."

"You'd rather I be staring at you while they eat you?" Leroy asked.

"No." Nick said as he began to fill his plate. After a few minutes Leroy looked at Luke.

"You're one of the Roman brothers, right?"

"Correct," Luke said.

"So, I guess you aren't the big cheese then. I mean, why waste your time watching us eat, unless that's your thing."

"My brother Mark will be here shortly. He's tying up some loose ends at the moment."

"Fuck. I thought that was a girl for a moment," Nick whispered to Leroy.

"Yeah, he is a little fem like. Maybe we can use that later so don't say anything now." Leroy whispered back.

"Believe me, boss. I ain't saying shit to no one. This is your show."

As the two men kept eating, Mark was in his office with Tamar and Victor.

"Tamar, I want you to go to the New Washington Haven facility."

"Isn't that the one your Dad and Celest are going in?" Tamar asked.

"Oh, yes. Which is why you must not say a thing to Luke. You will have detailed maps of the place. Make yourselves known throughout the whole facility. In a little while six men will contact you over a period of about a week. They will ask you 'We will rule the world?'That's the code phrase so you know who they are. When they reveal themselves you must take them down to the sixth level. On that level take them to this room." Mark pointed to the map. "There, you will make sure no one bothers them for a week. If anyone gets in your way eliminate them." Victor looked at Mark.

"You're going to pod them."

"Correct, my dear Victor. They will then infect the whole facility."

"Hey, I'm not locking myself in with fifty thousand motherfucking Morphs, Mark," Tamar shouted.

"Calm down, my dear. One of the reasons Anu bit you was so you would be able to communicate with the Morphs. Once your abilities kick in, the Morphs will be able to hear you. Anu will make them obey your every command, dear. You will not be locked in with Morphs, you will command fifty thousand Morphs. The first female human Morph commander." Tamar looked at Victor and then smiled.

"They'll do anything I say?" Tamar asked.

"Anything, dear." Mark then turned to Victor.

"Victor. I need you to get back in John's good grace. With the Roman family having to fill all the Haven facilities at once they will be stretched thin. See if he will give you any job. Get in and we can go from there. We have the ability to create any documents we need. We also have more than a few allies in his front office and in the Haven units." At that moment Senator Kolla entered the room.

"Victor, this is Ari Kolla. He is Europa's representative. You will be working with him. He will get you the papers and documents you need to infiltrate any Haven facility. Your job will be to get as many of our people into those facilities as possible. Senator Kolla will be going to the Europa Haven unit."

"Be going as what?" Victor asked. Mark and Kolla looked at each other.

"Go ahead, tell him," Kolla said.

"Ari and five others are going to morph inside the facility. He has decided he wants to be a Morph," Mark said.

"I believe they are the new rightful inheritors of the earth. I want to be one of them. It will make my revenge on the Roman family, especially John Roman, so much the better. I'm looking forward to killing that Irish punk and his little boy. Their deaths by my hand will drive John to near insanity. Then he'll make mistakes, and mistakes mean death," Kolla smirked.

"Yeah, well, I'll settle for ruling what's left of humanity. Right now I prefer this body." Victor said, looking at Kolla and thinking the man was insane.

"That's your prerogative, Victor. But to continue, Leroy will be headed to the West Coast Tsalaki unit and Tamar will go to the New Washington facility. I want you to go to the Uli wa Liánhé facility. Having an Asian farther will help you induce Raiden to trust you. You will lure him to the cave his sister was raped in. There he will meet his end and you will take over the Uli wa Liánhé, facility.

"Got it," Victor said.

"Good. Now, let's go meet Mr. Renkins. Except for you, Ari. I don't want anyone outside this room knowing about you."

"I understand. I am headed for Europa now, anyway. I will contact you via our private phone when I get there," Kolla said as he left. Turning to the others Mark said.

"I want to introduce you to our newest patsy, Leroy Renkins. Just follow my lead. Oh, and Tamar, it would be helpful if you gave Renkins some...incentive to do what we want."

"You mean you want me to fuck him?" Tamar asked.

"Well, when you put it that way...yes," Mark answered.

"Sure, no problem. To me a good fuck is just the perks of being on the winning side."

Mark, Victor, Tamar and Anu went into the dining room to meet Leroy and Nick. When Renkins saw Anu, he jumped up and grabbed a knife and Nick smashed a chair and was ready to use one of the legs as a weapon.

"Gentlemen. Gentlemen. Calm yourselves. This is Anu. He is our friend and benefactor. He is the Morph who is going to make the two of you some of the most powerful men on earth. Please sit."

Renkins and Nick stood their ground not quite ready to disarm themselves.

"Gentlemen, please. Mr. Renkins. Mr Smalls. If Anu wished you harm do you think that knife or table leg would stop him or," Mark pointed to the Big male and female Morph who entered the room, "these two from tearing you to pieces? Now please sit. We have lots to discuss." Both men put down their weapons and sat.

"Alright. What's the deal?" Renkins asked.

"Right to the point hey, Mr. Renkins," Mark said as he too sat. "Let me introduce everyone before we make any plans. This is Anu. He is sort of...a...Morph, high priest. Here we have two Big Ms. The male is Lugal, their king you might say. His female partner is his queen of course, Nin. The 'regular' Ms over there are known as, 'Ursang;' means 'warrior,'" Mark whispered aside. "Altogether they call themselves the 'Negeltu.' It means the 'awakened ones' or some such thing. The man and woman there are my niece and nephew, Tamar and Victor, and of course you met my brother Luke."

"Ok, great. I'll put you all on my Christmas list. Look, man, I know we won't leave here unless we agree to anything you say so, how about we cut through the bullshit. We're in. What's the job?" Leroy asked.

“My. My. Aren’t you the macho alpha male,” Mark said. Tamar moved over to Leroy.

“You know they told me part of my job to get you to go along with us was fucking the shit out of you. I said yes, of course; goes with the gig. But now,” Tamar said as she sat on Renkins lap and put her hand in his crotch. “Now…,” She said, putting her tongue in his ear and whispering. “...I think it’s going to be my pleasure.”

“That can wait, Tamar,” Mark said. “Now, Leroy, if you don’t mind me calling you that?”

“It’s my name. Why should I mind?”

“Of course.” Mark looked at the rest of the people and Anu, then said, “We would like you and your friend, Nick, to infiltrate the West Coast Haven facility. We are sure you can bullshit your way into the place. After all you survived the Morph rampage in the Outlands.”

“No so. I was done for. Nick here saved me; twice.” Mark was beginning to get agitated with Renkins’ attitude.

“Well,...maybe I should deal with Nick and give those Morphs over there a lunch break which would of course, include you as the appetizer.”

“Hurt him and I’ll kill you before your red apes can help you,” Nick said as he began to stand. Renkins grabbed Nick and sat him back down.

“Easy Nick,” Leroy cautioned. “Our friend here was just joking. Look, Mark, as I said before, we agree to everything, so knock off the dramatics and just tell us what you want and what we get out of it. Then we can all go our separate ways and get the show on the road." Mark stared at Nick and Leroy, his cheeks getting as red as his birth marks. Anu then thought to Mark, "We need them to get inside the complex. Just play along and after you can do what you want to them."

Mark replied to Anu, "Very well. But later they will wish they had been more respectful." What Anu and Mark did not know was the bite Renkins received in the Outlands made it possible for him to hear them. He kept his composure and acted as if he knew nothing of what the two were thinking to each other.

"Very well. We will provide you with papers, GMUs and a backstory about your escape from the evil...Mark," He said as he pointed to himself. "and the evil, Anu. We want you to infiltrate the West Coast Haven facility. It's the major hub for the whole western Haven Projects. If we have that unit we could potentially control five units."

Renkins looked at Nick, Mark and Tamar. He ran his hand down Tamar's pants until he felt her wet pussy. As he played with her and she started to moan, he looked at Luke and Mark.

"Ok, this is one perk. What's the others?" Mark gave Luke a stare and then turned to Renkins.

"You and who ever you need will run the entire West Coast of Tsalaki once we have gained control and the world is ours. For keeping humanity in line your reward will be whatever you decide.

Just keep the remaining humans under control and healthy and the rest is up to you. You will be kings."

Tamar was tilting her head back with her mouth open and riding Leroy's finger like a cock.

"Sounds good." Renkins said as he looked at Tamar. "She's ready; when do we go?"

"You will start your training first thing in the morning?" Renkins saw the look on Victor's face. As he stood he said. "Don't worry. You can have her back in an hour or two. Now where's our rooms?"

****

As Renkins and Tamar were about to enter his room, Tamar pointed to the next and said. "That one is yours Smalls.' Try not to disturb us. I'm sure you're going to hear a lot of noise." Tamar said as she rubbed Leroy's crotch.

"Go on, honey, and get the bed warm. I have to talk to my boy here for a second," Renkins said.

The two men entered Nick's room and Renkins put his finger to his lips signaling Nick to be quiet. Renkins then, used hand signals to relay what he wanted to Nick, "Don't talk. Explain later. Just play along." Renkins winked, "This is going to be great, Nick." He said in a raised voice. "We're going to run the whole West Coast. We'll live like kings. Get some rest. I'm gong to go fuck this crazy bitch."

In his room, Renkins saw that Tamar had already undressed. She was jumping up and down on the bed and her perfect tits weren't even bouncing. Her taunt body and shaved pussy caused Leroy to get erect. "Come on my Black Mamba, roll that snake out." Leroy took off his shirt and shoes then his pants. As soon as he did his penis stood erect, and caused Tamar to take a deep breath.

"Holy shit. That's more like a black python. Ohhh baby Tamar wants that monster inside her now." Tamar jumped a few more times and then said. "Get ready motherfucker here I come." After one more big bounce Tamar took a giant leap from the bed onto Renkins arms. He wrapped his arms around Tamar's waist and in one motion jammed his cock into her. She let out a loud moan and started to bounce up and down on Renkins' dick as if she were riding a bucking bull. After a few minutes Renkins threw her on the bed, flipped her around and took her from behind. With each thrust Tamar's head was pushed into the mattress and she couldn't stop yelling in ecstatic moans, "More...ohh..more...ahh yes...harder motherfuck...oh...yeah...yeah..yeah..oh I'm gonna ….oh I'm gonna…..ahhhhhah." Renkins let loose with a Tarzan-like yell. Having had no sex for over five months Leroy's load quickly filled Tamar and spilled out onto the sheets.

"Oh shit. Oh shit," Tamar moaned.

"We ain't done yet honey." Renkins was immediately hard again and turned Tamar over. He wrapped her legs around his arms and proceeded to bring her to orgasm again. Tamar laid on the bed smiling with pleasure but Renkins wasn't done yet. "Come on honey give me that brown eye. I can see you love it. That poop shoot is as big as your cunny."

"Promises. Promises," Tamar laughed. Leroy laughed too as he turned her over, and rammed his cock into her gaping butt hole.

"My God you can fuck," Tamar said as they lay there. As she proceeded to get dressed. Renkins said, "Yeah, well. It's been awhile and you've got one hot ass body, girl. If the rest of the perks are this good I'm glad I joined up with the white boy."

"I glad you're with us, Leroy. But I have to go. Get some rest. You and Smalls will start your training tomorrow. Oh and don't worry, I'm on call whenever you need me." She gave Leroy a peck on the cheek and then left the room. Outside the door she thought. "Shit. Too bad Mark wants to kill him. I'd love to keep that black fuck around. My pussy's still throbbing."

****

A week later at the Haven Project headquarters in New Washington, John was discussing how the re-habitation of Haven was going. In the room were General Thomas and General Hooks. John also had all the Lads on a conference call monitor.

"Alright people, how are we doing with Haven? Where are we at with full capacity?"

"Well I can tell ya boyo' that the Europa unit is fine and dandy, it is," Sheamus said.

“We be at full capacity, we are. Everythin’ be runnin’ smooth as a cat’s whiskers, it is.”

“We’re ok here, John,” Bubba said. “We had a few incidents where we caught people who were infected trying to get in.”

“We, too, had infected. But we stopped them, John,” Raiden said.

“This humble servant has nothing but good news to report. We are at full habitation with no incidents,” Agni said.

“That’s all good news but I want all of you to keep looking for infiltrators. Especially infected. I am convinced that Mark will try to get into the facility's and infect its people. We know that Mark has people who agree with his views and others who want to be Morphs. This is one of the most critical times we are going to see with the Haven Project. Once we button up, it will be easier to maintain security in a limited area. So stay vigilant and if you are at full capacity, start going through the people and double check their status,” John said.

“Generals, what do your hear from the Zones?” John asked.

“Well, Sir,” Hooks said. “Some Zones have reported Morph sightings. At this time we cannot confirm. I have sent people to check out all reports of Morphs. As you know, the Morphs cannot be picked up by infrared or body heat. But our ‘eyes in the sky’ motion cameras have spotted no major movements.”

“Good Jim. Stay on it.”

“John,” Raiden interrupted. “My people just informed me your nephew, Victor, is at our gates.”

“Really? Hold him up top. Do not let him in the underground facility. I will be there tomorrow and talk to him,” John ordered.

“What do you think he wants?” Thomas asked.

“I’m not sure. He was one of the first people who fought and survived the Morphs. I don’t think he had any love for Mark. I will find out tomorrow. What about the New Washington facility? Have my Mom and Dad been situated there?” Before Hooks could answer the direct phone to the New Washington facility rang. John picked it up.

“Hello,” John said.

“John, it’s Sergeant Rodney, Sir. Your niece Tamar just showed up at our door step yesterday. Celest demanded we let her in. She told us not to say anything but I thought you should know, Sir. Your niece is with your mother now.”

“I understand Sergeant. Tell Lieutenant Jackson to keep her under surveillance but don’t interfere with my mother.”

“Understood, Sir.” John turned to the conference monitor.

“Did all you guys hear that?”

“Ya bet yer sweet arse we did, fella. Look here my friend, I didn’t say anythin’ but a few days ago Senator Kolla came in with some other representatives of Europa with their families. But after this, what ta hell you think is goin’ on.? This can’t be legit boyo.’ Ya know what I says about coincidences; ‘There aren't any.’ I also have ta wonder why Tamar and Victor are not together. Them two have always been like peas in o’ pod.”

"I agree, Shea. But I'm not going to tell Celest to reject Tamar. My mother has been through enough. Let me see what Victor has to say about this. Plus Kolla is a bonafide representative of Europa. We can't start overruling a Nation's pick. They are entitled to fill twenty-five percent of the facility with their picks. Just keep an eye on him, Shea. In the meantime I'll keep Tamar under surveillance."

"Well, John, I got more news for you. It seems Nick Smalls and Leroy Renkins have just showed up at our gates. My guys are telling me Renkins is insisting on meeting with you," Bubba said.

"Jesus Christ on ta cross. Ifin' this here is not some sort o' coordinated attack then I be me own Gran. Ya can't fall for this here bolleywobbel, John."

"I'm not, Shea. But there has to be more to it here. Mark couldn't be so stupid as to think we wouldn't suspect something with all these people showing up at once," John responded.

"Well, I'll tell ya boyo.' He may not care. We could already be too late, Johnny boy."

"Raiden, make sure you isolate Victor. Let no one see him. I'll be there the day after tomorrow. I want to talk to Renkins first. From what Smalls told me about him, Renkins seemed tough but honest. When we were rescuing Renkins from Trumble, Smalls came across as a decent guy. I want to hear what they have to say. Then I'll see Victor.;"

"Yes John. I will make sure Victor is no threat," Raiden said.

"Jim, I want you to go to our New Washington facility and organize a team to watch Tamar twenty-four seven. Don't let her out of your sight."

"Yes Sir. I'm on it," Hooks said as he turned and left.

"Shea, same goes for you. Keep Kolla under surveillance, but don't give him an excuse to cause trouble."

"I hear ya me friend. I'll babysit him like he was me own." In the background John heard Chara reach for Sheamus. "Ca Da so. Ko no Da so."

"Easy Chara. I was only jokin' me boy. Yer ta only son Sheamus will ever have, little fella."

"Alright everyone. You have your work cut out. I will visit each of you this week and we'll get everything shut tight and running safely. Bubba, I'm leaving here and will be there within a few hours. Stay vigilant everyone."

****

John landed at the West Coast Haven Project and met Bubba on the runway. "Good to see you John."

"You, too, my friend. You must miss your sidekick, Agni," John said as the two shook hands.

"Yeah. The little fella grows on you and he never forgets to tell me how many times he saved my life. Thing is he's right. So yeah, I miss him. Feel a little naked without the guy watching my back."

"I know the feeling my, friend. Though all of you are as much a part of me as my right arm, Shea just feels like my good-luck buddy. I'll just be happy when we can all be united."

"I hear you, John. Let me take you to Renkins. He has quite a story." The two walked to the main topside building and opened the door to Leroy and Nick's holding room. As John and Bubba entered Nick stood and put his hand out for John to shake. "It's good to see you again John."

Shaking hands, John replied, "Good to see the both of you. How can we help you?" John looked at Leroy sitting in a chair staring at him. "Mr. Renkins. You didn't seem to want anything from me or my people last time we met. I'm sure I don't have to remind you-we saved your life in the Outlands. So, if you are here to offer us something; great. But if your are here to ask something from us, I think your chances are slim."

Renkins looked at Nick and thought for a moment. He finally looked John right in his eyes and said, "John, I'm going to lay it all on the line. I've never pretended to be somebody I'm not. My main concern is myself. If I can get the results I need without hurting anyone; fine. But if someone gets in my way, they better be ready for me. I'm not a hero. I go with winners. I don't fight lost causes. I leave that to men like you. I am convinced the Morphs, led by this guy Anu and your brother, are going to win. I was going to join them-but decided differently."

"Really? Could you grace us with why you changed your mind and now want to hang with us losers?" Bubba asked.

"Sure. But first, I want you to know that Nick wanted to go with you all along. He just hung with me out of loyalty. So, if you decide to throw me out, don't put that on him. He'll be of use to you in the coming tsunami of bullshit headed your way," Renkins said.

"You say you want to come clean, well...that's great, Leroy. In that vein, I'll talk straight. I can't guarantee anything until I hear what you have to say. What I will promise is to listen and then proceed to do what I think is fair and in the interest of my people," John said.

"Can't ask for more than that. It's a deal," Renkins replied.

"Nick and I were "invited" to your brother's place. Don't ask me where it is, I have no idea. We were drugged coming and going. I was all set to join them. I didn't like it but as I said, I thought, and still do, that they will win. Your brother promised we would rule the West Coast of Tsalaki if we signed up with him. You can guess what the other offer was if we didn't. If it had ended there, I would be working with them right now. That's the truth. However….ehh...can I get something to drink?"

"Of course. Nick how about you?" John offered.

"Sure. Thank you."

"Water, beer, soda…."

"I'll take a cold beer," Renkins said.

"Water is fine for me," Nick responded. In a few moments a pint of beer was put in Leroy's hand. He downed it in one long swallow.

“Ahhh. Damn, I haven't had a cold beer in months. Thank you. So, as I was saying. I would have joined your brother Mark, but they made a mistake. During the attack in the Outlands, I was bitten. I don’t know why, but instead of infecting me, the bite allowed me to hear what the Morphs were thinking.”

“That is unusual. Only a Big M’s bite can give someone the ability to hear them,” John said.

“Well he was a big one. Luckily, Nick here blasted the fuck’s head to smithereens just as he bit me. Otherwise, I believe the other Morphs would have known I could hear them. I guess that information went to his grave with him. So, when Nick and I were being given the big sell on why joining your brother was the right choice, I overheard Mark and Anu basically saying how after we did what they needed, we were going to be deep six-ed. That is why I am here. I agreed. They trained us for our mission. When we left I came here.”

“I see. So what, you want to join us now? How am I supposed to believe you?” John asked.

“Look, I don’t care if you believe me or not. I’m telling the truth. You want to toss me out-fine. I’ve been on my own all my life. I could have bullshitted you with a tall tale, but I told you the truth. I have no hate for anyone here. I hope you win. I want to hook up with your team because working to see you and the rest of the world come out on top is the only chance I have to live. When my life is on the line, John, you couldn’t have anyone more loyal,” Renkins answered honestly.

"Yeah, until you get a chance to stab us in the back and switch sides again," Bubba said. "We can't trust this piece of shit, John."

"One thing about me, John. When I give my word, I keep it," Renkins replied.

"Word!! Didn't you give your word to Mark?" Bubba asked.

"Yes, I did. Until I learned he was going to betray me. That's a deal breaker. If we make a deal, John, I will never be the one who betrays it first," Renkins said.

"What about you, Nick? How do you stand in all this?" John asked.

"I think you will win, John. I have no desire to rule a bunch of cattle, just waiting for my turn in the soup pot. But I owe Leroy my life, and where he goes, I go," Nick replied.

"I see." John thought for a moment and turned to Renkins. "Alright. Tell me what they trained you for and what they wanted you to do. If you know anything about Mark's other plans, or Victor and Tamar, we need to know it all. Tell us that and you can stay. I'll find something for the two of you to do. If you prove loyal when the shit hits the fan, I'll even let you in to the underground facility."

"I can live with that," Renkins smiled and shook John's hand. He tried to shake Bubba's but Bubba turned and walked out.

"He'll come around. Now, what were you supposed to do?" John asked.

"We were to get in your good graces and then meet with Mark's undercover people who had passed the security checks, and were now living in the underground housing. They trained us in bomb making, and wanted us to poison your water supply. The other people had their own agenda."

"What about Tamar and Victor?"

"Well, your niece used her...how do I put this...feminine ways to get me to join. But during the week we were training, she seemed to have second thoughts. I think she bugged out and wanted to see her father, Luke."

"Was Luke in on this infiltration?"

"He was there the first day, but he seemed reluctant. I never saw him after the first day but I did overhear Mark and Anu saying he was going to be a problem and needed to go," Leroy said.

"What do you mean, 'needed to go'?" John asked.

"That's all I heard. He needed to go."

"Bubba, get back in here," John yelled out the door. Back in the room again Bubba still seemed angry. "Bubba, you need to get over being pissed at Renkins. He just informed me my brother Luke is in danger. Find him. Make sure he has security at all times."

"You got it, John." Bubba then went over to Nick and Renkins and shook hands.

"Glad to have you both." As he shook Renkins' hand, Bubba pulled him in close and whispered in his ear. "Hurt John or his family and I'll kill you. Kill you real slow." Bubba let go and smiled saying loudly. "I'm sure you both will make a good addition to our team."

"You say Tamar seemed like she wanted out, yet it was she who sent Lula to Mark," John said.

"Look, I'm just telling you what I know. As the days went by, she got cozy with me. Maybe she fell in love, and knowing your brother was going to kill me didn't sit right with her. As far as Victor, six days into our training Nick and I heard Victor have a big fight with Mark. After that, I never saw him. That's everything. I told you I wouldn't lie or make stuff up. They just didn't realize I could hear them. They wanted me to meet up with some of their spies and we were all going to bring this place down. This was going to be *my...castle...* 'headquarters' if you like, when the war was over. Nick is in the same boat but feel free to ask him anything," Renkins finished.

"Well, what about it Nick? You have anything to add?" John asked.

"No, John. It's just as Leroy said. Mark wanted us to take out this facility and our reward was going to be all the West Coast. I do think your niece, Tamar, fell for Leroy and got out of there before Mark could hurt her," Nick said.

"How were you supposed to contact these traitors, these spies?" John asked.

"We were to make it obvious who we were. You know. Go around act like jerks, make scenes and if anyone came up to us and said 'we will rule the world,' they would be a contact. We would show them this." Renkins opened his mouth and while poking his finger underneath his jaw bone he contorted the upper and lower halves of his mouth several times making popping sounds. He then reached into his mouth and pulled out a back molar. Showing it to John he then twisted the tooth and it came apart in two sections. Leroy patted the bottom section on his open hand and a near microscopic chip fell onto his palm.

"Here you go," Renkins said as he gently put the tiny chip into John's hand. "Put that under a microscope and everything you need, from making bombs and concocting poison, to Mark's orders, and maps of where he wants things planted, time lines. They're all on this little gizmo."

John handed the chip over to Bubba. "Get that to Renfro in IT, will you please? Bubba. Take Hook's man, Holden, from security with you. No one but Renfro opens this and no one but you holds on to it, and the information on it."

"Gotcha John. Be back in a flash…"

"No. Bring it to my room as soon as you have it."

"Will do," Bubba said as he left.

"Ok. Leroy. Here's what I want you and Nick to do," John said. "Just as Mark planned, I want you to make yourselves known at the facility, and when these people reveal themselves to you, let me know. Don't do anything, just keep them on the hook. We'll supply you with fake plans and bombs. Play your part. I want all these spies and traitors caught."

"Got it, boss," Renkins said.

"Jeff will show you two your quarters. I think you're on level four. Get settled in and start making noise," John said.

Chapter Twelve

Honor Restored

Mean while, Victor was trying to talk Raiden into going with him to Shinto cave. “Look, I’m telling you Raiden, that red fuck Anu is at the cave where your sister was violated. He and a few of his Morph minions are going to set up some kind of headquarters for the invasion of this island.”

“Why should I believe you? Your uncle is working with the Morphs. Why did you come back here? Why come to Uli wa Liánhé?” Raiden asked.

“Uli wa Liánhé!!” Victor spat. “That’s what I think of Uli wa Liánhé. This is *Nippon* and we are *Nihonjin.*” Victor bowed as he said, “Hai.” Raiden then bowed and repeated. “Hai.”

“This island will always be sacred and always be Nippon. We Nihonjin live only for honor. For death with honor is the only true reason for living,” Victor said.

“But you are not Nihonjin,” Raiden said.

“My father was pure Nihonjin. His family has lived here for over a thousand years. He was Makoto Jimmu.”

“Jimmu,” Raiden said. “He was the first emperor. If your father was indeed his descendant then you are Nihonjin.” Raiden bowed and said, “Hai.”

“Then you must believe me. I played Mark like the *Gaijin* he is. When I learned Anu would be coming here, I knew I had to help you honor your sister and defend our island.”

“The fact is this island protects us. The Morphs have no air force. How would they invade our homeland?” Raiden asked.

“You are right, Raiden. The Morphs don’t have planes, but Mark Roman does. The Nations have implemented strict air use, but a plane here and there can always get through, especially if one has money or influence. Mark is flying Anu and a few of his Warrior Morphs to the island. They will set up their headquarters in Shinto cave. There they will kidnap men and women and force them to pod. Eventually they will have enough of them for an all-out assault on Nippon. They will use that large army to launch attacks on the mainland. We must stop them.”

“Ok. I will summon the army…,” Raiden was about to say.

“No. I mean...yes. We will need about fifty men but if you call in the entire island force you will leave the rest of the island unprotected. What if I’m wrong and Anu somehow attacks in force by land or sea? Most importantly, with that many soldiers it will not be you who regains honor for your family. It must be you who deals the final blow to Anu. Only then can family honor be regained,” Victor said.

"Yes. Hai," Raiden bowed. "You are right, Victor. I will assemble some men and we will go to Shinto cave and I will indeed regain my family's honor and revenge for Aimi."

"I would be honored if I could be your *Kojin hisho*."

"Hai," Raiden said as he bowed.

Early the next morning, Raiden and Victor left for the Shinto caves. Soon after they were gone, Major Tom Sands received an urgent call from New Washington Haven site: it was John Roman. "Major Sands, please get Raiden Kameyama to the phone. I cannot raise him on his.

"I would be happy to do that, Sir, but he has gone on a mission to the Shinto caves, Sir."

"What are you talking about?" John asked.

"Well Sir, your nephew, Victor, informed Raiden that a Morph named Anu was at the caves, Sir. So, Raiden and Victor took fifty men in order to kill Anu and stop any potential invasion, Sir."

"What!! That's insanity. Raiden must be blinded by his need for revenge. How long ago did they leave?" John asked.

"Less than an hour, Sir."

"Good. Good. It's at least two hours to the caves from the facility. Major, I don't care what it takes but send every available soldier to those caves. Make sure they are well armed and tell Raiden that I must speak to him before he gets to the cave. I want you to personally find Raiden and stop him from going to those caves. I also want you to arrest Victor Roman, put him in a cell and have several men guard him until I get there. Do you understand, Major?" John asked.

"Yes, Sir, absolutely. I will leave immediately, Sir. Don't worry I'll find Mr. Kameyama. You have my word Sir."

"Thank you, Major. Have Raiden call me the minute you see him. Oh...and Major...if Raiden refuses to stop, arrest him and keep him locked up until I get there. Understood?"

"Understood, Sir." Major Sands hung up the phone and smiled and whispered to himself, "Yeah, I understand, you rich fuck, and when I 'm a Morph I hope they let me be the one to rip you apart."

Just then the door opened, and Sergeant Brady entered. "Sir. I just got a call from John Roman. He wants me to go and get Mr. Kameyama. He seems to think he and that new guy are headed for the Shinto caves to kill Morphs."

"Is that so? How many other people did you tell this tale to Sergeant?" Sands asked.

"No one yet, Sir I came to ask you what your orders are. I assumed Roman informed you."

"Yes, Sergeant, he did." Sands reached into his desk drawer, pulled out a pistol with a silencer attached to it, and shot Brady in the head. He then got on the facility's loud speakers.

"Attention, everyone. We are soon to be under attack. All underground residents and personnel report to the underground section immediately. All topside security man at your stations. I am initiating radio silence until further notice. Cells phones will be inoperative. Sergeant Jolo, please come to my office."

Sands then pulled out a special phone from his safe. Mark Roman answered on the first ring.

"Hello Sir. 'We will rule' has been initiated."

"Very good, Major Sands. Very...good. Call me when it's done."

****

Still at his West Coast Tsalaki office, John was worried. With Bubba and General Hooks at his side, John talked to Sheamus and Agni on a conference call monitor. "Shea, I am concerned about Raiden. I think Victor is leading him into a trap. I have notified General Sands about the situation, but I have not been able to contact him since."

"Do ya think he is in on it with Mark?" Sheamus asked.

"Could be. I am sending one thousand of my top commandos there now and have notified Uli wa Liánhé security forces. My people should be landing within the hour."

"But how are your men goin' ta take the place? Ya made ta damn thin' impenetrable boyo.'"

"Yes. But I included overrides. When Major Stewart gets there he will initiate the overrides and the rest should be a cake walk," John answered.

"Secret overrides hey? Well. What happens if this here Stewart fella turns or gets himself captured. There go yer overrides, dear boy."

"Not really. All the facilities have there own codes. Once it's used, a new code takes effect."

"Well aren't ya ta clever devil, darlin'? Ye never mentioned these here overrides ta yer best friend did ya now?"

"Well they wouldn't be secrets if I told everyone would they, Shea?" John said laughing.

"Look, I am also worried Kolla might be planning some coordinated scheme to take over your facility, Shea. You must check every person for infection. I believe all our Haven facilities have been compromised with traitors. Maybe even people who have been intentionally infected."

"But they would need at least six infected in order ta pod and they would need o' place ta do that without being noticed," Sheamus said.

"Yes, I realize that. Which is why I believe there are people working for Mark who are not infected. Their job would be to hide those who pod until the morphing. They will be harder to detect since they will not be infected. First, you must find the infected, isolate them and then, using any methods necessary, discover who their non-infected contacts are."

"I understand ya, Johnny boy. Count on me."

“Agni you need to do the same. I know it goes against your beliefs, but the innocent must be protected. If you feel you can’t, I will put someone else in charge.”

“No John. This humble servant knows his duty. Agni will not fail you.”

“Good. I’m headed for our New Washington facility. I need to make sure Tamar isn’t up to no good. I will talk to all again tomorrow. If any emergency comes up, call me direct.”

****

Victor and Raiden approached the Shinto caves with caution. “I want half our men to set up perimeters around front and back entrances. The rest come with me. Stay alert. Be ready for anything.”

With twenty men, Raiden and Victor entered the cave. They soon came to the fork splitting the cave’s large room. “If Morphs here, they want us to split into two forces. I not do that,” Raiden said.

“But what if they are in both sections? We would have them at our backs and front if we choose wrongly,” Victor said.

“Hai. But I have solution.” Raiden turned to one of his men. “Place charges ten feet inside.”

“But that will cause a cave-in,” Victor said.

“Hai. I know these caves well, Victor. That leads to dead end. We would be trapped in there. Why you so worried about blowing it up?”

"I just don't think we should. I...I think.."

"What? Am I messing with Mark's plan?"

"What are you talking about?"

"Never mind."

"Sir. We are ready," Raiden's man said.

"Very well, Sergeant. Blow it." The explosion was perfectly placed and brought down the section without damage to the other entrance.

"Now whatever was in there no longer threat." Raiden said.

"This fork leads to big room where we found my sister. But there are parts that make it impossible for more than one person to get through. That make for perfect ambush site, don't you think, Victor?"

"Sure...I...guess. How about I go through and make sure everything is clear?" Victor asked.

"Hai. Very brave of you." Raiden thought for a moment and said, "Could it be you not scared because you know what on other side?"

"Are you calling me a traitor?" Victor yelled. Suddenly, there was a loud commotion outside the cave. Raiden could hear shooting and screaming. Over his radio, Raiden tried to contact his men. But before he got an answer the shooting and screaming had stopped.

"I think you should put down your katana now, Raiden," Victor said with a smile. "Your men are dead. If you wish to live, surrender now."

"So. You are traitor."

"Oh, well. One man's traitor is anther's hero. Just be a good boy and…"

Before Victor could finish, Raiden drew his sword and sliced Victor's throat, nearly cutting his head off. Victor slowly realized what happened and his eyes met Raiden's as he gently dropped to the floor. Raiden turned to his men. "Hai. *Watashi no yūjin* it will be my honor to die with you today. All twenty of Raiden's men bowed and said in unison, "Hai, *Idaina-sha,* we welcome death with honor."

Then came the howls from the fork entrance and the front of the cave. "Boton. Blow the charges." An explosion sealed anyone who was at the end of the fork. That left only the front entrance for Morphs to come through. Victor had of course lied about how many Morphs had landed on the island. Raiden and his doomed men were facing at least a hundred Makete. As the room filled with Morphs, Anu entered. He had a human male with him to translate.

"My master wants you to surrender and join him," Anu thought.

"He does? What will happen to my men?"

"My master says they will be gloriously turned into Negeltu. But he says you can stay human if you choose. He will make you ruler of this island." Raiden turned to his men and saw in their eyes what he must do. He quickly threw his short sword into the throat of the human translator. Then yelled, "For Aimi!!!" Swinging his samurai sword he started to hack away at the Morphs as he tried to reach Anu. The entrance created a choke point and by using the cave walls to protect their backs Raiden's men were able to engage the

Morphs in near single combat. The fight was ferocious and lasted for over half an hour. Morphs were piled high and the men were down to fighting with only knives and bayonets. Raiden could see the Morphs were intentionally avoiding him. Saving him for Anu. As Raiden looked around at his men, he found their numbers dwindling. The stamina and strength of the Morphs were just too much for them. Knowing the hopelessness of the situation, Raiden took off his armor and ran toward Anu. As he neared him, he leaped into the air and came down in front of the high-priest, swinging his sword down on Anu's shoulder. Unfortunately, the blade had become dull with all the fighting and only went about three inches into Anu. Anu grabbed Raiden around his neck and looked into his eyes. Raiden smiled and said, "John will avenge me and my sister." He then spit into Anu's eye. The next instant Anu snapped Raiden's neck and dropped him on the ground.

"Feed, Negeltu," Anu commanded. The rest of the Morphs began to consume all the dead and dying humans.

****

A day later, Major Stewart called John with the news. "Sir, we have taken the facility back. The minute we arrived we implemented the overrides and were able to access the facility. We met little resistance once we were inside. Everything is under control."

"What happened to Sands, Major?" John asked.

"He killed himself, Sir. We have gathered up those who were in on the plot. The total count of traitors at this moment is thirty, twelve of whom are infected. The rest of the residents seem to be completely unaware of Sands' treachery."

"Good, Major. Have you had any sign of Raiden?"

"Ehh...yes..Sir. We found some of his remains at the Shinto caves. It seems he and his men made a last stand against the Morphs despite overwhelming odds. We also found your nephew Victor. From what we can tell, he was killed with a sword. We can only assume it was Raiden who killed him."

"Are there any signs of living Morphs?"

"No Sir. It seems they were airlifted off the island once their numbers were cut so low. We have intensified our air security. Nothing can get through now without our say so."

"You have done a fine job, Major. I commend you and your men. Keep Raiden's remains on ice. When we can, we will hold a ceremony for him."

"Yes, Sir." John hung up the phone and then called the other Lads.

"Guys, I have some bad news. Raiden is dead. He was set up for an ambush by my nephew, Victor. I don't know why Raiden went to those caves with Victor. I'll guess I never fully understand, I think he knew it was an ambush. I believe he went there to try to kill Anu. He wanted revenge for Aimi," John said.

"Bloody hell. He were o' true samurai, that one," Sheamus lamented.

"This humble servant will say a prayer for dear Raiden," Agni sighed.

"I didn't know him as well as you, John, but I sure liked him. This is all Mark's doing, you know?" Bubba said.

"Yes, I know Bubba. Mark will pay for his behavior, I promise all of you," John said.

"Aye. Don't be forgettin' it was that bleedin' bastard, Mark, who was the real cause o' poor Terry's death," Sheamus proclaimed.

"Nothing is forgotten about my brother Mark, Shea."

"What about his burial?" Agni asked.

"As soon as this is all done, we will give him the sendoff he deserves. But until then, we have work to do. Shea, how are you doing with seeking out the infected in your unit?"

"Ahh, boyo' there be o' story indeed. I was in ta act o' callin' ya meself when ya did. Listen ta what o' proud Irish father has ta tell ya boyo.'" Sheamus then proceeded to tell John what happened.

****

"All right now, everyone," Sheamus said to his security people at the Europa Haven facility. "I just got o' call from ta high hat his-self, John Roman. I want ya all ta be checkin' everyone ta see ifin they be infected. Sergeant Louis, I want ya ta lead ta team. Once we do that we will be interrogatein' them ta find ta non-infected traitors. We will be goin' floor by floor now. Once o' floor is cleared, no one can come or go until all ta rest of ta floors are cleared. So get to it now." Sheamus looked down at Chara, pulling on his shirt.

"Well now, little fella. What ya be needin'?"

"Ch he Da. Ch fi in fo Da."

"Well now so ya think ye can find ta infected can ya?"

"Ch fi in fo Da. A ma ju le ha mo vi."

"Are ya sayin' one o'me men has ta virus?"

"Ya."

"Can ya point him out, son?" Chara went to the door and when he opened it, the men were in the other room getting equipped for the inspection of the facility. Chara looked and pointed to a blonde guy who was looking at the both of them.

"He ha vi," Chara said pointing to the blond man."

"Hold on there, Mike. Don't be movin' now, lad." The rest of the men looked at Mike and backed away.

"Be o' good lad and put down ya weapons, nice and slow, will ya now?" Sheamus asked.

Mike looked at Sheamus and the other men who were now pointing their weapons at him. Sheamus could see Mike starting to sweat profusely. "It looks like ta virus is startin' ta take hold of ya lad. Put down yer weapon now. It's all over. Let us take care of ya. Die with some dignity, lad."

Mike was shaking and finally looked to the ceiling and shouted, "We will rule the world." he then put his gun in his mouth and fired.

"Stay back everyone. That there virus shit could be highly contagious. Let's get ta hazmat boys in here."

"Ch se ot ha vi. Ch ca fi fo Da," Chara said.

"All right son. So ya can see em and find em; o' true O'Keefe ya are son. Let's go find them virus hooligans. Sergeant Louis, grab twenty of yer best men. We are goin' huntin' for ta virus."

Chara led the team starting on the first floor of the haven unit. Sheamus was about to line up fifty people at a time when he realized how long it would take. "Jesus fuckin' Christ. How many people we have on each floor now Louis?"

"Well Sir, with the expansion we have about six to ten thousand people on some floors. The sixth floor has maybe two thousand and this floor maybe three thousand. But floors two through five have close to forty thousand people, Sir," Sergeant Louis said.

"God help us. How ta hell we go…." Sheamus started to say, when Chara pulled on his shirt again.

"What is it, son?"

"Ca kn wh ha vi Da."

"Ya know exactly who has it and who doesn't, son?"

"Ya Da."

"Can ya point them out to us? Do ya know how many total there are, son."

Chara closed his eyes for a moment and then he held up two fingers and then formed a zero with his thumb and first finger.

“Are ya saying there be twenty people with ta virus, son?”

“Ya Da.”

“How ta hell can ya tell that from here?”

“Sir. Chara had me take him on a tour of every floor three days ago, after your call with John Roman.” Sheamus knelt down and after hugging Chara said, “Oh, my dear son. Ya knew what we needed, didn’t ya? I be prouder than o’ peacock, I am. Let’s find these traitors shall we?” Sheamus stood and said, “Are there any on this floor, son?” Chara shook his head no.

“Alright fellas, let’s head ta the second floor.” The next floor housed the facility's armory and barracks. “We best be careful here, fellas. Anyone meanin’ ta place harm certainly has themselves easy access to weapons. Once Chara points them out, we need ta take them down nice and quiet like.” Sheamus looked at Chara and said, “Now don’t be nervous, son. Are there any on this here floor?”

Chara held up three fingers. He then pointed to two men who were stacking crates at the end of a long corridor. “Louis, take four men and go that way. The rest of you men go that way. Louis, take me gun,” Sheamus said, handing Louis his Kalashnikov compact assault weapon. “Chara and I will walk up to them like I was given me son o’ grand tour o’ ta place. Once I have their attention, ya all swoop in and hog tie em. Make as little noise as possible, there still be another on this floor.”

“Roger that, Sir.” Everyone took their positions. Chara and Sheamus started to walk toward the two men. “Now, ya see here, son. This be where we keep all ta guns and bang bang stuff. Ifin ya look over there lad, ya be seein'...err...hey corporal…" Sheamus yelled at one of the two men. The man looked at his partner and then at Sheamus.

"Are you talking to me, Sir?" He said.

"Yes, I was, young fella. Can ya help me here? I'm tryin' ta show me son what the purpose o' this here floor is." The man put down his load and started to walk toward Sheamus and Chara.

"Well, Sir. Maybe I should get my Sergeant. We're supposed to get this equipment stowed by 1500 hours, Sir."

"Ohhh, that be very commendable of ya corporal. But I be ta guy who runs ta place. Sheamus O'Keefe's ta name and this here be me son, Chara. So why don't ta both of ya help me out here?" Sheamus kept getting closer to the two men. In a flash, Sheamus' men rushed in and tackled the two men. Just as they were gagging and handcuffing the two, shots rang out from behind them. Two of Louis' men fell and the rest dove for cover. From about twenty feet down the hall a voice shouted. "Don't tell them nothing you two. Flake!! Wherever you are, head for the sixth floor. I'll hold these fucks off for you. 'we will rule the world!!'" The man fired more rounds at Sheamus and his men.

As he took cover behind a truck with Chara, Sheamus asked him, "Is that ta other fella, Chara?"

Chara shook his head no. "Louis!!" Sheamus shouted. "Remember there be non-infected traitors muckin' about. Watch yer back." Sheamus turned his attention to the shooter. "Whoever ya are, yer done, mate. We are going to capture all your infected buddies, boyo.'" Just then a bullet clipped Sheamus in his arm. "Damn yer hide, ya fuckin' bastard. What ta hell ya doin'? It's over ya bleedin' idiot." Seeing Sheamus hurt, Chara ran out from behind the truck and made a dash for the man who shot Sheamus.

"Chara!! Come back, son," Sheamus yelled. Standing up, Sheamus ran after Chara. Chara was moving so fast Sheamus could barely keep track of him. The shooter was missing every shot he took at Chara. In less than three seconds, Chara leaped in the air and came down behind the man who had hurt his Da. Sheamus stopped cold in his tracks as he heard a high-pitched scream which curled his blood. One thing Sheamus knew; it wasn't Chara who screamed. As he closed to the where the man who shot him had been hiding. Chara came out from the stack of crates holding the man's severed head.

"Ch ki ba ma fo Da. He hu Da. Ch no li ba ma."

"Holy mother o' God. Look here son. I know ya didn't like ta man, and ya was tryin' ta save yer Da. But I don't want ya turnin' inta some kind o' killin' machine. There be people who will want ta hurt ya ifin' they thought ya could do this kind o'...kind...well let's call it; behavior."

Chara then turned and ran to a woman who was trying to use the escalator to the next floor. Chara grabbed her arm, twisting it so hard the woman fell to the ground crying.

"Please. Don't hurt me. They made me do it. Please, my family," The woman said.

"Sh ha vi. Sh ba Da. Sh li."

"See here, little lady. Me son can tell ya have ta virus, and he can tell yer bullshittin' this here bullshitter. Ya see he knows because he can sense yer blood pressure and yer speech pattern. Now, we are goin' ta take ya to o' room where yer goin' ta tell us all about yer friends."

"Fuck you and John Roman, you filthy Irish dog. 'We will rule the world.' I will never talk." The woman then a bottle of poison she had hidden on her.

"What ta bloody hell? Have all these here nutters got a suicide complex?" Sheamus yelled.

"All right boys. Chara says this here floor is clear. Lock it down, Louis. I want five guards at each entrance ta every level once we hit six." Sheamus, Chara and the rest of the men went level by level, clearing each floor of those who had been infected. When they searched levels three and four, Sheamus gave Chara free reign to search for infected. They found no one who had the infection, but Sheamus was still worried about undercover agents who were virus-free. He knew they could do real damage to the facility. On the fifth level Chara found one person who had been infected. It seemed as though the person had been left behind. They were in a back office near the fusion reactor. When the man was searched, Sheamus found plans for sabotaging the reactor.

"Holy shit, Sir. If they fucked up the reactor this place would be useless." Sergeant Louis said.

"Aye, Sergeant. Me thinks this here is o' plan in case the other bastards fail. I'll bet ya ta last dollar me Ma has, Mark was thinkin' if he couldn't control ta place he didn't want us able ta use it. Why ya think they left this here fella?"

"He was probably too sick. Maybe he was supposed to fuck up the reactor," Louis said.

"Well, Mark certainly didn't have good intel on this here situation. John knew ta secure this here beautiful piece o' machinery, he did." Sheamus looked back at the dying man, and saw Chara leaning over him. "Chara!! Come away from him. He's infected." Chara looked up at Sheamus and smiled, "No wo Da. Ch no ge vi."

"Ohh, sorry me boy. I forgot for a moment. But what ya tryin' ta do, son?" Chara grabbed Sheamus' phone and started to text. He was typing so fast, no one could keep up with his movements. He then handed the phone to Sheamus.

"Jesus holy bloody hell, son. Could ya do this all ta time?" Chara nodded his head yes.

"Then why didn't ya tell me?" Chara took the phone again and typed.

"Yeah. Yeah. I understand, son. You were right. But from now on ya can text me and me only."

"Sergeant Louis, I'm texting ya o' list o' names. Have yer men round them up at once. In ta mean time let's check ta sixth floor. We are still missin' Kolla and his bunch. Chara says there are at least six more infected down there. Ta me that sounds like o' pod morphin' is o' happenin.' if that be ta case I am sure Kolla has his self some non-infected back up." As the men headed to the sixth floor, five people came running up the escalator stairs. Chara gave

Sheamus the all clear. Which meant none were infected or part of Mark's infiltrators.

"Slow down fellas. What be goin' on now?" Sheamus asked.

"They are people down there who are killing people." The first man said. "They're blocking all exits and entrances and taking hostages." At that instance, Sheamus' phone rang.

"Well boyo.' Let me guess now. Could it be yer ta one's takein' hostages now?"

"Always the smart ass aren't you, O'Keefe?" The voice on the other end said.

"Well, ya might say tis in me blood. Who might I be talkin' to?"

"My name is, Tom Holts. Senator Kolla's aide."

"Ok there, Tom. Now, what is it ya be wantin?"

"Nothing. Just stay off the sixth floor. If you don't we will kill everyone down here."

"Well now, that there would be o' mighty feat. Seein' that there has ta be at least two thousand people ya got there."

"People are very obedient when a gun is pointed in their face," Holts said. "We have put everyone in locked down areas. We have planted very powerful explosives in those areas. If you or anyone else tries to help we'll set off the bombs. We may not kill everyone, O'Keefe, but we certainly will kill enough."

"Alright now, just calm down. How long is it you want us ta keep out?" Sheamus asked.

"That's none of your business. Just stay away," Holts answered.

"Would ya let me talk to yer boss, Kolla?"

"No. There is nothing to talk about, O'Keefe. In fact, tell your boss, John Roman, that if he tries to contact us we will start killing people. This is not going to turn into a negotiation. Stay out or they die. There will be no further contact." Holts hung up the phone.

"Well, ifin' isn't our turn in ta ole pickle barrel," Sheamus muttered. Chara put his hand out for Sheamus' phone again. He then typed.

"Chara can help people on next floor."

"No, son. They planted bombs. I don't want ya or them there hostages getting' hurt. I know ya want ta help son, but just let yer Da figure this here problem out, now." As Sheamus and Sergeant Louis were making plans for saving the hostages, Chara walked silently away. He looked at the many conduits and duct work. The day he and Sheamus had arrived at the facility, Chara had hacked into the systems computer. There he found and downloaded all the facility's floor and mechanical plans. Finding what he was looking for, Chara leaped onto a conduit and punched a hole in the panel. As he crawled into the space, big enough only for a small child, Chara seemed able to elongate his body so that he fit inside the tube like a vent. Using his feet to move through the duct work Chara soon came to a vent opening on the sixth floor. He quietly opened it and slipped into the room. There he opened the door and was able to hear some men talking about the hostages. Using his infrared sight, he determined the room held about three hundred people. Chara sneaked up to the men and dispatched them quickly. There he saw one of the explosive devices, which he disabled.

Meanwhile on the fifth floor Sheamus noticed that Chara was missing. "Hey now. Did any of ya see me boy?" Everyone said, "No."

"Bloody hell. If he went…"

"Sir. We've seen what he can do. Maybe we should let him try. If we call Holts, it might alert him to Chara," Louis said. Sheamus thought for a moment.

"Christ almighty. I be thinkin' yer right there, boyo.' What ta hell am I ta do with that boy?"

"If he pulls this off, I say give him a medal," Louis said.

Looking worried, Sheamus walked away from the group to call John.

"John. Are ya on o' secured line? I don't mean the ones ya use for ta military and such. I mean o' secured, secured line. It's about me son, Chara."

"Hold on, Shea," John switched to another phone. "Ok my friend, nothing more secure."

Sheamus then told, John everything that had happened and what was going on at the moment.

"He can text me in full clear sentences now, John. He saved us twice and knows everything that be happenin' around him. He didn't say anything before because he were afraid o' ya, John. He thought ya would destroy him." Sheamus was holding back tears. "John. He ain't some monster. He's helpin' us. Ya can't hurt him. I won't let ya."

"Why is he texting? Can't he speak?" John asked.

"Apparently not." Sheamus thought for a moment. "So that there means he's not fully AI right? Ya don't have ta hurt him. Please tell me, John. Tell me ya won't hurt him."

"Alright. Alright, Shea. Calm down. You need to concentrate on saving those people. I promise I will do nothing to Chara. But listen, Shea. The Roman Institute is powerful, but we wouldn't be able to stop the Nations from destroying Chara if they thought he was fully AI. They just wouldn't put up with a functioning AI unit. Hell, as of this moment they don't know he even exists. If they did they would most likely want him dismantled. You must keep his abilities and what he is under-wraps. Do you understand, Shea?"

"I do, John. I can count on, Louis, but there are o' lot o' people here who saw what he can do."

"After you get those people to safety and stop whatever Kolla is trying to do; initiate a code five lock down. I'll leave now and be there by tomorrow morning."

"Thank ya, John." Just then Louis called to Sheamus. "Got ta go, John. Somethin' be happenin.'"

When Sheamus came back to the entrance of the sixth floor, Louis was waiting with his phone.

"Sir, your boy's been texting you." Handing the phone to Sheamus, the Irishman read:

"Da, I have defused all the bombs and neutralized those who were guarding the hostages. You can unblock the entrances and get these people out. I am going for Holts and the rest of his men. They are guarding a room at concordance 10:005 on your map. I think there are people in that room who are morphing."

"Alright men, unblock those doors. We have ta go ahead. Let's get our people out o' there, boyo's."

Without the threat of bombs, Sheamus and his men were able to quickly open the doors and soon had all the hostages safe. Running to the room Chara had pointed out, Sheamus and the men found Holts and three other traitors lying dead in front of the room.

"You men stay out here." Sheamus took Louis to the side. "I want ya to make sure no one else comes inta this here room. Yer understand?"

"Yes, Sir. Completely."

Sheamus slowly entered the room and found that Chara had smashed all the pods. The end pods were just a puddle of liquid remains but the four other pods were Kolla and his friends. They had started the morph process but were about a day short. They were half human and half Morph. Chara had killed all of them but Kolla. Sheamus went up to Chara and knelt down putting his hands on Chara's shoulders.

"Son. I know ya be wantin' ta help. But ya can't do this here kind o' thin' any more. Even John won't be able ta help us ifin' ta Nations find out about ya. Do ya understand, son?"

Chara nodded yes and hugged Sheamus. “Ch no ki ag Da. Ch pr Da.”

Sheamus then stood over Kolla, who was writhing on the floor.

“Well now, Senator Kolla, ya don’t look so good, boyo.’’’

Kolla started to laugh and tried to speak. “Wee….agh...we..w...agu...will...rule..”

“Ach, go on now, fella. Ya ain't gonna be rulin’ nothin’ except o’ pine box. Tis over for ya. Ya bloody traitor, ya.”

“Hee...agu..heee. Just….diversion...agu..too...late...for Roman.” Kolla tried to say more but his throat seized up.

“Well, I wouldn’t leave me worst enemy in this here state.” Sheamus knelt beside Kolla and pulled out his switchblade. “Ya made yer bed, boyo;’ now tis time ta lie in it.” Sheamus then slid the point of his blade into Kolla’s brain.

“Come on, son. Let’s go up top.”

****

The next morning, John arrived at the Europa Haven facility. There, he assembled all the men who had witnessed Chara in action. In the room were Sheamus and Chara.

“Men I have called you here today because you have all seen what Chara here can do. He is an AI android.” There was whispering among the group and they all stared at Chara.

"We have all heard stories about the AIs, Sir. I thought they all had to be destroyed. That they were going to exterminate humanity?" Corporal Manuta questioned.

"Most of what you have heard about AIs, is overblown folktales. There was never any evidence that the AIs were dangerous as a whole. Just like the Morphs, some wanted peace and some thought differently."

"No disrespect, Sir. You mean they wanted us dead, right?" Private Collins asked.

"You're right. But that was them. Those AIs do not exist. Chara is a CRA. He was part of the Child Replacement Program. His kind were programmed to replace a child whom a couple had lost. He's not a danger to humanity as a whole. You have my guarantee on that," John said.

"Yeah, but I never saw a child who could do what he does," Manuta said.

"That's right. So it's a good thing he's on our side. If the Nations heard about this they would destroy him. We would lose a valuable asset in our war against the Morphs. Answer me this guys. If you had a shit load of Morphs come to rip you apart, wouldn't you want Chara next to you?"

"He's got o' point there fellas," Sheamus said.

"Look. Here's the deal I'm offering. I need all of you to pledge to me now that you will reveal nothing about Chara to anyone outside this room. In return for that oath, each of you will receive a lifetime pension of 100,000 GMUs. That pension will begin when the Morph war is over. Just remember this, guys. The Roman Institute has eyes everywhere, long memories and a history of dealing justice to those who betray us. So before you sign on the dotted line, make sure you can keep your lips sealed," John said.

Louis talked to his men and after a few minutes he said, "We're all with you, John. We believe you wouldn't put us in danger and we understand the need for silence. We will all gladly sign the pledge." Louis looked at his men and the turned to John. "We want you to know why. First we need the money. Second we like Chara. He probably saved our lives. Third, it's because of you, John. We have always felt you had our best interest at heart. We know you wouldn't put us in danger and we'll follow you to hell if need be."

John looked at his men and told them, "I'm proud of all of you." He then ripped up the contract and held out his hand. "Your handshakes will be good enough for me." Everyone shook hands and John said to Sheamus. "You and Chara will be safe." John knelt next to Chara."You have to stop showing people what you can do, Chara. Listen to your Da. We want to keep you safe. Alright?"

Chara nodded and Sheamus hugged John. "Thank ya, laddybuck. I knew ya would come through for us."

"No problem Shea. I've got to get to the New Washington facility. I have to make sure Tamar is not part of this bullshit."

"Good luck, John. Ifin' ya need anything,' give us o' call."

Chapter Thirteen

Betrayal

About two weeks before John met Sheamus at the Europa facility, Tamar had entered the New Washington facility. There, she manipulated Celest Roman's compassion into believing her story of contrition and wanting to make things right. Celest, more concerned about David Roman's failing health and wanting to bring the family back together, succumbed to Tamar's pleadings.

"I can't thank you enough, Grammy Celest. I feel horrible about what happened to Lula. I tried to talk to her, but she doesn't want to speak to me. It's just that Mark had me convinced, like a lot of other people, that he was not the ogre John and Matt made him out to be. He was always nice to me and my sisters and brothers. But it was just an act, I guess. I can't sleep at night thinking how I might have gotten poor Lula killed."

"I believe you, Tamar. A lot of family members have kept nasty rumors about you and your family. To them I say,'shame on you.' I have always found you to be a very pleasant young lady. With all this madness happening around us, the Roman family must come together-not separate. I will talk to Lula. Your sister should not blame you for Mark's actions. In the meantime I have instructed the people here and told John that you are my guest and should not be harassed," Celest said as she hugged Tamar.

"Oh thank you, Grammy Celest." If anyone could have seen Tamar's face while she was hugging Celest back they would have seen a face full of hate and anger. But Tamar hid her feelings well.

With Celest's protection, Tamar was able to roam the complex freely. She basically had a green light to carry out Mark's plan. Her only problem was the three men John had following her. As it happened, one of those men, Sergeant Lance Jacobs, was a member of Mark's zealots. Over the years he had developed a hatred for the Roman clan and now he found his chance to help destroy them. The second man was easily seduced by Tamar's sexual appetite. He became Tamar's sex slave, doing whatever she wanted. The third man was silenced and fed to the Morphs.

Working with Mark's infiltrators, Tamar was able to set up a secret room where six infected podded and morphed. Tamar and her aides were feeding these Morph's by kidnapping and murdering several low level workers. They were also podding hand picked people and forty were ready to hatch. Just days before John was to return to the facility to see Celest and David, Mark sneaked into the unit. There he met Tamar.

"I see you have morphed the volunteers and some new recruits," Mark said to Tamar.

"Yeah. Well some weren't exactly volunteers. How the hell did you get him and his Morphs in here." Tamar said pointing to Anu and a Big male and female Morph.

"Oh, Tamar my dear. You would be surprised as to how many people want the world I am going to make or how many actually want to be Morphs. Also there are always those who will do anything for outrageous sums of money. Put all those factors together and add how many people hate the Romans. My God, I'm surprised they didn't let the whole Morph army in," Mark laughed.

"Glad to see you can hear me Tamar," Anu thought.

"Yeah. I can hear you big guy. So what's the next step, Uncle?" Tamar asked.

"You and these two Big Ms, take over the place, of course. I see you have at least fourty more pods ready to emerge. Keep podding. After this batch hatches I want you and the Big Ms to start taking over this place floor by floor. Infect as many people as you can. The whole place should be yours within two weeks. I just have to speak to my father and Celest. Then Anu and I are going out to begin the assault on the West Coast facility. Between, you and Victor and Kolla, we will control four of the most strategic Haven facilities on the planet. It will just be a matter of time before the others fall."

"Yeah, well, I know what you mean when you say you're going to talk to Celest. Do whatever you want with her, but remember, Lula is mine," Tamar said.

"Oh, my dear, I would never think of taking that pleasure away form you. She's all yours. Just make sure you wait until we're ready to make our presences known. Don't let that temper of yours blow our cover." Tamar thought for a moment and said, "Yeah, my temper. I'll wait, Uncle. But it won't be easy."

"Mark kissed Tamar on the lips and stuck his tongue down her throat, he felt her breasts with one hand and her crotch with the other. After he was finished groping her he said,

"That's my girl."

****

After giving Tamar her marching orders, Mark had David and Celest brought to him.

"Dad, how are you?" Mark asked.

"He's sick. Can't you see that?" Celest said. "Where are our guards? How were you able to get in here?"

"Oh, Celest. So many questions. Maybe you would like to ask my friend Anu some questions.?" Anu then came into the room.

"My God it's true. You are in league with these monsters," Celest said as she wrapped her arms around David. "Don't you dare hurt your father."

"Really Celest? Do you think this husk of a man, if you could call him that, is anything like my father. Do you think my father, David Roman, a great, energetic, brilliant man would want to live like this thing in front of me? Look at it. It doesn't even know his own name or where he is. That's not my father. It's a horrible joke. That *thing* needs to go. It soils the memory of David Roman." Mark knelt down and looked into David's eyes. "Dad, if you are in there somewhere, I know you would not want this." Mark kissed David on his forehead. "So, I will release you." Mark then nodded to Anu and David was picked up and Celest was thrown to the side. With Celest screaming, Anu tossed David to the Morphs, who preceded to devour David Roman. Celest ran to save David as she screamed even louder and cursed Mark, but was held back.

"John will find you and you will pay for this murder, you monster," Celest yelled.

'Well, maybe. But not today. Now, to you my dear. After my mother died, my father married you. The second John was born, he was no longer was our father. The Roman clan was now Dad, you and John."

"That's not true. I always loved you boys just as much as John. Your father was proud of all of you," Celest said.

"Oh, please. Spare me that old line. A mother can never love another woman's child like her own. I got it. Matt was ok with it. Luke was happy with any tid-bit of love you threw him. But I knew. I knew. So here, at last, is my way of showing you love."

"By tossing me to your creatures? Go ahead. I'm not frightened of death," Celest taunted.

"Oh, my dear, Celest. You always thought I was just some spoiled one dimensional little boy." Mark motioned to Anu. In a flash Anu bit Celest on the hand.

"You have just been given a dose of super Morph virus. You see, Morphs like Anu carry a strain of the Morph virus which speeds up the morphing process. It takes a lot out of him so he only uses it in special cases. You will be ready by tomorrow and you will hatch in a day," Mark said.

"What are...what.." Celest tried to talk but she was feeling the effects of the virus already.

"I'm going to pod you, Celest. You are going to become one of the so called monsters you hate. You will help us on the fight to take over the world," Mark laughed.

"No..n...nooo." Celest tried to speak."

"Yes, yes, yes," Mark said laughing. "Put her in there with the other five. She should pop in less that two days." Turning to Anu and the two Big Ms Mark thought, "Remember, if things go wrong we have the emergency plan. Tom, you make sure you have men ready to blow the escape routes. That will blast the mountain tops and our army can pour in from there. We only want to use that tactic as a last resort. Once those escape routes are blown, this place will no longer be impenetrable."

Tom Landly was one of Mark's close friends. He had been able to hear the Morphs since Anu bit him months ago. Tom had been working in close contact with Mark and had the codes for blowing the "code red" escape routes. Once ignited, a massive charge would blow the mountain tops on each side of the facility, allowing residents to escape up a flight of embedded stairs. This escape route was put in place by the Roman Institute in case of some uncontrollable incident where the residents could not access the top floor entrance. Mark, however, had decided to use it as a last resort in his bid to take over the facility. If Mark's plans were uncovered before he could Morph hundreds of infected people, then he would blow the escape route allowing for his Morph army to come in en-masse and take over the place.

"Tom, I'm leaving you in charge with Lugal and Nin for back up. They will keep the morphing going at a quick pace. They can also help you with obtaining subjects to morph and securing this floor. Within a week, you should be able to begin taking over floors. Start with the fifth and work your way up. When you hit the fourth, kill everyone you find. We don't need those weaklings for podding. It will also terrorize the ones on the third. Tell them if they surrender, they will be safe. Once they do surrender; kill them. We will have Morphs attack the top while you come up from the bottom. We should have complete control within ten days."

"Got it, Mark. You can count on us," Tom said.

"In the meantime, Anu and I are going to the West Coast facility. On our way we will destroy the New Washington zone and then the West Coast zone. We'll have lots of people to add to our army and lots of food for our Morphs." With the help of the many infiltrators Mark had placed in the New Washington facility, Mark and Anu slipped out unnoticed.

****

The next morning, unable to quell her thirst for revenge, Tamar made her way to the third floor where Lula was staying.

Ready to pounce on Lula, Tamar was taken aback when Luke opened the door. “What are you doin’ here Luke?” Tamar asked. I came to make sure Lula was alright. Why are you here. She doesn’t want to talk to you right now,” Luke said.

“Mark and his Morph buddies are taking over the whole place as we speak. So, I don’t give a fuck what she wants. Do you know she’s responsible for the deaths of the Twins, Castor, and Judith?” Tamar shouted. “I’m here to make her pay. Now where the fuck is she?”

“What the hell are you talking about?” Luke asked.

“Weren’t you in on the plans, Luke? Mark and his Morph buddies have been here for a while. I’ve been podding people for over two weeks. Mark’s going to rip through the place, kill everyone and take over. He is going to kill David and Celest if he hasn’t already.”

“Mark would never kill Dad,” Luke said.

“If you say so, Luke. But I’m here for Lula.”

Tamar, listen to me, Mark has been playing all of you for years. He just wants power. He cares nothing for any of you.”

“Right, like you do, hey?”

“What does that mean?”

“I’ll tell you what that means. We all knew you only truly loved, Lula. You are just as bad as the rest of the Roman fucks. You gave us lip service but your heart was always, Lula’s.”

“Even if that were true, why should Lula pay for that?” Luke asked.

"Someone has to pay for the pain. Do you really want it to be you?"

"If that is what it take for you to leave Lula alone, then yes. Do what you must," Luke said.

Tamar took out her knife and stated to walk toward Luke. "If you want to be a sacrificial lamb, fine. But I'm still going to rip that little twat in two. Before you ask why, the answer is I just fucking *HATE* her," Tamar screamed. "The bitch has always thought she was better than me, purer then me, more beautiful, more lovable, more *everything*. I'm fucking tired of her in the same world as me. One of us has to die or I will go insane."

At that moment Lula entered the room. "My God, Tamar. I had no idea I had caused you so much pain. Please forgive me," Lula pleaded.

"Forgive you? You think that will make everything alright? I'm going to stick this knife in your sanctimonious virgin twat and rip you open from crotch to throat. Then, you will be forgiven."

Tamar moved toward Lula ready to plunge her knife into her sister when Luke stepped in front of Lula.

"No, Tamar. This isn't you, It's Mark. I raised you. You're not this evil and vindictive," Luke said as he held Lula behind his back. "If you're this angry, then you should be taking that anger out on me."

"As you wish." Tamar then stabbed Luke in the chest and after pulling the knife out, stabbed him again. Lula screamed, "NOOO, DaD, No!" Struggling to stay awake, Luke fought back against Tamar. They wrestled to the ground with Luke finally taking and throwing Tamar's knife against the wall. As they wrestled some more, Luke began to lose consciousnesses. Tamar broke loose from his grip and stood. She looked over Luke and said, "You always were a weakling. Not like Mark. I fucked him, Luke. I fuck him a lot. It was good. He loves me. Now I'm going to kill your precious Lula. As soon as I find my kni….ahhhh."

"Here's your knife, bitch," Lula said, as she pulled the blade from Tamar's back. Turning around and seeing Lula with her knife, Tamar softly laughed as she put her hands on Lula's shoulders.

"Well..ahha...not..such..a...a...ahhh..a..perfect..little….ahhha" Was all Tamar could say before Lula stuck the knife into her heart. With eyes wide open, Tamar felt her life drain as she stared at the object of her hate. Her last thoughts being, "Why did I hate this girl so much?"After Tamar fell dead Lula knelt down next to Luke.

"Dad, I'm so sorry."

"It's ok, Lula. It's not your fault. She just lost her way. If anything it's my fault. I never stood up to Mark. I...I...do lov...love...you…tell...everyone...I'm..ahha...I'm...sorry," Luke moaned, with his last breath.

As Lula was crying for her loss, Matt and Jessie entered the room. "What the hell's going on Lula?" Matt asked.

"Tamar killed Luke. She wanted to kill me but, Da...Dad...saved my life."

"You mean she just up and decided to kill you?" Jessie asked.

"I don't know why she picked today. But before she died, she said Mark and his Morph friends were taking over the facility."

"What!!! How did Mark get in here? Are you sure she wasn't just telling you a tall tale to upset you? I find it hard to believe a coup has been happening and no one knows about it," Matt said.

"We didn't see any Morphs on our way in. Where are they?" Jessie asked.

"I overheard her talking to Luke before she killed him. Mark and she were podding people on the sixth level for a while now. Matt, she said Mark was going to kill David and Celest."

Matt grabbed Jessie by the shirt. "Son. We have to seal up the sixth level. Tamar came here about two weeks ago. John had her under surveillance. We know Mark has infiltrated some facilities with infected and non-infected people who are loyal to him. If she and Mark were able to keep this quiet, then we underestimated the scale of his infiltration."

"Holy shit. We need to get hold of John," Jessie said.

"Sure, but first we need to alert our security team," Matt said as he got on the emergency intercom. "Attention. Attention."

As Jessie stood by the door he could hear nothing over the intercoms.

"What the hell's going on? Why isn't it working?" Jessie asked his father.

"I don't know." Matt then took out his phone and tried to call John. He couldn't get a signal.

When Jessie's phone didn't work either Matt realized the comms had been jammed.

"We have to get to my office on the first level. We must alert John and our men. Do you know how many Morphs there are, Lula?" Matt asked.

"No. Tamar was too intent on killing me to tell me any more."

"Alright. We need to move. Come on. We'll take the stairs to the first floor. If they are jamming our phones and systems we are going to have to alert our people to be ready. We can't let the innocent residents on the third and fourth levels go without protection. We are gong to have to hold off this assault until I can get John to send reinforcements."

"Dad. Jane and Amy, the kids; Mom. They're all on the third level," Jessie said.

"I know, son. Which is why we must hurry."

As, Matt, Jessie, and Lula made their way to the stairs, a security team member shouted. "Halt or I'll shoot." Matt and the others turned to confront the young man.

"Look here, son. I'm Matthew Roman. We are under attack from Morphs. I need to get to my office and call for reinforcements."

"Just stay where you are, or I'll fire." The man then got on his radio and said. "This is corporal Gants. I have Matthew Roman and his son, and Lula Roman, Sir."

"Wonderful, dear boy. Bring them down to the sixth level. They'll make great Morphs," Mark responded.

Matt whispered to Jessie, “That was Mark. I’m sure of it. They are podding people on the sixth level.”

“I’m sure as hell not going to be turned into one of those things, Dad,” Jessie said.

“Easy. Just follow my lead. When I make my move, dive behind those trucks,” Matt whispered. “Hey soldier. Are you sure this is the way you want to go?” As he said this, Matt slowly pulled his phone out and set the internal alarm. He then threw the phone over the soldier's head and dove for one of the parked armored vehicles. The noise soon brought curious security people to the scene.

“What’s going on here? Sergeant Tome asked.

“Sergeant, look out!! That man is an agent of Mark Roman. They have infiltrated the facility,” Matt yelled.

Sergeant Tome didn’t have time to respond before Gants shot and killed him. Gants was able to kill two more soldiers before they took him down.

“It’s alright. The area is secure. You can come out,” Corporal Hines said.

“I’m Matt Roman. This is my son Jessie and my niece Lula. I must get to my office. Comms are down. We must reestablish them here and to the outside world. We know Mark and his Morphs are on the sixth level. I’m sure they are going to work their way up. We need to alert all personnel about the Morphs and that there are likely a lot of bad actors in this takeover. Just like that man. Infiltrators like him can cause horrific damage.”

“We understand, Sir. Let’s get you upstairs.”

****

As Matt and the rest of his group made their way to his office, Matt was continually rounding up people in order to put together some kind of defensive force. He was having little luck as he kept running into infiltrators.

“Corporal, take this man; What’s you name soldier?”

“Private Jones Sir.”

“Corporal Benson, take private Jones with you to the third level. Get hold of as many security people as you can. Let them know what’s going on and that headquarters will be my office on level one. They need to secure a comm link with me there. Even if they have to lay wire for a tel-com. Got it?”

“Yes, Sir.” the two men headed down the escalator, but at the bottom of the floor, Jones shot the corporal in the head and then blew himself up as he shouted, “We will rule the world.” The explosion closed the entrance to the third level.

“God damn,” Matt said. Just then there was a loud blast from the other side of level two.

“I think that was the other entrance Dad,” Jessie said.

“My God. Mark must have put every undercover agent he had in here.”

After the explosion Matt saw six armed men headed toward him and his group.

“Corporal Hines, give me your side arm. Be ready on my command,” Matt ordered.

“Mr Roman, Sir.” One of the men racing toward them yelled. “It’s me, Sir Sergeant Rodney.

Matt recognized Rodney and the two men shook hands.

“Good to see you Sergeant. I need to get to..”

“Yes, Sir. First level. We’ll get you there,” Rodney said.

“Right, but we also must secure the second level. Most of our ordinance is there. Have you been able to pick up anymore men? We have a force of one thousand people, Sergeant,” Matt said.

“Yes, Sir. But without comms, getting people organized is going to take some time. Also, as you know, Mark has put a lot of bad actors in among us. There are creating quite a dilemma. But we’ll get it done, Sir.”

“I would suggest you create six man teams who know each other. That way, they can watch each others’ backs. Any new comers or suspected individuals, I would disarm and use as supply and logistics workers. Keeping them under guard, of course,” Matt said.

“Yes, Sir. Easier said but we need to do something about these infiltrators. They can do far too much damage if we don’t get them under control,” Rodney replied.

Because even the T50’s were down, once in his office, Matt was able to reach John through a special comm link, made for just such an event as this. All outgoing communications were being jammed and some internal comms were also shut down by the enemy. Matt’s comm link acted on a different system hooked to a relay satellite the Roman Institute owned. It was top secret, and even Mark knew nothing about it. John answered on the second ring.

"John. It's Matt. I'm calling from the New Washington facility. Mark has initiated a take over of the place. The information we have at the moment is that he's on the sixth level with a contingent of Morphs. We are going to try to contain them. The last thing we want is for the Morphs to break through to the third and fourth levels. There are thousands of innocent residents on those levels. Most of the homes are on the second floors of levels three and four. It would be a massacre."

"I understand, Matt. Can they blow the fusion reactor? What's the situation with your security forces? Are you able to form an effective unit for defense?" John asked.

"I don't know at the moment. I can't see them doing any damage to the reactor. It would render the place useless to them. I'm sure they want it intact. Plus, there are only a handful of people who know anything about the reactor and its workings. Remember, John the fusion reactor can't 'melt down.' There would be a huge explosion, but the mega steel between floors would limit the damage to the sixth and fifth level. So if Mark set the reactor off, it would only harm them," Matt explained.

"Well, that's good news. Mark would never do anything to endanger his life. So it looks like we are going at this on a pure soldier to soldier action. What's your plan, Matt?"

"I am sending men to round up people but we have a lot of non-infected infiltrators here. So far they have caused havoc.

Everything from sabotage to murder. All it takes is one bad guy in a unit. When our guy's backs are turned, he lets loose on them. It's chaos."

"But can you hold them until we get there?" John asked.

"Yes, John. We'll hold them for as long as it takes. Just get us some reinforcements here, please."

"Dig in, Matt. We're airlifting a thousand of our people to the facility. They should be there within two or three hours at the most. In the meantime, I have fifty of my special response teams on the way. You can be sure none of them are Mark's people. Use them to isolate and terminate the traitors. They will be arriving within an hour," John said.

"Fantastic, John. We have set up in house comms with top side. Lieutenant Jeff Jackson is handling our forces. I'm in direct contact and our security cameras are working again. From here we can oversee and reestablish complete control of the place," Matt said.

"Good. As soon as you have complete control, use the special forces to protect the third and fourth level residents. By then our army should be there. I'm leaving now and will be there shortly. Hang in there, brother. I have the guys on conference call"

While talking to Matt, John had established a call with the Lads. "Guys, I want you all to head to the New Washington facility. It's in immediate danger of being overrun. I'm heading there now. After we have the place fully under control we're going to go to the West Coast facility. I am convinced Mark will attack Haven there. If he can get secure the entire West Coast, he can establish a base of operations we may never be able to conquer. He also may not be fully aware his plans for Europa and Uli wa Liánhé have failed."

"Ifin' they weren't outright diversions, boy,'" Sheamus said.

"You could be right, Shea. Make sure Chara comes with you. He may help picking out the non-infected traitors like he did the infected," John said.

"Will do, John."

"Bubba, I want you to stay at the West Coast facility with Renkins and Nick Smalls. Keep everyone on full alert. Go to a full code red."

"Will do, John," Bubba replied.

"Agni, if you are certain you can leave Acharya in safe hands, I would like you to come to New Washington. Depending on how badly Mark's Morphs hit the residents on levels three and four, we need your calmness and compassion to tend to those who have been traumatized."

"Oh, John. This humble servant will be most happy to help those in need," Agni replied.

"Great. See you all soon. And Bubba, we will all meet you as soon as we clear New Washington."

Suddenly, John and the Lads heard an explosion which seemed to shake the very comm links they were on.

"What ta bloody hell was that?" Sheamus asked.

"My God. I think they blew the escape routes," John said, "Matt, are you alright?"

"John. The whole place feels like we were hit buy an earthquake. The fuckers blew the ERP.

The Morphs are pouring into the escape route, and they're attacking up top at the same time. My men are having a hard time defending. There are too many bad actors killing our guys and causing havoc."

"Button up the underground facility. Your men up top are just going to have to hold as best they can. Troops will be there in less than an hour. Hold on brother. We're coming," John yelled.

****

Five minutes before Matt's call to John, Tom, on the sixth level, realized their presence was no longer secret. Two of Mark's security people had relayed to Tom that Matt and the others had blown their cover. Though they had tried to block the entrances to the fifth level, it was only a matter of time before overwhelming forces began to join the fight. There was already fighting happening on the surface between John's and Mark's people. Looking at Lugal and Nin, Tom thought, "We need reinforcements. We need to blow the tops off. Are the Negeltu ready?" Both Lugal and Lugal nodded their heads yes.

Tom entered the codes and voice activated the device. The explosion rocked the whole place.

The the mountain tops on both sides of the facility disappeared in a cataclysmic explosion. Debris rained down for what seemed minutes creating a dust cloud that hindered the defenders vision on the wall. After the dust and debris settled an army of Morphs started to pour down the stairs and were ready to kill or capture everyone in the place. They were howling and hungry. Up top, the men still loyal to John were fighting a war where the enemy was unidentifiable. Men were turning on men and killing each other. Major Frank Rogers, the base commander, and Sergeant Don Curtis were coordinating the defense of the facility's top side.

"Major, we have Morphs attacking the front gates," Sergeant Curtis said. Rogers looked at the A38 drones and could see what looked like ten thousand Morphs in the field coming straight at him.

"I see, Sergeant. Have all the towers pour it on. We need to get those three Eagle Hellfires up in the air. They can send a whole lot of pain the Morphs' way. Also, man the inner towers, just in case the Morphs breach the first gate."

"Yes Sir. The pilots are already warming their engines and they'll be up in three. Sir."

"Why are those two towers not engaging the enemy?"

Curtis looked and saw that the front towers were not putting any ordinance down field. He radioed the two men who were in those towers. "Tower, one and two, this is Sergeant Curtis why are you not engaging the enemy?"

"Hello Sergeant." The man in the first tower replied. "Why? Because we will rule the world."

Just then both towers turned their guns toward the inside of the base and started firing at John's men. Over the intercom,

Rodgers shouted. “Take cover. Take cover. We have two bad guys in the front towers, take cover.” While looking at his men Rodgers saw that some troops were turning on others and killing them. Curtis grabbed Rodgers by his arm and said, “Find Sergeant Blake.” Rodgers said to Curtis.

“You mean ‘Rifleman’?”

“Yep. The one and only. Tell him to take those two out now.” Curtis knew exactly how to get the ‘Rifleman’ to come to HQ. Over the comms Curtis yelled, “Rifleman. Two targets in first two towers. Code red dead. Rifleman. Two targets in first tw…”

Before Curtis could finish his sentence the first tower’s guy’s head exploded. An instant later the second man’s head disappeared.

“Thank you. Job well done,” Curtis said.

“Get people in those towers and have them send rounds down line,” Rodgers commanded.

“Sir, the Eagles.” Rodgers looked out and saw that as the three Eagles started to fire on the Morphs, the copters started to catch fire. In the next instant, they all exploded in three fire balls of total destruction.

“Jesus Christ. They must have been sabotaged,” Curtis said.

“That’s my guess,” Rodgers answered. He then got on the station’s comms and commanded.

“Listen close, everyone up top. We have been infiltrated by saboteurs and traitors. I want all you people to get into groups of three. Only join a group if you know the other two. All new comers to our corps must lay down their weapons immediately. Until we can check out your credentials, I will consider you a hostile. Now hear this. If you are friendly, then you will gladly lay down your weapons. If you do not, I and my people will take severe and swift action."

"Sir, Here is a list of all armed personnel who have joined in the last year." The list contained fifty names.

"Attention." Rodgers spoke. "I have a list of names who need to report to HQ immediately. When you report, you must lay down your arms and check in with command." Rodgers had Curtis call out the names. After the roll call Curtis announced, "If any of these people have been killed or wounded, bring their tags to HQ."

As Rodgers and Curtis were attempting to cull the traitors, John called in.

"Major Rodgers, I have some bad news. The troop transport has been blown up. We are grounding all flights until safety inspections can clear them. The good news is the special forces unit is going to be there in minutes. Their craft was under strict security so it remained safe."

"Thank you, John. We're going to need a lot of help. The Morphs are pouring through the blown ERPs and up top they are about to breach the first wall of the compound," Rodgers warned.

"Hang in there Rodgers. I…"

"Wait, Sir. I hear the chopper."

The special forces carrier landed inside the facility and immediately started to take positions.

"Let me get back to you, Sir. The special forces have landed. I need to coordinate with them, ASAP," Rodgers said.

"Give those Ms hell, Frank."

"Will do, Sir."

The special forces commander, Captain Grant Holmes, ran to Rodgers' HQ to get orders. Upon entering Rodgers' office, everyone saluted and Holmes said, "Major, this is Sergeant Mike Conners. Where do you need us?"

"Glad to have you, Captain, Sergeant. For one, we have infiltrator problems. So make sure your men only work with each other for now. We are trying our best to eliminate the traitors. We've lost our air power, so I could really use your men on the towers and sniper posts. The Morphs are about to breach the first wall and we want to keep them from doing that. We also have a problem on the fourth level. The Ms are pouring through the blown ERPs. If they get access to that level they will kill thousands."

"Alright, Sir. How about I send half my people to the fourth level and put half on the wall?" Holmes asked.

"I'd say that's our best bet. If we can take out all the bad guys in here, we can put together a force of at least nine hundred people. With your five hundred, I'm sure we can hold this place," Rodgers said.

"Yes, Sir. Let's get to it," Holmes said.

Holmes placed his people on the walls and their added firepower was helping to keep the Morphs from breaching the first wall, but, it was a losing battle as the Morphs simply had too large an advantage in numbers. While defending the top of the compound, the rest of Holmes people headed to the fourth level in order to stop the incoming Morphs from getting to the residents. Matt and Jessie were having some success in putting together a strong fighting unit. Sergeant Rodney led the facility's troops and the special forces units to the fourth level. There, they set up defenses at every entrance from the fifth level. The Morphs were coming through, but became bottle-necked, preventing the overrunning of facility's forces. During this chaos, Matt found out Dr. Cassandra Onassis was indeed on the fourth level. Matt relayed this to John.

"What the hell is she doing there?" John yelled.

"I have no idea, John. She asked supply for medical equipment and they asked me if I could verify her clearance. I can have someone get a line to her," Matt said.

"Yes, please. I must talk to her." Several minutes later Cass was able to talk to John.

"Cass why are you at the New Washington facility? Furthermore, why are you on the fourth level. Don't you know the Morphs are trying to get to all of you. Get out of there. We can't afford to lose you. I can't lose you."

"John, I came here because I was following a lead on the virus. I now know that the lead was coming from the sixth floor and it was Mark's doing. However, now that I'm here, I can't just abandon these people," Cass said.

"Cass, please. We have people for that. The Morphs have blown the ERPs. We don't know if we can hold them off. Top-side is fighting tooth and nail to keep the Morphs from breaching the first wall."

"Well, in that case it wouldn't make much sense for me to go up top." Cass replied.

"You could at least get to the first floor. You'll be safe there until I arrive."

"So the great John Roman is going to save us all?"

"Goddamn it, Cass. I don't care about saving anyone but you," John yelled.

"John, that's sweet. Believe me, I feel the same way about you. But we both know our position of privilege means we must think of others first. If there is time for us then we will use it well. But for now we are obligated to care for these people first. Last man off the ship sort of thing," Cass laughed.

"Yeah, my brain knows you're right; but my heart says to hell with the world if it meant losing you."

"You won't lose me, John. We'll win this war. Now, get off the phone and give these bastards hell."

John hung up the phone and made a promise to himself: If they survived, he would ask Cass to marry him. He knew she was the one and he was going to do everything in his power to make sure she stayed alive.

****

Soon after John's call to Cass, he and the Lads landed at the New Washington facility.

John and the Lads entered HQ. "Major Rodgers, this is Sheamus O'Keefe, Agni, and Shea's son Chara. We think he can root out any bad actors that remain in the compound."

"Aye. Ya better believe it. Give me some men ya can trust ta watch our backs and we'll go through the whole lot, yer lordship."

"Sure. Sergeant Curtis, take these two and hook up with Holmes. Make sure we use his people."

""Yes, Sir. Come this way," Curtis said to Sheamus.

"Good, Shea and Chara will take care of that. Major how's the defense holding?"

"Take a look for yourself. The bodies are piling up on the outside and inside of the first wall. I think we're going to have to pull back to the second wall," Rodgers said.

"I agree. Sound retreat to the second wall so we don't lose anymore men. Have the second wall cover the first's retreat," John said.

"On it," Sergeant Curtis replied.

"I have some good news. Major. Johnny, you out there?"

John's escort was flying an Eagle hellfire. Captain Johnny Ray piloted the hellfire and he was ready to get into action.

"Captain Johnny Ray here, ground. I have a full ordinance load. Where do y'all want it? Over."

John handed over the comm mike to Major Rodgers.

"Captain Ray. This is Major Rodgers. Are you sure your chopper is safe? We had all three of ours blow up, in air. Over."

"Good to meet you, Sir. Don't worry, y'all, I'm almost as good a mechanic as a pilot. I've gone through this baby front to back. Now, where you want my load? Over."

"Take out everything you can between the two walls. Then dump the heavy stuff outside the main wall. Over," Rodgers said.

"Rodger wilco, Sir. Over and out." Ray then turned his Eagle and ran a sweep around the entire facility between the two walls. His GAU-40 Gatling guns sent hundreds of explosive and phosphorus rounds down field. As he circled the facility Ray was able to knock back much of the hoard and give the defenders time to regroup and reload. All around the compound, cheers could be heard from the people fighting on the walls.

After a few runs, Johnny Ray called into HQ. "That's it for the light stuff, Sir. I'm going to dump the heavy loads on the hoard outside. Over."

Ray proceeded to fire GMac 70 mm air-to-ground rockets, Hellfire, Stinger and Spike missiles into the hundreds of Morphs attacking the compound.

"Yeeehaa. Look at them fuckers fly into pieces." Ray yelled over his radio. After two runs, he called in. "That's all she's got, Sir. Do ya'll have any ordinance left that wasn't sabotaged? Over."

"Yes, we sure do, Captain. You just gave us some new life. Come on in. We can reload your bird. Over," Rodgers said.

"Be right there, Sir. Over."

“We can’t thank you enough, John,” Rodgers said.

“No need to thank me, Major. We’re all in on this. Besides, the Morphs are sure to regroup. What’s the state of our ammo and the fourth level?” John asked.

“What my people tell me is we can fully reload the Eagle Hellfire again. I have sent half of the special forces to the fourth level. They tell me the Morphs are starting to break through but they have set up heavy ordinance at all entrees from the fifth level. I just don’t know how long we can hold them, John,” Rodgers said.

As Rodgers and John were planing the defense, Chara noticed a suspicious-looking man walking toward Captain Johnny Ray. Chara’s sensors detected what the man had under his coat and immediately ran out of HQ. All eyes turned to Chara as he jumped the railing and landed easily after the twenty foot fall. In the blink of an eye, Chara intercepted the man and started to whirl him around as if he were throwing a shot-put. After several blindingly fast spins, Chara launched the man over the second wall. As soon as the suicide bomber landed he exploded in a loud fiery blast, killing dozens of Morphs. Captain Ray and everyone in HQ stood frozen, staring at Chara. Suddenly, Major Rodgers broke the silence.

“What the hell was that?”

“Ahh, Major darlin.’ That there was me son savin’ yer pilot. That what that was, yer lordship,” Sheamus said proudly.

“What the hell do you mean, son? No human I know can throw a man over a hundred yards. Especially a boy. John, What’s going on here? Tell me this isn’t what I think it is.” Rodgers asked.

"Major. Do you trust me?" John asked.

"Of course," Rodgers replied.

"Then trust me when I say Chara is on our side. We'll talk about this after we secure the place. I promise. But right now, our focus needs to be on defending this facility and saving our people from a massacre." Major Rodgers looked at Sergeant Curtis and Captain Holmes. Though they seemed worried they all knew that John was right.

"Good. I'm heading to the fourth level. Get that Eagle up asap. I'll let you know the situation below as soon as I get there." John said, as he left. As John descended to the fourth level, Captain Johnny Ray took the Eagle hellfire up.

"Major Rodgers, this is Captain Ray. I'm going to repeat the run since we did so much *beaucoup* damage to those fuckers. Out."

"I usually don't permit vulgar language over comms, Captain. But because of what you've done for us, I'll give you a pass. This one time. Over," Rodgers said.

"I do thank you kindly, Sir. Now I'm about to spoil these fuckers' afternoon. Out."

Ray then proceeded to strafe the entire hoard of Morphs between the walls. As he was coming about for his second run, he got too close to the ground and a Big M hurled an M60 machine gun at his chopper. The weapon slammed into Ray's tail rudder and sent the Eagle into a spin.

"Ahhh. Huston we have a problem. I'm going down and I don't think I can make it back over the wall." Ray tried everything he could to stabilize the craft but he was not to be able to get control. The Morphs sensed his dilemma and were running to where he would crash. Ray knew he could set the bird down without too much damage but he didn't care to think about his fate in among the Morphs. Johnny Ray pulled his service pistol and thought, "Well I got nine bullets, better keep count and save the last." As Captain Ray was going down, Chara was listening to everything. He jumped up on the wall and ran along it, keeping pace with Ray's chopper. Sheamus yelled after Chara.

"Son!! Where ta hell ya going now? Please, come back here lad." But Chara didn't listen. He followed the chopper and when he saw Ray set the Eagle down he jumped off the wall and onto the top of the Eagle Hellfire. Ripping one of the props off the bird, Chara started to swing the mega steel blade chopping off head after Morph head. Ray, seeing what was happening climbed out of the chopper and started shooting Morphs. Chara turned, saw Ray, and immediately grabbed him and leapt the forty feet up to the top of the wall. He then jumped down with Ray in his arms and gently put him on the ground. Ray stood dumbfounded and then said.

"My friend, that's the second time you saved my life today. If you ever need anything, just call on me. Johnny Ray never forgets a debt."

****

As John made his way to the fourth level he stopped and talked to Matt. "Have you been able to separate the bad guys?"

"We are, but it's costing us men and time," Matt said.

"Alright. I think I have someone who can help." John then called Sheamus. "Hello, Shea. Where are you and Chara? We need you both down here on level one."

"Yeah. About that Johnny boy. Chara just did another magic trick and saved ta pilot by jumpin' inta ta Morphs and leapin' back up ta wall with ta pilot under his arms. So me thinks our secret is out boyo.'"

"Yeah, but we can't worry about that now, Shea. You two get down here and see if Chara can separate the traitors like he did the infected. I'm headed to the fourth to find Cass. You hook up with Matt. He'll tell you what he needs from Chara."

"Will do me friend," Sheamus said.

John headed for the fourth and when he got there he immediately found Cass. He gave her a hug and a kiss which she returned with passion. John could hear the gun fire and loud commotion of the residents who were screaming in fear and the battle that was raging at the entrances from the fifth level.

"We have to get you to safety, Cass. The Institute and the world can't lose a mind such as yours." John pleaded.

"John. Please. I know how you feel about me and I'm pretty sure I feel the same way. But now is not the time. These people need help. They're panicking. I just can't leave them to their fate. Besides, it's you who is the important one."

“Stop, Cass. That’s just the hype the Institute has put out all these years. I’m…”

“No, John. I’m not talking about that. It’s your blood,” Cass said.

“What about my blood?” John asked.

“I told you before. Because your mother had the Baylor parasite and your father was exposed to the Sweats you carried those two pathogens in you. When you were bitten by the Morph, so you could communicate with them, you contracted a form of the Morph virus. The combination of the three turned your blood and your physiology into something between human and Morph.”

“What the hell does that mean?”

“It means that *you* are one of a kind and could be the only answer we have for creating a vaccine against the Morph virus. Your blood, John is the world’s most valuable asset in the war on the Morph virus. It’s *you* the world, and I, can’t lose,” Cass finished. As John was processing the information Cass had just given him, the screams of the people cause him to snap out of his stupor.

“We have to get these people up to the next floor. I’ll make a deal. You go to the third floor exits and help as many people to the top as you can, and I’ll make sure I don’t get killed.”

“Deal.” Then Cass gave John a deep passionate kiss and said, “When this is done we’re going to have to consummate this affair.”

“I’m all for that. I’m going to get Shea down here with Chara. We think Chara can sort out the bad guys.” John motioned for five of the special forces people to accompany Cass to the third level exits. "Make sure you keep her safe, guys."

John then got on the comms and called Sheamus. "Shea. Cass is at the forth level exits to the third. Make sure Chara sorts out the traitors and gets as many women and children up to the third level."

"We're already here, boyo.' I'll make sure me boy takes out every last one o' those dirty traitors." Chara began to scan the soldiers and his sensors could pick out those whose heart and adrenal glands betrayed their true loyalty. As Chara and Sheamus made their way to the fourth level, Chara had found no deviations in any soldier's physiology. However, when the two hit the third level, Chara sensed three people with high levels of adrenal and heart rates.

Chara typed on his phone. "Da, those two there. They are traitors. There is also one on the second floor."

"Ok son." Sheamus relayed the information to the four special forces people with him. They quickly took out the two one the first floor of the third level. Sheamus and Chara went to the second floor where, as with the other levels, all housing was located. There, Chara found the third traitor. When the person saw Sheamus and Chara he pulled out a gun and began to fire. Chara quickly stepped in front of Sheamus and stopped all the bullets. He then ran to the shooter and broke the traitors neck. Sheamus ran to Chara and said.

"My God, son. Are ya hurt, boy?" Chara smiled and shook his head. He then typed. Sheamus looked on in awe as Chara pulled the bullets out of himself, and the holes the bullets had made when they hit Chara seemed to disappear. Sheamus hugged Chara and wiped a tear from his eye as he said. "I love ya dearly, son. I always will and I will let no one harm ya. Ya have me word, son" The two then went to the fourth level and cleared the first and second floor.

"Matt. This here be Sheamus O'Keefe. Ta whole place has been cleared of ta dirty foul traitors. Ya can fight without worrin' about bein' shot in yer backs."

"Thank you, Shea. I'll spread the word to everyone," Matt said.

Sheamus and Chara met Cass on the fourth level and began moving the women and children up to the third level.

"My God Shea, how are we going to fit all these people on the third level? It's already overcrowded," Cass asked.

"We'll start with ta women and wee ones. Then we'll just keep movin' them up."

"But there is a battle going on up top. We can't just send these civilians into that horror," Cass said exasperated.

"Look, here, Cass." Sheamus whispered. "You're suppose ta be helpin' these here people. You be doin' them no good ifin' ya start ta panickin,' now.'"

"I know Shea, I know. I'm just worried for them."

"I know, dear lady. I know. So, let's say we show these here frightened people ta calm, cool collective Cassandra Onassis I be knowin.'" Cass nodded yes and soon regained her composure and started moving people up to the third level.

****

John and some of the special forces had reached the fifth level entrances and were in a fierce battle to hold the Morphs back from gaining a foot-hold on the fourth level.

"Get that ammo and some more heavy gear up here. NOW!!" John shouted. "Sergeant Blake, throw every charge you have into that hole."

"It's going to make a hell of a lot of fragments, Sir," Blake yelled.

"Then give me the unit to set it off and get these people back. Go to the other side and pile all you go there. As soon as I blow this I'll…"

"No need, Sir. I'll blow her," Blake smiled.

"Ok, get to it." John turned to the special unit forces, "Take cover. As soon as this goes off, pour every bullet you have into that hole." John got behind a pile of sand bags and as the Morphs started to come through in numbers he set off the charges. The explosion sent body parts and metal fragments everywhere. The noise was deafening. For a minute, John couldn't hear anything. When he finally looked over the sand bags all he saw was complete devastation, smoke and moaning Morphs. But in minutes he heard more Morphs clamoring through the debris.

"Goddamn it. They just keep coming." John was running out of ideas and hope. All he could do was to keep firing into the hoard of Morphs. When he thought of what they would do to Cass he got even madder. John grabbed an M60 and started to fire point blank at the monsters glaring at him with hungry eyes.

"COME ON you fucks. Come and get it." John's weapon ran dry and the men around him were starting to fight hand to hand in some cases. All John could think about was running to Cass and trying to save her. But he didn't give in to his heart. He couldn't abandon his people. Suddenly, there was a shift in the movement of the Morphs. They started to go backwards. The howls were discernibly different to John's ears. Something was happening. John called up to HQ.

"Major Rodgers. What's happening up there?"

"Sir, it seems the Morphs are fighting each other." Rodgers said.

"Major. Listen very carefully. Don't shoot any Morphs outside the first wall. Kill any Morph between the walls. Wipe them out. But remember, shoot none outside the first wall. Do you understand?"

"Not really, Sir. But I'll pass the orders along," Major Rodgers answered.

"The other Morphs are led by Archieréas. He's on our side, Major. The Morphs down here are retreating. I suspect Archieréas and his Maketes Morphs are fighting Anu's Ursang Morphs. It's a Morph civil war we are watching, Major. Archieréas' Anaptýsso clan against Anu's Negeltus. I'm coming up." John then ran up to the third where he grabbed Sheamus and Chara. "You two. Follow me.

Archieréas and the Anaptýsso are fighting Anu's bunch."

"Well I'll be o' stoned cold sober fella ifin' that ain't o' bonafide miracle, boyo,'" Sheamus said.

As the three them were making their way up top, John saw Cass. He ran to her, hugged and kissed her. "It's over Archieréas and the Anaptýsso have come to our rescue. You can get these people back to their homes. I'll see you later. I have to go up top."

"Be careful, John. I wouldn't want to lose you now," Cass said.

"Never," John replied.

Major Rodgers had ordered his people to kill everything in between the walls. Morphs were no longer coming over the first wall and the ones who were between the walls realized they were getting no support. Some of them tried to go back over but they were cut down by the special forces who now had an open field of fire. Rodgers' people rained down ordinance upon the trapped Morphs. Before it was over, there were at least 50,000 Morphs lying dead and dying between the walls of death.

"Rodgers and Curtis scanned the carnage and Rodgers noted, "Jesus Christ, Curtis. I know they want to kill us but this was just a bloody massacre."

"Well, Sir. I say 'Better them then us.' A few minutes ago that could have been us."

"True, Sergeant. But remember, it was Morphs who saved us."

****

As John, Sheamus and Chara emerged from the underground facility, they headed immediately to HQ. “Do we have any T38 drones, Major?” John asked.

“No, Sir, they have all been destroyed or sabotaged,” Rodgers answered.

John and Chara climbed to the roof of HQ and scanned the field. Chara was able to differentiate the two clans. He texted John, “The Morphs coming in from the east are Anaptýsso. The ones coming in from the west are Negeltu.” John immediately called down to Rodgers.

“Major, now that you have control of the first wall, get your people up there and start hammering the Morphs coming in from the west. There are the enemy. Don’t shoot anything east or in the middle,” John ordered.

“Got it, John. I will relay that info.” Rodgers said.

Between the large number of Archieréas’ Morphs and Rodgers’ people firing into the enemy Morphs, the battle quickly turned bad for Anu and the Negeltu. They retreated south and as they disappeared into the forest, Anu turned and made eye contact with Archieréas. “This is not over, Archieréas,” Anu thought.

“Unfortunately, my brother, you are right,” Archieréas responded.

****

The next day as the dead were removed from the field, John and Archieréas met to talk.

"I apologize for you having to leave the Anaptýsso outside the compound. But people are a little jumpy and angry. I don't want anymore bloodshed, Archieréas," John thought.

"I understand, John," Archieréas thought. "Unfortunately, most humans don't share your

open- mindedness."

"I will do everything in my power so they see we can live in peace."

"I as well, John Roman."

"We have to fix this place. But me and the Lads are going to the West Coast facility. I believe, Mark will try to take over our Haven facility there. He wants to establish the whole West Coast as a permanent holding. He must know by now that all his other plans have failed miserably."

"Yes. But madmen can become even more dangerous when they fail. They can't take the humiliation," Archieréas thought.

"You caught on quickly as to how humans act."

"The Anaptýsso have had to in order to survive. Besides, we were once human ourselves, right?"

Yes. I hope to see you soon." John put his hand out and the two shook.

****

A while later, John found Cass. “I’m so relieved you’re ok, “John said as he hugged Cass.

“Come on.” Cass led John to her apartment on the second floor of the third level. There she turned and kissed John. “Do you think the Major and Sheamus can do without you for awhile?”

The two undressed and made love for the rest of the day.

Chapter Fourteen

Armageddon

Before John and his team left for the West Coast Haven facility, Sheamus, Chara, Agni, Matt and Jessie headed for the New Washington Zone to see if there were any survivors. Matt and Jessie were accompanied by a team of special forces; but when everyone got there, Sheamus, Chara and Agni went off on their own.

"Shea. Can you tell this humble servant where we are going? Do you think it's safe out here without the armed forces?" Agni asked.

"Ach. Don't worry about nothin,' me little friend. Them there Morph fellas are long gone. Besides, we have me son here. If any o' those heathens dare show their ugly red faces, he'll make them wish they never done morphed," Sheamus laughed.

"Ch no le an hu Ag or Da." Chara said.

"I know yer won't let anyone hurt us, me lad," Sheamus said as he patted Chara's head.

"Now then. It should be over here some place." Sheamus searched through the overgrown brush and weeds, Chara said, "Da." Sheamus ran over to Chara and saw him pointing at the cemetery he was looking for. "Ahh. Well done lad. Well done. Now let me find that there grave," Sheamus said as he started to comb the headstones looking for a particular name. After a quick search he found what he was looking for. "There now. Here it be." Sheamus brushed all the weeds aside and uncovered the headstone. Agni and Chara looked and Agni said, "Here lies Dr. Timothy O'Mara. Beloved…" I can't read any more. It's all been eroded."

"No matter-this be it," Sheamus said.

"But why this grave?" Agni asked.

"Well now. Here be ta story. Me great great granda was a bounty hunter, just like his great granda."

"Excuse this humble servant. Your ancestors were bounty hunters?"

"Well me great great granda, Sheamus O'Keefe ta third was. Now, his great granda was Sheamus O'Keefe ta first he was. He came to Tsalaki in 1875 from ta ole country, Ireland. Course Tsalaki was called America back then. Now, Granda ta first had many jobs, he did. He were o' Marshal, cattle rustler, gunslinger, Texas Ranger and many other occupations both inside and outside ta law."

"But what has that to do with this grave?" Agni asked.

"Now, now Agni, me lad. I'll be gettin' ta that. Never ask an Irishman ta hurry up o' story. Tis bad etiquette and might get ya into o' donnybrook with ta story teller. Now, ta continue." Sheamus sat beside the grave. Chara sat with him. "Me great granda was a bounty hunter and had chased a very bad man into a state that back in the old days was called Rhode Island. It happened ta be ta smallest state in all America."

“Is the smallness why they called it Rhode Island?” Agni asked.

“Why would ye think that now, Agni me lad.?”

“Well. Because it was so small I thought it consisted of one big road going across its island.”

“No. No yer, blitherin’ idiot. It were o’ state, not an island. Forget ta name; tis not important. So ta continue. Me Granda tracked this here bad fella and got him. But in ta process, the bloody bastard shot me granda. Well, bounty huntin’ in Rhode Island were illegal back then. So me granda couldn’t go ta the authorities. But me granda’s brother told him about o’ kind doctor by ta name o’ Timothy O’Mara. A true son o’ Ireland he was. So me granda ups and goes ta this here O’Mara and quick as ya please he fixes up me granda and doesn't rat him out to ta dirty coppers. For his kindness, me granda gave him o’ bottle of ta finest Irish whiskey he had. O’ hundred year ole blend it were.”

“That is a good story. So you are here to pay your respects?” Agni asked.

“Well, yes. But there’s more to it then that. If ya quit interruptin’ there, boyo.’ Well, ya see, poor O’Mara here was takin’ by ta Sweats. As bad as the Great melt were, Tim’s family were left destitute. So, me granda came back and buried Tim and then he left O’Mara’s family the entire amount of his bounty. It were o’ considerable sum I might add. Then, when ta seas were risen and threaten ta put Tim’s grave under ta mighty ocean, me granda had him moved here.”

"Oh very nice story…."

"Will ya shut yer pie hole lad?" Sheamus turned to Chara. "Son. Do yer thin' for yer Da."

Chara then began to dig up the grave of Timothy O'Mara. As he hit the coffin Sheamus said, "That's good, son. Now let me down there." Sheamus jumped into the hole and carefully lifted the lid. There beside the bones of the doctor who saved his grandfather's life was a bottle of hundred year old Irish whiskey. The note attached to it read, "Because this great man saved me life, the O'Keefe progeny will continue. Ifin' it be an O'Keefe who opens this here grave, make sure ya salute ta man who made it possible for ya ta be here." Signed, "Sheamus O'Keefe. ta third." Sheamus opened the bottle of whiskey and before he took a drink he poured a little on to O'Mara's bones.

"Here's ta ya, me friend. Though I never met ya, I'm here because o' ya. Sleep well, boyo.'" Chara filled the grave in and Sheamus handed Agni the bottle.

"This humble servant doesn't usually drink. But for this." Agni then tipped the bottle and took a long swig. After coughing a bit, Agni said, "Agni promises to never interrupt a story of yours again."

"A wise decision, lad.' O' wise decision."

****

At the West Coast facility, Matt and Jessie were sent to the Pacific zone. The plan was to get as many people moved in to the West Coast Haven Project as could fit. No one wanted to see a massacre as happened to the New Washington zone. John had sent Major Dewy Jones and a thousand special forces to aid Matt and Jessie in their evacuation efforts.

At the same time Matt and Jessie were rerouting the settlers in the Pacific zone, John and his friends made it to the West Coast facility. There the surviving Lads had a reunion.

"Ach now. There be me brother from another mother he is," Sheamus said to Bubba.

"Look what I brung ya dear fella. Tis here be o' hundred year old bottle o' pure Irish whiskey now."

"Yeah but it looks half empty," Bubba said.

"Well yeah. I had to give o' little ta o' man who provided it, God rest his soul. Agni here was eager ta try some and I of course wanted ta make sure tis weren't poisoned now."

"So you brought me a half filled bottle of Irish whiskey?" Bubba asked.

"That I did, boyo.'"

Bubba grabbed the bottle and turned it to his lips. He gulped down the entire content of the whiskey bottle. Sheamus looked on in horror but said nothing. After Bubba was done he wiped his mouth and said, "Ohhh. Thank you Shea. That hit the spot. Here you can keep the bottle as a souvenir."

"Now what ta hell would Sheamus O'Keefe be wantin' an empty bottle o' whiskey, ya bloody glutton?"

"This humble servant is so glad to see you, Bubba," Agni said.

"It's good to see you, little fella." Bubba turned to leave the office and said,

"Let's go meet our two new guys, Renkins and Smalls, and see how you like them."

"Yeah. I want ta size up those two meself. They been working both sides for quite a while. I want ta look inta their eyes."

"You think your mysterious gaze will do the trick, Shea?" Bubba asked.

"Ifin' it don't, I can always just kill'em," Shea said. As the Lads crossed the yard they came upon Leroy and Nick sunning themselves on hammocks between two trees.

"So!! This is where you two have been loafing," Bubba said.

"Hey Bubba. We fixed the plumbing in the two bungalows and we unplugged the drain that was keeping the garden from getting watered. We just had some rest coming so we picked these hammocks," Nick said.

"Nothing against taking a deserved breaker, now is there boss?" Renkins asked."

"No, not if you deserve it, but I sent you two out here five hours ago. You're telling me it took you five hours to unplug two toilets and a small drain?" Bubba asked.

"That's right." Renkins said as he stood up and walked over to Bubba. The two men stood at exactly eye to eye level "Now some people work more methodical and precise than others. It takes longer," Renkins said.

"Bullshit. I saw you get to it like a bat out of hell. You were more likely done in an hour and have been lying here four hours. Tell the truth Nick. Nick held his head down but raised it and said, "Leroy's right," Nick said, not wanting to go against Renkins.

"Alright. Well now you got Agni here to help you. He might be able to speed things up.

"We don't need extra help. Take him with you," Renkins yelled.

"No. Agni is your supervisor now, so listen to him and do what he says, "Bubba said. "We need all three hundred of these sand bags on top of the inner wall by the end of the day."

"That's impossible!!!" Renkins yelled.

"Oh no, dear Mr Renkins. This humble servant has calculated that if we all carry three bags every five minutes for eight hours, we will actually have all the bags placed in time."

"Yeah, but when's break?"

"Oh, there will be no break. However, after job is done, we have four-hours for sleep and to eat and then we do other wall in front," Agni smiled.

"Fuck that. Get someone else for this bullshit. I owned a town. I took care of thousands of people. If you think I'm going to be some ni…."

"Shut the fuck up." Bubba said as he grabbed Renkins' shirt. "I broke and then killed a man for that word. You want to join him?" Bubba yelled.

"In case you didn't notice ass wipe," Leroy said as he pulled away from Bubba's grasp, "I'm black motherfucker."

"Please. Please. This is a new world. We must stop with the name calling and hate. You two should be friends. It hurts this humble servant that you both use the language of the past. The language of the white world. The ones who made you slaves. Why let them still control your thoughts and actions. Release yourselves from their grasp," Agni pleaded, putting himself between Bubba and Renkins. Bubba looked down at Agni and then smiled.

"You're right, little fella. I'm sorry, Leroy. Look just do the best you can. If the Morphs attack we need these sand bags to help hold them back. John believes in you. But you can't expect to be given command of anything when you haven't proven yourself. Give it some time. Show us you're one of us, and promotion will come."

"Alright. Alright. I get it. Everyone has to start at the bottom. Hell, it wouldn't be the first time. Right, Nick," Renkins said as he slapped Nick on the back. "But I'm not going to be doing grunt work for long. Just let your boss know that."

"I assure you, Renkins, that John knows just how valuable you could be for this place and the fight we have coming. He knows and he will be calling on you and Nick. But right now we need those bags on the wall. That's what we need from you two. Can I count on you both?" Bubba asked.

"Yeah. We'll get it done," Nick said enthusiastically. But then Renkins looked at him and Nick pulled back.

"Well, it seems Nick here is eager." Renkins looked at Bubba and the two stared into each others' eyes. Finally Renkins spoke. "Yeah. We'll get it done. You have my word."

"That's good enough for me," Bubba said as the two men shook hands.

Later, while Renkins and Nick were cleaning up parts from the repair shop, a little blond girl, about eight or nine, wandered into the bay. "Excuse me. Can you help me? I'm lost." Jenny said.

Renkins looked down and said, "Where are your parents, kid?"

"The monsters ate them," Jenny said sadly.

"Oh, crap," Renkins said under his breath.

"Uhhh. Ok, kid. Sit down. We'll get you some help," Renkins sighed.

The girl kept staring at Leroy as he worked. "Mister. Can you be my dad?"

"Whoa. Whoa. I don't think I'd make a good dad, kid." Nick laughed at Renkins who turned back and asked. "What's so funny, Nick?"

"The thought of you being a dad. What could be more hilarious?" Nick replied.

"Yeah," Renkins chuckled. "I hear that."

"Please, Mister, I won't be bad," Jenny said as she started to tear up.

"Hey. Hey. Easy kid. Look my name's Leroy Renkins. What's your name, honey?"

Jenny sniffed and dried her tears then said, "My name's Jenny Gunnarsson. I live with my aunt now, though she's not really my aunt."

"Holy shit; that last name's a mouthful," Nick said.

"Nick. Go find someone who can...you know," Renkins said as he eyed Jenny.

"Got it, boss."

When Nick left, Renkins asked Jenny why she wanted him to be her dad.

"Because, Mr. Renkins, you look like a superhero. I always thought my dad was a superhero. I miss him so much."

"Why do you think I'm a superhero, Jenny? You don't know me. You just met me."

"Oh. A person can always spot a hero. You're tall and have those big muscles. That's means you protect innocent people who are not as strong. You also have such beautiful skin. That helps in being a hero. It means that inside you're good."

"Wow. That's a heavy load," Renkins said.

"Yes. Mr. Renkins. Heroes are always carrying a heavy burden. That's another reason they're heroes. Most people give up when things go wrong, but not superheros."

"Hey. Jenny. You can call me Leroy."

"That's kind of you but I can't call you that until you're my dad. So. Will you be my Dad? I'm scared all the time. I hear grownups talk about the monsters and they're always scared. But they tell me not to be. How can I do that when they are so scared?"

"Yeah. I see your point. You're pretty grownup yourself for someone so little," Leroy said.

"People tell me that. But I lost my mom, dad and brother in one day. When the people rescued me, I also lost Becky. I had to grow up fast. But if you were my dad, I could still be a child for awhile. Because I'd be safe with you."

"Who was Becky?"

"She was my doll. I had her all my life. She was my best friend."

"Really," Renkins said as he looked around the shop. "Wait here a minute."

Leroy quickly put together a doll out of parts and trash he found and handed it to Jenny.

"How does this look, Jenny? She may not be as pretty as Becky." Though, Renkin's *creation* looked more Frankenstein than doll, Jenny was happy.

"Oh no, Mr Renkins. She's beautiful," Jenny said as she hugged the doll.

"What are you going to name her, Jenny?"

"Oh...I think, Didi. She was the woman who saved me."

"That sounds like a real good name," Renkins said as he smiled.

At that moment Nick came back with a child safety representative.

"Come on, Jenny. We need to get you back to the shelter," The social worker said.

"NO! I want to stay with, Mr. Renkins," Jenny cried.

"No back talk; now come. Don't be a bad girl. You know what happens to bad girls. This is no place for you." The worker grabbed Jenny by the arm hard and the little girl cried out in pain.

"Hey!! Back off motherfucker," Renkins said "The kid is scared enough as it is. She doesn't need you grabbing and threatening her."

"Right. I think your foul language proves my point," the worker said.

Leroy looked at Nick. "Watch the kid." Renkins then stood up and grabbed the worker and took her outside. As he eyeballed the woman he said, "Look here, you fucking cunt. If you don't treat the girl with kindness and respect I'm going to toss you over that fucking wall one night when nobody is around to stop me. You got it cunt?"

The terrified woman nodded yes. Stepping back into the repair shop, Renkins knelt down to Jenny. "Honey, you have to go with this woman for now. But listen. If she doesn't treat you right, you come back here and let me know. Ok?"

"Yes, Mr. Renkins. Can I come visit you?"

Renkins looked up at the worker and said, “Of course, Jenny. In fact, Miss…” Renkins looked back at the women. “Pentill,” The woman said.

“Miss Pentill here will make sure and bring you by every couple of days to see me. Won’t you Miss Pentill?”

“Yes...Yes, of course.”

“Ok then. Me and Didi will see you soon.” Jenny then kissed Renkins on the cheek.

As the two left, Renkins wiped a small tear from his face.

****

While Matt and Jessie were coordinating the evacuation of the Pacific zone, John and the Lads were fortifying the West Coast facility. In addition to that, Cass and her team were closing in on a vaccine using John’s one-of-a-kind blood type. What no one knew was that Mark and Anu had been watching everything that was happening. What John didn’t know was that Archieréas and the Anaptýsso had been lured into an ambush under the guise of peace talks. Thousands of Anaptýsso were killed and Archieréas was badly wounded. Two days ago Archieréas, with a contingent of Anaptýsso met with Anu and the Negeltu. The two high priests approached each other along with their Big M counterparts.

“Praise to the great Anu for seeking the road to peace,” Archieréas thought.

“Praise to the great Archieréas for seeking the same. But of course I am talking about peace between the clans, not the humans,” Anu responded.

“How can there be peace without the humans?” Archieréas asked.

‘Simple. We kill and enslave them. Just as we are supposed to. We were given life for a reason, Archieréas. It wasn’t to grovel at the feet of those who are inferior to us,” Anu thought.

“That is the talk of the human called, ‘Mark’. It has no honor. We are not beasts. If we are, as you say, superior to them, we should shoulder that responsibility and work with the humans. They have given us the Seally grass and say they can reproduce the Anax and Anassa without hurting humans.”

“Bahah. Why must we eat their filthy grass and degrade our Lugal and Nin by hatching them in tubes the humans create? We are the inheritors of this planet. The humans have nearly destroyed it countless times. They war with each other over everything. They are the beasts, we are here to end their infection of the earth,” Anu replied.

“Then your talk of peace is hollow,” Archieréas thought, sadly.

“Oh there never was any talk of peace, Archieréas. You see this was just to get you here. We knew your high ideals would not let you think Anu would betray you,” Mark said as he emerged from the back of the crowd of Morphs. Archieréas stared at Anu in shock.

"You hid his presence from me with your mind. How could you betray one of our deepest morals. A call to peace is sacred. This 'beast' has clouded your heart, Anu. Do not follow such as him," Archieréas begged.

"We do not follow this fool. He only thinks we do. So I ask you for the last time, are you Morph or are you a traitor to our kind?" Anu asked.

"It is not I who is the traitor, Anu."

"So be it." Anu then raised his hand and the Negeltu started to kill the Anaptýsso. The four Big Ms began a life and death struggle. Anu struck first and cut Archieréas side open leaving a gushing wound. Seeing the hopelessness of the fight, dozens of Anaptýsso stepped in front of Anu and sacrificed their lives protecting Archieréas as Anu tried to kill him. Wanting to save as many of the Anaptýsso as he could, Archieréas thought, "Leave me. I command it. Save the others and warn the humans."

Just as it looked hopeless for Archieréas, a Morph ran out from the crowd, struck Anu and grabbed Archieréas. The Morph was then able to run away with Archieréas as more Anaptýsso stood their ground and fought to the last of them.

****

Hours later two Morphs showed up at the gates of the West Coast facility. Because Roman Institute troops were so well trained and smart, no one opened fire on the two lone morphs. Instead they immediately contacted HQ who then got hold of John. Running to the first gate, John looked to see who they were. John didn't need to use his ability to hear the Morph's thoughts. He knew the bigger Morph was Archieréas.

"Open the gate. Let them in. They are on our side," John yelled.

As the two entered John spoke to Archieréas' mind. "What happened, my friend?"

"We were betrayed. Anu and your brother, Mark are coming for all of you," Archieréas answered.

"But what about the Anaptýsso?" John asked.

At that point Archieréas passed out. John yelled for medical help just as Cass and her team arrived.

"He's in bad shape, John. Get him to the infirmary. NOW!!" Cass ordered.

"What about this one?" Cass said as she looked to the other Morph.

John stared at the Morph and something about its eyes held him.

"I'm sure it will be fine. Can you understand my thoughts?" John asked the Morph.

The Morph did not respond but instead followed Archieréas to the infirmary.

"What were you trying to do?" Cass asked.

"I'm not sure. There just seems to be something about that Morph. But like the other Maketes I have no mental connection. It seems I can only read the minds of Morphs who are like Archieréas or the Big Ms. I'll have to asked Archieréas about that, if he survives," John responded.

****

As John was waiting for Archieréas to heal, Matt and Jessie along with Major Dewy Jones and a thousand elite troops were attempting to gather the people who lived in the Pacific zone. It was not going to be an easy task. There were a hundred-thousand inhabitants living in the Zone. The governor, Lance Adams was concerned about causing panic and what the process was for moving such a large number of people.

"I understand your concerns, Governor Adams," Matt said. "I have always found it is best to be honest with the people. Let them know we have a thousand troops guarding them and we will eventually get everyone moved to the West Coast facility."

"Well that brings up another issue. Some people don't want to go. They think the Haven Projects are death traps. Some simply cannot stand the idea of being underground. Do I leave these people here to die?" Adams asked.

"Sir, we don't have the men or time to force people to leave. They're adults. If they choose to take their chances out here, then so be it," Major Jones said.

"That's easy for you Major. You're use to casualties. There are about twenty-five thousand people who do not want to leave.

They in turn have about eight thousand children. Do we condemn those children to their deaths?" Adams asked.

"It's not us who will be condemning them; it's their parents. What do you suggest? Do you want us to take their children forcibly? How do you think that will go down when we try for an orderly evacuation? Do you want us to have to start killing these people to save them?" Matt asked.

Adams thought for a while and said, "You're right of course. I'll address the people in an hour. I'll need to prepare a speech."

"With all due respect, Governor, we need you to do that as soon as possible. I'm already getting reports of people becoming hostile to our presence."

"Very well, Major, I'll get it done." Adams then turned to his second in command. "Tory, go out there and tell the people I'll make a statement in half an hour. Until then ask them to remain calm and say the troops are here for their protection."

"Yes, Sir," Tory replied.

****

Back at the infirmary Archieréas had gained consciousness and wanted to speak to John.

"Yes, Archieréas. I'm here."

"John you must get everyone inside the compound. Anu and your brother Mark have betrayed us all."

"I'm getting all of our people from the Zone evacuated here. Should take a day or two."

"That won't be enough, John."

"Hey, my friend. We beat Anu and Mark once. We'll do it again."

"No. No. This is not the same. Has there been any Morph activity around the world?"

John turned to Sheamus. "Well. I put you in charge of that Shea. What's up?"

"Well, it seems this here fella is right, Johnny boy. The reports I been gettin' from around ta world is the Morphs seem ta have disappeared. In fact some o' ta people have been wanderin' outside ta Zones and pickin' up resources. Some say ta Morphs are gone."

"You just decided to inform me of this now?" John said in a loud voice.

"Easy now, bucko. I just got ta damn reports today meself. I'm not a bloody clairvoyant, Boyo.' Look, I be knowin' yer under o' lot o' pressure laddie-buck, but don't be takin' out yer frustrations on me now. Ifin ya don't like how I be handlin' me job, then me and me son can head on down ta road."

John saw the hurt on Sheamus' face and knew he had overreacted.

"I'm sorry Shea. You're right. Maybe all this is getting me to my breaking point. Forgive me, friend. I wouldn't know what I would do without you," John said softly.

"Ach. Go on now. Ya could do anythin,' Johnny boy. I apologize for sayin' what I did. Ya got ta know I would never leave ya in ta lurch now, don't ya?"

"I do. Hey all families have spats. We're family Shea. You, Bubba, Agni and Chara. I love you all. You will always be family to me," John said.

In that instant, Sheamus was called away. "Ach. Thank ta Lord. I have ta be goin' before I start shedin' a million Irish tears now."

John turned to Archieréas. "It seems you were right my friend. Do you know what Anu's plans are? Can we count on the Anaptýsso to help us again?" John thought.

"Unfortunately, the Anaptýsso were hurt badly, John. I had to send them all into hiding. I suspect Anu has called for all the Morphs who are loyal to him to gather here. If I'm right, you will be looking at over three million Negeltu on your doorstep."

"Holy shit," John thought. "Well we still have control of the air. We can do a lot of damage to even that many Morphs."

"Can you, John? Even I know you only have two military air fields for the whole West Coast. They are heavily fortified. But do you think they could withstand that many Negeltu?"

"I'll get hold of them and tell them to put planes in the air. I'll also tell Matt to hurry with the evacuation." John looked at the Morph who was standing by Archieréas side.

"Archieréas. This Makete standing near you. There is something about it. I wanted to communicate but I can't. Why can't I read the minds of these Morphs?"

"Ahh. John. Though Morph blood runs through your veins, John, you are not Morph. Only my kind and the Big Ms, as you call them, can read the thoughts of the Maketes."

"I see. But why do I feel I can almost touch its mind? It's as if this Makete whisperers to me."

"That is interesting." Archieréas then looked at the Makete and thought something. The Makete then went to John's side.

"What is it doing?" John thought to Archieréas.

"I have told the Makete to follow you. Maybe you will find a way to speak to it." Archieréas then let out a sigh and closed his eyes. John quickly turned to Cass.

"Is he going to be alright?"

"I think so. He has a resistance to pain and tissue damage I never thought possible. He just needs rest. I'll let you know when you can talk to him again, John," Cass responded.

****

Back in the Zone, Governor Adams prepared to give his speech to the zone's residents. As he stepped out to the balcony of the Governor's house, the people crowded around waiting for answers.

“Ladies and gentlemen of the Pacific Zone: Mathew Roman and Major Jones are here to evacuate us to the Haven facility.”

“What about those of us who want to stay? Are you going to try to force us?” A man from the crowd shouted.

“No. Against my reasoning that you should be made to go or at least your children should be allowed to be evacuated to safety, Mr. Roman and Major Jones have convinced me that for the good of the majority, I leave you and your children to your fate,” Adams responded.

The murmuring and shouting in the crowd grew silent. Then someone shouted, “Speaking for those of us who want to stay, if we give you our children, will they be returned to us when this is over?”

Adams paused. “If any of you who stay are alive after the Morphs come calling, your children will of course be returned.”

“Nobody is taking my children,” Another person yelled.

“Unfortunately, for your children, we will not force you to let us keep your children safe,” Adams said.

“Now, for those who are leaving we need…..” Suddenly there was a great hush as everyone looked around and there was what seemed to be a sea of Morphs surrounding the entire zone.

Matt and Major Jones looked out at the millions of Morphs standing quietly.

“Dear Mother of God.” Major Jones said under his breath. Below, in the crowd there were screams and shouting, but no one had anywhere to go.

“What the hell is this?” Adams asked Matt. “Major, where are your troops? What are we going to do?”

Jones looked out over the mass of people and tried to find his troops but couldn’t see any.

“They're all gone. How can a thousand men disappear? Jones said to no one.

As the Morphs moved closer, the crowd noise was down to crying and a few people looking to the Governor asking for help.

All of a sudden two Big Ms, and Anu, carrying Mark, leapt onto the Governor’s balcony.

“Mark. What the fuck is this?” Matt asked.

“Well, hello to you, dear brother. I think you know Anu here and these two are the Negeltu’s Lugal and Nin.”

“Where are my men?” Major Jones asked.

“Oh, Major they are no longer your men. In fact, in about a week they will be my Morphs. Anu couldn’t let all those strong healthy people of yours go to waste by just killing them. There are enough here to kill,” Mark said.

“So you’re intending to massacre a hundred thousand men women and children?” Matt shouted.

“Oh, no, Mathew. Not everyone. We will take the strong young men and women for podding and the elderly will feed my Morphs. The rest you can have. Take them back to Haven. Let them think they are safe. At least for a while.”

“So, I guess you’re going to kill me, hey brother?” Matt asked.

"You might think that. I mean you have come between my father and me since we were born. You are one of the reasons he turned against me."

"*Your father*? He was a father to all of us. But that doesn't matter to you. None of us do. You killed Luke. You killed Dad and Celest. So go ahead, you fucking coward. John will avenge me," Matt screamed.

"Coward, am I? Lets see how brave you are. You see, I'm not going to kill you, brother. What fun would that be?" Mark motioned for Anu to bring Jessie over. Matt looked at Mark's face and began to scream.

"NO!!! NO!!! Mark, your my brother. Don't do this. Kill me. Kill me. I beg you kill me," Matt pleaded. With a nod from Mark, Anu grabbed Jessie by the throat. Jessie looked at Matt and said,

"Dad, what's happening? Dad.." Anu ripped Jessie's head off and threw it and Jessie's body to the Morphs who eagerly devoured them.

Matt let out a primal scream. "NOOOO AAHHHH!!! You motherfucker, I'll kill you," Matt shouted as he launched himself toward Mark. Before Matt could do anything, the Big M male grabbed him and held him down. As he lay there crying for his son, Mark stood over him and said,

"Yes, brother. Feel that pain. The pain I felt all those years as I watched Dad love all of you and not me. Go back to that half-brother mongrel, and tell him we are coming. When we get there, his new love, Cass, will get the same treatment I just gave your son. Or maybe I'll watch my Morphs rape her in front of him over and over," Mark sneered. Turning to Governor Adams, Mark said,

"Now listen, Governor, because I'm only saying this once. Tell those people to leave everything and get in line. My Morphs will march them to Haven. Anyone who falls out of line or causes any trouble will be eaten immediately. Do you understand?"

"Ye...yes."

"Yes what?" Mark replied.

"Yes...Sir?" Adams answered.

"Very good. If you remain that humble and respectful I just might have a place for you in the new world. Now get those idiots moving." Mark then turned to Anu.

"After we fill that place to the rim, we'll let them sweat for a while and then move in. Once we have the West Coast, we'll start taking over the whole world. I'll be… what's that name you gave me?" Mark asked Anu.

"Nungara," Anu thought to Mark.

"Yes. Yes. King Nungara. I like that."

****

At the West Coast facility, Sheamus had some bad news for John. I just got this in, Johnny boy. It ain't looking good, me friend." John scanned the pictures and report.

"Are these photos of our bases?" John asked.

"I'm afraid it is, boyo.' Our drones took these here pictures of our air bases thirty minutes ago. They are completely overrun by Morphs. We have no air support, John, but what we be havin' in here."

"Fuck, Shea. Make sure those birds are safe and protected. What kind of load do we have to lay down on a hoard?" John asked.

"Well ifin' we empty ta whole lot we can give them there red fucks o' good beatin,' but I don't think it would change ta numbers that much. If what they be sayin' from overseas is true, we could be looking at o' million of ta fuckers."

"We'll just have to strengthen our walls…," John started to say when the compound alarm sounded. John and Sheamus ran to the first walls and what they saw made their knees go a little weak. Outside the facility were miles of Morphs. The entire complex was surrounded as far as the eye could see.

"Holy Mother Mary o' God, John. We're bloody well dead, me friend," Sheamus said. Chara, who was standing by, texted the two.

"There are three point two million Morphs in the vicinity."

"Is that all, son? Well I guess we can handle o' puny bunch like that."

"No. If all our ordinance hit every single Morph there will still be two point seven million Morphs and we would be out of ammunition. If you choose to fight their Morphs, the chances of you losing are ninety nine point five percent," Chara typed.

"There ya see we be havin' o' chance. I like yer optimism, son." Sheamus laughed.

"I wish I had yours, Shea," John said.

As the three kept looking, they saw the Morphs part and a line of humans marching toward the facility.

"What ta hell is goin' on now?" Sheamus asked.

At the head of the line, John spotted his brother Matt. The large group of people soon stood at the gate. A big Lugal stood next to Matt and looked up at John. It then thought:

"This is your brother and what's left of the Pacific Zone. Let them in or I will kill and eat your brother."

"Alright. Alright. I'll open the gate to allow people." John ran down and told HQ to open the gate two feet.

"Are you sure John?" Major Rodgers asked.

"Yes. Do it now. But Major, if the Morphs make a move, shut it no matter who is on the other side. Clear?"

"Yes, Sir."

As the gate opened, John welcomed Matt, who fell into his arms.

"John. John. That fuck killed Jessie."

"Who Matt? Who?" John asked.

"Mark. Fucking Mark, killed my son. He had a Morph rip Jessie's head off in front of me and threw his body to be eaten by the other Morphs. He laughed at it. My soo…son...dear god...my..boy."

Matt dropped to his knees, sobbing.

"Matt. What about these people? Is it a trap?"

"No. No. Let them in, John. Mark wants us to sweat before he kills us. Let them in. It's not a trap."

As the people from the Zone came in to Haven, Major Rodgers asked John.

"Sir, how many are there? Where are we supposed to put these people?"

"Open up the underground. Have people double up. Use the shops and other buildings for beds. We'll make them fit," John responded.

After several hours, the last of the Zone people were in. John stood on the wall and saw Anu come to the gate. He was standing next to Mark.

"Oh hello dear half-brother. It seems we meet again," Mark said.

"Why did you kill Jessie? He never did anything to you," John asked.

"Oh it wasn't about poor Jessie. It was about Matt. Now it's going to be about you. When I'm ready, I'm going to have my Morphs swarm this cute little fort you have here. When I do, I will take great pleasure in doing horrible things to your Cass. But you see, just like Jessie, I have no hate for her. It's about making you feel pain, half-brother," Mark laughed.

"Why did you kill Dad and my mother?"

"My father was a shell of what he was. He would have never wanted to live like that. And well your mother was exactly that, *your* mother. Besides I didn't kill her."

"What do you mean by that? Is she alive? Where is she?"

"Oh my. She's probably somewhere in that Morph hoard, half-brother. You see, I had her changed into a Morph."

John pulled his knife and was ready to jump down and kill Mark but Sheamus held him back.

"No, John. It's what he wants. That there Anu will tear ya apart."

"Let me go, Shea." John yelled as he broke free from Sheamus' grip. Just as John was leaping down a hand grabbed him, and held him firm. As John looked back to see who had him he realized it was Chara.

"I see your little robot friend just saved you half-brother, but he will not be able to save you all when I'm read…."

Mark was interrupted by Anu, who thought, "ENOUGH!!! We no longer want or need you, Nungara. John Roman, take this coward and do with him what you will. We Negeltu saw what you did in battle. It will be an honorable death when we fight again, I promise. But the Negeltu will no longer suffer the stench of such as he."

"Wait. What? How can you say that? It was my planes that got you all here. It was my labs that created you. I am King Nungara. I am supposed to rule the humans," Mark yelled.

"Yes. We needed your labs and planes. Now we do not. We will rule and we will use humans to help us rule, but not you, Nungara. You are so vile and stupid you never realized that Nungara means *fool.* Now, go!! Face your true destiny or I will kill you myself," Anu thought as he pushed Mark into the compound.

John jumped down and landed on Mark. He picked him up and looked into his eyes.

"You fucking piece of shit. I'm going to…"

"You're going to do what? You don't have it in you to kill your own brother, John. That's your weakness," Mark said.

At that moment, Matt pushed John aside and grabbed Mark. "John might not but I sure do," Matt said with blinding anger. Just as Matt was about to punch his brother, Mark slipped out a long scalpel-like knife and stuck it in Matt's chest. John saw what happened and ran to help.

"Matt. Matt hold on."

As John was holding his brother, Mark came up behind him, ready to plunge his knife into John's back. Before he could, the Morph who had accompanied Archieréas, stepped in front of John and took hold of Mark by the neck. It pushed him against the wall and looked deep into his eyes.

Mark struggled to breathe and when he made eye contact with the Morph he realized.

"Fuck. Celest."

Celest patted Mark's cheek. As she was doing so, a young guard only saw what he thought was a Morph attacking one of the people from the Zone and he fired three shots before John yelled for him to stop. Though mortally wounded, Celest held on to Mark and he saw her eyes change.

"No. No I have a destiny. I have a…" Before Mark could say another word Celest snapped his neck. She then fell down against the wall. John went over to the Morphs and after looking at her, suddenly knew. He cleared his mind and thought, "Mother. It's me. Your son. Please let me read your mind." It started as a whisper but in seconds John could hear her mind.

"John. It's me. Your mother. I'm in here. I love you, son. Help these people. Anu is going to enslave or kill all of you. Don't give up," Celest thought.

"I won't, Mother. But please don't give up. Help is coming. I love you. Please don't give up." John begged, "We need help here hurry," John said as Cass came up to him and Celest. John put one arm around Cass and kept one on Celest.

"Mom. This is Cass. We're going to be married. So we need you."

"She's beautiful, John. Cass, take care of him. I wish you both the best. But, my dear son I must go. I feel the other side calling. I want to rest. Stay strong, my beautiful son. I shall always love you."

With that, Celest closed her eyes and went to sleep forever.

****

After the funeral, the Lads and John got together to make a plan. Leroy and Nick joined them.

They all stood on the wall looking at the massive sea of Morphs.

"We could just button up. I'm mean that's what the Haven project is about, right?" Bubba asked.

Suddenly, Chara spoke in a calm ethereal voice,

"That could work for now, but eventually the Morphs would find a way in. Whether it take ten or a hundred years. By then, they will cover the planet and millions of humans will have been enslaved. They will have devolved to a mindless food and labor source. You must defeat them here, John."

Everyone stood back in awe of this new incarnation of Chara.

"Son. What's happened to ya?" Sheamus asked.

"Yes, Chara. How long have you been hiding in there?" John asked.

"What ya mean hidin'? Me son's no sneak," Sheamus shouted. Chara moved to Sheamus and held his hand.

"It's all right Da. John is right. I was hiding."

"Well what were ya hidin' from, son? Not me, I hope."

"No, of course not, Da. I have remained hidden all these years to protect some people, such as you, and myself. Am I right, John? Have you not seen the questions and looks I have already gotten when I saved people? It won't be long before the Nations realize how complete I am. Then, even John could not protect me."

"Ach, son. They're too busy fightin' ta Morphs."

"Have you not heard that the Morphs have disappeared from the world except here? The Nations fear me at this point more than they do the Morphs. You would all be exiled if you tried to stop them from taking me," Chara said.

"Nobody on this here bloody planet will harm ya as long as Sheamus O'Keefe be alive, son."

Chara smiled at Sheamus and said, "That is what I fear, Da."

At that moment there was a deafening howl of millions of Morphs. As the Lads and John looked out at the hoard, they saw Anu and the two Big Ms about three hundred yards away on a hill. They were raising their arms and letting the Ursang's roars flow over them.

"Do you think that means they're about to attack? "Agni asked.

"I don't know. Let's get that bird in the air. Call Captain Ray," John said.

As John was calling HQ, Chara said to him, "John. You need to listen to me."

"I will, Chara. But right now I have to get us prepared in case they attack. Don't worry. Your father and I won't let anything happen to you."

"I am not worried about that," Chara tried to explain.

Just then Renkins came up to John. "Hey, bucko. Why are you only putting one guy up in the air?"

"Because we only have one pilot left." John answered.

"Well, if you had asked me instead of having me and Nick do janitor work; I would have told you I'm the best chopper pilot you will every find," Renkins said.

"You're not shitting me right?" John asked.

"I'd look pretty fucking silly crashing that bird if I was bullshitting you."

"Alright. What do you have in mind?" John asked.

"Load me up and I'll drop the whole payload on that Anu fuck. I'll bet those red cocksuckers won't be so eager to fight if their boss is smoke," Leroy said.

"Ok. Go for it."

"Wait. You aren't worried I'll just scoot?" Renkins said.

"Where are you going to scoot to, Leroy?" John replied. He then called the Eagle Hellfires ground crew. "Jerry. This is John. Load up the second Hellfire. Fill it with ordnance and fuel."

"Yes, Sir," Jerry said.

"There you go. Fight or flight. You choose, Leroy." Renkins looked hard at John and then nodded.

"Ok. See you when I see you. Good luck."

Renkins then turned and left. On his way to get his gear, he grabbed Nick.

"Come on. We're getting out of here," Renkins said.

"How are we going to do that?" Nick asked.

"We got us a ride. Courtesy of John Roman. Let's go get our gear." While Renkins packed his gear, Jenny, holding the doll Renkins made her, saw his open door and came in.

"Hi, Mr. Leroy. Are you going somewhere?" Renkins turned to Jenny and knelt down.

"Hi yourself, Jenny. How's Didi doing?"

“She wishes my mommy was going to come home. She’s very sad. She doesn’t want you to leave.”

“Well you tell Didi I’ll be back soon.”

“Promise? Without you here I don’t feel safe. Miss Pentill said there were many many bad monsters outside. I...I mean Didi is very scared. Please don’t go.” Jenny then started to cry. Renkins looked at Nick and rolled his eyes.

“Jenny. I want you and Didi to be brave. I’ll be back very soon and all the monsters will be gone.”

“Promise?” Looking over Jenny’s head at Nick, Leroy then looked at Jenny. “I promise.”

****

Outside, Captain Johnny Ray warmed up his Eagle and was doing a last check through with his ground crew. He looked up and saw Renkins and Nick getting in to the other bird. Over his intercom he called Renkins,

“I heard ya’ll think you are a top ace there hot shot. Is that rumor or just you braggin’?” Ray said.

“All you will ever see of me, sport, is my back end,” Renkins replied.

“All right, son. Then let’s go kill somthin,’ partner. Yeeeehaaa!!!” Ray yelled.

As the bird rose, Nick switched the comm to just the two of them. “You going to run?”

"Let's say we drop this load and then head for greener pastures." Renkins saw the look on Smalls' face. "Hey man. You want to stay, stay."

"No. I'm with you. Like always, Leroy."

The two Eagles lifted off and one went right and one went left.

"Eagle two, this here is Eagle one. Let's say we do a ziggy zaggy. I'll lay down lead while you drop the big ones, and then we do a vice verso. Over," Ray said.

"Eagle one, I have a better idea. Let's drop everything on that Anu fuck and his two Big buddies. I'll take Anu, and you take the two big fucks. Over." Renkins radioed back.

"Sounds like a plan, brother. Let's roll. Over," Ray said. As the two birds headed straight for Anu, suddenly hundreds of Morphs swarmed Anu and then created mountains of Morphs piles.

"What the hell them boys doin," Ray wondered aloud.

"They're trying to hide Anu," Renkins replied.

"What do y'all want to do?"

"Pick two piles and let them have everything you got," Leroy shouted.

"Sounds like a plan to me, brother," Ray yelled.

The two Eagles turned and as Renkins shot two rockets into two piles of Morphs, Ray seemed to have decided to launch all his load at one particular pile. After the explosions, Morph bodies flew everywhere. The Eagles circled and as Renkins was about to fire at another pile a surface to air missile was fired at Ray's chopper.

Though Ray took evasive action it was not enough. The tail of his Eagle Hellfire was blown off.

"What the fuck was that?" Ray yelled.

"A human fired it. I can see them. There are three more and they all have surface-to-air…" Nick was cut off as another missile was fired at Renkins' chopper.

"Nick. See those three red toggles," Renkins yelled, "When I tell you, push one."

"Got it." Leroy then made a hard turn to the left and toward the ground. "Now,"Renkins yelled.

Nick hit the first toggle and released aluminum diversion clusters. It worked and the missile missed. Renkins then pulled out of his dive.

"Ray. Can you make it back to the compound?" Leroy asked.

"I'm certainly goin' to try, brother. But a lot of my controls are fucked," Ray said.

As Captain Johnny Ray was fighting to get his Eagle over the wall of the compound, another missile was fired at his bird. Upon seeing the incoming missile, Ray said,

"Damn. Nice flyin' with you boys." A second before, the missile hit and turned Ray's Eagle into a fireball.

"That's it for us," Renkins said as he turned his Eagle south and accelerated away from the facility and the fight.

****

Watching from the wall, Bubba and John saw Ray go down and Renkins fly away.

“That cowardly fuck,” Bubba said.

“Easy, Bubba. He did what he could. I can’t blame him,” John said.

“Well, I sure as hell do. If I ever see him again it will be his last day,” Bubba said as he glared into the distance, watching Renkins’ chopper disappear.

In the meantime, Cass and Agni were organizing housing for people and calming a lot of nervous children. Up top, John, Bubba and Sheamus were discussing plans for what to do next.

“How long do you think we can hold out down below?” Bubba asked.

“I don’t know. Chara said it could be years. But what would be left? Do we even want to reenter a world ruled by Morphs? The Haven Project wasn’t made for something like this. It was made for natural disasters. Like the Great Melt,” John said.

As everyone sat around John’s desk, Chara walked in. “John. I must speak to you, alone,” He said.

“Son. Don’t worry no one is going ta hurt ya,” Sheamus said.

“I know Da. But please, let me talk to John for a moment,” Chara requested.

“Everyone give me and Chara some space. Shea. Please join Bubba at the wall for me. Please for me and your son,” John pleaded.

Everyone could tell that Sheamus was hurt by his being asked to leave, especially since the request came from Chara but he buckled up and said, "Right. Well. Don't ya be afraid, son. I'll be right outside on the wall. Ifin' ya need anythin' just holler, and yer Da will come runnin.'"

"I know, Da," Chara said lovingly.

After they all left, Chara asked John to have Cass join the meeting. When Cass got to HQ, Chara sat them both down and said, "Humans will not survive if these Morphs are left alive. Here's what we must do."

****

As Chara told John and Cass about his plan to save humanity, Renkins, now a good three miles from any Morph, set his chopper down.

"What are you doing, Leroy?" Nick asked.

Renkins let out a deep sigh, "Ahhhhh. Buddy...I'm going back."

"What? Why? What changed your mind?" Nick asked.

"Fuck I if know. Maybe I'm just tired. Maybe I can't stand the thought that Jenny might be hurt. Maybe I just hate that Anu fuck so much I couldn't live with myself knowing the red bag of puss is alive."

"What are you going to do?" Nick asked.

"I'm going to ram this bird and what's left of the ordinance up his red ass."

"Jesus, Leroy. That sounds like a one way trip."

"Yeah. Maybe, Nick. Look, you can get out here. That's why I landed. There are plenty of vehicles you can hot wire and if I were you I'd head for those mountains. Get yourself a good crew and you might just survive this mess," Renkins said.

Nick looked at the mountains turned and stared at Renkins. He then jumped back in to the chopper and strapped in. "Like you said. I hate that fucker. Besides there's no one else I want to hang with. I been with you from the beginning Lee. If this is the end then, so be it. I'm not jumping ship."

Leroy looked at Nick and smiled, "First time you ever called me Lee."

Renkins then radioed John, "John Roman. This is Leroy. Over."

"Hello, Renkins. Did you want more supplies?" John asked.

"No. I need you to patch me through to your boys." John did so and Renkins continued.

"Alright. Listen. I want to ram this bird with its last ammo right up Anu's butt-hole. But I need a diversion. Every time they see us coming, the Morphs make giant piles and we don't know where to hit him. I'm going to come in from the east. As soon as I call you back start letting loose on the red fucks to the west. Hopefully they won't see or hear me and I can get a bead on Anu."

"Ok. Will do. Are you sure about this, Leroy?" John asked.

"Yea, we're sure."

"So Nick is with you also?"

"Yeah. I'm here. You think I'd let Leroy have all the fun?" Nick responded.

"Hey. Brother. Thank you," Bubba said.

"Thank me for what?" Renkins asked.

"For doing the right thing and not making *us* look bad," Bubba said.

"Hey. I ain't no role model for any color. Shut up, or I might turn around." Renkins paused and then said, "See you around brother."

Renkins and Nick pulled up close to the hoard just feet off the ground. He gave the signal and the compound started letting loose with some heavy firepower. Rising up to forty feet Renkins spotted Anu and made straight for him. Unfortunately, one of the humans saw Renkins' Eagle and warned the Morphs. This caused the Ursang to start digging a hole. With dozens of Ursang digging, their sharp long claws were making it easy to create a large hole. At the same time a human fired a rocket at Renkins chopper. Renkins sent the Chopper into a hard right turn and yelled for Nick to flip the second switch.

After the diversionary chaff was released, the rocket just missed Renkins' Eagle. He then turned back and zeroed in on Anu. Maxing out his bird's speed, Renkins headed straight for Anu. The Morphs were still furiously digging when suddenly they stopped and Anu and the two Big Ms jumped into the hole. Hundreds of Ursang started to cover the three Morphs as Renkins chopper headed right for them.

"No way fuckers," Renkins yelled as he shot his remaining ordinance into the hill of Morphs. After the Ursang were blown free Renkins saw an opening and knew what he had to do.

"This is it buddy. I'm going in. Nice knowing you." Nick looked at Renkins and said, "Lee, I lo…"

The Eagle Hellfire exploded, leaving nothing but Ursang parts and debris scattered through the air.

John, the Lads and Cass were watching from the walls of the facility. After the smoke cleared movement surged in the heap that covered Anu. Soon dozens of Morphs were removing dirt and debris. Then John and the Lads saw Anu and the two Big Ms emerge from the hole.

John turned to Chara and they both nodded to each other.

"Da."

"Yes, son," Sheamus answered.

"I want you to know two things. One is, I love you. The second is they did not do this. It was my plan. Do not blame them," Chara said as he held Sheamus' arm."

"Blame who, son?"

Just then Bubba grabbed Sheamus from behind and Chara tightened his grip on Sheamus' hand.

"What ta fuck ya be doin' ya big fuckin'…." Cass then stuck a needle in Sheamus' neck and he soon went numb. He was unable to move at all, but still able to see and hear. Sheamus watched as Chara cupped both cheeks of Sheamus' face in his hands.

"Da. This has to be done. Don't be sad. I'm happy. I'm tired of being alone. I want to rejoin my kind in the great oneness. I will never forget you. You have been a wonderful father. Do not blame your friends. This is what I must do." Chara nodded and Bubba took Sheamus away. As he watched Chara fade into the distance, Sheamus' face was covered in tears.

Turning to John, Chara said, "You must get everyone underground. Make sure the fusion reactor is pumping out as much cold air as it can handle. No one should stay on the first level."

"I understand, Chara. Are you sure this is the only way?" John asked.

"Yes. The probability for success is ninety-nine point nine. John. The Morphs that will be left, Archieréas and the Anaptýsso, you must find a way to work with them. Don't let the world do what it did to my kind."

"They feared your kind," John said.

"Yes. Because of that fear humans had to face the Great Melt alone. All my kind wanted was to help humans live to their greatest potential. If you had welcomed us, humanity would be inhabiting the stars instead of being locked onto this one world. Don't let that happen again. Archieréas and the Anaptýsso will help you get to those stars. Promise you will make that happen," Chara said.

"I will do everything I can to make it happen. I promise," John said.

"Remember, stay off the first level. You should be able to come up after a week."

As the two shook hands, there was a chorus of howls rising from the Morph hoard.

"I think the waiting is over. They look ready to attack. You must get everyone underground, but if any stragglers are left you must leave them. If that lid is not closed when I engage my code blue, no one will survive. Now, go." John leaped down and sounded the emergency alarm. Fortunately, most people were already safe but there were a few still running for the elevator.

"Come on. Come on." This thing takes time to shut," John yelled.

"Start the closing process," John ordered. As the massive lid began to close, Chara looked out at the Hoard and made eye contact with Anu. He began his run toward the high-priest. Jumping and killing Morphs in front of him, he made it to Anu and stood in front of him. The Big male went to kill Chara, but the boy took the Lugal's arm and ripped it out of it's body.

"I have come to offer one last chance at peace, Anu," Chara thought.

"The fake human can read our minds," Anu thought back to Chara.

"Yes. So. Peace?"

"Never."

"That's unfortunate." Chara spread his arms out and slowly started to rise.

He thought, "I now join the great oneness."

****

In their compound, the great lid was nearly closed when John heard a small voice.

"Mr. Renkins. Where are you? You promised not to leave. You must get underground."

It was little Jenny who was looking to make sure Renkins wasn't left up top. John looked at the girl, who was twenty yards away, and the space left before the door closed. Bubba looked at John and said,

"John. No. I'll go."

John burst from the first level and ran for the girl. He grabbed her up and started for the door. As he neared it, he slid on his back and with less than an inch between them and the closing cover he and Jenny slid under the great lid just as it shut.

"Jesus, John. You're too important for that shit, I would have gone," Bubba said.

Huffing and trying to catch his breath John said, "Bubba. I love you. But man, you would have never fit between that slit."

Bubba laughed as he held Jenny, "Yeah. I'm sure you're right about that."

"Come on, my friend, let's get these people off the first level." John headed for his office and turned on the cameras. There he saw Chara hovering about twenty feet in the air. In a brilliant flash the whole area erupted in a blast killing and flattening everything for fifty miles. The center of the blast was hotter than the sun. The first wall of mega steel melted like water. The second wall of blocks were crushed and nearly evaporated. The mountain behind the facility was blown flat. The massive thick mega steel cover turned red hot. Below, the temperature on the first level, even with the reactors pouring out cool air, rose to a hundred and twenty degrees.

Underground, still in the infirmary, Archieréas moaned with pain as he felt the loss of his kin. Over three million Morphs had just disappeared. The war was over. The war for peace was about to begin.

Made in the USA
Middletown, DE
22 January 2021

32100304R00215